MOON BOUND

PACK BOUND SERIES BOOK 2

LEISL LEIGHTON

PERMIEN PRESS

Published by Leisl Leighton as Permien Press. For more information, email: leisl@leislleighton.com

First published 2018 by Escape Publishing Australia. Rewritten and republished 2022 by Permien Press.

Cover design – Samantha Marshall

Ebook ISBN: 978-1-922836-02-1

Print ISBN: 978-1-922836-03-8

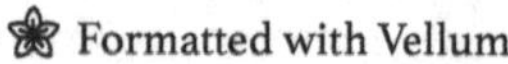 Formatted with Vellum

PRAISE FOR MOON BOUND

"Moon Bound is one thrilling read that had me glued to the pages … The Pack Bound world is definitely fascinating and full of intrigue which ensures that I am going to keep coming back for more."

— EVA MILLIEN - STORMY VIXEN'S BOOK REVIEWS

"A fabulous storyline, with exciting characters and an intensity that leads the reader to want so much more. I'm absolutely looking forward to the next book in this wonderful series."

— KAREN ROMA – GOODREADS REVIEWER

"I love this book!"

— JESSICA – GOODREADS REVIEWER

"Second book just as good as the first! The world building continues to enthrall, the storyline is action packed and exciting, gripping and entertaining and I just couldn't put it down. Filled with danger and suspense and twists and turns to keep you guessing as the story continues on from book one."

— DEBBIE - AMAZON REVIEWER

"Head over heels for tortured hottie River and gentle soul Bron! Adored this latest installment in the Pack Bound series and eagerly awaiting more."

— MARNIE - AMAZON REVIEWER

MOON BOUND

To my boys, Jacob and Nathaniel.
This book is dedicated to you to remind you to trust your instincts and to
never give up.

PROLOGUE

Edinburgh 1502

Morrigan stood on the rise looking down on the village that had once, many years ago, been a sanctuary to her before the Witch Finder had come and turned its people against her and her kind. She'd run, but her sister—heaven damn her —had obviously followed a long cold trail here, seeking to find her.

The panic that had been a clawing cold in her chest when she'd felt Morghanna's fear days ago, now turned into something hot and bubbling as she saw what they'd done to her sister. The animals that were supposed to protect her were nowhere in evidence.

Her face twisted as the Witch Finder lowered the torch to the kindling surrounding the pyre that was Morghanna's judgement. The crowd of villagers cheered.

Traitors! Murderers! She would not allow them to do this. They would not murder her beautiful, gentle sister, the woman who'd brought comfort and help to so many.

She lifted her hands and began to incant, drawing power.

'No Morrigan.' Morghanna's voice, carried by the Goddess on the wind, sounded in her ear. *'The Witch Finder will see you. Do not bring*

destruction upon yourself. Carry our line through the ages or all I have suffered will have been for nought.'

The power fell away. Morrigan's hands dropped to her side. Devastation and grief pulled at her. How could she stand by and let this happen to the most beloved person in her life? She might have run away from her sister and a life tied to the Were, might not have seen Morghanna for ten years, but she could never truly turn her back on the only person who had ever had faith in her and had never stopped fighting for her.

Morghanna had been more than her sister. She had been mother after their mother and father had died in a backlash of power, their lives ended in a cruel blaze.

And now, it seemed, her sister's life was to end in another kind of cruel and unjust blaze. It could have been prevented if only Morghanna had listened.

Morrigan seethed, shouting into the night, 'I told you this would happen. I warned you no good could come from aligning with those animals.'

'I know what you said. But I was right too. For many of our kind, the Pact has been a blessing.'

'How can you defend them?'

'Morrigan, listen. Not all of them are bad. Just this pack, and not even all of them.'

'Is that so? Then where are they now? These so-called good Were? They are supposed to protect you, so where are they?'

'I forced them away, to build a pack of their own where all of our coven can be safe.'

'And they let you?'

'They had no choice.'

'If you love some of them still, then why did you invoke that curse?'

'I had to. I had to ensure they protect Alistair's and my—' Her voice cut off as the flames licked closer and a cry of pain left her lips.

'Morghanna! I will kill them for doing this to you.'

'No Morrigan. Do not go down that path. Believe me when I say, those

responsible will pay. As will any others who seek to treat their covens as Iain McCrae and his ilk treated ours. The Curse will make certain this happens to no other witch or warlock again.'

this happens to no other witch or warlock again.'

Morrigan shook her head. No curse could ever be enough to assuage her grief when her sister was gone. Especially the one her sister had invoked only minutes ago as they bound her to the stake. It would only kill off the pack who had not protected her sister and were therefore responsible for her capture.

It wasn't enough. It would never be enough.

'Please, Morrigan. Listen to me. You are inviting the Darkness to you. Can you not feel it all around you? It is what we have fought off with the Pact. Please, do not allow it entry into your heart. I beg of you not to—'

The words ended on a cry of pain. Morrigan stumbled. Linked as she was to her sister, she could feel the terrifying heat, the smoke burning in her sister's throat, making each breath an agony. Grief and rage tore through her.

In that moment, the Darkness crept forward, edging into her line of sight. She had long fought its influence, but she didn't want to fight it any longer. Not if it would help in her revenge. She reached out, inviting it in.

'No Morrigan. Don't! Not for me. Never for me.'

'Only for you,' she cried as the Darkness touched her outstretched fingers. It curled around her, its touch icy, soothing the burn, whispering along her skin, wrapping around her; a lover's touch long denied. 'They will pay for this. Everyone responsible, every man, woman and child taking delight in this horror, will feel each moment of terror and agony you endure.'

'No, Morrigan. It does not have to be like this.'

'You are wrong. They sealed their fate the moment they laid hands on you.'

'Then you give me no choice.' Morghanna looked up to the heavens and cried out, her voice carrying over the rabble, over the crackle of flames, 'Please, my Goddess. End this now. Take me as you always promised you would.' There was no answer and as the flames licked her skin, Morghanna screamed.

'Our Goddess has failed you,' Morrigan cried. 'I will not.' She lifted her hands, despite her sister's plea to not bring notice to her magic. The Darkness would protect her.

Before Morrigan could utter a word, light streamed from the heavens, surrounding her sister in a golden glow. Morghanna lifted her head, her face glowing with an expression of such devotion and happiness that Morrigan could see it clearly even from this distance.

It brought an ache to her heart. A longing she'd thought never to feel again.

'I knew my Goddess would never forsake me,' Morghanna cried out. Then in Morrigan's head, Morghanna said, *It is not too late for you either my beloved sister to change your path. Fill yourself with the Goddess' light and love. Do not let the darkness have you.*

Morrigan reached out towards her sister, wanting to experience the bliss Morghanna so obviously felt. As she did, the Darkness hissed, but began to lift from where it twisted around her.

The light around Morghanna brightened, white and pure. Villagers cried out, shielding their eyes. Morrigan stumbled forward as the ropes tying Morghanna to the stake disintegrated to nothing. 'Sister, don't leave me!'

Morghanna didn't seem to hear her. She lifted her hands and cried out to the stars above, *'Save me.'*

Flames exploded, whipping into a tornado that shot up into the sky. Screams sang out on the air as the mob of villagers ran away from the explosion of white-hot heat and flame.

Morrigan shielded her eyes from the flare. The force of the explosion shoved her back. She fell, tumbling up the hill.

Then the wind died, the force dissipated and the light blinked out.

Morrigan gained her feet and spun around, ready to run forward and pull her sister from the dead pyre before the villagers realised what had happened.

She stumbled to a stop.

The pyre was nothing but ash. Morghanna was gone. 'No!' She fell to her knees, tearing at her hair, her clothes, rubbing dirt across her skin. Trembling, hot tears poured down her cheeks. She threw her head back and stared up at the sky. 'Please, Goddess,' she sobbed. 'Take me too.'

There was silence. No peace or warmth touched her soul. Just the cool Darkness as it flew back to her, surrounding her once more.

Grief dug its claws in, but not enough to dull the rage burning in her heart. She stood shakily and cried to the sky, 'You have turned your back on me, my Goddess, so now I finally turn my back on you. Revenge will be mine. This I promise on the ashes of my beloved sister.'

In her mind, a voice pleaded with her not to take this step, but she ignored it, allowing the Darkness to snap out and silence it. She had no time for mercy. There was a job to do.

She stalked towards the village. People ran around like chickens with their heads cut off, their fear and confusion alive in the air, feeding the Darkness inside her. She came to the open square where they had tried to put her sister to death. The Witch Finder still stood there, his shrieks heard above the fearful cries of the people as they ran to find shelter from whatever evil had taken the witch into its fold. He turned to face her as she drew near, jowls wobbling as he spat, 'Who are you?'

'Your death.' She lifted her hands and called power. A fae wind whirled, blowing her hair from her face. Dark clouds bloomed on the horizon. Lightning broke the gloom, crashing into the thatched roof of the church—the place of the trial; the place where they'd damned her sister—and setting it aflame. Another bolt hit the Witch Finder, cutting off his scream as he was lit from within. He fell to the ground, a smoking ruin.

Screams rose on the wind, winding around Morrigan, making the Darkness writhe in delight. She laughed, the sound whipped away on the wind, smothered by the crack of another bolt of lightning. It struck another building. More flames. Pushed by the wind, they flared, leaped to another building and another until the entire village surrounding her was alight.

'*They try to escape,*' the Darkness whispered.

She turned to see people running through the street that led straight into the nearby forest, obviously trying to seek refuge. They would find none. She cried out:

'Hear my words, make them true

Never stop 'til vengeance is through.

Three times three times three times three

So I say, so mote it be.'

She lifted her hands, directing her storm towards the forest. Lightning bolts blazed down into the trees until the sky was lit with the false dawn of licking flames and the cries for mercy were silenced.

Then the sky cracked with a rumble of thunder. Rain poured down to dampen the earth and the angry, flesh-seeking flames.

It fell on Morrigan, sizzling on her cold skin. Lifting her face she screamed at the sky, 'You are too late. They are already gone.' She could feel it in her heart, the knowledge a balm to her soul. Thunder rumbled in the distance, but she laughed in the face of the power that had dampened her flames. She had taken her revenge.

They were dead and there was no power in the heavens that could bring them back.

Hair plastered to her face, her dress now a sodden, muddy, torn mess, she turned her back on the destruction she'd wrought and swept out of the village. A smile bloomed on her lips. Yet as she passed out of the village and walked back up the hill she'd run down only minutes ago, the Darkness began to whisper to her.

'*Destroying the villagers hasn't made a difference. Morghanna is still gone and you are all alone, just as I have been alone these many years.*'

Her smile faltered. The Darkness was right. Cold crept into her heart where her sister had always brought such warmth. She was alone.

'*You have lost everything. But you know who is to blame.*'

She nodded, her lip curling as she spat, 'The Were.'

'*Make them pay. All of them. Take back what they stole from you and your people.*'

'Yes. But how will I manage it?'

'*I will help you. Find others who feel the same. Together, we will build a family to fight against those who have hurt us both.*'

She hugged her arms around her chest, stroking above her heart where the Darkness rested. She was not alone.

A smile broke out on her face again and, grimly determined, she strode forward into the night, listening to the whispers filling the empty place in her heart.

1

River sat up, the breath exploding from his lungs as he opened his eyes to the semi-dark of the room he'd been given at the McVale Packhouse.

He panted, shook his head, trying to rid himself of the image that had followed him from the nightmare; of Skye calling on moondust, forcing him to change, and in reaction, he wrapped his hands around her throat and squeezed.

Exactly as he'd done on their tenth birthday. Except in the nightmare, he wasn't an enraged and out of his mind 10-year-old Were-boy, he was an adult.

But he would never do that to her now. Never.

Except, that part of him that grew stronger every day. It wanted it. It wanted it more than it wanted anything else.

'Fuck. Fuck.' He took in a shaky breath, hand passing over his face to wipe the sick sweat away, brushing over the scars that were a constant reminder of that day. Skye hated herself for those scars. But if she hadn't burned him, she'd be dead by his hands—and he never could have lived with that. He loved her more than anything. She was his twin. The better part of him. Yet with the nightmare fresh in his mind, his skin tingling with remembered pain, and that part of him he tried so very hard to ignore whispering him to take what he wanted, he had trouble remembering that.

He didn't want to have trouble remembering. He needed to cling to it. To cling to his love for his twin. It was the only thing that had saved him from giving in years ago.

Why wasn't it working now?

He threaded his shaking fingers into his shaggy hair, pressing against his skull, blowing out shallow, fast breaths. His heart was like an oversized hummingbird trying to tear out of his chest. He ground his fist against it, willing it to slow. It didn't do any good.

Swinging his legs over the edge of his bed, he stood up, staggered, caught himself on the wall. His knees gave way and he fell to the floor, knocking over the bedside lamp and upending the table as he went. The noise reverberated through the room.

In the distance he heard a sharp cry, his name called. A door slammed.

Fuck!

Skye was coming. She'd felt him through the twin-bond. But he couldn't face her. Not now. Not like this. So desperately close to the edge.

Pushing to his feet, shaky, heart still beating frantically, he staggered over to the balcony door and wrenched it open. Cold night air hit his face, his naked chest, the scent of spring roses a lush caress covered in frost. He breathed it in, the coolness a sharp knife in his throat and nose. He didn't care. The pain was a welcome distraction from the turmoil inside.

He'd tried to choke his sister to death all those years ago and right now, he was afraid he would do it again. His wolf howled and struggled inside him, tearing at him with frustrated anger. River didn't blame it. It just wanted to be free. But these feelings weren't coming from his wolf. There was another force inside him: ravening, angry and strong. So strong. And it had been getting stronger since he'd woken from his drug-induced stupor.

Skye's tread sounded near the door to his room, Jason's less familiar tread close behind. River put his hands on the balcony and leapt despite the two-story height. He landed hard on the grass below, his knees and ankles protesting the impact. But he couldn't stop to nurse the pain. They were already at his door, calling for him, banging to get in. Ignoring them, he rose from his sprawl and ran towards the park that beckoned at the edge of the garden.

Bare feet pounded on the hard ground. Stones and twigs dug into his soles. He didn't care. Had to get away. He couldn't face her. Not with those images swirling in his head. Not when his hands itched to wrap around flesh, crushing the life within. He was cursed. An animal made rabid because it was caught in a trap, unable to get free.

His wolf snarled at the other thing inside him, lashed with a claw that felt like it ripped open his chest. He cried out, clutched at his ribs. The sensation of being torn from throat to stomach wasn't real, but Gods, it felt like it was. In his mind, his wolf was real. But he was the only one his wolf was real to. Nobody else had seen it for nineteen years, even though it had been howling and crying for attention, lashing out as its needs were ignored. Kept down by the drugs his grandmother fed him and ignored by his twin who blocked him off from their bond and shut from her mind all memory of their past that could have told her who he truly was.

That had changed in the last few days. She knew now. The spell woven around her, which had blocked her powers and memories, was gone. But she still didn't remember everything. Much of what had happened before the accident was still locked away in her mind because of the trauma of losing their parents.

He would have liked to have blocked it out, too. But that moment lived large in his mind. It fed the angry thing inside him, trapping his wolf as if he was still on the drugs his grandmother had given him. The anger stood between them. An ugly monstrous thing. A Beast. He'd seen his reflection in a mirror the night before as Adam had carried him through the portal before he'd passed out. The sight had driven an agony of shame through him and his wolf.

Neither man nor wolf, it was a half thing.

He couldn't be that. His wolf couldn't be that. It was beautiful, its nature gentle and fun-loving. It gloried in the beauty all around, especially at home outside, with the heavy scents of freshly turned earth and the fresh green scents of plants, the sweet honey of pollen.

That's who his wolf was. Who *he* was. Not this snarling angry thing, a thing made out of the fractured, tortured parts of himself and his wolf. That part had formed into a whole and it wanted to rip. To tear. To kill.

And it wanted out. Now.

His hands started to shift. Not the glorious, melting shift of the full change. This was agony, the bones crunching, ligaments popping as they reshaped themselves into claws. He came to a halt, half bent over, hands pressed to his middle, willing it to stop. But the tearing pain didn't stop.

His heart beat faster. His breath hitched in his throat.

Fear.

The thick sour taste of it in his mouth.

No. He couldn't half change. Not out here. Not feeling like this. He knew he wouldn't have control over his actions if he did. He remembered what it had felt like when he'd changed in the cave, although his rage and need for blood had a focus then—Morrigan and her puppet, Alfrere Juneau. Alfrere had died at Jason's hand before the dark warlock could rape Skye as part of the ritual to separate her from her powers and break the bond between witch and Were. But Morrigan ...

She was still out there. He wanted to slash her jugular open with his teeth, shove his claws into her chest, tear her heart from her body and bathe in her blood. He wanted—

River shook his head, trying to rid himself of the horrifying thoughts assaulting his mind. Killing anyone, even someone as deserving of death as Morrigan, went against everything he believed in. And he knew his wolf agreed. Lifting his head, he howled his defiance at the moon.

Oh Gods! The moon. The waning moon. The last day of the full moon cycle. The Beast surged forward at the beckoning of the moon. Violence threaded through River's thoughts. No! He shook his head, gritted his teeth and pushed back the ugly, seething thoughts. He had to go back. No matter his need to be alone, he needed to return to Jason and tell his Alpha to lock him up.

Freedom—the one thing he and his wolf had always craved—slipped from his grasping hands again. He might be free of the drugs, but he was still caged by his cursed nature.

Claws clenched, he turned and ran back towards the house, trying to ignore the snarl of rage from the Beast. It took everything in him to fight it. The Beast kept pushing forward, make him change direction. To hunt. To kill. To glory in the warm rush of blood as it sunk its teeth into flesh.

'No!' His denial echoed in the bush around him.

The Beast snarled again. The muscles of his face pulled, elongating. He fought against the change. Fought for control of his body, bones groaning under the pressure.

The waning moon glowed down on him, making a mockery of his efforts to wrestle with centuries of conditioning.

'River.' River's head snapped up. Skye. She was calling to him, still some distance away, but her voice was clear to his Were hearing. 'River. Come home.'

The image from his nightmare snapped into his mind and he stopped. His wolf howled as the Beast pushed it aside, the ferociousness of its hatred overriding the love River and his wolf felt for his sister.

The Beast snarled, its contempt sliding into River like a saw-toothed knife.

'River! Please. Let us help.'

The snarling was cut off by a choked laugh. Help? Now she wanted to help? It was too late to help him. Didn't she realise that? Didn't she know?

'Please, River. Don't cut me out. Not when we've just got our twin-bond back.'

The pounding of her feet on the ground as she ran, searching for him, following the tug of the twin-bond, thudded through his entire body.

Others were with her too. Were in human and wolf form.

No! He couldn't see Skye when he longed to choke the breath from her. He began to run, the Beast pushing painfully at his flesh, longing to dance in the light of the moon. River gritted his jaw until it ached, curled his talons into his hands until they cut his flesh. He couldn't change. He wouldn't.

Flesh. Blood. The perfume of sweat-scented skin. The panted breaths of a jogger. Sneaker-clad feet beating a rhythm on the path to his right, an even more enticing rhythm fluttering behind the sound —heartbeat. The Beast stilled inside him, then with a howl, burst through his skin.

River fell. Skin tore on his knees and hands as he hit the earth. The stinging pain was nothing compared to the agony of his limbs and ligaments stretching. Hair sprouted from his skin, his face pushed out, lips thinned, teeth turned into razor-sharp fangs. He couldn't make a sound; the agony stole his breath, choking him.

Then it stopped.

He drew in a deep shuddering breath. The wolf in his mind pushed for prominence. But it couldn't get out. The Beast was in the way.

And it had scented the prey.

Its nose twitched as it drank in the mouth-watering scents. Before River could protest, the Beast was in his limbs and he was off.

The jogger was nearby. Musky cologne over sweat: a man. Faint music tinkled in the air from the jogger's earbuds. The sound and scent guided him to his prey.

Just up ahead.

He could see him now, the straight line of his back, the muscles of his legs and arms, sweat glistening in the moonlight. Warm. He could almost taste the heat of exertion on those muscles. Delicious—salted meat.

The wolf took prey from behind, quick and clean. But the Beast wanted to skirt around, to be seen, leaping as terror shot through the prey, adrenaline surging, making the blood so very sweet as teeth sank into shoulder and neck, tearing out the jugular. The prey wasn't

Morrigan, but he would do for now. It would lap of this blood tonight. It would taste good.

With a low growl, it drew closer.

'*River, no.*' Jason tackled him to the ground as the Alpha-command vibrated through him.

The Beast rolled with the impact, disentangling itself from the giant silver and gold wolf, and found its feet, coming up into a half crouch with a snarl.

The runner, feet slapping the hard path, was about to disappear over the rise. The Beast turned. It couldn't let the prey get away. It was hungry. It needed to feast as it hadn't been able to feast for years.

But the gold and silver wolf crouched, ready to spring again. In the way.

The Beast growled. Lips pulled away from fangs, claw swiping. The gold and silver wolf, the Alpha, sprang aside.

'*River. No.*'

That voice reverberated in its head again, through its body, pulling at the man inside the Beast. It tried to shake off the command's influence. Now that the Alpha was no longer standing in the way, the Beast could see that the runner had almost disappeared, the music channelled through the earbuds making him oblivious to death stalking so close behind. The prey wasn't going to get away. The Beast leapt up the path.

'*River. Stop.*'

Those half parts that made the Beast—man and wolf—wanted to obey.

'*River. I command you. Stop.*'

Muscles spasmed, quivered. But the Alpha-command didn't have the influence it would normally have on a Were. The Beast was not truly Were. It could fight the command if only it could hold on.

But the man and wolf inside were fighting too, spurred on by the Alpha-command and the twin-bond. Its movements slowed under their combined force. The Beast howled. The prey was getting away!

Enraged, it tore at the fetters of the bond, catching them all by surprise. Freed, it leapt forward towards the warm flesh a hundred metres ahead.

'River.'

Every muscle quivered at the sound of that sweet voice; the only voice with the capability of stopping the man and wolf in their tracks. The shock of it stopped the Beast too.

River surged forward, enough to grasp a little control. Breath tight in his chest, in his throat, he turned to face the source of that voice.

Bronwyn emerged from the woods at the base of the rise, panting hard, with Skye, equally breathless, at her side.

'River, please.' His sister.

He growled. Bronwyn raised her hand, stepping in front of Skye.

'Bron, no. He's not himself. He might hurt you.' Skye grabbed Bronwyn's arm, pulling her back.

River quivered with rage that someone else would put their hands on Bronwyn. She was his. Snarling, he snapped his teeth together, his muscles bunched to leap.

'No. He's there. Can't you feel him?' Bronwyn pulled out of Skye's grasp and quickly moved forward, hand outstretched. 'River, please, let me help.'

He quivered in place, confused.

His Bronwyn wanted to help.

He knew she was his. Had known it the moment he opened his eyes and saw her standing there looking down at him the night before. It was a knowing that sank its claws deep into his soul, and no matter how much he longed to deny it, it wouldn't shake free.

She belonged to him. Yet she could never belong to him.

He focused on his clawed hands, the fur standing erect on his arms. He wasn't whole. He was dangerous. And yet she was here, walking towards him, compassion in her eyes despite the fear he could smell on her, the fear in the fast-paced patter of her heart, her short, sharp breaths as she tried to calm her breathing after her desperate run.

'Don't come near me,' he growled. 'I might hurt you.'

'You didn't hurt me last night. You won't hurt me now,' she said, moving closer hand still outstretched. 'Let us help.'

'Yes, River. Let us help.' The Alpha-command suddenly had more sway, backed up with the plea of the woman who would have been his mate if Morrigan and her rogue coven hadn't intervened in his life. A growl burst to life in his throat, but the blood-slavering viciousness of before was gone.

'It's working, Jason. Keep doing whatever you're doing.'

'That's right, River. Just back down and let us help.'

River almost choked on a laugh. They thought Jason's Alpha-command was making the difference. They were wrong.

Bronwyn had almost reached him. A black wolf appeared at her side, pushing in front of her. She reached out to pat his head. 'It's okay, Adam. River won't hurt me.'

Adam's wolf nudged at her leg.

River snarled at the black wolf. He didn't like how close it was to Bronwyn. Didn't like the way she touched Adam-wolf, that gentle stroke across ruffled fur that spoke of familiarity, friendship ... love?

Fuck!

The thought was a jagged tear in his heart. He gasped out a pained breath.

'He's hurting. Jason, quick.' Bronwyn turned to wave the gold and silver wolf forward. 'I can see it. The damage to his aura is worse in this form than in his human one. It's covered in darkness.'

There was a shower of golden-rainbow glow and then Jason stood before him. Bronwyn didn't spare the Alpha's nakedness a second glance as she grabbed his hand and pulled him forward. 'I need you to touch River.'

'Can you force him to change?'

She nodded at Skye's question. 'I can, like I did last night. But I couldn't do it without help. That darkness in his aura fights me. Healing him through pack-touch was the only thing that worked last night. I think it's the only thing that will work now.'

Jason nodded and let her guide him. Skye appeared just beyond his shoulder.

River couldn't look at her. He no longer wished to hurt her, but he was ashamed of how much he'd wanted to only moments ago and was so terribly afraid she would be able to read those thoughts in his mind.

'Oh, River,' Skye whispered, voice trembling.

'Don't,' he managed through a throat raw with banked violence. He stood tall, towering over even his Alpha in this form, his moonlit shadow cast long on the ground, a grotesque melding of wolf and man. He closed his eyes against the sight and whispered, 'Help.'

Jason's warm hand splayed over his chest. His wolf surged forward, writhing under the exquisite rightness of his Alpha's touch. But there was another touch it longed for more.

Bronwyn placed her hand next to Jason's. The Beast snarled. She recoiled as if she'd been burned.

'Bron? Are you all right?' Skye grabbed Bronwyn's shoulder, but she shrugged from the touch.

'I'm fine. That thing inside him lashed out. It doesn't want me to touch him.' She stared at him, her eyes on the spot where Jason's hand was splayed over his chest. Then she smiled and reached forward again. 'If I can just ...'

He tried to cry out a warning, but the Beast was in his throat again and snarled a warning. She didn't listen. Trembling, River did all he could to rope the Beast in, the violence inside him urging him to do horrible things as Bronwyn moved closer.

She didn't touch him as he longed for and feared.

Instead, she placed her hand over Jason's and he sensed as she slipped into the warm rightness of his Alpha's touch. He shuddered as the Beast tried to surge forward again, but something stopped it. It was tethered, pushed back by the warmth, the glow of her as she reached inside him through the Alpha-bond.

The warmth melted through him and he gave himself over to it. And as his wolf and his mind accepted the Healing warmth, he noticed something in the sweet happiness she used to push the Beast aside. Something deep at her core that she didn't even let her best friends see. But he saw it. Felt it. And as she sent her magic into him, he knew deep in his soul that he knew her better than anyone had ever known her before. He alone knew of that kernel of pain and mistrust of herself deep inside.

She had a flaw, his mate. And she was ever the more perfect because of it.

His grotesque wolf lips pull up into something like a smile. There was hope in her future. That would have to be enough.

'I think it's working,' Skye whispered.

She was right. The terrible grinding, snapping pain as his limbs contracted made him want to scream. But he held it in, even as the patches of fur dissolved from his skin in a heated, hurtful parody of the golden glow of the Were change. His eyes watered, heart pounded under the stress, nostrils flared as he tried to breathe. His legs trembled, but he held on, kept himself upright through force of will.

He would not be weak before his pack.

More of them had arrived to witness his torment, their glowing eyes staring at him out of the dark. He wished they'd go away. Hadn't he kept himself together all these years without them? He didn't need them. Didn't need any of them.

'River, are you okay?' The tears in Skye's voice almost undid him. As the grinding pain in his face came to an end, and he knew the change had finished, he managed to nod.

Jason's hand left his skin. The warm imprint turned quickly cold, but he didn't miss it. He missed the sweet glow that had come through that hand from Bronwyn. He longed to feel her hand on his flesh. Longed to have it stroke over him, bringing bliss, chasing the remnants of pain and fear and violence away. But he couldn't have that and he had to stop thinking about wanting it. He took a deep breath, suddenly aware of the sweat prickling his skin, cold in the spring night air.

'River. Thank God you're back. Thank you, Bron.'

He opened his eyes as Skye reached for him. 'Don't.' He stepped back. The pain in her eyes stabbed at him. He gentled his expression. 'I just need a moment, okay? My wolf is riding me hard.' It was a lie. A necessary one. They could never know what this had cost him.

His wolf whimpered, ashamed of what it had nearly done. *Not you*, he whispered to it. *Me. It was me.* It howled its denial. It wouldn't let him take the burden alone. *We can't let it happen again.* The wolf agreed. River turned to Jason. 'You need to lock put me back under.'

'River, no,' Skye protested. 'We've only just got you out of that cage of drugs Grandma had you in. You can't think I'd let that happen again? I w—'

'It isn't your choice. It's mine.'

'I won't do what your grandmother did to you,' Jason said. 'Don't ask me to do that.'

'But the drugs my grandmother gave me just suppressed what was growing inside. They might be necessary.'

'They caused the fracture,' Skye insisted.

He shook his head. 'No. You're wrong. I mean, maybe, in the long run, they made it worse, but that fracture was caused by something else. Or else I would never have hurt Skye when we were ten. Grandmother knew I couldn't live with myself if I did that again. She loved me enough to know that. So she caged me and my wolf with the drugs.' He flexed his fingers. 'But I'm drug free now and I almost killed someone tonight. You can't put me through that again. So if you won't give me the drugs, you'll have to at least lock me up.'

'But you didn't kill someone. You stopped. Jason stopped you.' Her hand fluttered as if she wanted to touch him, but thankfully she pulled back before she did. 'I've just got you back, River. I don't want to lose you again.'

'You might not have any choice. If I can't control the Beast, then I will kill. Do you want to let me be a killer?'

'No! Don't talk like that, River. Please.'

'One of us has to be realistic. There's something broken inside me. If I can't change in full, I'll go rabid. And Jason will have to hunt me down and kill me.'

'No!' She turned, gripped her mate's arm. 'Jason wouldn't do that. He'd find another way.' Jason didn't say anything, but his gaze was too full of the truth for him to hide it. 'No!' she cried, letting him go, her hands clutching over her heart.

River couldn't bear to see her anguish. He reached out to touch her face, his hand trembling with the strength it took to be gentle right now. 'You never saw me for what I truly am and you're not seeing it now.'

'I am.' She reached up to press his hand more firmly to her cheek. 'You're strong. So strong. It's you who doesn't see yourself clearly. You've held on for all these years. Can't you hold on a little longer? We'll find a cure. We started looking through the diaries today. Shelley and Bron and I. We'll study and learn and Bron will learn about her Healer abilities and we'll find a way. Won't we, Bron?'

Bronwyn didn't answer. He turned. The slight Healer was leaning against the big black wolf, her face pale, shadows like bruises under her eyes. And those eyes—the cinnamon irises were almost swallowed by the black of her pupil as she stared at them blankly.

'Bron?' Jason said.

'Are you okay?' Skye asked.

Bronwyn's gaze shifted to them, unfocused. She wobbled and gave a faint, drunken smile. 'I'mokay. Jushtoomushpower.' She crumpled.

River caught her before she hit the ground. He pulled her against his chest, revelling in the feel of her weight in his arms while worry skated through his veins like cold fire. 'Bronwyn,' he whispered.

She looked up at him and smiled again. 'River.' Her eyes rolled up, her head fell back.

'Bron?' Skye was at his side, her voice shaking and high.

River shifted Bronwyn so that her head lay on his shoulder.

'It's okay. She's just passed out.' Jason came up behind Skye and hugged her. 'She channelled an incredible amount of power into River just then. I felt it flow through me.'

'You should have stopped her,' River snapped.

Jason's electric blue eyes were dark with sincerity as he said, 'I would have if I'd known another way, but for now, that seems to be the only way to bring you back from the edge.'

'Not the only way,' River growled. He began to stalk back down the path he'd hunted on only a few minutes earlier.

'I won't lock you up. Not while you're lucid,' Jason called behind him. 'That won't help you or your wolf.'

'Fine,' River snarled, turning around to pierce his Alpha with a glare. 'But you will need to keep a guard on me, because I can't guarantee how long this lucidity will last.'

Jason nodded.

'But during the full moon cycle, you *will* lock me up. If you don't, I'll do it myself. This can never happen again.' And so saying, he continued down the path, past all the wolves who stared at him like he was a curiosity, Bronwyn a warm weight in his arms.

2

'Did you feel that?' Morrigan Cantrae asked, her head snapping up as she stared around, half expecting to see the air electrified or the world to ripple.

'Feel what?' Eloise O'Brien—the acolyte who was seeing to Morrigan's needs for the day—asked in that little mouse voice that she couldn't stand.

Letting out a hiss of frustration, Morrigan said, 'That shift in the power lanes is what. It almost felt like ...'

'Felt like what, Mistress?'

Morrigan didn't answer, just closed her eyes and concentrated. Something had changed. She reached out with her mind, but exhaustion caused her usually dextrous touch on the power lanes to be more like a groping hand in the dark.

Anger grew from a little kernel in her chest. 'Damn them all to hell that they laid me low like this.' Everything was ruined. Centuries of waiting and planning and building had all come to nought. Her sister was unavenged and much of her power had been channelled into Alfrere so he could do what he'd been moulded to do. And now he was gone and she was back to where she'd started all those years ago.

Unable to use her powers, she picked up the bowl and threw it against the wall.

Eloise flinched as water and pottery exploded, showering over them both. The acolyte immediately grabbed a cloth to wipe it from Morrigan's skin before it could get into the wounds on her face and upper body.

The cloth touched the edge of the deepest gash on Morrigan's face. 'Ow. Be careful.' Morrigan sat up, swiping away Eloise's help. It was useless. Everything was useless. She wanted to cry, to bury herself in the ancient grief that had dug a hole in her heart. She pushed her burned fist against her chest, tears pricking her eyes at the double pain, breath hitching, heart thundering. She began to rock. 'I'm sorry. I'm so sorry,' she whispered.

'Mistress, you need to calm yourself. You're still not healed yet.'

Morrigan's head snapped up as she rocked, eyes pinning Eloise with her stare. 'I would be if you were any kind of proper Healer.'

Head bowed, the acolyte clenched her hands in front of her. 'I'm sorry, Mistress. I know my efforts aren't good enough. I *will* try harder. For you. I will do anything for you.'

Something stirred inside Morrigan at those words. She stopped rocking and peered along her nose at Eloise, bowing before her like a supplicant. Water dripped down her face, bits of pottery were in her tawny hair. She bled from small cuts on her cheek. And yet she'd not ministered to herself at all. She'd thought first of Morrigan. As a proper acolyte should.

'*The girl is more than an acolyte.*'

Morrigan let out a sobbing sigh of relief as she heard the Darkness' whisper. 'You're back.'

'*I never left. I'm just not whole as I was. But you can fix that. This girl can help you. You chose her along with her brother Cain and their cousin Ben for that reason.*'

'Yes.' Morrigan nodded. Their powers were unique. But they needed to be strengthened to suit her needs. This girl, Eloise, was even more unique. She had strengths in a number of areas, strengths that Morrigan had kept repressed because she didn't want any of the coven to rise up higher than her.

'*This is but a setback. All is not lost. There is another way.*'

Like a blinding flash, one face appeared before her eyes.

River.

He stood in beast form, half man, half wolf, the moon high in the sky behind him, the body of a woman at his feet, blood dripping red from his hands. He howled to the moon. A kernel of blackness nothing more than an inky sludge, spread between his double auras. It writhed and spread its tentacles, planting itself firmly, separating man and wolf.

She gasped. The Darkness had got inside River!

At some time in the past he'd invited it in.

It was only a sliver, but with the right impetus, sometimes a sliver was enough. It was hope, the heart of her deepest desires. A way forward.

She just had to find a way to tap into it, make it grow.

'*We started the beginnings of this transformation twenty years ago. You felt a whisper of it coming to life just now. And it's tangled up with that Wiccan-witch Healer. I know you felt it. So use that. Move forward.*'

'But how?'

'*Train Eloise as you train her brother. Use her. Infiltration is the key.*'

'Yes.' The Darkness was right. His council was sound.

'*She can be our true family. If moulded correctly, she will allow me in, just as her brethren did centuries ago. Just as you did.*'

'*Then you must complete her now.*'

'*No. I must be invited in. You know this. I need you to …*'

Morrigan sighed as the whisper faded. The Darkness had been drained too by the events on Samhain. They both needed to heal, but now, at least, she had a plan. A way forward, even if it was still unclear.

She reached out to touch Eloise's chin, tipping her head up to look in the clear, strange yellow-green eyes of this girl who did not know what she truly was. But Morrigan did, because of the Darkness.

She was the vessel. The way forward. As was River and somehow, that meddling Wiccan-witch, Bronwyn.

Through them, Morrigan would have her revenge.

3

'Are you sure you're okay in there by yourself?'

'More than okay,' Bron said to Iain, her Shadow for the day. She slipped the key into the lock and opened the door of her shop. Plastering a smile across her face, hoping it would convince him in the same way it had convinced Patrick, her Shadow for the past two weeks, she turned. 'I've got some reading to do and some spells to try.' She tapped the Pack Diary in her arms. 'And I need some peace and quiet to concentrate.'

'But shutting down your shop ...' He cocked his head as he looked at the dark shop behind her. 'That seems a bit extreme. I'm sure we could find somewhere for you to have peace and quiet at the Packhouse while your assistant continues to run the shop.'

'You're kidding, right?' She laughed, the sound a tad hysterical. His dark brown gaze swung to her, piercing in its intensity. 'Not about my assistant,' she hedged. 'She'd run the place no problems.'

'I know the Packhouse can be busy, but we all know the importance of the work you, Skye and Shelley are doing. Jason would kick everyone out if you asked.'

'I know he would. But I wouldn't do that to the pack.' Her smile gentled as she touched his arm; her new pack didn't just responded favourably to touch, they needed it. Although Iain didn't flinch away, her touch didn't seem to settle him like it did the others—in fact, it seemed to make him study her even more closely.

She let her hand drop back to her side. 'The pack need their Alpha to be accessible and he's not leaving Skye's side any time soon, so it makes more sense that seeing I'm the one with the problem, I should take care of it myself, not dump it on others.'

'You don't have to work alone.'

'I know. But I want to. It's only a few weeks until the next full moon and I need to find a way to help River.'

'He told Adam he doesn't want your help if it means you flare out again.'

She let out a puff of annoyed breath. 'Is that why he's been avoiding me?'

Iain shrugged, his dark gaze boring into her. 'Will you? Flare out again?'

Bron's mouth tightened and she looked away. She didn't know. She had no idea why she'd flared out that night or why her powers had gone haywire ever since. But she wasn't about to admit that to Iain. So she said, 'River's aura fought me that night and I had to push too hard to get in. I won't do it that way again. I need to research, to think. That's why I'm here.' That was partly true. River *had* fought her and she'd barely managed to get past his barriers and quiet the thing that raged inside him—and that was when she had some semblance of control. Now ...

She didn't dare touch him until she was certain of what she was doing. And she couldn't concentrate on gaining back her control with the urgent expectation in Skye's eyes haunting her.

Not that she blamed her friend. They were running out of time. All of them knew it. Bron just didn't need the emotionally draining reminder every time she caught her friend's gaze.

Iain began to say something else, but movement caught her eye in the trees at the side of the road and she tuned out. Those trees led back to the clearing where her grandma used to perform her most powerful spells and worship the Mother Goddess.

She frowned. Nobody should be back there. It was private property, part of the land Adeline Kincaid had bought because of the ancient power of the untouched bushland there. 'Is someone else shadowing me today?'

Iain followed the direction of her gaze. 'No. I'm your only Shadow. Why?'

She shook her head slowly. 'I don't know. I just thought I saw someone standing over there.'

Iain's body shifted, tensed as he turned to stand in front of her. 'Who?'

'I don't know. I couldn't see them clearly. It was probably nothing,' she said, shrugging. 'Probably just the trees shifting in the breeze. I am pretty tired. I could be seeing things.'

He frowned. 'You shouldn't be so flippant in the face of possible danger.'

'I'm not being flippant.' He raised his brow at her. 'Okay, maybe a little flippant,' she said, entering her shop. 'But really, something being in those bushes is more a *you* problem than a me problem, right?'

'Right.'

'So perhaps you should go check it out.'

'I'll go and check it out, right after I've checked in here.'

He moved past her too quickly for her to protest.

She sighed in aggravation—honestly, the Were really could afford to take a class in getting a clue at some stage. 'My shop is safe,' she called out as he disappeared into the back section.

'You can't know that for certain,' he called back.

'Oh, but I can,' she said to herself. She could feel it in her bones; the deep sense of welcome and homecoming as if the building itself was alive. Adeline had always said she would know if there was something wrong with her shop, and now it was Bron's, she understood what her grandma meant.

Iain was back a few moments later after checking out the client rooms, the storeroom, the office upstairs and her workroom. 'Everything seems fine in here,' he said, stalking behind the front counter.

'That was quick.'

'Not really.' He turned to face at her.

She didn't expect the usual smile she got from Patrick—Iain was a different kettle of fish altogether from his brother—but she didn't expect him to look so grim.

'I'm going to go and check outside. I want you to lock the door and stay away from the windows. You've got my mobile number if you need me.'

'You don't have to do that,' she began, but it was too late. He was already gone. A sigh of relief escaped her lips. She knew she needed a Shadow to protect her from Morrigan and her rogue coven, but she was kind of glad right now that Iain had gone. He was far too canny —more so than the fun-loving Patrick—and she was afraid he would discover her secret and let the others know. That was the last thing she needed right now. She couldn't stand their pity and worry bearing down on her too.

Just as she was about to lock the door, a small shape darted into the shop. Stopping before her, the little tawny cat twirled around Bron's legs, meowing loudly. 'Bluebelle,' Bron cooed. She bent and picked up the cat, careful of its sensitive back leg that had obviously been broken at some stage and not healed properly. 'You felt my need, didn't you?' she asked, stroking the cat's small head.

The cat, her new Familiar, meowed and rubbed her face against Bron's before jumping down and scampering off with a limping gate into Bron's workroom. 'I'll feed you in a minute,' Bron called out. But instead of following the little cat, her gaze was drawn outside to the quiet streetscape.

There were only a few shops along this stretch of road that lay at the peak of the hill—an enticing building that had been modelled to look like a gingerbread house that sold the boiled lollies that were Shelley's only food weakness, an antique store, and an old-fashioned café that did the best Devonshire teas in the whole of Victoria as far as Bron was concerned. Each shop was lined up on her side of the road, because the other side was almost cliff-like and afforded a deli-cious view of the rolling hills and dense bushland that stretched out from Kangaroo Grounds to Sugarloaf Reservoir and beyond. On a clear day, she fancied she could see all the way to the Victorian Alps.

The peacefulness of that view usually filled her with such contentment. Today, it filled her with something else. An itchy longing for something more, something ...

She shook her head, cursing herself for an idiot. She had important things to concentrate on—and getting her powers to behave so she could heal River properly and stop him from turning into the Beast again was at the top of that list.

Shoving the door closed, the bell tinkling madly above her head, she spun and faced her shop. Pleasure filled her despite the turmoil in her mind as she looked over the shelves of creams and ointments she'd made, the clean lines of the sales desk and the jewellery and crystals they sold, glinting in the light coming in through the window to the right. Perhaps she should rearrange the display? She hadn't done that for a while. Or she could dust and check the dates on the bottles of medicinals she sold.

A loud meow sounded from her workroom, jolting her back to reality. She was procrastinating. Nothing needed to be dusted or checked or rearranged. Everything was as it should be. She was the only thing here out of step.

Another plaintive meow made her smile. 'I'm coming,' she called. But instead of moving, she sighed again. She couldn't be sorry for the spell she and Shelley had canted to help their friend win against that mad witch, Morrigan Cantrae, but what they said about consequences was true—she was paying for hers now.

Another meow echoed through the room and Bluebelle darted out from the workroom and stared at her from the doorway as if to say, 'What's more important than feeding me?'

Bron chuckled, a bitter edge to the sound. 'I wish that was all I had to worry about.' Bluebell meowed again. 'I know. You're hungry. I'm coming now.' Shaking off the lethargy that kept seeking to take a hold of her, lethargy that would have once seemed alien but was now almost a friend, she took a deep, calming breath and made her way to the workroom.

As she passed the shelves that stood to the right of the door, a set of candles caught her eye. Excitement flickered in her chest as she came to a halt, staring at them. Bluebelle meowed again as she noticed Bron halt. Bron looked down at the cat. 'Just a minute, sweetie. I've had an idea.' She put the Pack Diary she'd brought with her on the shelf and picked up the frankincense candle—nothing was quite like frankincense for inspiration—and then darted over to another shelf and picked up a large moonstone. The crystal, alive with earth energy, buzzed and tingled in her hand. A sense of peace settled over her telling her this was right.

Bluebelle meowed at Bron again and she turned, a smile that felt true for the first time in days parting her lips. 'Thanks Bluebelle. You're right. Start at the basics. You are hungry, so I feed you—the hunger goes away. My magic isn't working, so I need to feed it with basic magic and retrain it.' She hurried into her workroom, put the candle and moonstone on the round table in the centre of the room, placed some smoked salmon—Bluebelle had a discerning palate and would only eat smoked salmon and cooked chicken—on a plate on the floor. She rushed back into the shop and gathered up a few more things, almost running back into the workroom.

She forced herself to take some calming breaths then put the frankincense candle on the shelf near the table and lit it. She sat at the table, placed a plain beeswax candle on the plate in front of her and breathed in the rich aroma of frankincense. Holding the moonstone clutched in one hand, she took twenty deep, calming breaths until her heart was beating slow and steady. 'Right. Start with basics,' she whispered. 'Concentrate, Bron. Light the candle.'

Closing her eyes, she settled into an old familiar cantrip to put her mind at rest, and then gathering the magic she borrowed from her Goddess—a teeth-clenching moment as it resisted her manipulation—she built the image of flame flickering to life on the wick in front of her. Once the image was stable, she filled it with the energy of her magic and as she sent that image out of her mind, centring the energy on the beeswax candle, said, 'Light.'

The magical energy skittered off to the side and slid away. She didn't even have to open her eyes to know the candle hadn't lit. Firming her lips, she took in another breath and tried again. Patience. That's all this would take. A little retraining led by patience.

A pity patience had never been her strong suit.

But today, with desperation filling her and an emptiness she'd not experienced since her grandma's death waiting to swallow her whole, she would become more patient than even the Dalai Lama.

At least, she would try.

Teeth clenched, she pulled on the resisting magic and tried again.

SHELLEY HOPPED out of the car and had to grab hold of the door to stop herself from wobbling. The last thing she wanted was for annoying Adam to do the caveman thing and pick her up and cart her home again. She was just tired. Not to mention feeling the stress of trying to keep all the spirits away. The extra power she'd taken on to save her friend had unexpected side effects. It was as if she was a mozzie-light for spirits. They'd always hung around, but not like this.

She glared at them as they rushed her now, wispy tendrils of fog that left shivers on her skin as they tried to touch her, begging for her attention. Her head throbbed. 'Piss off,' she said, in a low, harsh whisper. 'Leave me alone.'

'You know I can't do that.'

The tendrils parted to show Adam in front of her. 'I'm not talking to you,' she said testily. 'I'm talking to them.' She waved her hand.

Adam's eyes didn't waver from her like most people when she indicated spirits were around. 'Are they hurting you?'

The growl in his voice made them tumble away. She would have laughed if she wasn't so relieved. 'No. They can't hurt me.'

'Liar. I can see your headache has got worse.'

She gaped at him. 'How did you know I have a headache?'

'You're grumpier than usual.'

'I am not grumpy.'

'Yes you are. Normally you're just tetchy, but today you're down-right grumpy.'

She was about to bark at him when she saw the twitch on his annoying lips. He was laughing at her! She whacked him across the shoulder with the diary she held in her hand.

'Ow! Why do people keep hitting me?'

'Because you deserve it,' she said, glaring at him with what she hoped was a death-stare. By the way his lips twitched, she'd missed by a mile. Fuck. So she poked him in the chest with a hard finger. 'I am not tetchy or grumpy. I'm just tired because I've come off a very long night shift and need some sleep.'

'Firstly, ow! Again.' He captured her finger, holding it against his chest. She tried to pull it out of his grasp but failed—he didn't even seem to notice her pathetic attempt, as he said, 'Secondly, if you're so tired, perhaps I should take you home now and tuck you into bed.'

She glared at him—not that glaring at him had any effect whatso-ever. Which was even more annoying. She knew she gave good glare. Many a belligerent patient became meek and compliant under that glare. But the more she glared, the more he smiled. 'Argh,' she said, finally managing to pull out of his grasp—which allowed her to turn on her heel and stalk towards Bron's shop.

He caught up with her in a stride.

'Go away,' she said, purposefully not looking at him.

'Are the spirits here again? If I wave my hands around, will that make them go away?'

She snort-laughed as he began to do just that. 'No. Your hands just pass right through them. But I wasn't talking to them anyway. I was talking to you. Can't somebody else be my Shadow?'

'Nope. Where you go, I go too, I'm afraid,' he said in a doleful voice that made her want to start giggling again.

She coughed to hide it, telling herself she was just punch drunk from tiredness, and marched even faster.

'Why are we here?'

'Ah, to visit Bron. I thought that would be obvious given you've driven me over here and now I'm walking to the front door.'

'Ah, good, we're back to tetchy.'

She threw him a look.

He just smiled and said, 'I meant, why are we visiting Bron? You barrelled out of the house so quickly, I didn't have a chance to ask.'

'No, you were too busy singing "Suicide Blonde" all the way over here to ask a question.'

'I like that song, so sue me.' He smirked when she glowered her annoyance. 'Besides, I'm asking now. Why did you suddenly feel the need to come over and visit with Bron? I'm sure a phone call would have done the trick.'

'No it wouldn't.'

'And why not?'

She turned to face him after stepping up onto the porch of the shop, the extra foot of height allowing her to look down at him a little. 'I was doing some reading when I got home from my shift and—'

'You should have gone to bed, given how exhausted you are.'

She would have snapped at him again, except his tone this time wasn't joking, but concerned. She swallowed down the lump that note of concern brought and said, 'Yeah, well, I often can't sleep after shifts like that. I need to wind down.'

'I wouldn't think wading through one of these would be the answer,' he said, flicking his finger over the corner of the diary. 'Wouldn't a romance book or something light be better?'

'If you like that kind of thing.' His brow raised at her bitter tone, but he didn't make a quip, just crossed his arms in an attitude of listening. It made her uncomfortable. Shuffling back, she hugged the diary to her chest. 'These diaries are fascinating, not to mention that aside from video messaging with Cordy, they're our only way of learning anything about our powers now. So I have to read them.'

Adam stepped up onto the porch, crowding into her space, and tapped the book. 'What's so important that made you come rushing over here, even though you should be in bed?'

Shelley edged towards the front door, not liking how intimate he made that sound. 'I found something that indicates Morrigan is still in Skye's grandma's body and won't be able to change out of it until Yule.'

'What?' He grabbed her, stopping her backwards movement. 'Jason needs to know this now.'

She shrugged out of his hold. 'Then you can go and tell him. I need to talk to Bron.'

'I think it's more important you tell Jason first. This could make all the difference to us catching the evil bitch.'

'Maybe. Not that I think she's going to be out and about any time soon. Her power will be depleted and she won't be able to fully juice up until the next threefold flux of power.'

'Which is when?'

'Yule. There'll be another full moon then. She'll be able to pull on its power and the festival's power of rebirth.'

'That's only two. You said a threefold flux. What's the third?'

'Sacrifice. She has to kill someone to take over their body. Somebody with a bit of their own power, but not too much, otherwise they might fight back.'

'Like she did with Skye's grandma?'

Shelley nodded. That's why I have to talk to Bron. She's better at this kind of thing than I am.'

'What kind of thing?'

Shelley frowned at him. 'The kind of thing where you have to tell your best friend that the woman who killed her grandma is still in her body and the only way she can get out of it is to kill someone else just before Christmas.'

'Is anybody good at that kind of thing?'

'Better than I am.' Shelley turned from him and came to a stop as she noticed the sign on the door. 'Closed? Why is Bron's shop closed?'

Adam shrugged and whistled. A moment later, Iain rounded the corner and bounded onto the porch.

Shelley pointed at the sign. 'Why has Bron closed her shop?'

'She didn't tell me why, but Patrick told me when I got here that she's had the sign up all week. She apparently called her assistant and told her to go on a holiday for a while.'

'What?'

Adam gripped her shoulder as she reached for the door handle. 'What's wrong?'

'Bron hasn't closed her shop for one day since she inherited it from her grandma. If she was sick or on holiday, then she's had Helen or one of her grandma's old coven run it for her. Something's terribly wrong.' She turned the handle. The door clicked and pushed open.

'She was supposed to lock that,' Iain grumbled.

He and Adam moved forward as if to follow her, but Shelley held up her hand. 'Stay here. It's better I find out what's going on first. If you come in she'll put on her "happy" face and I'll get nothing out of her.' Adam opened his mouth to protest, but she put her hand on his chest, stopping him from moving past her. 'Trust me on this, Adam. Despite how close you've become, I know her better than you do. If there's a problem, I'll call. You can both come in and do your hero thing then.'

'I don't do the hero thing,' Adam protested.

Shelley rolled her eyes at Iain, who grinned and said, 'Let the lady talk to her friend, Adam.'

He subsided, but she heard the wolf in his voice as he said, 'I'll be right here.'

Shelley nodded, stepped inside and closed the door behind her. A chill chased over her skin as she stepped over the threshold, followed by a terrible feeling of doubt, depression chasing hard on its heels. There was frustration too, and anxiety. Not good. Sounds were coming from the workroom to the right of the main shop. Then she heard a voice.

'Oh, Goddess, I call on thee. Three times three times three times three, bring light to me, so mote it be.'

A sensation, like static electricity, chased across Shelley's skin and she hugged her arms to herself. 'What is she doing?' she whispered.

'Trying to light the candle.'

Shelley whipped around as a spirit manifested beside her. 'Adeline!' she said. 'Do you have to creep up on me like that?'

'I don't creep, *mo daor*. I'm an apparition. So I appear.' She gestured widely, like a magician at the end of a trick.

Shelley rolled her eyes. There was little point having an argument with this particular spirit. Bron's grandma had been stubborn in life and had become even more so in spirit.

'What are you doing here?'

'I'm here to help.' She gestured at Shelley. 'Do you mind?'

Shelley's eyes widened. 'Yes I bloody well do mind. Help in some other way.'

Adeline shook her head sadly and inched closer. 'I would if it would do any good. But it's too time consuming and tiring to go through you as an intermediary.'

'Then I'll let her hear you, like I did with Harrison.'

Adeline stopped and seemed to consider for a moment before shaking her head. 'No. I'm afraid this will be better.'

Shelley desperately tried to raise her barriers, but they wouldn't respond—she was simply too exhausted. She shuffled back, hands out defensively. 'Please don't. You know—'

Adeline rushed at her. Shelley made a choking sound and shuddered, eyes rolling in her head as the spirit connected and sank into her. Her bag and the diary thumped to the ground as the spirit of Adeline Kincaid pushed her consciousness aside and took over her body.

Shelley yelled and fought back, but Adeline made her limbs move, catching herself on a nearby shelf before she fell to the floor. After a moment of making certain she had control, Adeline forced her to walk towards the mirror hanging on the far wall. Shelley tried to fight but it was no use—Adeline was too strong.

Then she was staring at her reflection, the strange black of her eyes, the slightly dishevelled tumble of blonde hair and the grimace on her lips.

Hands rising jerkily, she pushed her hair back, patting it into place. Then her mouth open and with the distinctive Irish lilt of Adeline Kincaid, said, 'I'm sorry, *mo daor*, but it's the best way of reaching my Bronwyn. Perhaps she would listen to you, but this way is certain. I'll give you back to yourself as soon as I'm done. And promise I won't do it again for long while.'

'*Only because you won't have the energy.*' Shelley's railed, her voice an echo in her mind. '*Don't think I'm going to forgive you for this.*'

'We'll see,' Adeline Kincaid said. 'Now, let's go help my grand-daughter.' She moved towards the workroom, a little unsteadily at first, but with each step she sank deeper into Shelley's body and took firmer control until she was gliding along the floor with the same gentle grace she'd moved with in life.

She opened the door.

4

'**B**loody hell! What's wrong with this thing, Bluebelle? Why won't it fucking work?'

'Yelling at it won't make it light, *mo daor*.'

Bron jumped at the sound of her grandma's amused voice and looked up. 'Shelley?'

'No, *mo daor*. Shelley has stepped out for a moment.'

Bron's eyes narrowed as she looked at her friend, noting the differences in the way she held herself and her black eyes, not to mention the voice that carried the distinctive accent of her grandma. 'Did Shelley agree to "step out"?'

Adeline made a little moue with her mouth. 'She'll come around.'

'Grandma!'

'Don't you Grandma me. I'm here to help.'

'I don't need help. I should be able to do this. I've always been able to do this.'

'That might be the case but ... good Goddess, what is that?'

Bron looked down at the scrap of cat that had just jumped into her lap. 'This is Bluebelle, my new Familiar.'

'I'm sure you could find a better Familiar than that bedraggled beastie. It looks like it's been mauled.'

Bron picked Bluebelle up and nuzzled the scrawny cat's tawny head. 'I know. Poor thing. I found her out the back last week, mewling for help. She was covered in blood and her back leg was hurt. She'd obviously been going it alone for a while too—she was so scrawny.'

'Was? She still *is* scrawny.'

'Oh, no. This is plump by comparison. I brought her in and Helen helped me patch her up—she's got an affinity with animals I think will be quite useful if I can just manage my own powers so I can train her up in hers. Anyway, I couldn't just toss poor Bluebelle out once we'd patched her up and fed her. She needs someone to look after her. So I kept her.'

'That doesn't make her a Familiar.'

Bron turned Bluebelle around and peered in the cat's peridot-coloured eyes. 'I know. But there's something about her that speaks to me. She's a young cat too, so I know I can train her.' She kissed Bluebelle between the eyes and settled her back on her lap, stroking her head. 'The only thing is, she's frightened of the Were so I've been leaving her here rather than taking her home or to the Packhouse. But she'll get used to them soon.'

Adeline pursed her lips. 'Yes, well, that's all very well, but why did you lie to your friends about going to work?'

Bron's hand stilled on Bluebelle's head. 'I didn't lie. I just didn't want to burden them with my problems.'

'And closing up your shop and yelling at the candle to light is supposed to help this problem?'

'Yes. No. I don't know. All I know is, Skye—who has spent most of her life fearful of her powers and never learned anything about them —is taking control of hers. Shelley doesn't seem to have any kind of problem at all adjusting to the new powers we got on Samhain. Yet I, despite all my years of study and practice in spells and borrowing power from the Goddess, can't manage to make even the simplest of spells work right since then.' She glared at the candle. 'Yelling at it makes me feel better.'

'Does it?' Her grandma sat opposite her at the table, an unlit candle between them. Bron stuck her tongue out.

Adeline Kincaid's husky laugh rang around the room.

Bluebelle jumped at the noise, her claws digging into Bron's leg before she jumped down and limped across the floor to a patch of sun. She promptly laid down and closed her eyes. Rubbing her leg, Bron wished she could find peace so easily. Turning back to her grandmother she said, 'I know Shelley is probably hating every moment of this, but I'm so glad you're here.'

Adeline squeezed Bron's hand and then sat back. 'So, *mo daor*, tell me, why are you trying to light a candle?'

Bron blinked at her grandma and then frowned. 'I thought if I started with the basics, it might help, but I can't even do that right.' She knocked the candle over in disgust.

'Got out of bed on the wrong side this morning, did we?' Adeline chuckled. 'Let me fix that for you.' Hands flat on the table, she stared at the candle. It wobbled and then righted itself, the wick flickering into blue and orange flame.

Bron made a disgusted noise. 'You're dead and you can do that with ease. Why can't I?'

'Because you are not me. Don't wish yourself other than you are, Bronwyn. It's part of the reason your powers aren't working properly. Not to mention you came back to work before you were fully recovered from healing River. Shelley was right, by the way. That was foolish.'

'I had clients who needed me.'

'And you always have to make other people happy, don't you?'

Bron crossed her arms over her chest and stared mutinously at her grandma. 'I don't *have* to make other people happy.'

'Well, you made those clients you saw very happy.'

Bron glared harder at her grandma as she began to chuckle. 'It's not funny. Meg O'Brien has alopecia. Then overnight she got a full head of hair and thinks I'm a miracle worker. And I put Tracey Knight to sleep.'

'She had insomnia. You cured it.'

'I put her to sleep for a week. Her family were about to sue me when she woke up declaring she'd never felt so good. A newspaper reporter caught wind of it and I've had calls about my "miracle cures".' She snorted. 'There's no miracle. Just some screwed-up powers that I can't control. The last few weeks since Samhain have been a nightmare. I can't heal or help anyone else while I'm like this. Surely you see that's true? What if I hurt rather than help next time?'

Adeline squeezed her hands. 'You're a Healer. You aren't capable of hurting anyone.'

Bron laughed bitterly. 'Tell River that. I couldn't touch him without it causing him pain. I had to go through an intermediary to heal him.'

'I think that has more to do with his problem than your own.'

'I'm not so sure about that.' She shrugged and pulled her hands out of her grandma's grasp, looking down at them, the chewed nails, the burn scar on her thumb she'd got when she'd not been careful in chemistry class in year twelve, the pink scar across her palm from when she'd used blood magic on Skye on Samhain. She'd always trusted those hands, the power she'd harness from her Goddess that came through them when needed. Now ... She shoved them between her legs. 'If anyone would be used to Skye's power, it would be River, and yet now it's in me, it doesn't seem to work right even on him.'

'As long as you think of your new power as "Skye's power", you will have trouble with it.'

'What do you mean?'

Adeline spread her hands. 'Do you still think of this shop as mine?'

Bron looked around her at the workroom full of stills and shelves of spices and roots and herbs. 'No. You are here in everything I do and everything I've learned, but you left the shop to me when you passed on. I worked hard to expand it, to make a name for myself. It's mine.'

'As you should. And this is how you must think of the power Skye shared with you. Now you have ownership of it, you can't give it back. Now it's in you, it's changed and won't recognise her as master. It wants to recognise you; if you would only let it.'

Bron scratched at her brow as she took in her grandma's words. 'You think I'm pushing Skye's power away?'

'Yes. If you kept calling this shop "my grandma's shop", do you think it would ever come to feel like yours?'

'That's not the same thing. I spent years studying what I needed to run this business successfully. I didn't do anything to gain a portion of Skye's power.'

Adeline pressed her lips together, leaned back in her chair and crossed her arms. 'I think Skye and the pack would have something different to say about that. You and Shelley worked an incredibly difficult and dangerous piece of magic that night that could have backfired on you in horrifying ways. And yet you did it, to save them. Your willingness to do what must be done earned you this new power. It's yours to use at will if only you would accept the change this makes to the way you think everything must be done.'

'I ... That's not ...'

'Don't choke on your words, *mo daor*. Spit them out.'

Bron pressed her lips together, trying not to swear. She loved her grandma and valued her thoughts and opinions, but she could also be the most exasperating person Bron knew—alive or dead. She took a deep breath and tried again. 'I don't mind change. I made the biggest change of my life when I followed you into this business rather than doing what Mother and Father required.'

'I know you did, and that was very laudable, but then you stopped. On the outside it might look like you shift and change with the flow, but inside, your heart and soul haven't moved on from my death. They still fear change.' She leaned forward to cup Bron's face. 'This is an opportunity. You've been given a gift. It's up to you to stop your hands from shaking and open the gift. Only once you've opened it can you learn to use it.'

Hurt by her grandma's words, Bron pouted. 'That's not true. I'm the one who's open to these things. I want to use this new power.'

'But you fear it and that stops you from embracing it.'

'I don't fear it. Why should I fear it?'

'Because it's expanding you, making you into something more, something outside your knowledge. And that unknown frightens the hell out of you.'

Bron's nostrils flared, the muscles around her mouth and eyes pinched as she tried to hold back the tears. 'You're talking about this power like it's a fairy tale.'

'Now you sound like your mother.'

Bron jerked at the admonishment. 'I'm nothing like my mother.'

'You're more like her in some ways than you think. But you must stop thinking of them as weaknesses if you are to move forward. And you must stop focusing on the past.'

'I'm not,' she croaked. She didn't want to look back. She'd told herself long ago it didn't serve any purpose. She didn't even particularly like looking forward. That's why she put everything she was into living the now.

But for once, her grandma seemed oblivious to how she was feeling. 'You are. You do it every day when you try with everything in you not to be your mother and focus all your energies on being me.'

Bron sucked in a breath. 'That's not what I've done.'

Adeline looked around, a sad smile on her face. 'Yes, you have. And the pity of it is, you have more power and talent than I ever did, even before you took on this new power; yet you limit yourself to only doing the magic I did. I left you the family grimoires for a reason, *mo daor*. They were to teach you of possibilities. But you didn't learn from them in that way and it makes me sad to see it.'

Bron began to shake. It wasn't true. It couldn't be true. She looked up to argue further and saw that Adeline-Shelley was leaning against the table, her face ashen, the black in her eyes swirling wildly. 'Grandma?'

Adeline turned her head groggily, as if she'd lost control of her movement, and smiled weakly. 'I'm afraid my time with you has come to an end.' She reached out and Bron stood, grasping her hand. 'But please, think on what I've said to you today, *mo daor*. Be yourself. Do the work. Become something far grander than I ever was. Promise me.'

'I promise.'

'That's all I ask.'

She shook violently, teeth rattling in her head, and then she slumped. Bron threw herself forward to catch her friend before she hit the floor. She grunted as she tried to angle her back to the chair—but she was a dead-weight. Shelley was so much taller and bigger than she was and Adeline had used up too much of her energy. Her head lolled, her limbs floppy and weak. It was all she could do to lower her to the floor and hold her friend's body upright against hers.

'Help! Somebody help,' Bron called out, hoping one of the Shadows was nearby.

Shelley started to make a rattling sound in her throat. 'Oh Goddess, Shelley. I'm so sorry.'

The door banged open. She looked up to see Adam at the door, Iain just behind him.

'Shelley!' Adam cried and ran over to her. As he passed Bluebelle she hissed and shot under the shelves. 'What happened?' He scooped Shelley into his arms. Somehow, he made Shelley look small despite the fact she was built like an Amazonian or a Viking shield-maiden.

'Grandma took her over so we could have a chat.'

'Shit. Why'd you let her do that?'

Bron gaped at him. 'I didn't let her. She sauntered in like that.'

'You should have told her to get the fuck out!'

Bron crossed her arms over her chest, sick of people telling her what she should do. 'Don't shout at me.'

'Hey, guys. Whoa.' Iain stood between them, hands out. 'Nobody is at fault here. Bron can't control the spirits—that's Shelley's thing. And if she couldn't keep Bron's grandma out, then it's not likely Bron could.' He turned his back on Bron to face Adam. 'How about we give Cordy a call. She'll know what to do.'

Adam didn't answer, just carried Shelley over to the couch under the high window and placed her down carefully. 'Have you got a blanket? She's cold?'

As Bron darted to the cupboard in the corner, he took his phone out of his back pocket and flicked it open. 'Face time, Cordy,' he snapped into the phone. A moment later, Cordy's smiling face appeared. 'Who is that?' a voice grumbled behind her.

'It's Adam,' she said, laughing. 'To what do I owe this pleasure?'

Another face appeared beside hers; a harshly masculine face darkened by a five o'clock shadow and a deep scowl that didn't hide the shocking blue of his eyes. 'You're interrupting a moment, Trickster. Call back later.' He reached for the phone, but Cordy slapped his hand aside.

'Marcus, you're being rude,' Cordy said, flipping her straight red hair over her shoulder. 'Now go and make me a cup of tea while I talk to Adam. I'm sure he called for something important?'

'Shelley was taken over by Bron's grandma's spirit and now she's passed out.' He turned the phone to show Cordy Shelley's unconscious form.

Bron rushed over with a blanket just as Adam turned the phone back around and saw Marcus roll his eyes then sigh. 'Fine.' He gave Cordy a rough kiss. Pointing at the phone, he barked, 'Don't keep her long,' then stomped away.

Adam winced. 'Sorry, Cordy. I wouldn't have called if it wasn't urgent.'

'I know,' she said. 'I'll make sure he gets over his grump later.'

Bron placed the blanket on her friend then pulled on Adam's hand enough so he lowered the phone so she could see the other witch. 'Hey Cordy.'

'Hey Bron.' Her warm smile shone from the small screen. 'Now, is one of you going to tell me what happened?'

Adam waved to Bron. She explained as concisely as she could, with Adam throwing in the few bits he knew.

Cordy sighed and shook her head. 'The spirits around Shelley are much stronger than she has let on.'

Bron winced. She'd thought Shelley was doing so well. She should have known otherwise. Some great Healer she was!

'My great-grandmother was an extremely strong medium,' Cordy continued. 'There might be something in her diaries to help Shelley control her power more effectively. I'll search it out and send it down. If I can talk Marcus into it, I'll come down with it.'

Adam sighed. 'That would be great, Cordy. But what do we do right now? She's passed out cold.'

'It takes a lot out of a medium to be possessed like that, but it's nothing that some rest won't fix. Just take her home and let her sleep. And when she wakes up, a good bowl of that hearty bolognaise you make, Adam, would be the ticket to get her up and going. And some of that heavenly chocolate cake you made for me after Samhain wouldn't go astray, either.'

'I'll make two and bring it up to you especially. Thanks Cordy.'

'My pleasure. Call me if there's any more problems.'

'I will.' He flipped the phone closed and shoved it back in his pocket before turning to Bron. 'Sorry I snapped at you. It's just ...' He waved at Shelley. 'I'm her Shadow.'

Bron rubbed his arm soothingly. 'I know.' She knew how Adam felt about responsibility.

He patted her hand then asked, 'Are you coming?'

She shook her head. She was still upset about what Adeline had said to her and didn't feel like being around anyone. But she couldn't tell them that. Waving her hand at the tidy space she said, 'I've got things to do here. Cleaning and tidying.'

Adam's brow rose. 'Yeah. I think I see a speck of dust in the corner that needs to be taken care of. What are you doing here, Bron?'

'Just trying to figure some stuff out. Which I can do better if left alone.'

Adam held up his hand. 'Okay, don't bite my head off. I was just asking. But if you need me, you know where I'll be.'

'I'll be fine,' she said as he bent to pick Shelley up. 'Besides, Iain will be right outside. Just take Shelley home and look after her, okay. That's the best thing you can do for me.'

'You heard the lady,' Adam said to Iain. 'We're not wanted in here right now.'

Bron's chest clenched at his words. She wished she trusted herself like he trusted her. 'Thank you.'

He looked pointedly at her. 'No heroics though.'

Iain touched her shoulder. 'I'm here if you need me.'

Bron nodded, swallowing down the sudden tears.

As soon as the door closed behind them, she began to shake, her discussion with her grandma hitting her in full. It wasn't true. She hadn't turned from being a carbon copy of her parents into a carbon copy of her grandma. She wouldn't do that. She was her own person.

Wasn't she?

Every single last bit of energy left her as realisation hit with the speed of a freight train. She staggered. Goddess! Her grandma had forced herself into Shelley's body—Adeline hadn't done that just on a whim.

Hell! She'd thought she'd done the right thing. The respectful thing. Had thought she'd been following her own dreams. But now, everything just felt wrong.

Her head pounded with the wrongness, chest tightening. Grabbing hold of the back of the chair, she tried to take some deep, calming breaths, but they just hitched in her throat. Nausea swirled. She pulled the chair around with rubbery arms and plonked down in it. But that little amount of exertion made her pant, the breath squeezing through lungs like they were filled with fluid. She rubbed at her chest, trying to relieve the pressure but it didn't help.

A panic attack?

She hadn't had one of those since just before her grandma died eight years earlier. But this certainly felt like a panic attack. Sweat pricked her skin, tears swam in her eyes, she couldn't breathe and her heart was racing.

Fuck-fuck-fuck-fuck-fuck.

The room swam as she tried to focus on the shelves that were only a few metres away. Bluebelle's yellow-green eyes glowed at her from the darkness of the bottom shelf.

'Meow,' she said, head jerking up as if gesturing to the shelves above her.

'Yes,' Bron nodded sluggishly. 'I should make myself a tonic.' She tried to focus on the shelves Bluebelle hid under. Those shelves held all the ingredients her grandma had used to make a calming steam infusion when she was a child—lavender, ylang-ylang and frankincense, among other things. She just needed to put the ingredients together and turn the kettle on. If only she could do that, she'd be fine.

She tried to stand, but the room swung wildly and her legs shook. Breath rasped through her throat at the effort, the fist of panic squeezing her chest even tighter. She slammed back into her chair, fingers digging into the arms as she concentrated on pulling in her next breath. She tried to call out, but there was no sound.

No sound.

No help.

No breath.

She felt like she was going to die.

5

River didn't move as Adam slammed into Bronwyn's shop, Iain hot on his tail. The look on the Trickster's face would normally have made River race in after him to protect the women inside, except he knew Adam would never hurt a hair on Bronwyn or Shelley's heads. Besides, going in there himself would serve no purpose, other than to make him hurt even more than he already did.

He slunk back into the woods where Iain had found him earlier. His wolf whimpered. He wanted to follow. Wanted to go in, to make sure their mate was okay.

'We can't,' he whispered. 'This close but no closer.'

His wolf growled, even though he knew they had to stay away. They weren't safe. And she was too important.

She was the pack's new Healer Witch. They hadn't had a Healer Witch for nearly a century. The pack wouldn't want to see her or her talents squandered on a broken excuse of a Were like him. He had nothing to offer. Nothing to give.

He didn't even have himself.

Having spent too many years drugged out and verging on insane, he didn't know where he ended and the insanity began. Yet he had to be near her because he had to know she was safe, so he haunted the woods near her work every day. He felt her worry and pain when she couldn't harness her power to help her clients. His heart bled with hers when she hung the "Closed" sign on her door. He wanted to go to her and hold her while she cried. Wanted to find a way to make things easier, to show her a way. He wanted to be her muse for her powers as she was for him when he worked on the gardens that had been given over to his care in the past few weeks.

He'd never worked so hard or so well, turning dead and dying things into a wilderness of beauty and wonder. A reflection of what he saw in her, what she brought out in him, despite the over-whelming sensation of panic and rising fear.

Time was running out.

But first, at least, he could create some beauty to leave behind.

He had plans for the garden at her house that he would start today. Although he'd have to say he was doing it for Skye as he'd done with the garden at the Packhouse. He could never let on it was all for Bronwyn. The pack already watched him with a wariness that was a tether on his soul. If they pitied him too, a lock would fall into place and he would never be able to free himself when the time came.

So he pretended and acted as if he was trying to find a way to mend himself, showing a stability he did not feel as the moon's steady progress through its cycle pulled at him, calling to him, to the Beast, causing insidious ideas and longings to infest his dreams.

He wished there was some way of stopping the Beast from erupt-ing, but he was afraid that even his grandmother's drugs would be of no use now. The spells the ancient witch Morrigan had used on Samhain Eve had opened up something inside him; some primal, ancient thing that was the historical source of the Were, and there was nothing anyone could do to send it back to where it had come from. It was too strong. It had its claws in him and it wasn't going to let go.

But it needed the moon.

He looked up at the day shadow of the partial moon in the sky, his hackles rising at the taunting pale crescent. River was going to make damned sure the Beast never saw another full moon again.

As he dropped his gaze, he realised he'd circled back to a point where he had a view of the shopfront. Adam was leaving, Shelley in his arms. He carried her like she weighed nothing, even though she was six foot and built like a warrior. Iain followed. They seemed to be arguing as Adam lowered Shelley into his car. Their voices were too low for River to hear, but Adam gave an order and Iain nodded, then headed to take up sentry duty outside the shop.

Adam's car pulled out a moment later. Just as it disappeared around the corner, the world tipped and River stumbled. Panic flared through him, burning his chest, searing his nerves. Nausea swirled in his stomach and sweat drenched his skin.

The vision of a room appeared in front of his eyes; a room full of shelves containing bottles. He needed some of what was inside those bottles, and yet were too far away. He reached for them ... And grasped air.

The vision broke and he knew ... he knew he'd seen from Bronwyn's eyes.

And she couldn't breathe.

'Bronwyn!' He broke into a run, panic a hot lick of flame in his throat, a squeezing hand around his heart. She was alone. He had to help her.

'River!' Patrick, River's Shadow for the day, called after him.

River didn't stop to explain, just shouted, 'Bronwyn'.

Iain looked up, startled, as River raced onto the porch, opened the door with a jangle of the bell and pelted inside.

Behind him he heard Iain say, 'What the hell?'

'Bron. He sensed something wrong with Bron,' Patrick answered as he caught up. They both entered the shop behind River. 'Where is she?' Patrick asked.

River was already heading over to the back left hand side of the shop to the room that had 'Staff only' written on the door. 'Bronwyn!'

AT THE SOUND of the voice, River's voice, Bronwyn managed to take in a shuddering breath. Then another. Oh Goddess. She could breathe! She could breathe.

The door to the workroom slammed open and there he was, his height and breadth blocking the view of the room behind him.

Bluebelle hissed and skittered backwards under the shelving.

'Bronwyn.' He reached out to her but then his arms dropped back to his side as he halted just inside the room.

She wanted him to take her in his arms. Wanted the warmth of them around her. But he was too far away.

'You're all right. I thought I felt a ...'

His words died. She waited for him to continue, needed him to talk. The more he spoke in that deep, husky voice, the more the tightness in her chest loosened.

'Bronwyn? You are okay, aren't you?'

Bron blinked, nodded. 'Just a ... panic attack. I'll be ... fine in a minute.' She took in more deep breaths as he stood there, hovering.

Bluebelle growled as Patrick and Iain came to stand in the doorway behind River, trying to peer around him.

Oh Goddess! Did they have to be here too? She was supposed to be their Pack Healer; strong and together and always there for them in a crisis. Not someone who fell apart at the drop of a hat. Taking herself in hand, she decided it was time to stop trembling pathetically.

Using the arms of the chair, she pushed up. Dizziness overcame her and she stumbled.

Warm, strong hands caught her, stopped her from crashing to the floor.

She looked up. Met River's gaze. His eyes were like molten bronze poured onto emeralds with licks of gold—hot, deep, intense. And they were filled with worry. 'What are you doing here?'

'I was worried about you.'

She frowned. 'About me?'

He smiled. 'Yes, about you.'

Bron had trouble concentrating as she looked up at his smile. He so rarely smiled. She reached up, her fingers trembling for a moment on the edge of his lips. 'You have a beautiful smile.'

The smile faded. He lowered her into the chair behind her, then let go and stepped back. She started to shiver again without the warmth of his touch.

'Is she okay?' Iain asked from his position in the doorway.

River nodded. 'Just been pushing herself too hard again.'

'Should we stay?'

'I think she needs a few moments to catch her breath. Then I'll make sure she goes home to rest properly.' Something jangled and River lifted his hand to catch it as Patrick threw it at him.

'Keys to her car. Iain will keep guard outside. I'll let Jason know.'

There was a look on River's face she couldn't decipher as he stared at the keys in his hands then threw them back to Patrick. 'You forget. I can't drive.'

Patrick nodded. 'Iain will take you when you're done here.' He clapped his brother on the back. 'Come on.'

Iain nodded and followed Patrick out the door. River watched them go, then turned away from her to look over the room.

Bron frowned. Was he avoiding looking at her now? Was he embarrassed that she knew he couldn't drive? Of course he couldn't drive. He'd been locked away in Cantrae House out of his mind on drugs since he was a little boy. There was probably a whole bunch of things he'd never done. 'River?'

'Have you been trying to tap into your powers?'

Her mouth gaped. 'How ...' She shook her head. He couldn't know.

'I know why you closed your shop. Why you've suddenly been spending so much time alone. You're having trouble with your powers.' She gaped at him again. 'You shouldn't drive yourself so hard. You managed to heal me.'

She snapped her mouth closed. She wasn't going to say anything. She didn't want to admit it. Not yet. She opened her mouth to change the subject, but the truth tumbled out. 'I didn't heal you properly.

And I needed a lot of help from Jason. I couldn't have done it without his link to you.'

'But you did it.'

'I know. The problem is, I haven't even been able to tap into that in the last two weeks. And if I want to keep my business and be of use to the pack, then I have to figure out what's going on.' She clapped her hand over her mouth. Why on earth had she told him that?

'Is that why Shelley was here?'

She jerked. 'How did you know Shelley was here?' Had he been watching her?

He turned his face to the side as he reached out to lift a jar from a shelf, his nose twitching. 'Her scent is everywhere ... and it's strong.'

Of course! He could smell that Shelley had been here. She kept forgetting how good the Were sense of smell was. Unclenching her hands, she sighed. 'I'm not sure why she came, actually. My grandma took her over before she could tell me.'

'Your grandma? Ah, so that's why you got so upset. You didn't want to see your grandma?'

She bit her lip. She hadn't meant to share this with anyone. But for someone who rarely said a word to anyone, he was surprisingly easy to talk to. 'No. It was kind of nice to talk to her. But she spoke through Shelley and told me some home truths that were difficult to swallow. And if she's right—which I'm desperately afraid she is—I'm not sure how to go about fixing it. And if I can't fix it, then I'll never be able to do my job properly or help the Were. Or help you.'

River shook his head. Still not looking at her, he placed the bottle back on the shelf and ran his finger over the next one. 'Don't worry about helping me. I'm beyond help.'

Bron sucked in a breath, as if he'd punched her—his meaning was clear. 'You mean, you're beyond my help. That I'm not powerful enough, not good enough, to help you.'

He was by her side before she'd even seen him move. 'I could never mean that. You don't see yourself clearly.'

She frowned, his words echoing familiarly in her ears. 'That's what my grandma said.'

'Then she was right.' He reached out, brushed his thumb over her face where a tear had dried. Her skin tingled; her breath caught in her throat. 'You don't trust yourself or your access to these new powers. I understand that.' He looked down, his lips twisted wryly. 'I'm having trouble dealing with this new world I find myself in, too. But you will get this. You're powerful and clever and so full of life and joy it takes my breath away.'

His words brushed over her skin, leaving tremors in their wake. How could he know the doubts in her soul when even her closest friends didn't know?

Their eyes met. Held.

He leaned forward at the same time she did. His warmth washed over her, his scent an intoxication that made her breathe in more deeply. 'River.'

He rocked back on his heels, his hand dropping to his side as his gaze slid away.

She wanted to grab it, bring it back to her face. It was so much easier to believe everything he was saying when he was touching her. And yet ... 'You don't know me.'

'I feel like I have always known you,' he said softly. Her brows raised and he hurriedly said, 'Because of Skye. I've sensed you through the twin-bond.'

'Of course. What else could it be?' She tipped her head to the side, staring at him, wondering why she was certain he wasn't telling her the full truth.

He sighed. 'You don't believe me?'

'About the twin-bond?'

'No. About how capable you are.'

Her eyes narrowed. 'How can I when you obviously don't believe I can help you?'

'I ... That's not what I meant. You are a powerful Healer. You could do anything you wished. I trust you will find your way.' He stood, paced away, turned back. 'It's just, you've got a lot on your plate and I'm the last thing you should concentrate on.'

Bron sat forward. 'That's not true.' A surge of hope swept through her with his words—they echoed what her grandma had said. 'Do you really trust me?'

'Of course.'

'Do you really think I'm capable of learning how to become Pack Healer? Learning how to use these new powers?'

'Yes. Look what you've done so far. If not for you, I would still be swathed in bandages and look like a horror-movie reject.'

Laughter bubbled out of Bron and she clapped her hand over her mouth. 'Sorry. I know you weren't trying to be funny.'

He took her hand, pulled it from her mouth. 'Don't ever apologise for laughing. Your ability to see the light side is one of the things I ...' He dropped her hand, a look on his face that both disturbed and fascinated her.

She grabbed his hand, stopping him from turning back to his perusal of her workshop. 'It's one of the things what?'

His gaze slid to her and then away. 'Just one of those things that draws people to you.'

She let go of his hand, disappointment she didn't understand lodged in her chest. 'Yeah. I bring the fun. It's great. It's my purpose.'

'That's not what I meant. And nobody thinks that of you. I certainly don't.'

She could see he didn't. It was a relief. 'Then why won't you let me try to heal you? If you think I can do this, then why don't you want me to try?'

'I ...'

'It will help me to learn,' she rushed on before he could make more excuses. 'I learned so much the other times I tried to use my power on you. I learned how to channel through the Packbond, and even though I know that's not the ultimate answer, that I need to learn how to do it myself, you are the only one I've had any real success with.'

He watched her carefully, gaze racing over her face, but even though he gave nothing away, she got the sense he was wavering.

'My grandma told me the problem is I don't think of the power as mine. Well, I think the only way I can feel it is mine is to use it doing something I really want to do. And I really want to help you. In fact, I have to help you.' She put her fist against her chest. 'I never felt quite as ... whole ... as those times I healed you through the Packbond. I need to feel that again. I need to understand it.'

'But you passed out. I can't let that happen again.'

She waved her hand. 'That was nothing.' She pushed up from the chair and began to pace as her swirling thoughts cleared and one thought took their place. 'I just used too much power because I don't know what I'm doing. But I won't know what I'm doing unless I try. Unless I learn. Unless I accept what I can and should be.'

She was lost in her thoughts, so bound up with the idea of healing him that she wasn't even looking at him. River was thankful she wasn't. He was afraid she might see something in his expression he didn't want her to see. The thought of spending time with her, of her hands on him, of helping her, was a dream he couldn't allow himself to live. 'Bronwyn, I don't think this is a good idea. I'm a loner.'

'If that were true, you wouldn't have sought me out today.'

She was right, but he wasn't going to admit to it. 'I'm not the best person for this. Cordelia could help you. You should talk to her. And there are other Were you could help.'

'I've spoken to Cordy, and I know I'll be able to learn a lot from her when I've got a handle on this new power. But everything she's suggested to try to help me to meld the part of me that's used to borrowing power from my Goddess and the new side that has power that doesn't need to be borrowed, hasn't worked.' She took a deep breath, turning to face him, her cinnamon eyes huge in her pale face. 'And the other Were ... they're not like you. The others want me to succeed so badly, they're pushing at me through the Packbond. I'm still not sure exactly what that bond is and how it's going to affect me, but I know what I'm feeling from it. I won't know if they're healed because of what I'm doing, or because of what they're helping me to do. You're different.' Her cinnamon eyes burned with a fire of hope and excitement as she stepped closer. 'I can't feel you through the Packbond. But it's not just that.'

Her brow creased and she bit the corner of her lip as she paced.

He wanted to grab her, stop her restless movement, push her teeth away from the plump corner of her lips with his own and lick away any hurt they might have caused. Withholding a groan, he pressed his fingers against his legs, hard, willing the pain to bank the fire that ran along his nerve endings at the thought of kissing her.

She stopped pacing and swung around to face him. *Please, Gods. Don't let her notice how hard I am.* Someone was listening, because her gaze arrowed in on his.

'You are so different from the rest. Your wolf responds to my power in a strange way, almost like it's pushing me away, but I think that's because I'm not accepting it or trusting it and your wolf is just protecting you.'

River tensed—her words were far too close to the truth for comfort. His wolf was protecting him, but it was also protecting her—from him.

She didn't seem to notice his tension as she began to pace again. 'It's a slap in the face,' she huffed out a harsh chuckle. 'But that slap in the face made me think outside the square the other night. And I need that.' She cocked her head again, paused, a smile brightening her face as she turned back to him. 'Although, your wolf allowed you to touch me just now, so there is hope. Not to mention I have a connection with you already.'

He jerked back at her words.

'You can't deny it. You came here now because you felt there was something wrong.'

River shook his head, panicked at the thought of how close she was to the truth. 'That's not ... The Packbond is why ... I'm not used to being with people.'

'And that's why it's even more important for you to help me. You have to learn to be part of the pack again. Your wolf needs it. You do.' She stopped pacing right in front of him, her hands clasped before her as she looked up at him. 'We both need to find and understand the Packbond. With you by my side, holding my hand, it will make the journey easier. Don't you see?'

River's wolf whimpered. How could he deny those pleading eyes?

She didn't even need to say the words and he was already giving in. He was so weak where she was concerned. It was pathetic. But somehow, he made himself say, 'Being part of the pack won't help anything.'

'I think it will. But I'm not going to force you to go to Packland and live with them. I just want you to work with me for now. I think I can learn what I need to learn by finding out more about what happened when I healed you and trying to find a better way of doing it.'

She laughed, obviously excited by the ideas formulating in her head. Her laugh was a drug. It bubbled inside him, a golden elixir warming and brightening the cold, dark places. He wanted to make her laugh all the time.

She began to pace again, the words bubbling from her, and he listened, lapping up her enthusiasm as if he was a starving man and it was manna.

'I know you're afraid of what will happen at the next full moon— that whatever is stopping you from making the full change will bring forth that beast again. But I think I can help you.' She spun, pinned him with her cinnamon eyes. 'Healing you can help us both, don't you see? Please, River. Let me try. Let me help you.'

River closed his eyes. He had to say no. He couldn't be around her more than was necessary. He was broken deep inside and no Healer in the world could fix that. 'What if you fail?'

'Then I fail. But I'll never know if I don't try and I can't try if you won't let me.' She reached out to touch his arm, hesitated for a moment.

He held his breath, stealing himself against the impact of that touch. But no matter how many walls he built, the moment her cool fingers touched him, a silken caress on his skin, those walls crumbled and it was all he could do not to pull her into his arms and crush her mouth under his.

'Is that hurting you?' she asked, her voice a little breathless.

He was trembling. 'No. It's just ... I'm not used to being touched by anyone but Skye and my grandmother. It's ... difficult.'

'You are touch hungry.'

He almost choked on a laugh at her understatement. He wasn't just touch hungry in the normal Were sense. He was touch hungry for her. As any Were would be for his mate.

But he couldn't touch her in that way. She deserved so much better than him. Like Adam.

His wolf snarled.

She snatched back her hand. 'Your wolf doesn't like me touching you.'

'Why do you say that?'

'He just snarled at me.'

He frowned. 'You heard that?'

She bit her lip and cocked her head. 'Not hear as much as felt it.' She touched her chest. 'Here.'

Fuck. If she could hear his wolf through the bond, then he was further down the path to mating than he'd thought. 'I have to go.'

She reached out to touch him but then pulled her hand back. 'Sorry. I'm pushing. I don't mean to make you uncomfortable.' She looked away, the joy leaving her, despair surrounding her like a cloak. 'I didn't mean to lay my problems at your feet. I'm not your responsibility.'

Yes. You are.

She looked up at him as if she'd heard the words screaming in his head, searched his face then blinked and shook her head. 'Go. I'll be fine. Don't worry yourself about me. I'll bounce back.' She sighed. 'I always do.'

River watched her turn from him, the slump of her shoulders, the glow she usually wore fading before his eyes. He couldn't bear it. 'You can try to heal me. I'll work with you.'

She swung back to face him, expression so hopeful it made him ache. 'Really?'

Oh Gods, he was such a weak fool. 'Really.'

She bounced over to him laughing and threw her arms around him. For one glorious moment he gave himself over to the sensation. But the longing to hold her, to not let go, to laugh with her, live in her joy, was too intense, so instead of returning the hug, he stiffened. His wolf whimpered.

She let go abruptly, a look of chagrin on her face. 'Sorry. I forgot your wolf doesn't like me. But I'm going to work on that. Everyone always ends up liking me. I'm a likeable person.'

'My wolf already likes you.'

'But he doesn't trust me. That's okay. I don't trust myself. We'll work on that together.' She spun around in a circle. 'This is so fantastic. Thank you, River. I won't forget this and I promise, I'll find a way to help you. We're in this together now—you helping me and me helping you. It's symbiotic. Just like the Were-Witch Pact is meant to function. This is going to work. I know it's going to work.'

As she spun around, River sighed inside, praying to whatever Gods listened to Were prayers that this wouldn't make things so much worse than they already were.

Abruptly, she stopped spinning and began to flitter from shelf to shelf, gathering bottles and equipment into a basket.

'What are you doing?'

'I'm putting together some supplies.'

'Why?'

She looked over her shoulder, brows raised in obvious surprise. 'To help in your healing, of course.'

He almost choked. 'You want to start now?'

'The sooner the better.' She resumed collecting her supplies.

Shit! He thought he'd have some time to prepare himself and his wolf before she started. Perhaps he should go back on his word. His wolf snarled.

She spun. 'Did you say something?'

'No.'

She pierced him with a look he felt under his skin. 'You look on edge. Are you worried that I'll hurt you?'

'No.' His wolf lunged, wanting to get closer. He almost stumbled at the force of it in his mind, but rather than give in to its impulses, he stopped moving, forcing himself to stillness.

'I'm worried I'll hurt you.'

'You won't hurt me. You didn't the other night, even when the Beast was on the surface. But you are worried about something.'

Damn! How could she read him so well?

She folded her arms across the basket, her expression suddenly serious. 'You're humouring me, aren't you? You don't think I can help you.'

It took everything in him not to give in to his lunging wolf at the hint of hurt in her voice. He clenched his hands by his sides and shook his head. 'I think if anyone has a chance of helping me and my wolf, it's you.'

Her sudden smile was like sunrise breaking over him, banishing the nightmare, drying the horror-sweats from his skin, washing him clean.

'I needed to hear that. Thank you.' Her voice was a soft song weaving around him, lifting him with joy. Too overcome with sensation, he could only nod.

She turned back to gathering her things and night descended again, although in her presence, it was a night with the light of a million stars and no moon. A pretty night. A night he was happy to stand in forever.

'There, that should do it.'

He looked at the almost overflowing basket of bottles, herbs, candles and creams. 'What are those for?'

'Some are for me, to help centre myself so I can study my power and yours.'

'I don't have any power.'

'Yes you do,' she said. 'All Were have power flowing through them, otherwise you wouldn't be able to change.'

He snorted. 'Yeah, well, I can't change, can I?'

'No. Not entirely. Although, the fact you can partially change gives me hope.'

'Really?'

She nodded. 'It means what I originally thought is true, that whatever was done to you didn't irrevocably break your ability to change, it just blocked it. Or transmuted it.'

'That sounds very much like the Curse at play.'

Her brow creased and her fingers drummed against the handle of the basket. 'Yes, it does, doesn't it? But the Curse is broken, so that's not what your problem is. Maybe it made it worse, but the problem started with something else.'

'The rogue coven. They stopped my change with whatever they shot me with the night they tried to kidnap Skye and me.'

She nodded. 'Yes.' She bit her lip. 'If only I knew what they shot you with, it would help. But it was too many years ago and despite the fact it's still affecting you, I doubt there's a trace of it in your bloodstream. I wonder ...' Her gaze seemed to fog over for a moment as she fell silent.

'Bronwyn?' She didn't answer. He risked taking a step closer, touching her arm.

'Sorry.' She shook herself as if coming out of a daze and looked down at his hand on her arm. Then the full force of her beaming smile was aimed at him. 'See. Your wolf likes me better already.'

He forced himself to pull back. 'I promise you, that is not the problem.'

She looked at him curiously and then nodded. 'No. You said he isn't used to people. I get that. But he needs them. You need them.'

No. He only needed her.

She blew out a breath. 'So, let's get on with it.' She edged past him, careful not to touch him again, and dropped down in front of the bookcase. 'Are you going to come with me, Bluebelle?' The cat growled at her, hissing as River came closer. He backed up but Bluebelle still refused to come out. 'Okay,' Bron sighed. 'I get it. You need to get used to them. That's okay. I'll leave you some food and water and the window is a little ajar so you can get out. I'll be back tomorrow.'

She put some more salmon on a plate and filled a bowl with milk and one with water before scooping up her basket. She took an old book from the shelf to the left of the door as she walked past it and put it in the basket too.

River followed her. 'Why don't we just start here? Then you don't have to leave your cat.'

'Until I figure out how to use my power, the only way to study it without hurting you or me is to use the Packbond. I know Iain is here, but I don't know him very well, and I think it's better I use a Were I'm more familiar with as I study your auras. Adam will help.'

River nodded. His wolf snarled. *'Stop being such an arse. Adam will help her. We don't have to like it, but it's necessary.'*

He suddenly became aware Bronwyn was staring at him. 'What?'

'You were talking to your wolf, then. Weren't you?'

'How did you know?'

'You get this look on your face. And also, the black smudge that separates your auras was kind of pushed aside as the two parts of you reached for each other, like a caress. It was kind of lovely.'

River had to choke back an incredulous laugh. The snarling wolf inside his head was hardly lovely. 'So, Adam can help.'

'Yes. And Jason too, if Adam isn't available. Just until I get to know some of the other Were better.'

River didn't like the sound of Jason being involved. As his Alpha, Jason was already closer to him than he liked. He was also intuitive. A good thing in an Alpha. Not so good when you were trying to hide from your darkest fears. Not to mention he was Skye's mate, which gave him a triple link to River—through the Alpha bond, the Packbond and the twin-bond. He didn't need him to be involved in any more healings than necessary.

But he didn't say any of that to Bronwyn, just waited for her by the door as she checked her shop.

As she walked past the front counter, she bent and picked up a bag and a book. 'This is Shelley's bag and one of the Pack Diaries.' She frowned. 'I wonder why she brought this over with her.'

'Maybe she found something that could help you.'

'Maybe.' She tucked it in the handbag and slung it over her shoulder. 'But she didn't know how much trouble I was having. I'll read it when we get home.' She flashed a smile at him. He couldn't help but smile back. 'They're full of Healing lore and even though they don't particularly refer to someone in my situation—a half-blood Wiccan with powers gifted to me by a full-blooded witch—they might have something in them about you.'

River took the basket from her as she turned to lock the front door. 'I don't think there's been a broken half-Were before. I'm one of a kind.'

She turned to him, eyes filled with empathy, washing away the bitterness. 'So am I. Perhaps that's why this will work. Perhaps we were meant to be here, together. Because I feel broken and so do you; but together we can find a way to build something better. Something new.'

His breath, coming hard and fast at her words, fluttered the hair at her temples as it brushed over her face. 'Perhaps,' he managed, his voice husky with need.

She stared up at him for a long moment, then dropped the keys in her pocket, took the basket out of his numb fingers and headed towards the car park. 'Come on. Let's get started. It's going to take some time for me to figure out how to let my power free yours. Wouldn't it be great if I could do it before the next full moon cycle?'

His breath hitched in his throat at the thought of the next full moon. 'Yes, it would.'

6

‘**B**ron's running a little late, but she said to tell you she won't be long,' Shelley said as she closed the door behind him. 'Do you want something to eat or drink?'

River shook his head. 'You get back to what you were doing. I'll just head up to the treatment room.' Shelley nodded absently and drifted back into the study.

Nerves screaming with supressed energy, River headed upstairs, although what he really wanted to do was run away. Far away so he didn't have to go through the hell of a 'treatment' again.

The first one had been bad enough, and that had mostly consisted of Bronwyn staring at first him and then Jason—she said she was observing their auras—then placing her hand on Jason's chest while the Alpha placed his hand on River's chest. It had been uncomfortable, but he could stand it.

What he couldn't stand was that she then moved to touching him herself with her Healer powers engaged. Just like the night after Samhain, something inside him had lunged, snapping out at both her and him with some kind of electric jolt. It had left her rubbing her singed fingers and him prowling from the room, the wolf and the Beast growling for pre-eminence in his throat.

He'd hurt her and she wanted to try this again? It was crazy. *He* was crazy for agreeing. And yet, when she'd come looking for him afterwards, she'd shown him her hand when he'd told her to stay away.

'See, no permanent damage. It's already started healing. I want to try it again.'

'No. Absolutely not.'

'What if I promise not to touch you directly until I know how to do it without that reaction? I'll go through Jason until then. That seems to be better for you.'

'You weren't happy with just that.'

'No, but I've learned quite a bit about my new power and how to use the Packbond through Jason from just that one session. It could help me to reach others, not just you. Please, let me try again. Pretty please.'

How could he have said no to that?

So, here he was because she needed him and he was a big sucker with a lack of ability to stand his ground in the face of a pair of big, pleading, cinnamon-brown eyes.

He let himself into the room and stood there, breathing in the scent of her. He had a memory of being in a room similar to this when he was a boy. His mother's room. She was a teacher, but like so many of the pack, she had a secondary skillset—in this case, she was qualified in first aid and took care of the more minor injuries and illnesses the Pack Healer couldn't get to.

He had a distinct memory of sitting on a treatment table like the one by the far wall, his mother cooing over him as she patched up a cut on his knee. He still bore the scar from that wound, despite his mother's deft stitches. His mother had kissed his knee afterwards, 'to make it better' she'd said. The sticky sensation of her lip gloss left an imprint of warmth on his skin he could still feel the echo of.

He swallowed hard and paced to the French doors that opened onto a small balcony at the back of the house. He longed for nothing more than to escape through those doors, leap from the balcony and run far away.

Except, it would do no good. There was no escaping from memories and the melancholy they brought.

He absently scratched his scarred face as he pondered the change. His memories used to always be golden. They'd helped him to hold on through all the dark years, a glow of light—the warm, soft smile that always lit up his mother's face when she gazed upon her family or as she worked; the way Papa would ruffle his hair and sit River on his knee as he explained one thing or other about his role in pack life; the scent of his mother's cooking, especially when she baked his favourite apple and rhubarb pie, the fruit taken from their own garden and picked by him—his love of gardening had begun then; the scents of spices and herbs that always hung around his papa; Skye's laughter the first time she'd lit a candle with her power; the first time she'd levitated; when he would come to her in the night and beg her to join him for a run through the woods. They had been so safe and secure in their parents' love, the love and friendship of pack, sure of their place in the world.

Maybe that was the problem now. There was a hope for something better in Skye's future, but aside from being free from the drugs, nothing had really improved for him. In fact, it was a whole lot worse. He'd always hoped once Skye accepted her powers, once the Curse was reversed, he'd be free. But he wasn't. And it hurt to remember times when he'd been whole. When he'd been so sure of everything.

'What happened to protecting Bron from misuse of her powers?' River turned at the sound of Adam's voice to see the Trickster slipping into the room.

'What are you doing here?'

'Jason asked me to keep an eye on the situation. He's having a meeting with Marcus and isn't available today.'

'Good.' Hopefully it meant the session today couldn't go ahead. She'd promised not to touch him with her powers directly and if Jason wasn't here to channel through—

'Good that I'm here, or good that Jason's not?' Adam crossed his arms over his chest and leaned against the bookshelf that was filled with Bronwyn's little jars of lotions and potions.

River's mouth twitched. 'Both.'

Adam nodded. 'Is that because you know this shouldn't happen and yet you're too chicken to gainsay our Alpha?'

'Adam McVale!' Bronwyn said as she walked into the room. 'Did I just hear you call River chicken?'

Adam's lips formed a lopsided smile. 'It depends.'

'On what?'

'On if me saying yes will end in you hitting me.' He glanced over at River, laughter in his eyes. 'She may be small, but she packs a mean punch.'

She walked over and punched him in the arm, not once, but three times in quick secession.

'Ow,' Adam said, rubbing his arm. 'What was that for?'

'The first was for calling River a chicken—which he definitely isn't. The second was for calling me small.'

'But you are.'

She punched him again and, ignoring his protest, turned to the shelves next to him to dump a few more jars on them. 'And the third was just because you deserve it.'

'And the fourth?'

She turned and flashed him a smile. 'Because I felt like it.'

Adam gaped at her for a moment in false outrage, then turned to River and shook his head. 'I have to agree with that *Women are from Venus* book, because their reasoning is just not of this world.'

River couldn't help smiling, even though he didn't know what a 'women are from Venus' book was. 'I think Bronwyn's reasoning was quite sound. I wanted to hit you, too.'

Adam rolled his eyes and sighed theatrically. 'A Trickster's burden is to always be unappreciated and misunderstood.'

Bronwyn rubbed his arm where she'd just punched him. 'I get misunderstood too.' Her fingers wrapped around his arm as she leaned up on tiptoes and kissed his check. 'And even when you are annoying, I appreciate you.'

Adam's fondness for her clear for anyone to see as he smiled at her. 'And I you. We'll be misunderstood together.'

As he watched the friendly tableau, River knew he should feel grateful that Bronwyn had someone else to be interested in; that it was Adam seemed appropriate. They were alike in many ways, and there was something about Adam that River couldn't help but like. However, grateful wasn't the emotion simmering in his veins. He wanted to punch the Trickster in the face until that too charming smile disappeared and wouldn't be likely to make a reappearance any time soon.

Instead, he wrapped his arms around his chest, gripping into his sides, fingers digging painfully into his skin through his thin T-shirt. Through a throat filled with razor blades of emotion, he said, 'Can we just get this done?'

Bronwyn let go of Adam with a start and turned to him, her beautiful eyes full of apologies. 'I'm sorry. I know this is hard for you. And I so appreciate you doing it for me.'

'It's not hard. And please, don't apologise to me. Ever.'

'I agree,' Adam said, arms crossed as he glared at River. 'Especially when you're not the one who's done anything wrong, Bron.'

Bronwyn glanced between the two men. 'What's going on here? What are you talking about, Adam? What's going on?'

River pressed his lips together.

Adam was the first to break. 'You passed out on Samhain, and the night after, both times because you used too much power healing River. Not that I'm against you healing River—it was necessary—' River snorted. Adam ignored him. 'But we kind of thought you shouldn't be allowed to attempt that kind of thing again until you were trained in your new abilities. I mean, it's obvious, from what you did, that you're powerful, but you put too much into him. We can't have you flaming out—you know how dangerous that is to a witch.' He glared at River. 'He was supposed to say no to you if you pressed the point.'

She crossed her arms, her finger tapping against her forearm. 'Oh, really?'

River sent a 'thanks a lot' glare to Adam and shook his head. 'Don't get angry. We are worried about you.'

'Obviously you aren't worried enough,' Adam quipped.

River's fists curled at his sides. 'You weren't there when she asked. You wouldn't have said "no" either.'

'Oh, I think I would have.'

'Yeah, because you've had so much practice saying no to women.'

'Jealous?'

'Enough!' Bron shouted, stepping between them. 'You can finish this pissing match later.' She turned on Adam. 'Stop picking at River for doing something you know you would have done if I'd turned my puppy-dog eyes on you and asked you to help me.'

'I'm not that much of a pushover.'

'No?' Her eyebrows went up. 'So you're saying that not only, as my friend, you wouldn't do something really important to me, but that you wouldn't do something your Pack Witch asked you to do for the good of the pack?'

'I ...'

'Yeah, as I thought.' She poked him in the chest. 'And don't pretend otherwise. Anyway,' she said, waving her hand. 'We had a Healing session the other day and all in all, it went pretty well.'

'He burned you.'

'No he didn't.' She held her hand up to stop River from saying anything. 'I did something wrong, so any pain I felt is all on me. But I'm learning. Which is what this is about. Now, why are you here?'

Adam blinked at her. 'To help with the Healing. Jason told me to come.'

'And despite your reservations you still came. How sweet.'

His mouth worked for a moment as if he were swallowing back some choice words, but then he just pointed at her and said, 'You'll keep.'

'I'm sure I will.' She flashed him a grin. 'But Jason was wrong. I don't need you in here today.'

'So we're not having a session?'

She frowned at River. 'Why wouldn't we have a session?'

'Umm, because Jason isn't here.'

'Oh, that. I don't think I need him to be here either. I worked some things out in my head while I was sleeping last night and I think it will be safe to touch you.'

'You promised you wouldn't try again.'

'I promised I wouldn't try until I knew how to do it without that reaction.'

'And you know this for an absolute certainty?'

She made a face. 'Well, there's no such thing as absolute certainty when doing a Healing, but I'm pretty confident. Don't you trust me?'

Ah hell. He was going to give in again.

She obviously saw it on his face because she spun to Adam, smiling. 'See. Everything is fine here. I don't need you, so you can go.'

Adam crossed his arms over his chest and leaned back against the treatment table. 'I think I should stick around anyway; just in case something goes wrong.'

'Don't you trust me?' she asked, trying the same tactic on Adam.

Adam threw his hands up in the air and said, 'All right. I give in.'

River was completely surprised by how quickly the other Were folded—he thought the Trickster would last a little longer than he had. 'Not so easy to resist, is it,' he whispered through his teeth so that only Adam could hear him.

The Trickster's eyes turned suddenly serious as he faced River. 'If you let her hurt herself again ...'

'As if I would,' he growled.

'Adam! Stop it. Nobody is going to hurt anyone. Now get out.'

'Call me if you need me. I'll be right outside.'

'I assure you, everything will be fine. Now close the door behind you and don't let anyone disturb us.'

The door closed with a quiet snick.

She turned to River. 'You need to stop letting him rile you. You've done a nice thing. Get over it.'

He just stared at her, suddenly too aware they were alone. 'Are you sure you don't need Adam?'

Her brow furrowed a little. 'I want to try something and I won't be able to do it with the distraction of him in the room. If it doesn't work, I'll just call him back in.'

'You said you worked something out in your sleep?'

'Yes.' She was rubbing her hands together, seeming nervous all of a sudden.

He wanted to put her at ease. 'Do you dream of solutions to Healing very often?'

'Sometimes that's how the Goddess chooses to speak to me.'

'Is it like a trance or a vision or something?'

Bron shook her head. 'No. The knowings simply come in my dreams. But I've learned to trust them.' She swallowed hard. 'Can you take your T-shirt off? I want to get started. I'm running late enough as it is and I've got things to do later.'

'Yes ma'am.'

If River's smile wasn't enough to drool over, Bron's mouth went dry as he reached for the hem of his T-shirt and pulled it up over his head. She'd seen him shirtless before with his clothes in rags, but both those times other people had been around and the urgency of the moment meant her mind was full of healing.

This was different.

He was undressing in front of her. And there was nobody else in the room. Suddenly the world receded and her attention was completely taken up with River.

He was still too thin for his frame, but oh she could see the promise there as his muscles flexed and rippled. He had that mouth-watering combination of wide shoulders, tapered waist and sixpack stomach, the muscles on his chest, back and arms shaped and firm. Even though he'd been drugged up for twenty years with all the medication his grandmother gave to him to keep his wolf at bay, he wasn't a couch potato. All that gardening he'd done in the grounds of Cantrae House had sculpted and toned him into male perfection. And that was before you even took in the magnetism of his Were genes.

He turned to lay his T-shirt on the chair near the head of the table, his gorgeous arse outlined as his jeans stretched tight. Was she drooling? She touched her mouth just as he turned back to her.

'Where do you want me?'

Oh Goddess! She knew where she wanted him, and it wasn't in her treatment room in the Packhouse, with Adam just outside the door, a listening audience. She wanted him ...

'Are you okay?'

She jumped as his voice rumbled close to her ear. She glanced back at him; he was frowning. What the hell was she thinking? This was River. Her best friend's twin. He needed her help. He wasn't someone she should be having sex fantasies about for Goddess' sake! Disgusted with herself—she knew better on so many levels not to look at patients like that—she said, 'Just hop on the table and lie down.'

River moved more like a cat than a wolf, his actions smooth and sinuous, muscles bunching as he hoisted himself up, then stretching as he lay down. Her mouth went dry again at the flex of his sixpack. She snapped her mouth shut and turned away to the shelves behind her.

'What are you going to do with me?'

A jolt of desire burned through her veins and pooled, molten, in her stomach. Why did he have to keep asking things that sounded so sexual? Perhaps she'd been wrong to send Adam away. Being alone with River was not working out how she'd planned. She had no idea what the hell was wrong with her all of a sudden. Although it wasn't all of a sudden.

There had been little flashes of this before. But it had never been as strong.

'Bronwyn? What are you doing?'

His voice jolted her out of her thoughts. She took in a deep breath.

I can do this. She didn't need someone else to be in here with them. This was a test of her willpower and abilities and she was more than up to it.

She pressed her lips into a smile and said, 'I've got to light some candles and prepare some scented oils. Part of what I'm doing today is an old ritual of cleansing I read about in the diaries.' Out of the corner of her eye, she saw River turn on his side. Her gaze was drawn to the dip in his waist, to the way his arm muscles stretched and bunched as he leaned on his elbow.

A rush of damp wet her underwear.

She clenched her muscles and turned back to the shelves, quickly lighting the nearest candle—lemongrass and sage—hoping the pungent citrusy smell would hide any sign of her unwanted reaction.

Gripping the edge of the shelves, she closed her eyes and breathed in the lemon scent she always used when she needed a pick-me-up. Although, if her reaction was anything to go by, she needed more than a pick-me-up. Something was very off inside her. She almost snorted out a laugh—well, she knew something was off. That was why she'd shut her business down and was doing these sessions with River to try to figure out how to deal with all the changes.

She'd learned so much from the other session and she tried to concentrate on that now. Studying the two different Were auras in such close detail had given her an idea about how they worked together and separately. The focused channelling through the Pack-bond had helped her to understand how the bond worked—between the Were, and also between them and their Pack Witches. It was symbiotic, taking power, but giving it back tenfold. It had been the strength of those bonds that had kept the McVale Pack together when their Pack Warlock was murdered and their Pack Witch kidnapped and hidden from them for all those years. So much strength. It flowed off them in waves.

And yet, it hadn't touched River in quite the same way. He was strong, but there was that dark smudge she'd noted before, wedged between his human and wolf auras, affecting the way the power syphoned from the pack and into them. The human aura was still strong, but the wolf one was sickening, tendrils of that dark smudge threaded through it more deeply.

The dream she'd had last night had made her see she needed to try to heal the wolf aura, but she couldn't do that through the Pack-bond, because it was somehow cut off. Also, she had to approach it in a different way than she'd ever approached a Healing before. She had to try to touch him first, dig in deeper and then activate her magic. Hopefully then, the thing that had lashed out at her wouldn't have time to respond.

But to do all that, she had to prepare herself and him. She'd been so confident when she'd woken up that morning, she'd not thought about her reaction to him and what that might do to her concentration.

The reality of him smiling at her, undressing before her, the muscles beneath his golden skin rippling over sinew and bone, those sinfully long lashes lowering over hooded hazel eyes with golden flicks of amber in their heart, the secrets hidden there in those painfilled depths ...

Heat seeped through her in a slow, delicious crawl.

Fuck, fuck, fuck. Stop thinking about him that way. He's a patient. Heal him.

She began to gather other candles, some essential oils and a base oil from the shelves. Things to calm and centre—she needed those most of all. She was restless, her skin itchy, her nerves tightly strung so that she was far more jumpy than usual. She really needed to get back to work. Yes, that was the true problem here. She needed to settle into some normalcy.

Dripping a few drops of lavender, sandalwood, patchouli and tangerine into a petri dish, she mixed them together and then dabbed the mix on her temples, the seat of her third eye, her pulse points on neck and wrist and then a dab over her heart. She lit another candle —eucalyptus, spruce, rosewood and Ravensara—for clarity and deep, calm breathing. As the scent lifted in the air, mixing with the lemongrass candle she'd already lit, a sense of calm drifted over her. It filled her with hope. And certainty.

She could do this. What had just happened was an anomaly caused by exhaustion, anxiety and fear. Her grandma was right. She needed to play to her strengths. Healing River was one of the ways she could do that, but it wasn't the only one. Perhaps closing down her shop was a panicked reaction.

Things weren't really all that bad. She could open up her shop at least, maybe take some clients on—those who just needed her 'creams and lotions and potions' as Skye called them. She may not be able to use her reiki, given she'd always tapped into the borrowed power of her Goddess to do it, but she could give normal massage therapy to her stressed-out clients.

Yes. That should be okay. Nothing untoward could happen then.

Aware River lay behind her, waiting, watching, she began to mix the oils she'd used on herself in a dish with some massage oil then added a drop of frankincense—men did seem to object to smelling of flowers. It smelled exotic, slightly spicy now—a scent no man could have an objection to. The mix would calm him, slow and deepen his breathing, allay his fears and inspire his trust and security. She needed him to trust her.

Mostly because his trust would help her to trust herself.

7

fter adding a few more drops of lavender, Bron was happy with the mix and how she was more settled than she'd been moments before.

With a deep breath in, she picked up the bowl and walked to his side. Tension still bristled between them, but the candles she'd lit and the massage oil she was about to ask River to rub on his chest would help with that.

'Here.' She held out the bowl of oil.

River hesitated. 'What is that?'

'It's acid and will burn your skin off,' she snapped. His startled expression made her turn and light another frankincense candle because she obviously needed a little more calming. Taking in a deep breath, she turned, plastered a smile to her face and said, 'Take two.' She held out the bowl. 'This is a mix of essential oils that will help calm you and build a sense of wellbeing and trust between us.'

'I trust you.'

'Yes, but I don't trust myself and that's part of the problem. So, I need all the help I can get.'

'Right.' He reached for the bowl.

'You need to rub it on your chest over your heart.' He opened his mouth as if to say something, but then thought better of it and began to rub the oil into his skin.

'What?' she asked, curious to know what he had been about to say.

'Stop questioning yourself.'

'I'm not ...'

'Yes, you are. I can see the cogs winding in your head all the time. But you have to stop questioning and just trust what you know to be true. Nobody would be happy being only ever half of what they were meant to be, and you shouldn't expect yourself to be happy with that either. You need to get back to work. Healing me is not enough.'

Bron gaped at him, heart in her throat, her breath caught as his words reached down and turned her inside out. 'How did you know?'

He rubbed the last of the oil into his chest and lay back on the treatment table. 'Because it's how I feel.' Before she could read the truth of his statement in his eyes, he closed them and said, 'Can we get started? I've got a delivery of plants arriving this afternoon and I want to get them in before dark.'

Swallowing hard, Bron nodded, then realised he couldn't see her. 'Yes. Let's start. I'm going to place my hands on you.'

His eyes flickered open and he levered himself up on his elbow before she could touch him. 'I don't want you to get hurt.'

Her lips wobbled as she smiled down at him. 'I'm just going to touch you without using my powers to begin with; have a poke around a bit with my third eye. What burned me last time doesn't seem to mind me doing that, it's only when I try to touch you with active powers it seems to have a problem.'

His eyes narrowed. 'But you are going to try to activate them, aren't you?'

'Yes,' she said, unable to lie to him again. 'But in my dream, it worked this way.'

'But that was just a dream.'

'You said you trusted me.' The silence was long, her nerves screaming with tension as she waited for his response.

'I do,' he said, and closed his eyes.

Her knees wobbled and she had to lock them so as not to fall in a crumpled heap on the floor. She let out her breath. 'Okay, here I go.'

He lay silent and still as she rubbed her hands together, then reached out and placed them over his chest as if she were about to do CPR.

The warmth of his skin under her hands was an exotic glide on her senses. Her breath sped up. She pulled her hands away.

'Bronwyn,' he whispered.

'Yes.'

'You can do this.'

She nodded, inexplicably calmed by his trust in her. Closing her eyes, she breathed in deeply, allowing the scents wafting in the air around her and rising from his warm skin to centre her.

'I can do this,' she whispered and placed her hands on his chest. Warmth surged forward and she let it fold around her, sliding into its depths, gliding past the little jerk that signified the opening of the pathways to her inner senses. On an exhaled breath, she opened her eyes.

Colour and energy waves fluctuated around her. As always, she took a moment to enjoy the beauty of colour and sensation that could so easily overwhelm a person when they entered onto this energy plane. Thanking the Goddess for allowing her the gift of seeing the world this way, she sank further into the sight that allowed her to see the colour of life all around her. It was like welcoming a friend.

River was right. The power was part of her. Now she just had to learn to claim that part so she wasn't half of who she was meant to be. If she could get through this Healing session without anything going awry, then she would open her business again and try to get back to normal.

River's auras were beautiful even though they were fractured by the dark smudge wedged between them, keeping them from being truly one. She tilted her head and moved sideways a bit to get a different perspective. Still keeping contact with one hand, she lifted the other to run her fingers along the outside of his human aura. It was thin. Thinner than it should be. But the wolf aura was even thinner.

'I can feel that,' River said, his voice tight, as if he was in pain.

'Does it hurt?'

'No. It just feels strange. Warm. Have you started the Healing yet?'

'No.' She moved her hand, nearing the smudge of darkness. It roiled, like a wave, the oily surge of it moving towards her hand. Beneath her other hand, River stiffened.

'What does that feel like to you?' she asked.

'It's not painful as such. It's more like something rising in me, something acidic.'

'Do you feel nauseous?'

'Yes, but that's not it. It's more like something burning in my head. And around my heart.'

She nodded. That made sense. The dark smudge had tentacles threaded throughout his auras, but the thickest parts were centred over his head and heart, and in those places his auras were the furthest apart. 'I'm just going to try something.'

'Be careful,' he said through gritted teeth. 'I can feel the Beast at the back of my mind, stirring. It doesn't like this.'

'It can't emerge until the full moon. I want to try to make certain it never does again.' She wasn't certain yet how to do that, but there was something here. If only she could figure out how to ...

She moved, swapping her hands over so that her right hand was now over his heart and her left could reach for his head. 'Stay still. I'm going to slip into a trance and then try to activate my Healer powers and see what happens.'

'Bronwyn. I don't know if that ...'

'Shh. Just let me try, River. Please.'

He did as she asked, but she could sense his tension. It seeped into her. She couldn't let it.

Closing her eyes again, she visualised the glowing colours of his aura, focusing on the glistening threads of bond tying him, whether he liked it or not, to his twin and to his pack. Her breathing evened, slowed, as she went deeper, following the pathways right into the centre of his auras.

The wolf aura was still blocked from both bonds. She looked closer. But there was something there. Something so fine, she'd almost missed it. She reached towards it with her mind, touching the glistening thread, the lightest of caresses.

A howl sounded in her mind, mournful and yearning. Power flared behind her eyes, golden and sparkling. Behind the howl she heard a growl and a hiss. Words, cold yet unintelligible, whispered across her mind, leaving a burn of despair in their wake. She cried out.

Beneath her hands, River jerked and swore, then rolled off the table, breaking the connection. 'Bronwyn, are you all right?'

She blinked. Partially lost in her trance, she saw the colours surge around him, the smudge's tentacles flaring out like hissing whips, sinking deeper into his wolf aura, dulling the vibrant colours further. 'Oh, Goddess, I've made it worse.'

'No, you didn't.' River leaned against the other side of the table. 'I felt that. You did something ... good.'

She blinked, shook her head. 'I don't know what.'

'You began to use your powers.'

'I didn't mean to. I wasn't ready for it. I don't know what happened.' She blinked again, her vision still wavering. 'Did I hurt you?'

'Don't worry about me. You look like hell. Adam, get in here. Something's happened.'

The door opened and strong hands gripped her shoulders, turning her around 'Bron. Come on, Bron. Come back to us.'

'Adam. Don't touch her.'

He let go of her and moved aside to make room for Shelley. 'What? What are you doing here?'

'I felt something fluctuate in the Packbond. By the looks of it, you felt it too.' Shelley began to rub Bron's hands.

'Is she safe?' River's tense voice snapped her the rest of the way out of the trance. But still, she couldn't seem to gather her thoughts enough to enter the conversation that whirled around her.

'You said you felt something,' Adam said. 'Was she pushing too hard? Is she about to pass out again?'

Shelley stopped and cocked her head. 'No. It's not coming from Bron. Harrison agrees.'

'He's with you again today?'

'Yes.' Shelley looked to her left and rolled her eyes. 'And no, you can't "pop into my body" again. It hurts and this isn't important enough.' She stopped, frowned.

'What's he saying?' Bron asked finally, aware of River coming to stand behind her. She could feel his presence like a soothing hand stroking up and down her back.

'He says it is important ...' She rolled her eyes again. 'Yeah, I think you're a little biased on this.'

'What is he saying?' Adam barked at her.

Shelley winced and she touched her head. 'Don't shout at me. Everyone's shouting at me.' Adam put out his hand to touch her, but she shrank back. 'I'm fine,' she snapped. 'It would be nice if everyone stopped shouting, that's all.' Turning back to Bron, she jerked her thumb towards the presence of Harrison Cantrae that only she could see. Although, as River stepped from behind her, she noticed his gaze was focused on the spot to Shelley's left.

'Can you see Harrison, River?'

He nodded briefly. 'Sometimes. Less now than before. But that doesn't matter. So you thinks it's coming from Skye, Grandpa?'

'What's coming from Skye?' Bron asked.

Shelley looked at her as if she were daft. 'The surge in our power. I know you can feel it.' Her gaze flickered down. 'Look at that.'

Bron glanced at her hands. 'Holy crap!' Licks of orange flame with a green heart sparked from the ends of them.

'Fucking hell!' River reached for her.

'No.' She held her hands behind her as she stepped away from him. 'Don't touch me. It might burn you.'

'Is it burning you?' His eyes were hot coals in his face, with licks of amber flame, nostrils flaring as his breathing became faster, shallower, as if he'd been running.

'What's wrong with you?' she asked, her focus suddenly entirely on him.

'That's not the question to ask right now,' he said.

'No? Then what is?'

'Your hands are on fire. What do you think the question should be?'

'It doesn't hurt.' But as she said the words, there was a lick of energy that raked along her nerve endings and she winced.

'Right. That does it.' River stepped towards her.

'Stop, River. Don't touch her.' Skye appeared in the doorway.

River didn't look at her, his gaze locked on Bron. 'Why shouldn't I touch my ...' He stumbled over the word, almost saying 'mate' in his haste to do what he felt was right by Bronwyn. Recovering, he said, '... my packmate?'

'Because my power has been building and it surged a few minutes ago. Jason wasn't nearby and I don't know how to syphon it straight into the pack without needing physical touch.' She clenched her fist by her side.

'You can't learn everything at once,' Adam said.

Skye's gaze met his. 'I need to. I'm not learning fast enough.'

River avoided her gaze as it landed on him. 'You'd learn faster if you didn't spend so much time trying to find a way to help me.'

Bron sucked in a breath. 'River! That's not very nice.'

'Nice or not, it's true. But it's also beside the point right now. I want to know what happened and why it's affecting Bronwyn ... and Shelley.'

Skye gripped her hands in front of her. 'I was about to call to Iain or Patrick, whoever was closest, when the power just disappeared. I thought at first perhaps I had managed to syphon it into Jason without him being there ...'

'But it hadn't,' Shelley said. 'It came into us.'

Skye nodded. 'I was outside having a run when it happened and raced home to make sure you were all right.'

'Why did it syphon into Bronwyn and Shelley?' Adam asked carefully.

'Because we're linked. I read about it in one of the old diaries about covens using each other to syphon excess power into before it became critical. It didn't always work because it required a certain closeness and also a blood tie to create the link. And even then, it wasn't always effective because sometimes the powers wouldn't meld and only tipped the other witch or warlock over the edge instead. It was why Bridgette Colliere created the Pact with the Were, because her friends and loved ones were a danger to themselves and each other.' Her gaze went to Shelley, then Bronwyn. 'I'm so sorry. The blood link you made with me on Halloween, saved me, but it could end up hurting you if I can't learn to channel this excess into the Were without them being there.'

'We'll figure it out.' Bronwyn began to edge past Adam, careful not to touch him given what had just been discussed, but the orange fire flickered out hitting him on the hand.

'Holy crap!' He grasped at his hand.

'Sorry,' Bron said, flinching back from him, her hands clasped under her armpits.

'No. It's okay. It didn't hurt. It just felt ...' His words died away as he lifted his hand up to look at it. 'What the fuck?'

'What is it?' Skye asked, stepping forward.

'I cut myself yesterday. We heal fast, but this was deep and was still pretty red and sore this morning.' He held his hand out towards them. 'It's gone.'

Skye grabbed his hand, running her fingers over the smooth skin. 'You're right. There's not even a scar.' Skye looked at Bronwyn and then her gaze slipped to River, her gaze lingering on the scars on his face, before coming back to Bronwyn.

'I can't,' Bronwyn said softly. 'I was just touching him when your power hit me. Something lashed out at both of us. It doesn't like me touching him with my power.'

'But this is different. It's my power channelled through you.'

'Is it?' Shelley asked, frowning down at her hands. 'There's no flame on my hands.'

Bronwyn held hers up. They all watched as the flame flared, brightened. 'It's getting worse.'

'It's orange and green.' Skye frowned. 'Not blue, like mine.'

Shelley's smile was crooked. 'The excess power has been channelled into us. But it's not your power anymore. It's changed to suit us. Healer flame for Bron.' She stopped, swallowed hard, her gaze flickering around her, not landing on any of them, but definitely seeing something. 'Something else entirely for me.'

'You're seeing more of them, aren't you?' Bronwyn asked.

Shelley nodded. 'It suddenly became much harder to block them out. It happened when the power surged through me. And it's getting worse, too.' She flinched. 'They're shouting at me. They're so loud. It hurts.'

Adam grabbed her hand. 'Is there something ...' His words choked to a halt as he stiffened.

Shelley's eyes widened and River could see her struggling to release her hand. But Adam didn't let go. Couldn't. River's breath hissed through his teeth, the sound echoed from Adam's mouth, as he power surged through the Packbond.

A golden-rainbow glow surrounded Adam until standing before Shelley was a big, black wolf.

Shelley shook as she looked down at the wolf. Slowly, she took in a deep breath and glanced around. 'They're gone.' A smile broke out on her face and on a laugh, she bent over and hugged the black wolf, ruffling its fur. 'Thank the Goddess, they're gone.'

The black Adam-wolf made a sound deep in its chest and rubbed his head against her shoulder. Shelley's laughter rippled on the air and she looked up at Bronwyn. 'It's a release. We have to release it into the pack. It's gone. It's all gone.'

River's attention turned to Bronwyn. She'd turned paler. There was tension around her eyes, her full lips pulled thin. 'Bronwyn. You have to release the power like Shelley did.'

Skye nodded. 'River's right. In the absence of Jason, my power sought out those I was closest to, to relieve the pressure on me. But you can't give it back to me. The only way to get rid of it is as Bridgette Colliere did—through the Were. They can use it to power and control their change.' Adam grunted. Skye smiled down at him. 'Okay, you weren't in control then, but I guess you could change back to human now and then go right back to wolf with no problems at all.'

Bronwyn nodded. 'I can see it in his aura. By transferring the power into Adam, Shelley brought the two parts of his aura into true harmony. It's like they're one.'

Skye clasped her hands together, gaze going to River. 'This could be it. This could be what helps River with his change.'

Bronwyn's gaze flickered to him and he could see the uncertainty there. 'I'm not sure about that. Something really strange happened before. I heard something ...' She shivered.

'But this is different, Bron. Can't you see that?' Skye gestured at Shelley and Adam. 'Shelley doesn't like Adam and yet her power harmlessly fed into him and changed him into his wolf.' Adam barked in protest at her words and nudged at Shelley, who was still ruffling his fur.

'If she didn't like me, she wouldn't still be touching me,' River heard in his head, Adam's distinctive wry tone coming through the Packbond.

River almost laughed. But he didn't because Skye ignored Adam's grizzling and continued with her argument.

'That's all River needs, for something to change him into his wolf. It can't be one of us.' She gestured to Shelley and herself. 'Shelley's already syphoned the excess into Adam, and mine went into you two. Besides, so far River hasn't responded to my power. Maybe it's because we're twins and he's immune to it in some way—otherwise, why wouldn't my power have helped him all those years ago before grandpa and grandmother made me bind it? No. You're the only one with the excess power left.' Her green eyes filled with worry. 'And if I'm not mistaken, you'll need to get rid of the excess soon or it will really start hurting you.'

Bronwyn swallowed hard. 'It's not so bad.'

'Liar,' River said. 'You're sweating and trembling.'

'No. I ...'

'Enough,' Shelley said, cutting between the two of them. 'Skye's right. Bron, you need to try releasing it into River. Slowly though.'

River nodded. 'Do it.'

Bronwyn held out her hand. The power glittered on the tips of her fingers. He almost flinched away from it—his memories of Skye's blue flame leaping over his face, burrowing into his skin, setting his hair on fire, were etched into his memory like a brand—but he was no coward. He took her hand.

Warmth filled him. He sighed at the bliss of it. Smiling, he opened his mouth to thank her. The words turned into a choked sound as the warmth became a burn. It sizzled through the skin of his fingers, through his nerves, racing like wildfire through his body. His teeth came together with a snap, his jaw clenched so hard he thought it might break. Instead of a golden glow, orange and green fire surrounded him. He began to shake, spittle frothing through clenched teeth as pain exploded in his head.

Black filled his vision. Bright sparks swirled towards him through the black. In the distance he heard shouting, curses, his name being called. But he didn't respond. Couldn't.

All he could concentrate on was the silver sparks swirling in the dark.

Moondust.

It looked just like the stuff Skye had called on and played with when they were children, using it to force a change on him. It landed on him now, each silver spark burning through his skin, turning it into ash, and through the ash, fur began to sprout.

His wolf howled in jubilation as it prepared to spring from his skin.

Then something grabbed at it. Black, spidery threads spread across his mind, like a sticky net, holding him and his wolf down. His wolf thrashed, its jubilant howl turning into a cry of utter frustration.

The black web thickened and began to spread, until black was all he could see once more. It tightened. Tightened. Cutting off his breath. Choking him.

He couldn't breathe.

A voice shouted at him, echoing in his mind.

'River. Stop. Come back to me.'

He opened his eyes to stare into cinnamon ones, bright with anguish. 'Bronwyn,' he whispered.

Then he fell into the dark.

8

Morrigan stiffened as the power surged through her, her fingers dipping into the water she was using to scry with. Warm Healer magic skated over her skin, power that sank its barbs into her, wanting to heal something that was not broken. She tried to turn it aside, but it was stubborn and strong. Hissing, she tried to pull her hands from the bowl, but she couldn't move.

'Mistress?' Eloise emerged from the shadows—the girl was very good at hiding her presence; too good. Morrigan hadn't even known she was there. 'Mistress, you're in pain.'

'The bowl,' Morrigan said through clenched teeth. 'Take the bowl.'

Scurrying forward as fast as her limping gait allowed, Eloise grabbed the bowl and whisked it away from the table. But the power wasn't ready to let go. It sparked out, a great orange-green flare, snapping at Morrigan's fingers, curling up her arm. She screamed as the agony of the power reached inside her and tried to mend her broken, twisted heart.

'No! You can't have my pain. I won't let you have my pain.'

She tried to push it away with her powers, but she was still so weak, the scrying had taken too much out of her. The flame stretched from the bowl of water held in Eloise's hand, across the table, tightened its grip on Morrigan's arm, curling towards her shoulder, flickering out towards her chest. 'No! No!' she screamed, batting at it. It hissed and sparked as it sought out the scars on her hands, her arms, her face.

She tried to stand—maybe if she dropped to the floor, grounding herself, it would kill the flame. Earth was the enemy of fire—but her legs refused to support her. She cried out as the flames reached her throat, edging up towards her face, seeking entry via mouth or nose. 'No!'

'Mistress!' With a cry, Eloise threw the bowl to the ground, the glazed blue pottery splintering into pieces, water splashing against her, the wall, pooling on the floor. The flame made a sound like the roaring of a bushfire as it consumed all before it—a great, howling whoosh of a noise, monstrous and threatening—and then it was gone.

Morrigan flopped onto the table, clutching at her throat. Catching her breath, she peered up at Eloise. 'Thank you. How did you know to do that?'

Eloise, her yellow-green eyes shining bright and large in the dark room, shook her head. 'I d-didn't know for certain.' She took a deep breath, clenching her shaking hands before her. 'It ... it just seemed like the only way to break the connection was to break the water's cohesion to the bowl.'

'You have good instincts, my dear.'

'What was that?'

'A very powerful witch was trying to weaken me. If not for your quick thinking, she might have succeeded.'

'Oh, Mistress. I'm glad I was here.'

'So am I.'

'You shouldn't do something like this without someone around.'

The genuine care in the girl's tone caught Morrigan by surprise.

Shaken, she blinked eyes that suddenly felt strangely burning and full. 'You're right. I'm not as strong as I need to be. I promise I won't scry again without one of you here.' She held out a shaking hand. 'Now, help me over to my bed. I need to lie down. And you can tell me what you've seen lately. Have you made it into the Packhouse yet?'

Eloise shook her head as she rushed over, careful not to step in the puddle of water on the floor. 'No. I haven't been able to muster the courage. I'm sorry.'

Morrigan patted Eloise's hand. 'I understand. They are monstrous.'

Eloise helped Morrigan to lie back on the bed, covering her with a soft patchwork quilt. 'You should rest now, Mistress. I can give you my report later when you are feeling better.'

Morrigan knew she should argue the point, but she felt too strange, too fractured. Besides, it was nice to be taken care of. So few people had done that for her. Since leaving her sister and the pack Morghanna had foolishly bound herself to all those years ago, she'd become accountable for the wellbeing of so many. 'Very well. But before you leave, you can get me that cup of your rejuvenating tea. I've got some there in the kitchenette.'

'Yes, Mistress. Right away.'

Morrigan closed her eyes and listened to the soft sounds as Eloise moved, as quiet as a cat, around the kitchenette, putting on the kettle, getting out cup and saucer, the shifting soft whisper of the tea in the canister as she pulled it down from the shelf.

It was soothing listening to the sounds of a properly steeped cup of tea being made. It was one of the things she'd made certain of in Eloise's training—that the girl knew how to make a proper cup of tea.

Of course, her being a perfect handmaiden wasn't the reason the witch-shifter was here.

Despite her deformity, Eloise was proving just as useful as the Darkness had suggested. As was her twin brother, Cain, even though he couldn't shift form. Not that it mattered. Unlike the Were, shifters could also carry power like witches and warlocks, and he was powerful. More powerful than any warlock had been in the coven for centuries. At times that power worried her, but given the Darkness wasn't worried, she supposed she shouldn't be either.

All-in-all, she was pleased with the results of kidnapping them from their shifter family and bringing them here for Simon O'Brien and his wife to rear as their own.

As she listened to the sounds of the tea being made, she allowed the familiar ritual of it to wash over her, soothing her jangled nerves. But nothing she did could stop the itch of healing in her skin. She opened her eyes and lifted her hands to the light, peering at them.

The scars were almost gone.

Dark Goddess! The power to do such a thing was incredible; and through a scrying medium what's more! This was proof that the previously useless Wiccan, Bronwyn Kincaid, was now turning into something she was never meant to be.

Damn her and that Skye. The power should have been hers, not some useless Wiccan's and a witch too gormless to learn how to control it!

Hot anger lashed through her, but the Darkness clamped a cold hand around the heat and brought her back to reason before she wreaked havoc on her surrounds again.

'Maybe we don't have the power, but the Wiccan-witch isn't in charge of it either. We have time. And we must use it.'

The Darkness was right, again. *'But how?'*

'The piece of me in the half-Were is not powerful enough to take over yet, but with some help from you and our little friend there, it can be. He has emotions he cannot control. He thinks he is broken. And you know what that means.'

'The bond,' she whispered. Excitement fluttered in Morrigan's chest as she remembered what she'd seen in the scrying—the bond Bronwyn had used to twine the fractured pieces of River's aura together. If there hadn't been that surge in her powers, a surge the Darkness in River had responded to violently, the Healer Witch might have dug it out and won. But she hadn't because the bond wasn't strong enough yet. But it was there. And it could be used.

'Yes. He loves her. He will protect her no matter the cost. Even from himself. We only have to help that along.'

Love. Morrigan's lip curled. Love was a weakness. One she could manipulate. And if she did it in the right way, the Darkness in River would grow and when it was ripe, she would pick it and twist it to shape him into the embodiment of her revenge.

She began to chuckle softly to herself.

9

Bron sat on a chair next to the bed, her fingers worrying at the edge of the diary she held in her lap.

She'd been trying to read it. Trying to find the answers for what had happened when she'd touched River with the excess power. But so far, she'd come across nothing that was remotely helpful. As far as she was aware, neither had Shelley nor Skye. And they'd been looking. Tirelessly.

She'd sent River into some kind of grand mal seizure that had knocked him unconscious before Iain and Patrick had managed to pry her hand away and take the excess power into themselves. But even after the seizure passed, River hadn't woken up.

Thankfully Shelley had kept her cool. She'd managed to ascertain River was simply unconscious and would probably wake up at any time. Adam had changed back and carried him up to the bedroom set aside for him, with Bron and Skye following in his wake.

Neither of them wanted to leave him, so the others had brought up some of the most ancient Pack Diaries, and they'd sat on the floor for the rest of the day and well into the night, trying to find an answer to the problems before them.

They had discovered many things. But nothing that could help them understand what had happened to River. Nothing that could help her to make sure it didn't happen again— short of never touching him. And certainly nothing that could suggest how she could cure him.

Her gaze wandered back to River again. He was lying in exactly the same stiff position he'd been in when Adam had placed him there. Skye had removed his shoes and jeans and had pulled the cover up over him, but he hadn't moved. Hadn't opened his eyes. Hadn't acknowledged a single one of them for a whole night and day. Bron refused to leave him, even after Jason had arrived back from his meeting with Marcus McClune and dragged Skye away to rest. Shelley had nagged at her to go and get some rest as well, but she shook her head and said it was her duty to stay.

That had been hours ago.

'You should go and get some sleep.'

She looked up to see Jason in the doorway and smiled tiredly at him. 'I'm good.'

He crouched beside her. 'Shelley said you haven't left his side since it happened.'

Dobber,' she grumbled.

'She's worried about you. As we all are.'

Bron tightened her grip on the diary, her gaze returning once more to River. 'I'm supposed to be a Pack Healer now, yet I was the one who hurt him. How can I leave him alone in the dark?'

'We'll leave a light on,' Jason said.

'I didn't mean that kind of dark.'

Jason touched her shoulder, a soft caress of friendship, of support. 'I know. I was just trying to make you laugh.' He sighed, ran his hand through his hair. 'I should leave that up to the Trickster, shouldn't I?'

Bron couldn't even make herself smile at that. 'Adam's gone for a run to get rid of the excess energy Shelley fed into him.'

Jason sat down next to her. 'I know.' He took her hand in his. 'It's not your fault. You didn't know what would happen. None of us did. But you had to try.'

Bron pressed her lips together as they trembled. It took a few moments to answer him and when she did, her voice was tight with the tears she refused to shed. 'I wasn't certain. I shouldn't have done it until I was certain.'

'None of us can be certain about any of this. It's new territory. Even Cordelia says there's no mention in their Pack Diaries of anything like this. But unless we try, we can't learn.'

She pierced him with a glare. 'But why is River the one to suffer? Why did the power rebound on him and not me?'

Jason shook his head. 'I don't know. I wish I did, but I don't. What I do know is that River won't thank you for exhausting yourself by sitting here with him and getting no rest. In fact, I'm pretty sure he'll rip through me if I let you ignore your need for rest for much longer.'

'I'm not ignoring it. I don't need it. Ever since the energy transfer, I've been on a high.'

'Yes, but all highs end with a crash.'

'Then I'll crash. But I'm not leaving River until I do. And nothing you or any of the others can do or say will make me forsake my Healer vows. I've done damage here. I must be the one to make amends in whatever way I can. And if sitting vigil is the only thing I can do, then I'm going to do it.'

'One of the pack will sit with him at all times.' Jason stood and held out his hand. 'I promise.'

'Not good enough.' She stared up at him, not caring that her eyes were full of unshed tears. 'It has to be me.' Her gaze was pulled back to River. 'I don't know why, but it has to be me.'

He sighed. 'I think I know.'

She tore her gaze away from the unconscious Were in the bed to look a question at Jason.

He answered the look with a sigh and a shake of his head.

'If you know why, then you must tell me.'

'It's not my secret to share.' He nodded at River. 'When he's ready, he'll let you know.' Leaning over, he kissed her on the forehead. 'Is there anything I can get for you?' he asked as he straightened.

'You can bring me another diary.'

'I'll bring a few more up.' His handsome features and lightning-blue eyes were full of empathy. She was so glad her friend had found such a good man. They deserved each other.

He was as good as his word and brought up a box of diaries fifteen minutes later. Then he left, but not before trying to convince her to rest once again.

She simply picked a diary out of the box and opened it.

He sighed and left her to it.

She pored over the diaries in the box in the long hours that followed, often struggling to understand the crabbed, ancient writing. There was a lot of very interesting information about pack and coven life, many interesting spells and medicinal remedies she would normally be itching to try, but she found nothing that would help River.

'This is pointless.' She snapped the last diary shut and pushed it off her lap, uncaring that not only was it precious to the Were, but as a document that was nearing five hundred years old, it was priceless. Pulling her feet up onto the chair in front of her, she buried her face in her knees and gave in to the tears that had been threatening since the day before.

'Bronwyn?'

Her head snapped up. 'River?'

His eyes, tired and red-rimmed, were open and looking at her as if he was a starving man and she was a feast. 'Bronwyn,' he whispered again, his hand reaching out to her.

She leaned forward to take his hand so fast she lost her balance, tumbled forward off the chair to sprawl on top of his chest.

'Bronwyn,' he whispered, his breath playing over her cheek, gaze falling to her lips, hand buried in her hair. 'Bronwyn.'

He tugged her slightly, and more off balance than her little fall could account for, she softened into him.

His lips met hers. Soft. So soft. And warm. Little, almost nibbling kisses at first then pressing harder—a sweet glide over super-sensitised skin. His fingers curled in her hair, pulling her more firmly against him, holding her in place.

Not that she could move. Or wanted to with this warmth flooding through her. She'd been so cold since yesterday. Cold to the bones. But now, with River's mouth on hers, hot breaths mingling, his tongue running along the seam of her lips, once, twice, enticing her to open, sliding into her mouth when she did, she felt warm. Warmer than she ever remembered feeling in her life.

She groaned as his tongue stroked over hers. His head angled to go deeper. The kiss changed from languid and warm to fast and hot. So hot. The burn of desire, sudden and unbidden, raced through her veins.

She groaned.

His mouth shifted from hers, and she clutched his shoulders as he worked a path of fire down her throat to secure over the juncture of her neck and shoulder, his teeth biting into the soft flesh there—a tang of pain followed by the lush lap of his tongue over the sting.

'River!' she moaned as the impact of what he was doing flooded through her system. 'Touch me. I need your hands on me. Touch me.'

River stilled with a suddenness that made her breath catch in her throat. For a terrible moment it reminded her of the night before when she'd touched him and he'd become as still as death just before the seizure had started.

Just as suddenly, he moved.

Bron spilled onto the bed, bouncing on the mattress as River lifted her off him and sprang away to come to a hunter's crouch on the far side of the room. 'Bronwyn? What are you doing?' His eyes were wary. 'What happened? What are you doing in my bedroom?'

Bron sat up slowly, cautious. 'Don't you remember what happened? What just happened?'

He uncurled from his crouch, but his body posture still screamed of tension. 'I was having a dream. You were there. We were ...' His eyes widened and he sucked in a breath, his gaze raking over her as she lay sprawled on his bed. 'We weren't ... I didn't ... I ... Oh fuck!' He swung away.

Bron's heart clutched in her chest. 'You were dreaming?'

'I was ... I didn't mean ...' He turned, his expression so full of self-hatred she felt lashed by it. 'I'm sorry. I was dreaming about ... I was confused. It shouldn't have happened.' He turned, grabbed his jeans, jerked them on and before she could say anything, was at the door to the balcony. 'I'm sorry,' he muttered. 'Please forget that happened. I'm going to try to.' Then he was gone. Out the door and over the balcony.

With a cry, she raced to the balcony. By the time she got there he was already through the garden and out the gate into the park. Another shadow followed him—Iain. 'Thank Goddess.' He'd make sure River didn't get into trouble.

Legs shaking, Bron sank onto the floor of the balcony and wrapped her arms around her legs. What had happened? River's kiss had been so unexpected, and maybe if she'd been thinking straight and hadn't been so upset, she would have pulled back, would have noticed that he wasn't fully awake. That he hadn't meant to share that passionate moment with her.

He had seemed embarrassed, and now, so was she. She was nowhere near a prude, and was fully in touch with her sexual appetites, but no girl liked to think a man kissed her by mistake.

That's what he'd said. He'd been dreaming. Probably thinking about someone else entirely. Then she'd gone and fallen on him and kissed him. She was pretty certain her lips had met his first. Hadn't they? Not that it mattered. She was awake and he'd been asleep and she'd taken advantage of him.

She groaned and hid her heated face against her raised legs. She would never forget that look on his face when he'd woken and realised he was kissing his twin's best friend, his Pack Healer. Embarrassment didn't cover it. He'd been horrified.

Goddess! She'd never disgusted a man before. Freaked some out with her frankness and with what she did for a living, but never disgust. She groaned again and pulled her arms more tightly around her legs.

Everything her mother and father had ever said to her about her life choices shouted for pre-eminence in her head. She'd been so cocky yesterday, thinking she was ready to open her business again, thinking she could figure out how to help River and to harness her power so she could be a worthy Pack Healer. How wrong could she be?

She couldn't even kiss a man worth a damn and make him want to stay with her.

She banged her head against her knees. She was such an idiot. How on earth was she going to face him again? She was just going to have to make certain he knew it had been a mistake for her, too. Something that wouldn't happen again. An accident.

Who kissed by accident?

She banged her head again. Think! Perhaps she could make him believe she'd been half asleep too; that she hadn't really been thinking straight because she'd been exhausted? Yes. There was a chance he'd buy that. But one thing was certain—she couldn't stay here berating herself when he was out there, embarrassed, hurting and confused.

Pulling herself up, she shoved her feet into her ballet flats and raced downstairs and into the kitchen. Skye and Adam were standing in the kitchen chatting as Adam mixed something with the blender. They looked up at her, startled. The blender stopped.

'Adam, where's River?'

Skye tensed. 'Upstairs in his bed.'

Bron shook her head. 'No. He woke up and I fell on him and we accidently kissed and then he got embarrassed and jumped off the balcony.'

'What?' Skye raced out onto the patio, as if she expected to see him splattered all over the lawn in the garden.

'You fell on him and accidently kissed him?' Adam asked, knocking the blender blades against the side of the bowl, a wide grin on his face. 'How does someone accidently kiss?'

'I don't know,' she said, wishing her face wasn't as red as a beet-root. 'It just happened.'

Skye came back from the window. 'He's not out there.'

'Of course he's not out there,' Bron snapped. 'He ran off. We have to find him. I have to explain. Apologise.'

Adam laughed. 'No man needs an apology when a good-looking

woman kisses him. Although, I suppose it depends on how well you did it.'

'Adam!' Skye barked. 'Can you be serious for once?'

He tipped his head as if to consider. 'When it warrants being serious, yes. But I'm yet to hear something to give me any concern.' He waved his hand. 'You kissed him, Bron. It's not a crime.'

'You didn't see his face.'

His grin widened. 'He's probably never been kissed before and you shocked him, which was why he ran off.'

'Oh shit,' Bron said, burying her head in her hands. She hadn't even thought about that.

Adam laughed. 'It's not the end of the world. He'll get over it and will most likely be back for more. Mark my words.'

'I don't want to wait for him to come back. I have to find him now. He's very fragile at the moment and I don't want to make his condition worse by chasing him away.'

'Fragile, my arse. He's a Were. We're hardly what you would call fragile.'

'I don't mean physically, you moron. I mean emotionally ...' Her eyes narrowed. 'You're trying to piss me off on purpose. Why?'

He shrugged. 'Being angry is better than being embarrassed, worried and afraid.' He cocked his head as if listening to something, and then waved out the window. 'Iain says he's out in the park watching Tom ride his new bike.'

'That connection between the Alpha and lieutenants sure comes in handy. Thanks,' Bron said.

'I'll come with you,' Skye said as Bron rounded the kitchen table to go to the door.

Adam was suddenly at Skye's side, his hand on Skye's shoulder, stopping her. 'No. There are some conversations best had alone.'

Bron didn't wait to hear Skye's argument. She ran out the door and down the steps into the garden. She wasn't surprised by Adam's intuition. It was becoming apparent to her that there was more to the Trickster designation than the name implied.

She ran down the sloping lawn and let herself out the back gate and into the park. Her feet pounded, sending up little puffs of dust on the gravel path that meandered through the wide-open spaces of fields and woods.

She hadn't got more than fifty metres from the house when River appeared around a bend in the path. He was jogging towards her, Tom in his arms, Iain close behind him carrying the bike over his shoulder. Suzie, a young maternal Were who was studying childcare and was Tom's nanny, scurried along beside him, a helmet in her hands.

'What's wrong? What's happened?' Bron cried, running to meet them, her attention split between the sobbing boy and the man who held him.

'Tom had a spill,' Suzie said. 'He's hurt himself.' She gestured to the two large grazes on his knees, watery blood dribbling from them. Patches of blood on River's shirt where the little boy was clasping him told her he'd injured his palms too.

Bron's empathy surged and she had to stop herself from wincing as the stinging pain of Tom's injuries became her own. She reached River and said to the boy in his arms, 'Oh, poor sausage. I've had plenty of spills off bikes in the past. It hurts, doesn't it?' The little Were nodded, his lip quivering, tears making tracks through his dust-stained face. She ran her hand over his head. 'You're so brave.' She turned his hands over, brows raising. 'You've already cleaned these?' she asked, glancing up at River and meeting his gaze for the first time since he'd jumped from the balcony to escape her.

'Yes. Suzie had some water and we tipped it over the sores to get the gravel out.' River's gaze slide quickly from hers.

Crap. He was embarrassed. She knew he would be. She wished she could address the kiss right now, apologise and just get past it, but with Tom watching them with big, wet eyes and Iain and Suzie there for the show too, she bit her tongue on the words she needed to say and concentrated on the issue at hand. 'Shall we get him up to the house and see if Shelley is back from her shift? If she's not there, I'm sure we could find some bandages and things in the house to treat the wounds until she gets back.'

'That won't be necessary, Bronwyn.' River's eyes burned with an intensity that made her shiver as he finally met her gaze.

Heart pounding, she whispered, 'But he needs to be healed.'

'Yes he does. You can do it.'

'Me?' Her hand fluttered against her chest.

'Who do you think I was bringing him to?'

'You know I can't,' she said, her voice a harsh whisper. She couldn't believe he was asking this of her, especially after what she'd done to him.

'Of course you can.'

He sounded so certain. Pity she wasn't.

Her gaze flew to Suzie and then Iain, not wanting them to be witness to her worry. To her failure.

A faint smile curled the corners of Iain's mouth, but he turned and gestured to Suzie. 'Come on. Bron doesn't need us watching.'

Suzie looked like she was about to argue the point, but a stern look from Iain made her snap her mouth shut and follow along behind him as he stalked up the path towards the house.

She turned back, aware of Tom's curious gaze on her. She shook her head at River, hoping he'd understand.

His gaze met hers, unerring and direct in a way she'd never experienced from him before now. 'You can do this,' he said quietly, firmly. 'You need to forget about what happened yesterday.'

What happened today.

She frowned at the unspoken words between them, confused by the apology in his eyes. He didn't need to apologise. She was the one at fault for the kiss. 'I can't do that. I need to talk ... Apologise.' Her gaze flicked to Tom, then back to River, cheeks heating again.

His lips softened into an almost smile. 'There's nothing to talk about and nothing to apologise for. But there will be if you don't start healing again. And you can start with Tom. Can't she, little man?'

Her fingers clenched to still their shaking. 'You know I'm not the best person to do that at the moment,' she whispered.

'But you're our Pack Healer,' Tom said simply. 'Who else will fix me?'

River's brow rose. 'Out of the mouths of babes. You healed Adam's scar yesterday.'

'That was different.'

River shook his head. 'I don't think so.' He crouched on the grass beside the path, settling Tom on his raised knee. Reaching up, tentative, he took her hand and gently pulled her down to kneel beside him. Placing her hand over Tom's knee, he held it there for a moment, the warmth of him seeping into her so deeply the sensation remained when he let go of her hand. 'You asked me to trust you, now I'm saying you have to trust yourself. You've fallen off the horse. Now it's time to get back on.'

'I don't know if it's safe for me to ride again.'

'You won't know if you don't try.'

'But is this the safest way to test your theory?' She glanced at Tom, who was looking at them curiously.

'You won't hurt Tom.'

'You don't know that.' She didn't understand his certainty, his confidence in her, particularly after what she'd done to him.

He smiled at her. 'Yes I do. I'm certain of it because this is what you do. It's who you are. Look.'

She did and gasped. She hadn't noticed the warm tingle in her palm—he'd distracted her from noticing—but when he'd placed her hand over Tom's wound, her instincts had kicked in and she'd begun to heal his wounds without even thinking about it.

Tom smiled up at her, then took her hand, guiding it to his other knee. 'Do the other one, Bronny. It kind of tickled.'

Her breath an excited puff in her chest, Bron sent her powers into him, the warmth tingling on her palm. Tom giggled and wriggled.

'Stay still, Tom, until Bronwyn has finished.'

'Okay.'

The little Were sat still as she completed the Healing.

When she moved her hand away, there was only a slight pinkness of skin, like the wounds were weeks old and almost fully healed. Bron swallowed hard. 'I've never done a Healing like that before. It's amazing.'

'No,' River said, his voice a whisper. '*You* are amazing. Now Tom, hold your hands out so Bronwyn can fix them too.'

The little boy held them out, palms up, his face serious and hopeful. She put her hands over his, careful not to touch River, and concentrated on healing the gashes on Tom's hands. Moments later, she lifted her hands.

Tom wriggled his fingers and laughed. He stood, spilling off River's lap, and gave Bron a hug. 'Thanks Bronny.' He kissed her cheek before taking off up the path, shouting to Iain and Suzie, who had stopped by the back gate, watching. 'Iain. Suzie. Look what Bronny did.'

Bron couldn't help but smile at his exuberance as Suzie put her arm around him and bundled him inside Iain following with the bike. She allowed the joy of it to wash over her, strengthen her for what needed to be said now they didn't have an audience.

River stood. Bron scrambled to her feet, careful not to touch him despite the fact he held out a hand to help her. 'How did you know?'

River almost groaned. How could he not know? It was like her desperate need to heal was his; a burning ache inside him. But he couldn't say that to her. 'You've just lost confidence because your magic feels different now. But it's not really different, it's just ...' He frowned, trying to think of the right word to explain what he could sense. 'More. It's just more.'

She gaped at him. 'How do you know that?'

He shrugged, looked away. The urgency of her question pressed on him and he wanted to turn and run from it again. But he'd seen the devastation in her eyes when he'd run from her before, the echo of it as she'd jogged up to him just now, and he didn't want to put it there again. He ran his hand over his face. 'I can feel it through the Packbond,' he lied.

She gasped. 'Does that mean everyone can feel it?'

'No.' He grasped her shoulders; her embarrassment at the thought everyone could feel her confusion, her worries that she was failing at this thing she'd always been so good at, were a knife in his gut. 'It's apparent to me because of my link with Skye. I can feel things through her the others can't. It's like she amplifies the Packbond.'

She nodded. His sigh of relief fluttered the hair at her temples and he suddenly became aware of how close they were, the softness of her skin under his fingers where they touched her arm, the fresh apple blossom and honey scent of her. His cock hardened in his jeans and he bit back on a groan.

Fuck.

He let her go. Backed up a few steps. But it wasn't enough. What the hell had he been thinking when he'd remained with her rather than following Tom? It wasn't a good idea, being here with her with nobody else around. Especially not after the kiss.

Hell. He'd told her to forget about the kiss, but he couldn't. The memory of it was like wildfire in his blood, a flame that seared images into his mind; the image of her face in his hands, the bliss of her lips on his, the slide of her tongue inside his mouth and his inside hers, her gasping breaths an echo of his, the warm, soft press of her body lying on top of him. It drove all other thoughts aside, until all he could think about was doing it again. Going further. Taking everything she offered, and more, until they were wrung out, sweaty and limp in each other's arms.

That's why he'd run. But he couldn't run now. She was hurting and unsure and he had to make her see what was so apparent to him. She wasn't just warmth and light for him—she was that to the whole pack. To her friends. To her clients.

Digging his fingernails into his palms, he forced his body to calm, so he could stay and help her. 'I'm the lost cause, Bronwyn, not you.'

'I don't believe that,' she said, a spark in her eyes now.

'I know you don't. I also know your confidence isn't being helped because you're not having any luck with healing the schism separating me from my wolf. But you shouldn't let what's happening with me knock your confidence. Skye says that even the McClune's Healer is stumped, and she's been using her magic to heal for a lot longer than you have. Once your new and old powers come into balance, I know you'll figure it out. But you've got to stop focusing on it and seeing it as a failure. I don't.' He wanted to touch her forehead, brush away that frown, cup the warmth of her cheek. He realised he'd raised his hand to do just that. Her gaze lowered to it, and she stepped forward, as if wanting the touch too.

He dropped his hand and stepped further back, surprised by the flash of disappointment in her eyes. No. He had to have been wrong. She couldn't have wanted him to touch her. Not in the way he needed to touch her. Maybe in the way pack did, to settle, comfort.

Damn it! He couldn't even give her that. But he could give her words. He could give her what she needed to hear. 'They need you to keep trying. I need you to keep trying.'

'But I hurt you.'

'No you didn't. I hurt myself. Something in me just can't accept the change your powers bring.'

Her brow furrowed and her eyes fogged over again, but not in confusion this time. It was as if she wasn't quite there with him; like she was seeing something else. 'The darkness in you. I felt it lash out, but you stopped it. Held it in.'

His muscles clenched, jaw tightening as he remembered the pain that had followed the glory of her Healing power when it had first channelled into him. Her power hadn't caused the pain. The dark thing inside him had done that. 'I couldn't let it hurt you.'

'You're my hero.'

He huffed out a laugh. 'I'm nobody's hero.'

'You were mine, yesterday.' She reached out tentatively, touched his clenched fist when he didn't pull away. A shy smile flirted on her lips. 'You're so strong.' Her gaze caught his, held him for one breathless moment so that he couldn't respond. Just stood there, caught in the magic that was this woman who could be his mate if only he wasn't so broken. Too broken for even her to fix.

She curled her fingers around his fist and his hand opened, welcoming the slide of her skin over his, the twining of their fingers. She stepped closer—maybe he pulled her closer, he didn't know. But suddenly, she stood so close her warmth spread across his chest, the brush of her breath on his neck. She lifted her face, her tongue brushing over her lips, wetting them. He couldn't look away.

'River?'

'Bron! You healed Tom.'

He wasn't sure who jerked away first at the sound of Skye calling out, but suddenly they were standing on opposite sides of the path, panting like they'd been running.

Skye didn't seem to notice. She practically danced up to them and threw her arms around Bronwyn. 'I knew you could do it. My power always settles around the children and does what it's meant to do. It seems yours does, too.' Her lips trembled. 'I'm so relieved. I thought my power had screwed yours up and it's been tearing at me. I know how much you need to heal.'

'It's not your fault, Skye.' Bronwyn wrapped her arms around her friend, but her gaze didn't move from River's. After a moment, she released him from the intensity of her gaze and pulled back to look at her friend. 'I healed Tom with no worries. I know I can do it again.'

He knew she wouldn't forget about what had just happened. That she was going to try to have a 'discussion' with him about it later. But he couldn't let that happen. As much as he wanted to build her confidence, talking about the attraction between them wouldn't change anything. It would just cut the wound open, make it deeper so it would never heal.

Not that he was worried about healing himself. He'd soon be dead. At the first sign that the true madness was coming on, that he would turn rabid, he would take matters into his own hands and put himself down. It was the right thing to do.

The only thing to do.

He just didn't want to leave more open wounds behind than he had to. So he had to stop Bronwyn from pursuing this heated desire that kept flaring between them. It would do neither of them any good. He could never allow the mating bond to snap into place. It might bring a few months or weeks of bliss to them both, but it would leave Bronwyn with a lifetime of grief.

He couldn't be responsible for making her light fade. He wouldn't.

So he shook his head at the question in her eyes and turned his attention to his twin.

'It was remarkable, Skye, how quickly she healed Tom. You should have seen it.'

Skye spun to face him, one arm slung around Bronwyn's shoulders, the touch filled with a casual intimacy he envied. 'I wish you'd brought him up to the house for the Healing.'

'He was in pain. Bronwyn needed to heal him right away.'

'Of course. I'm being selfish. I thought I'd be the one to talk some sense into you,' she said to Bronwyn, then laughed. 'Who would have guessed it would have been my quiet, reticent brother?' She skipped across the path and threw her arms around him.

He knew he should have flinched and pulled away, start the separation now, but he couldn't. He loved Skye more than he'd ever loved anyone until he'd clapped eyes on Bronwyn. They'd been separated for so long, by the lies told to her and the drugs he'd been fed. Being part of her again felt so right, and he couldn't let go of it fully. Not quite yet. So he wrapped his arms around her and hugged her back, chuckling when she grumbled he was holding her too tight and then gave him a smacking kiss on the cheek when he let go.

'Come on. Both of you. This deserves a celebratory drink.'

River shook his head. He couldn't go up to the house and pretend to be happy and part of the celebration. He couldn't chat with his fellow packmates and share the food Adam was making now for whoever would be around. His emotions were too raw. And the Beast stirred inside him, even though the full moon was weeks away. He had to get away from the cause.

'You go ahead. I want to go for a run. I'll be in later.'

'But don't you want to tell everyone about Bron healing Tom?'

'I'm sure Tom and Bronwyn will do a great job of that without my mumbled version of events.'

'You're being too hard on yourself.'

Her disappointment dripped over him like acid. But he couldn't let it affect his decision. 'You know I don't like big groups. I'm better by myself.'

'But if you go for a run, it means Iain has to miss out too. Don't you think that's a little selfish?'

She was pouting at him, just like she used to when they were kids. He'd always given in to her in the past when she did that, her eyes wide green pools filled with her plea. He would have given in to her now, except Bronwyn was standing there, a reminder of exactly why he couldn't.

Laughing off her appeal, he said, 'If anyone wouldn't care about missing out on a party, it would be Iain. He is a Lone Wolf after all.'

He glanced at where Iain now stood by the gate, watching them from the spot he'd been standing in since Skye had run out. He'd probably seen everything. Thank the Moon it hadn't been Patrick or one of the others shadowing him today. If it was, they'd have questions about his intentions towards their Healer. Questions he wasn't prepared to answer. But Iain knew the value of keeping his own counsel and he allowed others to keep theirs too. He was the perfect Shadow.

He gestured with his head towards the path, and Iain nodded, jogging towards them.

River turned back to Skye. 'You go on and celebrate Bronwyn's success. I need to run. My wolf needs to run.'

'But I need you to help me talk her into opening her business again.'

'I'm standing right here,' Bronwyn grumbled.

He couldn't help but smile. She stood there, hands on hips, eyes blazing with a fire it was a joy to see. 'Bronwyn knows she needs to open her business. She doesn't need me or you telling her to do it. Do you, Bronwyn?'

Bronwyn puffed out a little breath as if his words had popped her anger, deflating it. 'No. I don't.'

Skye spun on her. 'Does this mean you're going to go back to work tomorrow?'

Bronwyn shook her head, something like bemused wonder in her eyes. 'I suppose it does.' Her gaze flickered to River as Skye clapped her hands and hugged her again.

'This is terrific, especially as I've already got a client waiting to see you.'

Bronwyn looked sideways at her. 'Who?'

'Me.' Skye said. 'My neck is killing me after poring over those diaries for almost twenty-four hours straight, and Shelley isn't much better.'

'You, Miss "I don't trust anything but western medicine" Collins are willing for me to do some reiki on you?'

'Yep. And Shelley wants a Healing session, too. And we both want a massage.'

'Now you're asking for too much.'

Skye chuckled. 'I know. Great isn't it? So how about me for nine am and Shelley for ten?'

Bronwyn rolled her eyes then laughed.

That laughter was like a key undoing the lock that had held him there for the last few minutes. Smiling at both of them, he said, 'Now that that's all settled, I'm going for my run. Have a sparkling for me.' Turning before they could say anything else to hold him there, he took off, feet pounding on the dirt path, the fire in his blood pumping through his heart, making him aware that no matter how far or fast he ran, there were some things he couldn't run away from because he carried them with him.

But he was determined one of those things would not be Bronwyn's heart or her soul.

BRONWYN'S SHOULDERS slumped as River ran from her again. He'd tried to make it seem like he wasn't running away from *her*, but he was. Something had happened between them before, but she wasn't quite certain what. Skye had interrupted before she could sort meaning from the mire of her own emotions. She shook her head. If River thought he could run from her and that would be an end to it, he didn't know her very well. She wasn't leaving him alone to bury his feelings—whatever they were. He'd said she had to face up to the changes in her powers and accept them. But that wasn't the only thing she had to face up to.

She'd hurt him. She knew it even though he'd denied it. But denying it didn't make it less true. And hiding from it wasn't going to help her figure out why. And the fact that he'd encouraged her to heal Tom, that he'd known she could, that he'd made her see she was foolish for not following the needs of her heart and soul and opening her business again, just made her even more determined to figure out what was happening between them, why she'd hurt him and what the fuck those heated flashes of desire were about. They'd been about to kiss again when Skye had interrupted them. She was sure of it.

And oh, Goddess, she wished it had happened.

'Bron? Are you okay?'

She snapped around to face her friend. Skye's gaze was probing and Bron looked away, trying to suppress the burn in her cheeks and the shot of desire that had punched into her at the memory of River's lips on hers. 'I'm fine. Just a bit overwhelmed.'

Skye's gaze darted from her to River as he disappeared over a rise, Iain a few paces behind. 'And you're worried about River.'

Bron nodded, happy to let Skye think that was all it was. 'He wants me to heal, but he doesn't think I can heal him. It's almost like he doesn't want me to.'

Skye gripped her arm and pulled her around to face her, eyes blazing. 'You mustn't give up on him. Please. Jason told me if we can't find a way to free River's wolf, terrible things can happen. Locked-down wolves ... they go insane. Turn rabid. Try to kill their loved ones. And the Pack Hunter ... they'd have to hunt him down and ... kill him.' The last was a harsh, painfilled whisper. 'I can't lose him to that. I can't.'

Bron stilled, breath caught in her throat at the thought of that happening to River. She gripped her friend's hands. 'I won't give up on him. I promise.'

'Thank you,' Skye said, her eyes glistening. 'I know you'll be able to figure it out.'

Bron shook her head. 'Why do you have so much faith in me?'

'Because I know you. Because you canted the spell that allowed you to share in my powers to save my life and bring balance to the pack. You did this before you even got these powers. You were already strong in magic. Shelley and I have always known it, but for some reason, you never did.'

'You knew it?'

Skye nodded, blushing. 'Why do you think I was always so nervous whenever you threatened to take care of my aches and pains? I felt the power you had inside, even though I tried to ignore its existence because I so desperately needed you to be my friend. You don't need my power to be strong. You already were strong. My power is just a boost. Blended with yours, you will be able to do remarkable things.'

Bron was flabbergasted. She'd had no idea Skye had ever felt any of that. But she couldn't deny it was true. Sensing power in others was something Skye could do. She'd always thought it was part of the spell her grandparents had woven around her, but it wasn't. It was a part of her power and she was just starting to accept it and learn to use it, not out of fear, but to help the pack.

Skye laughed at the expression on Bron's face and slung her arm around her shoulders, giving her a squeeze. 'Aside from all that, I got you into this and I'm not going to let you suffer alone; or let you give up on yourself or River.' A tear trembled down Skye's cheek as she looked up at the moon rising in the sky.

Bron slipped her arm around her friend's waist and squeezed back. She had less than two weeks to try to figure out how to help River. She couldn't give up now. 'I'll try my best.'

'I always knew you would.' She hooked her arm around Bron's and started walking back up the path towards the Packhouse. 'Now, let's go and celebrate your success with Tom.'

'Okay. But I'll only be able to have a quick drink. If I'm opening tomorrow, I have a stack of things to do. I have to call Helen—I'll need her to come in. We'll have to call everyone who is waiting for appointments. And I'll have to look at my stock and see what I need. I'll need more if the bookings pick up quickly.'

Skye beamed at her. 'That's my girl. Straight back into the nitty gritty.' She sighed and nudged her shoulder against Bron's as they walked in the back gate. 'Everything's going to be okay.'

Bron nodded. Yes, everything was going to be okay because she'd make it that way.

10

B ron opened the shop the next day. Her clients rushed to make appointments, not even minding Bluebelle's presence when she pushed into the room and jumped up onto a shelf to watch what Bron was doing. It made Bron smile and feel easier. Bluebelle would warn her if something was going awry just as she had before.

She started off with easy stuff—massage, reiki, a few naturopathy sessions where she diagnosed irritable bowel syndrome, an allergy to yeast and a urinary tract infection. She was able to treat them with tonics and tablets already prepared, suggesting dietary changes and rest.

The remainder of the first week continued on in the same vein and she would have been happy except ...

River was avoiding her and the next full moon drew ever closer. Oh, Goddess. She'd promised Skye, promised herself, and yet she'd not been able to do anything because he made himself scarce when she was around.

The three-day cycle that will turn River into the Beast begins tomorrow.

I know! she said back to her consciousness, not needing the reminder. The moon's cycle pressed on her in a way it never had before. Was it because she was now tied to the pack and she was feeling it through them? Or was it simply concern for River that made her so aware of the moon's passage?

Maybe the latter.

Probably the latter.

Most definitely the latter mixed with more than simple concern.

She dreamed about him every night. Hot, needy dreams where his lips on hers, his skin rubbing against hers, his body under her, over her, *in* her, set her on fire. Those dreams made her feel more alive than she'd felt in years. But it wasn't just the dreams that had him on her mind. The need for him filled her every waking moment too. She just couldn't stop thinking about him and that kiss. And the almost kiss in the park. She'd kissed many men before, but this was something quite different. It disturbed her in a way a kiss never had.

She needed to talk to River, but he was proving just as slippery to grasp as full control over her powers had been. He would leave early in the morning and not come back until late at night. Iain and Patrick —his regular Shadows—said he spent most of that time gardening at the house she shared with Skye and Shelley, which was a few streets away from the Packhouse.

She was glad he was doing something he loved, but why hadn't he finished the garden at the Packhouse first? Especially as he needed to be around his pack. He needed the comfort of them after having been apart for so long. From what she was learning in the Pack Diaries and from Adam and Jason, spending time with one pack member standing at a distance wasn't enough.

So why would he do that to himself? Was it because of her and the kiss?

'His wolf is angry and mistrustful of everyone,' Adam had said when she asked him what he felt from River through the Packbond. 'I mean, wouldn't you be if you were locked away for almost twenty years?'

She nodded but didn't believe a word. Adam was just trying to make her feel better. She didn't need to feel better. She needed to make River feel better and she couldn't do that if her presence was keeping him away from what he needed to settle his soul and be whole. Without pack, he couldn't truly heal. The more time she spent with them, the more she was beginning to appreciate that. And the more annoyed she became with herself for being a coward and not tracking him down to face him. Since when had she hidden behind embarrassment?

Never. Certainly not over a little, harmless kiss. They hadn't even got naked. So why was she so reticent to confront him?

Her mobile rang, cutting into her thoughts as she packed up for the day. Bluebelle wound around her feet, purring, and she considered not answering in favour of a hug with her Familiar. But then again, what if it was Skye or Shelley with some new information? With a sigh, she bent and gave Bluebelle a stroke and then picked up her phone.

She didn't recognise the number. Maybe it was a client. 'Natural Goddess Health, this is Bron, how can I help you?'

'You still haven't changed that ridiculous name, I see.'

Bron almost dropped the phone in surprise. 'Mum?'

'Yes, it's me …' The phone crackled and her mother's voice lurched and hissed.

'Sorry, I didn't catch that, Mum. This line's terrible. Where are you?'

'I'm on a sat … ite phone. We're still … rundi. There's so much desol … here. More fighting … broken … People are terrified … hurt and … We're busier than … We could rea … more help.'

'It sounds terrible, Mum. Are you and Dad okay?'

'We're fine. But it's not us … I'm worried about you.'

Bron frowned. 'Me? Why?'

'I heard about … shop closing and Mrs … told me … mishaps.'

Bron rolled her eyes. This was unbelievable. Her mother was all the way around the other side of the world in a ravaged and violent place and yet she still heard about Bron closing her shop. 'It's fine, Mum. Nothing happened. I just wasn't feeling quite … right for a few weeks.'

'That's not what Mrs Riggs ... I heard ... magic. You promised you wouldn't use m ... Think what this does ... your father and ... reputations.'

'I hardly think any of what I do could affect your reputations, especially as you're on the other side of the world.'

'But the university ... Your father's nomination by the Royal Society of ... in question. If you'd done as we asked ... medicine and followed ... footsteps, none of this would have ...'

Bron clenched her jaw, holding back the words she wanted to say. Yelling and swearing at her mother wouldn't change anything. In fact, it would just make things worse. Besides, it was the same old refrain she'd endured for years: 'why didn't you choose medicine over that ridiculous natural healing rubbish? No self-respecting medical practitioner will take you seriously. Why can't you get a real profession,' blah, blah, blah. If she'd endured it then, she could endure it now. 'Nothing happened, Mum. Certainly nothing that would jeopardise Dad's humanitarian nomination. I can't believe Mrs Riggs called you to let you know about something as minor as me shutting up the shop for a few weeks.'

'She didn't ... I called her ... in our regular chat.'

Bron's eyes stung and her chin trembled. Her mother rang her friend, Patricia Riggs to have a chat—a regular chat. And the only time she bothered picking up a phone to call her own daughter was to tell her off. Well, that was fine. Bron didn't need her mother or father to call her and catch up or show they cared in any way. They'd been absent for a great deal of her childhood and now even more so for her adulthood. They weren't a part of her life. She didn't need them. She had Skye and Shelley. In fact, she had a whole pack now.

Then why did it sting so badly?

Shoving that thought aside, she smiled stiffly into the phone. 'That's lovely that you catch up with your old friend regularly, but I'm sorry she worried you. I'm fine and nothing happened that will hurt you or Dad. Happy now?'

'I'd be happier if ... gave up ... ridiculous natural ... Your grandma ... bad influence ... Wicca rubbish.'

Bron swallowed hard, her finger hovering over the red end call sign on the phone's face. She wanted to scream at her mother, tell her to shut up, that if she didn't have anything nice to say, she shouldn't bother calling. But she didn't. Despite the animosity, she couldn't cut her parents out of her life. She just couldn't. The pain of that would be greater than all these little stings of her mother's whip-like words put together. Clearing her throat, she tried out the smile again. It was a little stiff, but what did that matter? Her mother couldn't see it. 'Can we keep that conversation for another time Mum? I really don't want to argue with you down the phone.'

'It's not an argumen … my opinion.'

'Yes, and my opinion is different and let's just leave it at that.'

'You're so much like your grandmother.'

'Yes. I am.' And she was proud of it. 'Look, Mum, I've got to go. My next client has arrived. You and Dad take care of yourselves, okay and let me know how you are. You can call me to have a chat too.'

'What's the poi … nothing in common.'

Bron sucked in a breath and closed her eyes as if she could shut out the words. She'd heard them before, but they still stung. 'I'll talk with you later, Mum.'

'Please think abou … I said.'

Bron almost laughed. She would hardly do anything else for the next few days. Her mother's words would jab into her like well-flung spears, stabbing at her mind over and over in the middle of the night.

'Don't embarrass us.'

The phone went dead. 'Bye, Mum,' Bron whispered. She dropped the phone on the desk, slumped into the chair behind her and pressed the heels of her palms into her eyes. She wouldn't cry. She wouldn't.

There was a gentle thump on the desk and something nudged at her head.

Bluebelle.

The little cat meowed at her and then rubbed her soft face against Bron's cheek. With a sob, Bron pulled her Familiar into her arms and held her to her chest. Silent tears coursed down her face as she looked at the cat in her arms. 'Neither of us were wanted by our parents, hey? But we've got each other. That's all that matters.'

Bluebelle meowed again and rubbed against Bron's chin. Then she struggled out of Bron's grip and ran to the door. She turned and looked back at Bron when she got there. 'You want to go out?' Bluebelle shook and raced back as fast as her limping gait would let her. She stood at Bron's feet, meowed and then looked at the door. 'You want me to go out?' Bluebelle meowed, jumped onto the desk and nudged Bron's handbag. 'You want me to go home?' Bluebelle meowed and ran around in a little circle then jumped into Bron's startled arms. Bron laughed. 'I think maybe that's the best idea anyone's had all day.'

She quickly finished packing up, Bluebelle trailing her every movement. When she got to the door, the little cat bolted out of it in front of her. 'Got a hot date? At least one of us does.'

She locked up and made her way to her car, aware that her Shadow for the day, Patrick, tracked her every movement from his position in the woods—despite her telling both him and Iain that they could do their guarding inside, they wouldn't, saying the danger wouldn't come at her from inside her store. 'Besides,' Iain had told her, 'We don't want to frighten any of your clients away with our presence.'

She didn't think "frightened" was what any of her clients would be at the sight of two hot and sexy males wandering around the store. The Were definitely had the monopoly on outrageous good looks and animal magnetism.

'I'm going home,' she called out as she reached her car.

Patrick appeared as if from nowhere, a smile splitting his pretty-boy face as he looked past her to her car. 'I think someone is going with you.'

She looked behind her to see Bluebelle sitting next to the car, waiting. 'You want to come with me?' Bluebelle meowed as if to say, 'of course'. Bron opened the door and the cat jumped in and made herself at home on the back seat. Her parents might not like or trust her, but this little cat did. It was a soothing bandage over an open wound. She let out her breath in a big rush, blinking back the tears. 'Okay. To the Packhouse for both of us it is.'

She was about to close the door when she remembered a video she'd seen of a cat left to roam free in a moving car. She pointed at Bluebell and said, 'You should be in a carrier. Promise you won't play up while I drive? Distracting me could be dangerous.'

A meep of assent.

Very well.

She threw her bag into the car, closed the door and turned to Patrick. 'You want a lift?'

He shook his head. 'Nah. I feel like a run. I'll follow you home.'

Bron nodded and hopped in. Looking over her shoulder at the tawny cat curled into a ball on the back seat, she said, 'Remember, no carry on when we move. Or I'll be stopping at the pet store to get that carrier.' Bluebelle lifted her head and meeped again but this time with a look in her eyes that on a human would have been an eye-roll.

Bron chuckled and started the car.

As she drove along the familiar streets that led to the Packhouse, she noticed that spring was coming to a close and summer was on the way with Christmas just around the corner. Golden wattles were blooming in every second yard and the pink and white cherry blossoms that heralded spring were now gone, the cherry trees bright with green and red tipped leaves. The bark of the ghost gums that lined her street, having turned grey over winter, were now transformed into brilliant white and sunset colours, reflective of the ever-brightening sun and longer days. Her street was particularly golden and red, with some of the biggest ghost gums in the area lining the road and more waratah and wattle trees than in the other streets.

Her street? She hadn't meant to come down here. She'd been headed to the Packhouse. Glancing back at Bluebelle, she frowned. Jason had ordered everyone to stay away from her house while River was there working. Bron had tried to argue with him, telling him that she needed to see him, but he had been firm. And she knew the reason why. It was important for River to lose himself in the thing he loved. He couldn't do that if she was there, disturbing him.

But even though she hadn't meant to come here now, she had. Everyone kept saying she should trust her instincts. If her instincts had brought her here tonight, maybe this was where she needed to be. Besides, Bluebelle probably wouldn't do so well at the Packhouse. She hadn't run from Patrick like she normally would, but Bron knew the little cat was still wary of the Were. She didn't want to frighten her. 'Home it is,' she murmured.

As she turned into her drive, Iain emerged from the shadows at the side of the house. He jogged over to her car and opened the door, waving at Patrick as he took up sentry position on the street.

'What are you doing here?' he asked her.

'It's my house.'

He looked chagrined. 'I didn't mean it like that. But you know River is here, right?'

She nodded. 'Perhaps that's why I came here.'

'You know he doesn't want to see you at the moment. He doesn't want to see anyone.'

'I didn't mean to come home—I was headed to the Packhouse to do more research. But instinct led me here anyway, which means something is telling me I have to see him. You're not going to argue with instinct, are you?'

He looked at her for a long moment and then stepped aside. 'Okay.'

Relieved he wasn't going to send her away, she grabbed her bag and hopped out of the car. Bluebelle jumped out after her, staying close but edging away from Iain. She bent and picked the cat up, holding her protectively.

Iain reached out to pet Bluebelle. The cat swiped at him with a panicked hiss.

'Okay,' Iain said, holding his hands up. 'Angry little thing, isn't she?'

Bron nuzzled her chin against the cat's head. 'Not usually. I don't think she was treated well. It takes her a while to trust. Besides, you know how cats are with dogs.'

Iain huffed out a laugh. 'We're nothing like dogs.'

Bron nudged him with her shoulder as they walked up the path. 'You know what I mean.' She looked down at Bluebelle. 'And not being dogs probably makes it worse. I mean, being Were makes you a predator in her eyes with her as the prey.'

'We wouldn't hurt her.'

'I know that. And she will too when she gets comfortable with you all. It's just going to take her a while. She's been on her own for so long and is reticent to make friends. You more than any of the others should know what that's like.'

Iain's expression became shuttered. 'You don't know what you're talking about.'

Bron pulled a face. Oops. Something she shouldn't have mentioned. 'I'm sorry,' she said, regretting that her words had made him stiffen, his demeanour now as warm as an ice-shard.

He gestured for her to proceed up the front steps before him.

She couldn't let it drop. 'I've always been able to read auras which gives me insight into people and I know to be careful with that. It's just, these new powers. They let me see more and I'm still getting a handle on it. But I shouldn't have blurted that out. I know you're not comfortable talking about your past.'

He met her gaze. 'No. I'm not.'

'We won't mention it again, then. Unless you want to.' He nodded, but she could see from his expression that talking about himself was as likely to happen as him turning into a cat. As she opened the front door, Bluebelle jumped from her arms and ran down the hall to the open back door.

'You need to go out there with her,' Iain said.

'Why?'

'You need to see what River has done.'

'He's finished?'

'Yes.'

Something about how he said it made her nervous. 'What's it like?'

'Why don't you come and see.'

She swallowed hard. She wanted to see him. Needed to see him. 'Okay. Show me.'

Iain led her through her own house, obviously comfortable. She noted the dishes in the sink and the shirt slung across a chair at the kitchen table. Her gaze zeroed in on that shirt.

Oh, Goddess!

She wanted to put on the brakes, make an excuse and get out of there before she saw River without his shirt on. The last thing she needed right now was to be fighting desire. She needed to talk to him, calmly, in charge of herself and the situation. She needed to make him see that embarrassment over a little thing like a kiss was no reason to suffer through another moon with the Beast. That there was nothing between them other than friendship and she was perfectly capable of treating him like any other patient in need of a Healing. He didn't need to know about the desire that had played out in her dreams in many hot, crazy-making ways every night since. Just thinking of it made her skin start to tingle and warmth curl in her womb.

Crap! She stopped, clenching her muscles, all too aware of Iain walking behind her. She couldn't let the sensation of desire grow. Iain would scent it. River would scent it.

Shit!

She supposed she could say she was hot for Iain. Except Iain hadn't been in the treatment room at the Packhouse that day, nor had he been in River's room the following day or out in the park.

Fuck!

Bluebelle, who'd been circling just inside the back sliding glass door, shot outside as Iain opened it.

He glanced over his shoulder, brow raised as he saw her stopped halfway across the room. 'Are you coming?'

'Almost,' she grimaced, clenching her muscles even tighter and wrapping her arms across her tingling breasts.

'What?'

'Nothing.'

But it wasn't nothing. River was out there. Shirtless. Working.

Sweat probably glinted all over his hard frame in the late-afternoon sun. Her mouth went dry, her nipples turned into little pebbles, pressing against her soft cotton bra. She clasped her arms tighter across her front, and because she had no choice—Iain was standing there, his hand stretched out in an 'after you' gesture—she walked jerkily forward and out the door. Then stopped abruptly as she got to the edge of the patio.

Her sprawling backyard—usually a stretch of closely cropped grass with Australian drought-resistant shrubs bordering it—had undergone a complete metamorphosis.

In two weeks, River had made their backyard into wonderland of flowers and herbs. Creeping vines worked their way over a lattice archway built over the steps from the back patio. A pebbled pathway wound from the bottom of the steps through the now multi-layered and multi-levelled garden. To the right was a bowery of shrubs, small trees and flowering plants with a meandering pathway disappearing into it. To the left was a Japanese pebble garden. Beside the Japanese garden was a paved area set up in a circular design: a prayer spiral for meditation.

Neither Skye nor Shelley meditated. The prayer spiral was for her. 'Holy Goddess,' she whispered.

'I thought you'd be impressed.'

Iain's voice in her ear made her start. She'd forgotten he was there. 'What is this?'

'An apology, he called it.'

'An apology for what? Did he and Skye have a fight or something?'

Iain chuckled. 'For someone who can be so switched on, you're incredibly clueless.'

She dragged her gaze away from the garden long enough to scowl at him. 'What do you mean by that?'

'You'll have to ask River.'

11

She stopped herself from biting her lip at the thought and straightened her shoulders. She couldn't have Iain know how nervous the thought of seeing River right now was making her. 'Then I will. Where is he?'

Iain nodded towards the garden. 'In there somewhere.' He stepped back, cocked his thumb towards the door. 'I'm going out front to scout around a bit. If you need anything, call.'

She smiled briefly at him. 'It's my home. I think I'll be fine.'

The door slid closed behind her and she turned back to gaze at the garden. There was still no sign of River. She supposed she should go and look for him, ask him why he'd done this. But first, she wanted to look around a bit. The garden called to her. She longed to explore, lose herself in the scents and textures, the beauty of floral display borders set against spills of rock and stone and wood. The greenery of creepers—the way he'd taken the overgrown and straggly jasmine and turned it into a work of art that was a billowing fall of snowy pink and vivid green, the scent mingling on the air with roses, lemon scented verbena and brown boronia.

The tinkling music of falling water played on the air and she wanted to discover its source.

Her shoes crunched on the fine white pebbles as she stepped down onto the path. The peppery yet floral scent of wild thyme lifted to greet her as she brushed past it. She wandered forward, running her hand over the English lavender bordering the path. Around the bend in the path there were decorative pots of mint—peppermint, spearmint, apple mint. She bruised the skin of the leaves to breathe in their pungent scent. Other pots were filled with rosemary and lemongrass and horseradish, their scents green and bright and fragrant.

Borders of bobbing yellow daisies and sweet lilacs drew her further down the winding pebbled path towards the rear of the garden where, going by the fact the tinkling water sound was getting louder, she would find some kind of water feature.

The path ended in a mini-cul de sac, a bench made out of a twisted chunk of gumtree at its head inviting her to sit. She did.

The bench's surface was sanded and polished until it looked, and felt, like a flow of warm silk. It was set at the edge of a circle of pebbles so that she could view the garden but also enjoy the sound of trickling water from the mini waterfall set into the rock feature to her left.

It was beautiful. A place to come and relax, to centre and calm oneself. The bench was even wide enough to sit on in her meditation pose. It was astonishing.

She ran her fingers appreciatively over the silken wood of the bench, but stopped as another, delicious scent caught her attention—vanilla and chocolate. Two of her favourite smells. Rising, she followed her nose and discovered the scent belonged to a little tufted plant with a purple star-like flower. She had no idea what it was, but it smelled divine.

'That shouldn't be flowering now.' River's voice made her jerk upright so fast she almost lost her balance. He reached out and grabbed her arm, steadying her so she didn't fall backwards into the garden bed.

'What?' she blurted, unable to think with the heat of his fingers searing through her shirt and into her skin.

He stared into her eyes for a long, heart-stopping moment, then let go. Stepping back, he shoved his hands into his jeans' pockets. Even though they were tucked away, the hot imprint of his fingers on her arm lingered.

Swallowing compulsively, she tried to speak again. 'What did you say?' She noted he was wearing a worn and faded blue T-shirt—thank the Goddess for small mercies—although the way it clung to his frame showed enough to make her mouth go dry.

'I said that *Arthropodium fimbriatus* shouldn't be flowering now, but I ordered it especially from a supplier I know.'

'Why?'

His shoulders went up and he looked down at the path. 'I know you love chocolate and vanilla.'

'How could you know that?'

'Your hand cream is vanilla scented, as is your shampoo. You always keep chocolate in your bag and Skye says you will bake chocolate cookies or muffins or cake just so the smell of chocolate is in the house.'

'Oh.' She looked around, gesturing at the plants, the layout, the meditation circle. 'You did this for me?'

He shuffled his booted feet, pebbles scattering with a little skitter into the rock border. His hands were shoved so hard into his jeans' pockets, she was surprised the material didn't tear. For a long, breathless moment, the only thing she could hear was the trickling splash of the water feature, the twittering of a few birds as they greeted dusk and the slight breeze that ruffled her hair, carrying a multitude of delicious scents from the herbs, flowers and fresh mulch that surrounded her. She wanted him to answer, but there was also a part of her that didn't want him to.

If he said he'd done it for her, what was she supposed to do with that? How could this be an apology, as Iain suggested? That just didn't seem enough reason to do something this large, this personal, this wonderful. But then again, it didn't have to be about her at all. He loved working in gardens. He'd done some work on the gardens at the Packhouse—nothing like this, but still lovely. And there was the garden at Cantrae House, although he hadn't been allowed to go back there yet. Not until Jason said it was safe. So this was the only garden he had access to. She knew he needed gardening like she needed to heal. It was an expression of his heart, his soul. The plants and soil, the birds and insects, were friends to a man who had never had friends.

Jason's words also echoed in her mind. He needed it to help keep himself together.

Those reasons sounded far truer than him having done all of this for her. She wished she hadn't asked the question. His silence was killing her. She was about to tell him that the garden was lovely, to try to bypass her incredibly egocentric question, when Bluebelle shot out of the nearby shrubs and wound around her legs with a plaintive meow.

'Hello, Bluebelle,' River said, reaching to pet the cat.

Bron's mouth dropped open when the usually shy cat rubbed against River's outstretched hand. 'Oh, my god. How did you do that?'

'Do what?' He looked up at her with surprise as he picked up the cat and cradled her gently against his chest.

Bluebelle didn't nuzzle against him, but neither did she spit and scratch and struggle like she usually did around the Were. 'That,' Bron said, pointing at her cat. 'How did you get her to do that? She doesn't go near any other Were either. She just scratched and spat at Iain.'

'Well, I don't blame her for that,' River said, stroking her from head to tail. 'He is scary looking. I mean, he doesn't have my scars, but that scowl ...' River chuckled as Bluebelle meowed as if in assent.

'But how did you even get near her? The last time you two were in the same room together, she hid.'

'She was a bit skinny looking, so I brought some treats with me the day after we ...' He stopped, looked away. 'I came to your work, wanting to apologise, but I couldn't think of what to say. I was procrastinating in the woods outside your shop when Bluebelle came along. I gave her the treats and talked to her—she's fond of chocolate and apples. Even though I had to keep my distance, she sat and listened.' He scratched behind Bluebelle's ears and she purred loudly. 'She's a good listener.' His twisted smile widened. 'I've been sneaking back each day since to give her the treats while I tried to build up the courage to speak to you.'

'You missed all of your appointments.'

'I know.'

'But you need them. I need to help you. I wanted to find a way so you didn't have to suffer through another change like the last one. But you didn't come. You didn't let me.'

'I'm sorry.'

The smile—that rare smile—disappeared from his face. She couldn't tell what had changed, but suddenly the atmosphere in the garden was close. Heat shot through her despite the shade and the coolness of the breeze. 'You don't have to apologise, River. I know it was my fault you stayed away.'

'No,' River growled. Bluebelle stiffened at the sound. She leaped from his arms and with a frightened yowl, took off up the path. Silence simmered between them, unbearable and yet unbreakable.

But River was stronger than her. Breaking the silence he said, 'I shouldn't have ... You don't know ...' He stopped, shook his head and turned away.

Stunned, uncertain what had happened, Bron reached out for him. 'River ...' The minute her fingers touched his arm, she knew it was a mistake.

He whirled around so fast, she stumbled back, her feet catching on a rock at the edge of the garden bed. Arms wheeling, she began to fall.

He caught her, steadied her, held her pinned with his gold-flecked hazel eyes. His fingers flexed against her arms and he pulled her a little closer. Breath shuddered out of her and his gaze darted to her parted lips. They were dry, so dry, and only he could quench the thirst in them. She swayed forward.

His hold tightened, his breath a ragged puff against her face. 'Bronwyn,' he muttered, gaze chasing over her face to then anchor again on her lips. He leaned closer, mouth mere centimetres from hers, but then stopped, not giving her what she so desperately needed.

'River. Please.'

'Bronwyn, I can't.' Red flared in his eyes and his lips curled. An expression of pure hatred crossed his face, lashing out at her.

'River?' she said again, but this time her voice was husky with fear, not passion.

He made a sound, a violent growl, tearing and painful, and then let go of her so fast that she stumbled. Shock arced through her because of that look in his eyes—it pulled at her and shoved her away in one go. If eyes truly were the windows to the soul, then River's soul was in turmoil; desire so strong she could feel it lick at her with its hot need, mixed with pain and hatred and bitter regret.

In the face of such inner turmoil, a need in her clicked in place. Energy buzzed through her, sparking power to life. The warm heat of her powers rolled through her, pushing at her to allow it a channel, a form of expression. She lifted her hands. Orange-green magic glowed on her fingertips.

River growled again, stepping back from that glow.

She didn't blame him. That glow had brought him such pain a few weeks ago. 'I'm sorry.'

He shook his head. 'Don't be sorry. It's not your fault.'

'It is my fault. I don't know what to do. Your wolf won't accept what I need to do for it.' He shook his head but didn't say anything. 'What River? What can I do?'

'The moon. It's the moon, my child. It brings forward the darkness and the Beast with it.'

The voice in her head was barely a whisper, but even though it wasn't her voice, something about its musical tones, the sweet breath of it in her mind, made her want to trust. She looked up at the night sky, not understanding. And then she saw. She hadn't realised how dark it had become. River had strung fairy lights in the branches throughout the garden and the paths were lined with lights. They were all obviously on a timer, because as dusk had fallen over them, the lights had come on. The sight of the twinkling lights in the trees and glowing golden and green along the paths would normally have made her sigh in deep pleasure, except above the lights was the moon rising in the purpling night sky. An almost waxing moon.

'Oh, Goddess.' She looked from the moon to River and saw that he knew. Of course he knew! The pressure of the moon's cycle would be in his blood, in his nerves. It was probably driving his behaviour right now. That hatred she'd seen before, the loathing, it wasn't for her.

It was aimed at himself. At the Beast writhing inside, waiting for the moon to let it out. And she'd done nothing in this past month to help free him from it. Had discovered nothing about the dark smudge that kept his two halves apart, other than it hated her magic and it was what formed the Beast. 'River.' She shook her head, took a jerky step towards him.

He reared back.

'River. I'm so sorry. I should have done something sooner ... should have realised ...' She waved ineffectually at the moon. 'I've been researching. We've all been researching, but we've found nothing and I know I promised to free you of the Beast before the next moon and now I've let you down. No wonder you've stayed away. I'm sorry. I'm so sorry.'

'Don't be sorry, Bronwyn. There's something inside of me that can't be fixed. I feel it grow stronger every day. But it's not your fault, don't blame yourself. You've helped me more than you know. Just the fact you've tried has made all the difference in my keeping control up until now. That's what I wanted to tell you because I knew you'd blame yourself. But you can't. You mustn't.' He took a step back. 'I have to go. I've asked Jason to lock me up at Cantrae House. I don't want to hurt anyone again. He promised to strap me on the bed and lock me in my old room until it passes.'

'Oh, River, no! There has to be another way. Let me try ...'

He backed further away from her glowing hands. 'It's too late for that right now.' His fists balled at his sides as he glared at the moon, tendons so tight in his neck they looked like they might snap. 'I've got to go. The Beast is riding high in me tonight. It's more vicious than anything you can possibly imagine, and this close to the full moon, I'm afraid of what I'll do.'

'You won't hurt me.'

'I can't be sure of that.'

The anguish on his face was enough to bring anyone to their knees. But River didn't need her weak and blubbering. He needed strength. 'I am. You didn't let the Beast hurt me the night of the last full moon.'

'No. But that was the first time it had come out. When I said it's grown stronger, I wasn't kidding. I can feel it moving inside me all the time now. It wants to rip, to tear. It wants to feed on flesh, to glory in the warmth of blood trickling down its throat.' His voice had turned harsh. 'And God help me, but I want that, too.'

Chimes jingled in the distance, their fairy sound at odds with the danger and tension in the air. 'You don't. That's not you.'

'I know. But it could be if I let go for one second. And sometimes when I think ...' He swallowed, shook his head. 'Promise me one thing, Bronwyn.'

'What?'

'Don't come and visit me over the next few days.'

'What? Why?'

'I don't want you to see me like that.'

'But, I could help ... I have helped.'

'I don't want you to help me like that. I don't want to be responsible for your hurting yourself.'

'I didn't hurt myself. Besides, if I observed your aura while you are half-changed, it could give me some clue—'

'No. I don't want you to come. Promise me.'

'I don't want—'

'Promise.' He barked the word out at her, vibrating with the tension of his request, his veins standing out like thick ropes on his hands, arms and neck.

Shoulders slumping, she said, 'I promise.'

'Good,' he grated out. 'Thank you.' There was no relief in his words, only grim acceptance.

'River?' She took a step towards him and he tensed even more.

'Don't. I ...' His mouth worked as if he fought to say something more—or not to say it. 'I'll let you try after the full moon.'

'I won't let you down.'

'I know.' The words were an almost unintelligible growl. Fear and pain alive in his eyes, he shook his head in mute apology, let out a growling sound, and turning, took off up the path, disappearing into the dark.

Bron hugged her arms around her chest and shivered. But she didn't move. She stood there for a long time, thinking about what had just happened and trying to figure out what it meant. But none of it made sense. And as she looked around the garden River had created for her as an apology because he couldn't bring himself to see her face to face, she was even more confused. Why would he do this if he didn't like her?

He'd promised to let her try to heal him after the full moon, and during that time, maybe, just maybe, she'd be able to figure him out.

RIVER RACED to the SUV where Iain was already waiting for him, door open. He threw himself into the backseat and growled, 'Lock me up. Lock me up now.'

Face grim, Iain only nodded. He hopped into the driver's seat and they took off.

Inside him, the Beast snapped and snarled, raking its claws under his skin. It wanted to come out now, but the moon wasn't quite right, so it couldn't. But it was there, in his mind, filling it with images of hatred and revenge and violent, bloody death. It had been getting worse over the last few days. He could never remember it being this bad. He'd always felt the moon and the rage that had risen as it waxed and waned in its twenty-eight-day cycle. Three days of utter misery each month for twenty years, where he had been unable to control his emotions and actions and lashed out at those he loved.

The memories of what he did in those times before his grandparents had found the right cocktail of drugs to suppress his rage and knock him out, made something in him curl up like an autumn leaf; dry and dead and ready to crumble into pieces at the merest touch.

But even in those dark days, he couldn't remember it being this bad. Now, it had a name. The Beast. Back then it had been a nebulous thing. He'd thought it had been about the rage of his wolf unable to come out and commune with him and the world. But maybe it hadn't. Maybe he was wrong in thinking what was happening to him now was caused by something Morrigan did to him on Samhain. What if it had been the Beast all along, writhing under his skin, subdued by the drugs, but now freed, ready to wreak havoc and destruction on the world that had kept it trapped for so long.

The Beast snarled and lashed out a claw, clamping its teeth down. River gripped his hands against his stomach, bent over, gasping for breath against the sensation of something being torn apart inside him.

'River—are you okay, man?'

River clamped his teeth together over the growl that erupted from his mouth and shook his head, eyes tearing, vision shifting strangely so that everything was washed with a haze of red. 'Just get me there.'

'It won't come out now. The start of the full moon cycle is tomorrow night.'

'I know. But it's in me, filling me with urges that are getting harder and harder to ignore. It's never been this bad before. It wanted to hurt Bronwyn. I need to be locked up tonight.'

Iain didn't question him—River liked that about him—just nodded and put his foot down on the accelerator.

The Beast thrashed as it realised it was going to be chained again this moon. It wanted to smash open the door of the car, escape, run free. River's hand raised to the door handle, gripping, ready to pull. Trembling, pushing down on the urge to do what the Beast wanted, he thumped his fist against the seat, gripping onto the edge. The leather tore under his fingers. He held on tighter and slumped down, pressing his knees against the seat in front, his head against the back of the seat as hard as he could, and with jaw and teeth clenched so tight it hurt, sweat dripping from his aching brow, he pulled his hand away from the door handle and shifted it to the grip on the door. With all his strength, he yanked the door inward. There was a grinding of metal as the door bent towards him—it would be very difficult to open.

'Fuck, man. You're wrecking my car.'

'Trying not to jump out,' he gritted through clenched teeth.

Iain threw a look at him over his shoulder, his eyes wide as he saw the way River was sitting. 'Okay. We're almost there.'

River only nodded. The Beast was slashing and tearing at his insides. The Beast wasn't a physical thing inside him—it was a presence in the same way his wolf was a presence—but it was like it was really there. Its urges were as pressing as his own. And being with Bronwyn had just made it worse. He thought he was fine when he saw her in the garden, despite the fact that the Beast had been prowling closer to the surface over the last few days. But when he'd almost kissed her and the power had glowed on her fingertips, something inside him snapped and he couldn't fully control it.

The Beast hated her. Hated that she was the one person who could force it to stop, force it back inside. That she was trying to get rid of it. She was foremost in its thoughts. The first person it wanted to kill.

'No,' River sobbed through gritted teeth. 'I won't let you.'

The Beast howled.

'Here we are,' Iain said, yanking the car into a tight turn, the tires squealing as he stopped to wait for the gates to open, then the car lurched forward again, almost leaping up the driveway to the front of the house.

Before he had even pulled up at the front door, the car was surrounded by pack: Jason, Adam, Gareth and a half dozen others River didn't know. 'He's busted the door trying not to jump out.'

'Fuck.'

Jason began to spit out commands. 'Gareth, open the door, Marcus and I will restrain him. The rest of you, make a cordon around us and stay tight until we reach the door.'

Marcus? Was the Alpha of the McClune Pack here too? Another pack's Alpha couldn't command him, but he could reinforce another Alpha's strength with his own and completely tie a Were to the command of its Pack Leader. Jason must feel how bad things were if he'd called on another Alpha to help.

The Beast thrashed inside him.

'Fuck,' River swore, holding on tight. He coughed, the wetness of spittle on his lips, the dribble of something warmer and saltier down his chin. Rage, hot and vivid, rose inside him, turning his vision red and black. He wanted to lash out, punch something, tear it to shreds.

'Okay, now.'

The door flung open and Jason was there, reaching across the car, shackles and chains in his hands. 'I'm so sorry, River.'

'Do it quick. It wants me to do something terrible. You can't let it.'

Jason nodded, pain and sorrow in his eyes, understanding in the tightness of his expression.

He could feel an echo of what was happening inside River! That was why he was prepared in this way.

River hated that Jason knew so much of what was inside him, but right now he was grateful. His Alpha would make certain he didn't do anything to regret.

The chains snapped on his wrists and were tied around his middle, and then he was pulled from the car. He tried to help them hustle him up to the front door, but the Beast was strong enough to take partial control of his muscles, pulling on rage. He lashed out, punching, clawing, kicking and biting those who were only trying to help.

He'd have so much to apologise for later.

Finally, they got him inside and up the stairs to his old room. It took all of them to pin him down so they could tie him to the bed. He tried to speak past the growl in his throat, to thank them, but the word wouldn't come out.

'Should we get Bron? She'd be able to calm him down,' someone suggested.

'No!' he screamed.

Jason held him down by his shoulders, face just above his. 'She might be able to help, River.'

'No. No. No.'

'He's afraid he'll hurt her,' Iain said.

He moved his head, trying to nod, but all he could do was thrash.

'Bron could help you.'

'No. No. She can't … come here. Don't … bring her here. I don't want … her. Promise.' He wasn't even certain the words were coming out right but, thankfully, Jason seemed to be able to feel what he meant.

'I'll make sure she stays away.'

'Thank you.'

'Here, give him this.'

Something pricked in his arm and his eyes flashed to Jason, accusing.

'Sorry, River. It's for the best. You don't want Bron, but we can't have you hurting yourself.'

Blackness edged his vision and a howl filled his head. Then his eyes fluttered closed and he slumped into unconsciousness.

12

'So, tell me what you saw.'

Eloise sat down on the couch opposite Morrigan with a little sigh. 'I'm not sure where to begin.'

'You got close to them?'

Eloise nodded.

'They don't suspect you?'

She shook her head. 'Not at all. They're trusting by nature. The Healer especially.'

'Good. Good. Cain is still trying to get inside one of their minds, but until he's done that, you will have to try to get closer.'

Eloise swallowed hard, then nodded.

'I know it drains you, but you are strong. You are more like me than I could have imagined. So ...' Morrigan clapped her hands onto her lap, noting that the pain of her injuries was now completely gone —nothing but a ghost of memory. The power from the Healer had actually done her a favour. It would have taken her months more to heal to this stage. 'Tell me what is going on between the Healer and River.'

'I think she likes him. She's been muttering to herself about a kiss and yet she's avoided him, and him her. I thought at first it was because they didn't like each other, but then today, when they were together for the first time in weeks, there was definitely a different kind of tension between them.'

'This is unexpected.' River was horribly scarred. She couldn't understand anyone seeing something worthy of loving in him. 'Are you certain?'

'Yes. They touched a few times and when they did, there was a definite reaction from her. I smelled it.'

Morrigan wrinkled her nose. 'Smelled it?'

Eloise nodded. 'When I'm in the feline body, I take on its attributes.' She looked down at her deformed foot with a frown. 'Although, this never goes away.'

'Things that are part of the soul never do.' She waved her hand. 'But that is of no matter. What of him?'

Eloise straightened. 'He feels something for her too. He is definitely very prickly around her, and yet he keeps seeking her out and talks to me about her all the time. He has come to her shop every day but doesn't go in. He just stays outside and watches. I've been watching him as much as I can, allowing him to tempt me closer. He brings me treats and talks to me,' she said, her brow furrowed. 'He's ... kind.' She said this like it was confusing; like she was seeing something in the Were Morrigan did not want her to see. But before Morrigan could open her mouth to put paid to any such confusion, Eloise rushed on. 'And you should see the garden he has built for her.'

'You are certain it's for her?'

Eloise nodded. 'I've heard some of the others speculate about it. They're not sure what it means.'

'*This is it.*'

'Yes.' Excitement grew in Morrigan's chest. She stood, began to pace.

'Mistress? Do you know what this means?'

Morrigan didn't turn to look at her protégé as she stopped pacing, but instead stared at the painting she'd hung on the wall. A painting she'd painted centuries before, of her sister standing on the moors, her arms raised as she welcomed the man who was moving through the lavender towards her. They were both in shadow, and yet you could see the longing, the love, that drew them together. They would do anything for the other.

'Love. The eternal weakness.'

Slowly, she nodded. 'Yes. I know what this means.' She swung around to face Eloise. 'It means you've discovered the key we have been looking for.' Her gaze was drawn back to the painting. 'These feelings between them must be encouraged to grow.'

'But how can I do that?'

'Make him want to swoop in and save her from her problems. Men are suckers for a female in distress. They can't help but be the hero. And women love a hero.' She stopped, thought for a moment, tapping her finger against her chin. 'You must do anything you can to sabotage her healing efforts, make her doubt herself and her powers again. And I will do things that will ensure the same.' Pushing Skye's power again so that it went into the Healer when River was around might just do the trick.

'But how will that help us?'

'Because if he does love her, he will do anything to help her.' She reached out to the painting, her fingers searching the texture, touching the blur of features that was her sister's face. 'He will sacrifice everything. And that is something I can use.' She pulled her hand away with a jerk and began to laugh.

13

River crouched in the bushland just near The Point lookout. It was the best spot to watch Bronwyn's shop. He could see up and down the road at the front with a fair view of the back of the shop as well. If anyone approached, he'd see them.

He'd had a prickling up and down his spine ever since the full moon. The Beast snarled at the thought. The snarl was so strong, it rumbled in his throat. He buried his head in his hands, pressing into his temples, and whispered harshly, 'Go away.'

The snarling grew louder. River pressed back against it. Sweat trickled down his brow as he strained to push the ugly sensation of the Beast back into the recesses of his mind. 'You get to come out three nights every month. I won't let you take over any more of my days or nights.'

The Beast slashed at him with his claws. He clamped down on the cry of pain and pushed harder until he could feel it no more.

Panting and exhausted, River collapsed to his knees.

'Are you okay, man?'

River jerked at the sudden arrival of the Lone Wolf at his side—pushing the Beast down had taken up so much of his attention, he'd not heard or scented him drawing near. *Not much of a guardian, am I?*

'River?' Iain gently touched his shoulder.

'I'm fine,' he answered.

A long pause then, 'It's getting stronger, isn't it?'

'I'll stop it.'

'I know you will.'

River looked up at him, eyes burning as he stared at the Lone Wolf, the man who could have been a mentor, a best friend, in another life, giving him the kind of support he wasn't sure he deserved. Iain stared back, unflinching despite the fact what he saw must be ugly; an ugliness that had nothing to do with his scars.

An ugliness that was a cancer growing inside him.

Iain had seen firsthand the horror of it on those days of the full moon. He and Jason and Adam and Marcus had split the shifts between them, watching him, shooting him with stronger and stronger tranquillisers. They'd had no choice. When in Beast form that first night, he'd broken from the bonds tying him to the bed and tried to pound his way out of the room through the door, the walls. He only had hazy memories of what he'd done, but he remembered attacking Marcus and Iain. Remembered the scent of blood. The warm tear of flesh under his claws.

He pressed the nauseating sensations back and glanced up as Iain took a step closer to him. Iain and the other lieutenants had seen the absolute worst of him. He couldn't understand how any of them could be around him or trust him when they knew what was prowling inside. But here Iain stood, looking at him with an empathy he didn't deserve. In fact, in the last few weeks since the full moon, they'd drawn ever closer, their caring a warm stroke to his touch-hungry wolf.

He jerked away, unwilling to accept the connection, a growl rumbling deep in his chest.

'Perhaps you should see Bron earlier than your appointment? I'm sure she'd schedule you in.'

River shook his head. 'That's unnecessary. She's busy with her clients and I don't want to take her away from her business. It makes her happy.' He frowned as he said that. She hadn't been so happy lately. She put a good face on it for everyone, but he could see that something was bothering her. He just hoped it didn't have anything to do with him.

'It would make her happy to see you.'

River's head snapped up. 'No more than it would make her happy to see any of us.'

Iain's lips twitched. 'You can't tell me you really think that, River. She's your mate.'

River was on his feet, fists caught in the collar of Iain's coat before he'd even given it a thought. 'She is *not* my mate.'

Iain didn't blink. 'Only because you won't let it happen. I don't understand why you'd do that to yourself.'

'Don't you?' He let go and forced himself to take a step back, hands trembling. 'You saw what I was on the days and nights of the full moon.'

'But that's only three nights in a month, man. Bron wouldn't worry about that. Besides, when she heals you, there will be no problem. Unless of course you damage your wolf now in holding back; or hurt her so that she won't accept you.'

River flinched in the face of Iain's words. 'I would never hurt Bronwyn.'

'You will hurt her if you deny the mating.'

'You don't know what you're talking about.'

Iain shoved his hands in his pockets and sighed, his gaze travelling over the valley beneath the peak they stood on. 'Perhaps not. Lone Wolves rarely mate. And I don't really want that kind of complication in my life. But I can see it's hurting you, and if it's hurting you, it's hurting her.'

'It hasn't gone that far. She has no idea about the mating. And she won't if I have anything to do with it.'

Iain made a snorting noise. 'Fuck, man. You're living in a dream world if you believe that. She's your mate and an empathic Healer Witch. She has to be feeling it.'

'No. No. I'm blocking it.'

Iain shook his head again, sadness filling his eyes in a way that made River keen inside. 'Not enough, man. Not enough. Jason knows about it. I've noticed it. And I've seen her look at you in the way Skye looks at Jason. And if she's feeling it. How long do you think it's going to be before others notice it too? Even if she doesn't truly know, she will then. The pack won't let either her or you stuff up something as precious as a mating.'

River trembled at the thought. 'No. They can't know. Jason knows because he's the Alpha and the Alpha always knows. And you know because you're just one hell of a nosy bastard who can't help but stick his opinions into other people's business.'

Iain burst out laughing. 'Yeah, that's me. You've got me pegged.'

'And she can't know yet. Not really. Those looks are just pity.'

Iain snorted. 'Yeah, right.'

River turned away from Iain's sarcasm and stared down at Bronwyn's shop. 'If you tell her or anyone else ...'

Iain's hand landed on his shoulder. 'I would never do that, man. If you want it kept secret, then that's what it will be. But I'm telling you, you won't be able to keep it at bay for much longer. Others will start to figure it out, and when they do, you'll have to do something about it. Either choose her or walk away. But if you walk away ... I'll be one of those who'll come after you to make you pay for hurting our Healer.'

River's lips twitched. 'I'm doing everything I can to make sure that won't be necessary.'

Iain patted River's shoulder. 'Well, despite how interesting this all is, it's time we go, otherwise you're going to be late. And you know how much Bron hates it when people are late.'

River glanced at his watch and hissed out a breath. He thought he had more time. He wasn't ready to see Bronwyn yet—hadn't steeled himself against it. But then again, there was no steeling himself against the depth of his feelings for her. Not truly. Pushing to his feet, he began to jog down the hill, Iain right behind him.

ELOISE JUMPED down from her perch in the tree after River entered Bron's shop.

She had to let her mistress know he was there right now. This was what she'd been waiting for.

Running deeper into the woods, she made her way to the sacred circle Bron's grandma had used with her coven years earlier. Bron didn't use it anymore, but it still held magic. Enough for Eloise to use.

The heat of shame rose up over her again as she entered the circle of stones. She shouldn't have to use something like this. Morrigan had bound her with a blood spell, and yet she still couldn't truly communicate with her Mistress like Cain could. Another thing she was useless at.

But now wasn't the time to wallow in self-pity. Now was the time to send to her Mistress the message she was waiting for.

Quickly changing forms, she drew the circle's power to her and sent a single word through the aether. 'Now.'

BRON PACED, knowing she should be readying herself—incanting the calming cantrips to prepare her mind for the session ahead—but the edgy knowing that River was about to arrive crawled through her nerves, making her twitchy and unable to settle.

After he'd shown her the wonder of the garden he'd created for her, she had trouble thinking of anything but him in the weeks since.

And she needed to concentrate, to find a way to heal him, now, more than ever.

The Darkness—that's what she'd come to call the smudge between his two auras. It was more than it had been before the full moon. It had dug in deeper, spread further, looked stronger, more insidious. And nothing she did seemed to make any difference. In fact, all her efforts had done over the last few weeks since the full moon was to make it angry and cause River pain.

She was now officially annoyed. And officially worried. Everything else about her powers was coming along nicely. Sure, she wasn't doing her full work-load as she was still getting a feel for it and dealing with the kinks—completely fixing Mrs Jones' nasty tummy tuck scar had been a bit of an oops. But she'd been able to cover that up so that there would be no stories about 'miracle cures' popping up again.

What she couldn't understand was, if she could do that, why couldn't she heal River?

It made no sense.

The Darkness. It had to be the Darkness, but she couldn't figure out what it was or where it had come from. And she had no idea how to get rid of it. There was something oddly familiar about it. Like she'd seen it before. Except she hadn't. There was no mention of it or anything like it in the diaries she'd read so far. She wasn't even certain why she called it the Darkness—only that the name seemed right somehow.

The diary on the table flickered open and in her head she heard one word: '*Read.*'

She had no idea if the voice was her grandma or the Goddess or just some manifestation of her own subconscious, but whatever it was, it hadn't set her wrong so far. She plonked down on a chair, eyes focused on a word written in different coloured ink half way down the page.

Triad.

'Three witches tied together by blood and friendship,' she read out loud. 'One a Healer, one a Medium and the other an Elemental, the combination enhancing their powers threefold.'

A chill of excitement chased along her shoulders and down her arms, tingling in her fingers. 'It's us,' she whispered. 'Skye, Shelley and me. We're a Triad.' She read on, about the Elemental and the Medium, the descriptions perfectly outlining her friends and their power. This could be something they could use.

The page flipped over again and her eyes focused on the next passage. 'The Healer in the Triad is the soothing essence, balancing the others—' Bron snorted. Disappointment sank into her, chasing the tingling away. Looking up at the ceiling she asked, 'Is this your idea of a joke? I can't even balance myself. Besides, how is this supposed to help? I can't balance the Darkness out of existence.'

'Try your Grandma's massage oil from yesterday.'

'Oh,' she breathed out. 'Why didn't I think of that?'

'Think of what?'

Bron snapped upright, the chair spilling over behind her as she spun around to face the door. 'River.' His presence sent flickers of awareness to chase across her skin. 'You're here.'

He took a step into the room and looked at his watch. 'Am I early? I can come back.'

'No. Don't go.' Wow—did that sound desperate or what? She forced a smile to her face. 'I was just reading a diary and lost track of the time.'

'Did you find anything interesting?' He took another step into the room.

'Nothing.' She slammed the diary shut. 'But it made me realise that the Darkness didn't respond to that massage oil that got knocked over yesterday.'

'Why would it react to massage oil?' he asked, coming to sit down in the chair on the opposite side of the table.

'Well, it wouldn't. At least, not to something I didn't make, given it seems to only respond to me in a negative way. But what fell off that shelf yesterday and spilled on you, that was my Grandma's work. Full of her magic.' She nodded towards the shelf behind him. It had been really strange. The massage oil had practically flown off the shelf, the cork popping out as it bounced on the bench and splashed all over River. She hadn't thought about it at the time, being too busy cleaning it up and dealing with the sight of River's skin glistening with the oil, but now she realised it had possibly been Adeline telling her something. It was worth exploring.

'So, I was thinking that maybe I can rub some of that onto my hands and onto your shoulders—kind of give you a massage—and activate my powers slowly while doing that. See what happens. Is that okay?'

He stiffened and she thought he was going to refuse, but then he nodded.

She spun away, covering her sigh of relief. 'Take a seat. I'll just get everything ready.' A few moments later, she stood behind him. 'Okay, can you move the chair away from the table—I might need to move around you. Good. Ready?'

'As ready as I'll ever be,' he said tightly.

She poured massage oil into her palms, rubbed them together for a moment and then placed her oil-coated hands on his shoulders. Nothing happened. Encouraged, she moved her hands across his shoulders and back. Still nothing. Her grandma's magic tingled her fingertips, but the Darkness didn't seem to care it was there at all.

Interesting.

She moved her hands across his shoulders, fingertips digging into his smooth, warm skin. River stiffened. 'Sorry. Did I hurt you?'

'No. I'm just not used … to being touched.'

Bron cursed herself. He'd been kept segregated from everyone except his grandmother, Skye, their butler and the cook. Pack-touch would even seem strange to him. But she knew he needed it. Everyone needed touch, the Were even more so. Taking a steadying breath, she forced a smile into her voice. 'Take deep breaths. The scent in this oil should help calm you. Let it sink into your senses.'

River jerked his head in a tight nod and breathed in deeply. She moved her fingers along his shoulders, his neck, her fingers tingling, the sensation skating up her arms in a delightful shiver. Hell, was the room getting hotter? She pushed the sensation away—it was completely unprofessional to get turned on when touching a client.

She took some calming breaths then continued to massage up to the base of his scalp, around to touch his third eye. His breath hitched, fluttering over her wrists, and he became even more tense than before, which only served to make her more aware of her own reactions to him. She needed to hurry things up—for her as well as him.

'Concentrate on the Healing. Let go of everything else.'

With some effort, she calmed her mind again and did what the voice suggested. 'Okay. I'm just going to try a little something. Tell me if you feel anything ... untoward.'

Moving her hands so one splayed across his shoulder blade, the other on his chest over his heart, she pushed calm through her fingers and into him. It was a risk, but so far the Darkness hadn't reacted at all to the magic in the oil and she was hoping that it would be enough to mute its ability to sense what she was doing.

He stiffened.

Oh, Goddess. Please let this work.

His gaze snapped up to hers. 'Bronwyn?' he breathed, his shoulders relaxing; the rage that always seemed to be lurking in him faded from his eyes.

She almost cried in relief that it had worked, but there wasn't time for that. She pushed further in, using her grandma's magic as a conduit.

Colours sparked before her eyes as his auras came alive in her mind. The Darkness, turgid and glistening, still lay between them, and in the Darkness, the Beast paced, lunging to be allowed out to play. Its presence was bile in her throat, an icy prickling over her skin.

It was different from before, more present. It had pushed River's wolf further inside. A once proud wolf who due to years of imprisonment now cowered in the background, crying for help, begging not to be forgotten.

That plea broke her heart.

She sent calm and love and hope through her hands and into River, hoping the wolf would be able to sense some part of that. The Beast snapped at her, fighting, but she harnessed the spark of her grandma's magic in the cream, wrapped it around the calm and love and hope she pulled from inside herself, and shoved it towards the Beast. She felt the sting of its snarl in her mind, but then it backed away. It hadn't gone, but it had subsided to a place where it could do no more harm. At least for now.

A victory, no matter how small. She wanted to see what else she could do.

She pushed more calming and love through the medium of the magic in the cream.

The Darkness cringed back as the Beast had. It seemed unable to lash out at this new, unfamiliar magic. That was wholly unexpected and very interesting. She poured more oil onto her hands and then shifted, so that she could place both hands on his chest now.

His skin was so warm under hers, the muscles firm, his nipples pebbled. 'Are you cold?'

'No.' His voice sounded choked, his face turned away so she couldn't read his expression.

'This isn't hurting you?' He shook his head. 'Okay.'

Her fingers moved and she watched the impact her grandma's magic mixed with her own had on him. His auras, usually thin and dull, began to spark and pulse. They were far from healthy—the Darkness was still there exerting its influence—but they did look better. She pushed all negative thoughts aside and filled her mind with thoughts of sunshine and filtered the emotion through the conduit into him.

The Darkness seemed to dull.

Her insides trembled. She swept her hands over his shoulders, shaping the muscles in his arms, marvelling as the spark in his auras enveloped the length of his artistic fingers. It made sense that his hands would be the first to register the change in his auras—they were the conduit to his creativity. She brushed her hands up over his shoulders again and back to his chest, palms down; his nipples were hard pebbles under her palms.

His breath hitched.

Heat flushed her skin, but she tried to ignore it once more; tried to ignore her awareness of him and concentrate on what she was doing. The Healing was working. For the first time since she'd helped him change back from the Beast, her magic was working on him.

She bit her lip, closed her eyes and leaned closer, concentrating on what she could see in her mind's eye.

'Bronwyn?' River's shuddering voice broke into her thoughts. 'What are you doing?'

'I'm helping.' And she was. She actually was.

'Bronwyn. Can you just stop for a moment? I'm ...' He shifted and something hard brushed against her stomach.

She opened her eyes and stilled. His mouth was only inches from hers. How had he got so close? How had she come to stand in the v of his legs? If she leaned forward just a little, her lips would be on his.

No! She couldn't have that thought. *Look away. Don't think about his lips.* But it was so difficult with him so close, his legs surrounding her, his erection making itself known as it pressed against her stomach. Fire raged over her skin. 'Oh.'

His breath came hard and fast, fluttering the wisps of her hair, cool against her too-hot skin. His jaw was rigid, his lips pressed into a white line, nostrils flaring.

How had she not noticed how tense he'd become?

'Bronwyn, you need to move.' His husky voice would normally have tempted her closer, but his tension snapped through her, finally infiltrating the haze being so close to him brought to her mind. She stumbled back, banging into the table.

He reached for her, to steady her, but she twisted away.

'Are you okay?'

'Yes. I'm fine,' she managed. Silence fell between them as they stared at each other, the sound of their breathing heavy in the still room.

Goddess forgive her, she wanted to kiss him. She wanted to go over and slide her fingers into his soft hair and pull those full lips against hers, losing herself in the flavour of him. And she wanted to feel his erection pressing into something more than her stomach.

His nostrils flared and a sound like a groan broke from his throat as his hands gripped the arms of the chair he sat in, the wood grinding under his fingers.

Fuck. She was upsetting him. What kind of Healer was she? She was supposed to be calming him down, not rile him up.

She broke the grip of his gaze and lurched over to the sink, turning the tap on to wash her hands. She was suddenly so hot. Burning up. Her knees were shaking. She jerked off the tap and grabbed a cloth to wipe her hands. She had to calm down. Okay, so she'd almost climbed on top of River and attacked him, but she hadn't. Really, she shouldn't be having this much of an embarrassed reaction. She'd been sexually active since Ryan Callahan had taken her virginity after the school dance when she'd been sixteen. And she enjoyed being sexually active. Not that she was a promiscuous, but sex was a great tension reliever—among other, more pleasurable things.

So why was she reacting like this?

Heat flared through her and she almost swayed, dizzy. Shit. She wasn't going to pass out from desire like some ridiculous schoolgirl with a crush. Squaring her shoulders, she threw the cloth down turned. 'Look, River …'

'Bronwyn? What is that?'

She looked down at her hands. 'Crap.' Golden-orange flame with green at its heart flickered on her hands. Of course. She was reacting like this because there was a power-surge coming at her through her bond with Skye and Shelley.

Oh, no! 'River, you have to leave.'

'No.'

Eyes wide, her gaze slammed back into his; the power surged through her, arcing out of her fingers towards the one source in the room that could channel it from her. Desperately, she pulled it back into her, flinching at the sting. 'Don't be stupid. You have to leave now.'

His expression was full of steely determination as he took a step towards her. 'This is from Skye again, isn't it? Didn't you get any warning?'

'If I had, do you think I would have been touching you?'

'You need to touch me. You need to expel the energy in me.'

She shook her head. 'Not going to happen.' She backed away.

'It's how this is supposed to work.'

'Maybe for the others, but not with you. Not until we've figured out what the Darkness is and why it's stopping your change.' As she spoke, she began to shake, the power increasing in intensity more suddenly and voraciously than before. The heat of it moved from her fingertips to curl over her palms, across her wrists. It was coming on fast. Much faster than last time. It must have caught Skye by surprise with no Were around again.

Goddess, why did Iain and Patrick have to be running the perimeter? 'I'll phone Iain,' she said, her teeth chattering as the power wrapped around her chest, little licks of flame lunging up her neck. She winced. It wasn't burning her, but it was hot and uncomfortable all the same. She had to get her phone. But River was standing in the way. 'River, move. I can't ... touch you.'

'Use me.'

'No.'

'Because I'm broken? Because I'm useless?'

'No!' He stepped closer. She stepped back. 'River, please ...'

He shook his head. 'If you don't think I'm useless, use me. Don't be worried about hurting me. I was born for pain. It's so familiar, it's almost a friend.'

She wanted to cry. Not just because of the words, but because he meant them. 'No, you weren't.' Her teeth snapped closed as the pain increased, burrowing an ice-pick into her head. But still, she had to tell him, had to get him to understand. Through clenched teeth she gasped, 'You were born ... for love ... and friendship and beauty. Pain is not ... your friend.'

'It's more my friend than yours. Give it to me, before it finds a home in you.'

'No. Patrick and Iain ...' She cried out as the pain lacerated through her skull.

'Fuck this, Bronwyn. You have to use me before it's too late.' And then, in one of those lightning-fast moves she still hadn't got used to, River reached around her and grabbed her hands in his.

Shocked by the sensation of being encased in his arms, she didn't even have a chance to try to stop the power from lashing out and into him. 'River, no!'

He stiffened. His teeth snapped closed, lips pulled back in a rictus, the tendons in his neck standing out like hard wires. For a long moment she was caught in the grip of his arms, unable to move, unable to help or do anything but watch him twitch and try to hold back the moans as the power poured out of her and crashed through him, unable to find a home. He began to vibrate, his teeth clacking together, saliva foaming at the corners of his mouth. His arms tightened around her, almost crushing the air from her. She let out a gasp of pain.

He let go, his eyes rolling up into his head, and collapsed onto the floor with a thump.

'Bron, are you okay in here? I heard shouting.'

She didn't look up at Helen as her assistant opened the door, because her gaze was pinned on River.

Why had he done that? All he had to do was call the others. Even though the power was hurting her, she could have waited for them to get here. He didn't have to take on that pain for her. It didn't make sense. She wanted to drop to her knees, to check on him, to brush his hair back from his brow, to wipe the spittle from his lips, but she was afraid to touch him for fear of giving him more pain. Her fingers weren't hot anymore, but they were still tingling.

'Bron. What the hell happened? Are you okay?'

'I'm fine, Helen.'

'What happened to River?'

Bron shook her head. She couldn't tell Helen. Her fellow Wiccan had yet to be brought into the secret world of the Were. Although if things like this kept happening, she would have to be told. Tearing her gaze from River's prone form, she said, 'River's epileptic. I've got to ring Skye and Jason. Can you please check he's okay while I do that?'

'What do I do if he comes to?'

Bron's mouth twisted as she took in River's pale face. 'It was a grand mal seizure, so he probably won't come around for a while. Put him in the recovery position and make sure he's breathing. I'll be right back.'

She raced out of the room, ran over to the desk, made a quick call to Skye. Her friend picked up on the second ring.

'Are you okay? I didn't feel it coming on. Jason isn't here, otherwise I would have—'

'Skye, I'm fine.' She cut into her friend's rambling. 'It's River. He was with me.'

'You channelled it into him? How could you?'

The jab of Skye's words cut deep, tearing at the hole that the acid of guilt had already gnawed in her chest. 'I didn't mean to. I was trying to get him to call one of the others, but he's so stubborn, and before I could stop him, he grabbed me.'

'Oh, God! Why would he do that?'

'You tell me. But that doesn't matter now. I need help.'

'Where are your Shadows?'

'River said they were running the perimeter.'

'Fudge that. They shouldn't have left.'

'They trusted him. It's a good thing,' she said, as much to remind herself as her friend. 'But I need them back now. River has to be moved and I'd like to try a Healing on him, but I can't risk touching him myself.'

'I'll call Jason. He'll get them to you in a few minutes.'

'Is Adam with Shelley?'

'Yes.'

Bron breathed a sigh of relief. If it had been this bad for her, she was worried about what it had done to her friend.

'I'm coming now.'

'You don't have to.'

'I want to.'

Bron nodded and hung up. Her fingers still tingled with warmth. She was right about needing more than one person to channel the power into. She needed Patrick or Iain to get here soon, otherwise it would start hurting again.

Patrick chose that moment to enter the shop. She didn't need to explain—she could see the knowledge of what had happened on his face. He held out his hand and, with a sob, she grabbed hold of it and released the power into him.

A golden-rainbow light flared out around them and then a

gorgeous black and brown wolf stood in front of her, a cheeky expression on his face. Bron took his big face in her hands and kissed his snout. 'Thanks, Patrick. Now scoot before Helen comes out and sees you. I can't explain this to her yet.'

He licked her face before heading to the door. She opened it for him and he took off. Slamming the door shut, she raced back to the workroom and knelt beside River. She took the damp cloth from Helen's hand. 'Thanks Helen. You better get back to your client. I'll take care of this now.'

Helen rose. 'Let me know if you need anything else.'

'I'll be fine.'

Bron wiped the cloth over River's face, careful not to touch him, pleading with the Goddess that he would be all right. His skin was so hot it warmed the cloth. She rinsed it out again and returned to running it over his face, over the lumps of his scars—those vivid red ropes against stark white that twisted across his cheek and up into his hair.

'How can I help him when I can't even heal his scars?'

'*His scars are much deeper than this,*' the voice whispered in her mind. '*First you have to heal his soul.*'

Before she had a chance to question further, the front door crashed open, the bell jingling wildly, then Iain raced into the room.

'Should we take him back to the Packhouse?'

Bron shook her head. 'No. I don't want him jostled by a car ride. Just take him upstairs to my office. I can take care of him there.'

Nodding, he lifted River carefully, cradling him in his arms like a baby despite his rather large form, then with an ease that was almost frightening, carried him out of the room and headed upstairs.

14

River smiled as the dream whispered into his consciousness. Moondust. Skye called to it, playing their game—she made him change and he'd pop back, dance around, daring her to try to hit him with it again. He liked dreaming about turning into his wolf.

But something was different this time.

His smile slipped.

Skye called the moondust to her, but fear and dread shot through him, living things pounding on his chest, in his head. He couldn't move, even though he tried.

She tipped her head, eyes twinkling, the moondust sparkling on her fingers. 'I've got you this time, River.'

He screamed at her to stop—too late.

The sparkling moondust shot out from her fingers to arrow into him, cutting through his skin rather than caressing him. 'Skye!'

Her scream joined his as pain sliced through him.

'River?'

The sound of his name brought him surfacing up out of the nightmare. Cool fingers touched his forehead, stroked damp hair from his brow in a gesture of such familiarity it clutched at his heart.

'Skye.' Her name drummed in his head alongside the frantic beating of his heart. He'd been dreaming about her. He'd been fearful of her. Of something she was doing. But what? The dream had slipped away and now the horrific feelings it created were slipping away too. He grasped at them, but they swirled, nebulous as curls of mist in the dark of night and drifted away.

Pain rose up and slammed into his head. He groaned. 'Skye.'

'I'm here.'

He tried to open his eyes, but light stabbed at him. He closed them again. The room smelled of books and parchment, the lemon scent of furniture polish and another, more familiar scent of honey, oranges and spices: Bronwyn. It was warm and close—she was here, in the room. He relaxed a little to know she was here, safe. Behind her scent, there was an underlying nuance of older, fainter smells that told him it was a place Bronwyn spent time in. 'Where am I?'

'You're in Bron's office.'

'What happened? How did I get here?'

'Oh, River. I'm so sorry.'

'What are you sorry for?' He frowned, even though the action hurt.

She smoothed his frown away with a stroking caress. 'My power spiked suddenly and Jason wasn't around. I've still not got the hang of opening the channel to the Packbond when he's not nearby, so it spilled into the more familiar connection I have with Bron and Shelley. I didn't mean to do it. I certainly would have tried to find a way to hold it back if I'd known you were with Bron.'

So much worry, so much guilt, pouring from her in every word, in her scent, in the way she touched him. He had to stop her from allowing that guilt to eat her up. He tried to sit up, even though the pain clawed into his skull and shredded down his spine.

'Don't move.' Small, warm hands on his chest pushed him back. Bronwyn's hands. He'd know those hands anywhere. If it had been anyone else, he would have fought to sit up, but for Bronwyn ...

He lay back down without a protest and opened his eyes a crack, enough to see, but not enough to allow too much light to stab at him. 'I still don't understand what you're apologising for.'

'Because I should have called. Should have made certain one of the pack was close by to help Bron and Shelley release the energy safely. Should have made certain you weren't here for a treatment.'

She clasped his hands and he had to bite back a wince as pain jagged along his nerve endings from the tight grip on aching bones and ligaments. 'Did you have time to make a call?'

'No. The power spike hit me without warning.'

'Were you at work? With the kids?'

'Yes. But—'

'They could have been hurt if the power had lashed out at any one of them, couldn't they?'

'Yes.'

'Then you had no choice. You made the right decision. Don't apologise for protecting the children.'

She sat back, wringing her hands and biting her lip. 'I don't want to hurt you. Ever again.'

'I know you don't.' He reached out, muscles protesting, and took her hand in his. '*You* didn't hurt me. It was *my* choice.'

She shook his hand, anger suddenly spiking in her green eyes. 'And why would you do that?' She smacked his arm.

'Ow! What was that for?'

Her expression didn't change, but she rubbed his arm where the sting of the slap still vibrated. 'You should have let Bron call Iain or Patrick. Both of them would have been back here in under ten minutes. They could have channelled the power I pushed into Bron and done it safely. Instead, you had to go and do an idiot thing you knew would hurt you. Why?'

He could have said he'd done it because it was his job to take care of Bronwyn, but that would lead to questions he didn't want to answer. It was bad enough that Jason and Iain knew. So instead he said, 'It was hurting her and I was here.'

Skye's gaze whipped to Bronwyn. 'You never said it hurt you.'

Bronwyn shrugged. 'It doesn't always. Only when I fight not to release it.' Her cinnamon-coloured eyes narrowed on him. 'Which I was only doing because I didn't want to spill it into your idiot brother.'

'Oh, God! This is such a mess.' Skye stood and began to pace, her hands burrowing into her hair. 'Why can't I control my power? I should be able to control it. Papa thought I could, so why can't I learn? I mean, it happened when I was around the children. I would never have been there if I thought it might spike like that.'

'Of course you wouldn't,' Bronwyn soothed.

'But I didn't know. It had barely begun to build. I thought I had time—weeks—before I'd have to do another channelling session. But it hit me. Just like that. Oh, God! I'll have to give up work.'

River hid his wince as Skye's guilt—guilt that was tearing her apart—vibrated down their twin-bond to him. He wanted to offer words of comfort but bit them back too—she'd just slap them away. Instead, he asked, 'Why did it spike like that?'

Skye threw her hands in the air. 'I don't know. That's what I'm saying. I've got no control over it whatsoever. I thought I did, but today just showed me how far from control I really am.' She turned, face starkly pale in the dark room, wringing her hands so harshly he thought she might pull the flesh from her bones. 'I should never have done it. I should never have connected to Shelley and you.' Her gaze wavered on Bronwyn. 'I should never have completed the mating bond and pulled Jason and all of the pack into my shit.'

'I think Jason would think differently about that,' Bronwyn pointed out. 'I've never seen two people so in love. And I've never seen you more settled and happy than since you bonded with him.'

Skye raked her hands through her hair again. 'I know. I love him with every fibre in me, but how can I deserve that happiness when the cost to all those I love is so high? I mean, I hurt you and River; and Lord only knows what's going on with Shelley at the moment. What if Adam hadn't been with her?'

'But he is. Shelley is fine.'

Skye shook her head. 'I don't know how any of us can be fine when—'

Bronwyn bounced to her feet and grabbed Skye's hands, giving them a shake. 'Stop it, right now.'

Skye blinked. 'But—'

'No.' Another shake. River smiled as Bronwyn interrupted his sister again. He'd never seen anyone cut Skye off in her tracks like Bronwyn could. It was quite a talent. 'I know you're about to start blaming yourself for sharing your power with us, but I won't let you. You had the power of two people inside you. Nobody would be able to handle that by themselves, so give yourself a break.'

Skye looked like she was going to argue the point, but Bronwyn raised her hand. 'I will only say this once. The bond Shelley and I created with you was our choice, strengthened by ties of love and friendship, and it can't be taken back. Not only that, I won't let you take it back even if you tried.'

'You're only saying that because you all think I would have died if I hadn't shared the power with you.'

'Of course we were, but that's beside the point.' Bronwyn grasped Skye's shoulders and even though she was a good four inches shorter than Skye, it seemed to River she stared straight into his sister's eyes. 'That night, what we did, when we helped you by taking on some of your powers, linking ourselves to you for good or bad, it was our choice. Mine and Shelley's. Our gift to give to you. Our best friend. The sister of our hearts. You didn't force us. So stop wallowing in guilt and listen to the real intent behind River's question.'

River chuckled, even though it hurt his head. Only his Bronwyn would be able to snap his sister back like that, with love wrapped in a slap.

His Bronwyn.

He shoved that unwanted thought aside. She wasn't his Bronwyn. She could never be his Bronwyn. She had a manifest destiny that didn't include a scarred and twisted Were who was damaged beyond repair and could never be of real use to anyone. Despair clawed at him with its sharp talons, leaving permanent wounds that he could never fully heal with his will, but he wasn't going to let it take him down. Not while he had strength and sanity enough to ensure Bronwyn was safe and happy.

'Bronwyn is right, Skye.' Pushing himself up with a muffled groan, he faced down two sets of eyes that were now narrowed on him.

'I thought I told you not to move,' Bronwyn said, coming back over to him.

'I'm feeling better now, thanks.'

'You're a bad liar,' she retorted, repeating his words of earlier.

His lips twitched. 'Touché.'

She chuckled, as if, even in this serious discussion, she couldn't hold at bay the light and fun and laughter that seemed always to be bubbling out of her. It was nectar to him and it had been in short supply lately. His smile widened to match hers. But then he moved and pain sliced from his head, down through his body. He winced.

'I wish I could help you with the muscle pain.' Bronwyn's gaze became unfocused in that way it did when she looked at his aura—as if she both looked through him and around him. 'But the Darkness seems angrier. I don't think it'll let me use my power on you right now. Although ...' Her eyes brightened. 'The lotion that had my grandmother's power laced into it helped channel some calm into you before. Maybe if I—'

'No.' He couldn't let her touch him again. Not after the way he'd reacted to her. She'd thought she was helping him but he ... He swallowed hard. By the Moon, his erection had pressed up against her—she couldn't have missed it. Hopefully in all the fuss, she'd forgotten it. But if she touched him again—

'You don't need to be afraid,' she said, her brow furrowed as her gaze met his. 'I got rid of the extra power by channelling it into Patrick.'

'I know.' He'd known it when she pushed on his chest earlier, making him lie down. The soft warmth of her touch was still a golden glow in his chest, completely unlike the electric sharpness of the excess power. But of course, she didn't know that wasn't what he worried about. 'I need some space for a moment. Okay?'

Rejection flickered in her eyes. He was sorry to have put it there, but if she touched him right now, he wouldn't be able to stop from pulling her to him, taking her pink bow of a mouth with his, pushing his hands into the softness of her night-dark hair, before running them over her body to pull her luscious curves against his hungering hardness. He wouldn't be able to stop from kissing her even though his sister was there. And he would never be able to explain such an action or think that she might forget it. Or ignore it like she had the one and only time they'd kissed; the one that had made him run from her.

That kiss. It had played in his mind over and over; brought him screamingly awake, raging hot and hard from his dreams every night since. His wolf whimpered.

Bronwyn's gaze snapped to him, questioning, as if she'd once again heard his wolf. How could the connection between them be so strong when he kept cutting it off?

He edged back, into the corner of the couch. He knew she wouldn't come near him—her empathy wouldn't allow her to push him in that way, no matter how much her Healer instinct told her otherwise. But that pleading, hurt expression in her golden cinnamon eyes still tore at him.

She turned away, her footsteps muffled as she moved across the thick golden carpet towards her old and slightly banged-up desk. He expected her to sit in the worn, green leather chair, but she bypassed that and reached into a turquoise earthenware bowl on the windowsill behind the desk. The crystal she picked up glinted in the light, green with a golden light at its centre. The white lace curtains behind her fluttered gently in the early summer breeze; the soft rose light from the wood-nymph art deco lamp in the corner cast a nimbus of light around her.

Despite the fact that she wore her plain taupe uniform—a long tunic and loose pants—she looked like a Goddess. She always looked like a Goddess, but the light and the sense of rightness of this place, her utter belonging, made her seem even more so.

His eyes were drawn to the dormer window, a shadow shifting

there. Bluebelle. She sat, a sentinel, like the cats of the Egyptians who looked after their masters and mistresses.

A Familiar needed to be unswervingly loyal. It was good Bluebelle was there.

Bronwyn shifted, moving from her place in front of the window, breaking the spell. She grabbed a large jar at the end of the row on the shelf nearest the desk and brought it over to him, holding it out. He lifted his brow as he read the label: Eye of Newt.

The jar was full of gelatinous-looking eyes.

'They're jellies, left over from Halloween.'

'Halloween?'

She nodded. 'Kids from around here always come to the shop. It's a bit of a tradition that grandma set up—a bit of fun coming to the "witch house". She always did it up with fake cobwebs and pumpkin lanterns and covered all the lights with green shades so it looked spooky. Then she filled a whole pile of bottles with things that look like eyes and entrails and put them on the shelves. She always made us dress up like witches—usually like the three old hags in Macbeth. She had Halloween lollies shaped like eyes and fingers and spiders and frogs.' She looked down at the crystal in her hands, running it between her palms. 'I'd planned a big one this year but I missed it because I was ...' She glanced up at Skye. 'Well, you know. Busy. But Helen and her boyfriend held down the fort and I'm told it was popular as ever. The eyes are all that was left. Take one. You need a hit of sugar right about now. Chocolate would be better, but I don't have any. These might look disgusting, but they're quite nice for a massive hit of gelatinous sugar.'

River nodded. He usually didn't like sweets, but he popped an eye in his mouth surprised at how quickly it dissolved on his tongue, rather like cotton candy. Except, unlike cotton candy, it didn't just taste sweet. It tasted of a history vibrant and full of fun and love. Bronwyn's history.

Bronwyn offered one to Skye, who took two. When Bronwyn gave her a look, she shrugged and said, 'Two eyes are better than one.'

Bronwyn chuckled and shook her head. 'There was a time you

wouldn't touch a Halloween lolly with a stick just because of the magical, witchy overtones of the celebration. Times have changed.'

Skye smirked, one of the eyeballs creating a round mound in her cheek. 'It was hard though. You know I'm a sucker for anything sweet. You're not having one?' She gestured with the one in her hand as Bronwyn put the lid back on the bottle and slid it onto the shelf next to a thunder egg; an amethyst crystal that still wore its rough stone shell. It was ugly on the outside—how had anyone known of the beauty within enough to know to crack one open? Or was it simply a mistake that had found such hidden loveliness?

He tore his gaze away, an aching hardness in his chest, and tried to focus on their banter.

Bronwyn was saying, 'No. I never got a taste for raw sugar like you. Now, if they were chocolate on the other hand—'

'There wouldn't be any left in that jar.'

'You know me so well.' Bronwyn chuckled and picked up the green crystal she'd placed on the shelf when she picked up the bottle and began to rub it between her hands again. 'But enough about eyeballs and chocolate. Let's get back to the subject at hand.'

'Awwight,' Skye said, chewing on the eyeballs, which were now both in her mouth. 'Wha wa e ubje a and?'

River shook his head at his sister as he sucked the taste of sugar and fun from his mouth. 'We were talking about your power spike.'

'That's right. I think River asked the right question before,' Bronwyn said. 'Why did your power spike when there were no signs it would do anything of the sort?' Skye's mouth hung open—thankfully she'd swallowed the eyeballs. 'The last time this happened, you said there was a kind of build-up, although you didn't know what it meant. But this time, there was nothing.'

'I hadn't even thought of it that way.' Skye moved over to the couch and sat beside him, careful not to touch him.

'Do you think this could be Morrigan's influence?'

'No. That's not possible, is it?' Skye looked between them. 'You said she was terribly injured. We know from that diary Shelley found that she can't change bodies until Yule, and after what she tried on

Halloween, she wouldn't have the strength to heal herself let alone do something like this. For all we know, she's gone to ground and isn't even a threat.'

Bronwyn nodded, rubbing the crystal harder between her hands. 'I think it would be naive to think she isn't still a threat. She's had five hundred years to build up her resentments. She's not going to let it all go because of one setback.'

'Setback?' Skye's voice rose a little. 'But we completely thwarted her plans on Halloween. If she can't syphon my powers to use as her own, she has no use for either of us.'

Bronwyn's frown increased and her eyes darkened. 'That's wishful thinking, Skye. She has power unlike any of us or the other Pack Witches have seen before, according to what we've read in the diaries and what Cordy has told us.'

'But Cordy said ...'

'She said she didn't think you could be used again. Not in that way. But we don't know what Morrigan is truly capable of. I mean, she was going to murder River and have Alfrere rape you so she could tear your powers from you and use them to break the link between you and the Were, and therefore break the Pact. I don't think she'll stop now, do you?'

'I ... I ...' she looked around her wildly, fingernails digging into the cushion she'd grabbed.

A growl low in his throat, River grabbed her hand and said, 'That Morrigan bitch will not get my sister.'

15

River's words tore through the air with savage intensity.

Bronwyn visibly shivered, her eyes filling with worry as she met his gaze. 'I know you want revenge, but we can't let that cloud our minds.'

'My mind isn't clouded. I want Morrigan dead. She can never be allowed to hurt any of you again.'

Bronwyn snorted out a laugh. 'Oh, I don't disagree with that, but how can you protect Skye, or any of us, from a different kind of attack?'

'What do you mean?' Deep inside, his wolf became alert.

'What if Morrigan created a link with you that night,' she said to Skye, 'and can manipulate your powers from wherever she is?'

'No. She couldn't. That wouldn't be possible—would it?' Skye looked to him—for comfort, for denial—her body held stiffly as if she was trying not to tremble. He understood. She didn't want to appear weak, but that ancient witch had put her through hell. A hell nobody else had been there to stop.

Except for him.

Like he had on that night, he wanted to help her; help them. Yet he was as useless now as he'd been then, drugged and drained of all energy, unable to move or communicate until Skye had started to use her power to fight. The power had surged through him, bringing him out of his stupor and he'd tried to fight with her, to help, but the Beast had clawed to the surface. He'd fought it for control and in the process had been caught under a rock fall and knocked unconscious. He might as well be unconscious now for all the help he was to them.

'Skye. Are you okay?'

'Jason!'

Skye jumped to her feet as her mate rushed into the room. She ran to him and he scooped her into his arms, planting a long, lingering kiss on her lips before he leaned back, his gaze full of longing and completion as it met hers. A gaze returned by Skye in full.

River turned away. He was happy for his sister, but they had something he could never know. He hated the jealous rage that shot through him at that thought.

'Sorry I took so long,' Jason said. 'But it wasn't until Iain contacted me through the Alpha-lieutenant link that I knew you'd left me a message. Marcus has rules about mobile phones in the McClune compound being switched off.'

Skye's face glowed. 'So do you.'

He kissed her neck just below her jaw. 'Can you blame me? We don't know where Morrigan and the rogue coven are or what they might do next. I'm not going to hand them easy entry by allowing people to take photos that could be posted on the web or allow us to be tracked to our new base by our mobile phones.'

Skye shuddered. 'I think if she wants to track us, all she has to do is zero in on me.'

Jason didn't move, but River sensed the tension, the battle-ready alertness, shoot through his Alpha. 'Has she come after you?'

Skye took a deep breath. 'Not in person. But Bron and River think she did something to me today.'

'What do you mean?' Jason turned to look at River for the first time, firmly pulling Skye to his side, as if he needed the contact with her more than he needed to breathe.

River knew that feeling. He wouldn't give in to it, though. 'We think maybe somehow Morrigan is behind Skye's sudden spike in power.' He raised a brow at Bronwyn.

She nodded. 'I didn't feel anything building. And I know Shelley didn't either, otherwise she would have said something. There was nothing and then suddenly, bam! It has to have been influenced from something outside of us. And the only person I can think of who would have anything to gain by making Skye go kaboom is Morrigan.'

Jason's expression hardened, his eyes turning to steel and blood as he pulled Skye even more tightly into his side. 'How is that possible? You said she was badly injured when she came through the portal. Cordy didn't think she'd have much power right now and what Shelley discovered in that diary backs her up. How could she do something like this?'

'Morrigan had begun to create a link with Skye on Samhain to syphon her power,' Bronwyn said quietly. 'It's possible that link is still intact. If that's the case, she really wouldn't need much power at all.'

'Fuck!' the Alpha said, his wolf growling so they all could hear it.

River understood the need to fight and protect roiling through his Alpha because he experienced the same need every day towards the woman who was meant to be his. The need to protect warred against the need to allow her to be herself. It was a terrible, unending clash where one side never won entirely, but each held the other at bay. Instinct versus love. Could there ever be a winner?

Jason turned to Skye. 'I want to tell you that you can't leave the Packhouse, that I won't let you out of my sight, but I know I can't because it will crush you. So please, tell me how to deal with this.'

Skye reached up and cupped his face. 'I'm not going to work until we find a way of cutting this link, or whatever it is, between me and Morrigan. I won't endanger the children.'

Jason's sigh brushed the hair back from her face as he bent to lean his forehead against hers. 'Thank you.'

'I don't want you to stress about this. I'll let you put extra protection on me at the house and when I go out.'

'Why will you need to go out?'

She smiled indulgently. 'You don't imagine for one second that I can possibly stay in the house for weeks on end? I mean, who knows how long it will take to figure this out? I'm happy to bend to your need to protect, because it matches my need not to put those who can't protect themselves in danger, but I'm not going to hide away. I'll want to go out. I won't go shopping or anything, but I'll need to stretch my legs, perhaps go to my house for a change of scene. And I'd like to go to Cantrae House.'

He shook his head. 'Out of the question.'

She stepped out of his embrace, eyes sparking. 'You're not trying to tell me what to do, are you? Out of the two of us, who has won this argument in the past?'

Jason brushed his hands through his hair, and for a moment River felt sorry for him.

Bronwyn obviously didn't feel the same. There was an amused glint in her eyes as she leaned back against the desk, arms crossed over her chest and watched as if this was her favourite kind of entertainment.

By the Gods, she was magnificent.

'But it's not safe at Cantrae House,' Jason argued, pulling River's attention back to the Alpha-couple.

'We both know that's not true. River spent the whole of the full moon there and he's fine. Nothing tried to attack him and you've had it fully guarded ever since Halloween. And you said Marcus allowed Cordy to come down and check it out, so we know there's been no sign of anything magical clinging to the house. Nothing evil.'

'Except the ghosts of the past,' Jason said.

Skye flinched.

River growled. 'She doesn't need to be reminded about our grandmother, or Ferris. That memory lives large in both of our minds, I can promise you.'

'I'm sorry.' Jason gathered her into his arms. River expected his sister to deny his touch, but she did the opposite, flowing into him as if she could become one with him. 'I didn't mean—'

'I know,' she mumbled into his chest, hands stroking his back, giving comfort as much as taking it. 'You were talking about my past. My unhappy memories.'

'Yes.'

'But Gran and Ferris are part of all that. And I need to go back. I need to say goodbye to them both. I need to face what happened there.' She peered up at him. 'Besides, maybe being there will help me figure out why I'm still linked to Morrigan. Maybe it's got something to do with her being in my grandmother's body.'

'Could there be something in the Pack Diaries?' Bronwyn suggested.

'I'll get on to it right away,' Skye nodded.

'No. You've got to keep on with your own studies and doing the Skype tutorials with Cordy,' Bronwyn said. 'Shelley can look through the diaries. She loves researching this stuff.'

'What about you?' River asked.

'Adeline told me I should read the family grimoires. I thought she meant in relation to what was happening to me, but I think she meant more than that. I'll check them out and get back to you all.'

'Good,' Jason nodded.

'I can't believe Marcus won't let Cordy near me yet,' Skye grumbled.

'I'm working on it,' Jason said, kissing Skye's brow.

'I know you are. I suppose the Skype thing is okay for now, but I know I'd learn so much faster face to face.'

'She's working on Marcus, too.'

Her lips curved up as she brushed her fingers through the hair at his nape. 'I know. I'm lucky to have her, really. She's amazing.'

'I knew you'd love her.'

'I was bound to love her.' He looked at her with a query on his face. 'She helped you find me.'

Jason chuckled softly and kissed her.

River glared down at his lap, trying hard to stifle the jealousy that shot through him again. 'This is all fascinating, but we've kind of gotten off topic.'

Jason nodded. 'Tell me what happened today.'

River and Bronwyn explained as much as they could, with Skye adding in the bits she knew.

Jason shook his head. 'I'm sorry, brother. Are you okay?'

His words were accompanied by a gentle stroke through the Pack-bond; but River's wolf was buried too deep to feel the benefit of it. 'I'll survive.'

'He's being stupidly brave,' Bronwyn said, edging forward. 'It seriously hurt him. Unnecessarily so.' She crossed her arms. 'Can you please order him not to do something so stupid again?'

'I agree.'

River glared at his sister. 'Jason wouldn't do that. He knows the safety of the Pack Witch comes first. I took care of Bronwyn's safety. End of discussion.'

Bronwyn folded her arms in front of her and somehow managed to make her pixie-like features look stern. 'That is not the end of the discussion. You hurt yourself because of me. I will not allow that to happen again.'

'It was my choice. My pain to bear.'

'But you didn't have to bear it.'

He just stared her down. She threw her hands up in the air. 'You are so stubborn. And you're not listening.'

He tipped his head to one side then the other, cracking his neck to release the tension building in his muscles. 'I am listening. You just haven't given me a reason to change my mind.'

'Do you think we should leave them to it?' Jason whispered to Skye. She nudged him in the ribs.

River would have smiled at the interplay, but his attention was riveted to Bronwyn as she made a growling sound in her throat.

'Well how about this for a reason. I'm a Healer. Pain is my burden to bear.'

He went suddenly still. 'What do you mean by that?'

'Where do you think the pain goes when I heal someone?'

A shocked silence filled the room.

Skye was the first to break it as she whispered, 'I thought it just disappeared.'

Bronwyn snorted. 'That would be lovely, but that's not the way the Mother Goddess works. Life is cyclical. Birth, life, death to birth again and so on. What goes in must come out, but it also must go back in again. I'm able to heal because I take the pain away and put it into me.'

'Stop growling, River. It's not helping.'

Jason's voice rang in River's mind as Skye gasped, 'Oh, I never knew.'

River snapped the sound off in his throat, not because of Jason's words, but because of the way Bronwyn was looking at him—pride and hurt combined.

'You have no right to be angry with me,' she said stiffly.

River wanted to snarl again, wanted to tell Bronwyn she wasn't allowed to heal anyone ever again. But he didn't have the right to demand such a thing of her. He knew she wouldn't listen anyway. What he wanted to know though was ... 'Why do you do it?'

Bronwyn shrugged. 'I'm a Healer.' Her face broke into a smile. 'I've only just started to realise what that truly means. It's who I am.' She shrugged. 'Besides, it's not so bad. The pain doesn't stay with me for long because I turn it into a different kind of energy.'

He could see that she didn't mind it, but still ... To think he had caused her pain. 'I don't like it.'

'What's not to like?'

He stood up, began to pace, grateful that the shakes had now left his legs and his head was beginning to clear. 'I caused you pain. That's what I don't like.'

'But you didn't cause me pain.'

His gaze snapped to her at her lie. 'You healed my wounds on Samhain. By your own admission, that hurt you.'

'Oh, that.' She waved her hand. He gave her a flat look that made her huff out, 'It really wasn't that bad, River. You're making too much of this.'

'What did it do to you in our sessions?'

'That's completely different. That's not pain so much as a darkness.'

'A darkness that you take on?'

'Well, kind of. It doesn't truly let me take it on, which is part of the problem, but I can feel its coldness, its rage, and I take some of that from you.'

Her affirmation tore at him. 'And when you used your power to turn me from my Beast self, what happened then?' She looked uncertainly between him and Jason and over to Skye; from their expressions, it seemed they wanted to hear her answer as much as he did. 'Well?'

'I don't ... That's different. That's not like using my power normally.'

'It hurt you, didn't it? Was that why you passed out?'

'No.' Her jaw squared. 'I'm just not used to doing it, that's all. It was the shock of using so much power all at once. I'll get used to it. Wait until next time.'

'There won't be a next time,' he said, the words short and clipped to hide the anguish, the agony tearing through him.

Bronwyn's arms fell to her sides, the crystal dropping to the ground with a thud. 'Don't say that.'

'Why not? I might not be in charge of anything else, but I am in charge of that. I will not be responsible for causing you pain. I won't do any more sessions with you. End of story.'

Her jaw squared, the fire in her eyes sparking. 'That's not the end of the story.'

By the Moon he loved to see that spark of temper in her, but he wasn't going to give in to it. 'It is to me.'

'But I want to help you. I just need time. I'm so close to understanding what was done to you. And using the dregs of my grandma's power did something I know is important. I'm certain I can figure out how to undo it if you only give me time.'

'I don't want you to figure it out. Not for me. Not if it forces you to take something ugly and painful into yourself. I'm not worth it.'

'River,' Skye reprimanded. 'How can you say that?'

'Because it's true.'

Skye's eyes flashed. 'I've never let anyone else say such things about you. Why do you think I'm going to let you get away with it?'

He shoved his hands into his pockets. 'You can do what you like— as will I.'

He moved away from her as she reached for him through the twin-bond, trying to change his mind by pushing thoughts of need and empathy into his head. 'Don't try that trick on me. It won't work.'

Skye clasped her hands together. 'You have to let Bron help you.'

'No. I don't. I don't want her help. I don't want any of your help.' He headed to the door, snarling over his shoulder. 'Just leave me alone. All of you.'

'But River—'

'Skye. Let him go.'

The door slammed behind him and he began to run.

———

BLINDSIDED, Bron trembled and dropped down in the chair behind her. She pushed her knuckles into the tearing pain in her chest, but it didn't help. How could their discussion have turned into something so heated and filled with pain? 'What just happened?' Nobody answered. She looked up.

Skye was tugging against Jason's hold. 'Let me go.'

'No.'

'But I have to go to him.'

'No. You don't. Arguing with him now won't help. In fact, it will just entrench his belief further.'

'But he's pulling away.' A tear trembled down her cheek. 'Can't you feel him pulling away?'

'Of course I can,' Jason said, his voice a gentle caress. 'But I know the power of the wolf when it needs to be alone.' He stroked his finger down her cheek, brushing away the tear. 'He'll come back to us.'

'How do you know?'

'Because I'm the Alpha. It's my job to know. Besides, why do you think I've set a Shadow on him all these weeks?'

'Because you were worried about Morrigan and also about the Beast inside him and what it could do.'

He shook his head. 'No. He can take care of himself now. He's not the drugged-out male he was. He will not be so easily taken. He doesn't need a babysitter to keep him safe.'

'Then why have Iain and Patrick shadow him?' Skye asked.

'Because he needs to make connections with the pack,' Bron answered for him, her words slow and wondering as she stared at him. Despite the fact that he was a new Alpha of a pack slowly recovering from near disaster, he was already incredibly strong. And the pack was strong. Stronger than they should be—and all because he was their Alpha, holding them together with the sheer strength of his will, as he'd held them together from the moment his father had died. 'You're creating bonds, even when he's trying to deny them.'

He smiled at her. 'You truly are a Healer, to understand that so quickly.'

Bron huffed out a breath. 'Not true enough. I shouldn't have told River about what being a Healer really means.'

'We all make mistakes.'

'Yeah, but I seem to make more than most others. Me and my stupid mouth that doesn't know when to shut up.'

'Your honesty is what makes you special and so good at what you do. Don't let a few mistakes make you think otherwise.'

Bron bit her lip. Was he right? Not that it mattered. What did matter was that River had left worse off than when he'd arrived and she couldn't let that stand. 'I'm not sure you're right about him stomping out of here because his wolf wanted to be alone.' She frowned, trying to concentrate on what she'd seen. 'The Darkness has spread, like an infection. Little tendrils of it have burrowed in deep and are digging deeper.'

'Can you tell what it is?' Skye asked.

She shook her head. 'I have no idea. All I know is it responds negatively to my power. It's not his wolf that's been pushing me away.'

'You can't stop trying, though.'

'I'm not going to. Who is following him now?' she asked Jason.

'Patrick. He'll make sure River's all right. He's very good at drawing people out.'

Skye had been frowning at both of them, but now a smile slowly bloomed on her face. 'You chose each of them purposefully, didn't you?'

He nodded. 'They all remember River from when he was a boy. Patrick used to play with him—they're the same age. I've also got Liam flying in from Italy. He was always one of the group and should round it out nicely.'

'But why Iain? He's so ... rock-like. And alone.'

Jason smiled. 'He's a Lone Wolf—attached to the pack, but not. There is strength inherent in him because of that, one the pack needs, especially now. He came the moment I called, using that strength to buoy the pack, to help keep us standing.' Jason's smile widened. 'River and the others followed Iain around when they were pups—they kind of hero worshipped him because of what they instinctively felt in him.'

'So, you were betting on the bonds from those relationships to still be intact,' Skye said slowly.

'Yes. And it's worked. He doesn't seem to be able to stop himself from talking and interacting with them. And while he baulked at their presence to start off with, he's come to accept them in his life. The more time they spend together, the more the bond will strengthen and the more he'll be pulled into the arms of the pack.'

Tears glistened in Bron's eyes as Skye leaned up and kissed his cheek. 'You won't let him pull away.'

'Not in this lifetime.'

Skye brushed his hair back from his brow. 'Have I told you recently I love you?'

'You might have mentioned it once or twice. But I wouldn't mind hearing it again.'

'I love you, Jason McVale,' she whispered against his lips.

'I love you too, Skye Collins,' he said, cupping her face and kissing her.

Bron shifted, crossed her arms and coughed. They broke apart slowly and turned to look at her as if surprised to see someone was in the room with them.

'You know how annoying it is to feel like you've disappeared?'

Skye blinked and smiled softly. 'Sorry, Bron. I didn't forget you were here, it's just ...'

Bron waved her hand before picking up the crystal. It hadn't given her any comfort today like it normally did, so she put it back in the bowl. 'Yeah, I know. And I'm sorry to interrupt your session of getting so lost in each other that you forget I exist, but I need to go. I need to start being the Healer you think I am.'

Jason took her hand in his. 'I don't just think it. I know.'

She swallowed hard. 'Thank you. But I have to prove it to myself.'

'You're going after River?'

'I have to. I know you think we should leave him alone, but my Healer instincts are telling me I need to go to him now. I think it's being alone that's letting the Darkness sink in further. Patrick being with him is good, but it's me the Darkness responds to and I have to find out why.'

'You are the only person who can do this because you are more integral to River than you know. So trust your instincts. I do.' He gripped her shoulder and squeezed, then kissed her cheek—a brother to a treasured sister; an Alpha to one of his pack.

'Thank you,' she whispered, her voice husky.

'Make him better,' Skye said softly. 'Find out what's wrong. Bring him back to us.'

'I'll try.'

Turning, she picked up her bag and left them to find comfort in each other, knowing there would be no comfort of that sort for her for quite some time.

Not until she'd managed to make a certain broken Were feel whole.

16

As the sound of the engine faded into the distance, Bluebelle turned and peered back through the dormer window. Skye and Jason were on the couch, too wrapped up in themselves to notice anything else.

Good. Hopefully that meant she had time. She scurried down the roof, jumped onto the top of the brick wall at the side of the building, teetering as her malformed foot buckled under her. She fell awkwardly, scraping her chin along the brick and landing heavily on her shoulder. Bright sparks of pain shot through her, but she didn't have time to lick her wounds. Pushing to her feet, she shook herself, then gingerly made her way along the wall to where she could jump through the window that was always left open for her.

More carefully this time—she didn't want to make a noise by knocking over any of the glass bottles on the shelf under the window—she jumped down to the floor. The impact jarred up her leg, sending a bright shoot of pain into her shoulder. She'd injured herself more than she thought, but that didn't matter. She had to make a phone call and only had a little time in which to do it. Helen would still be busy with her client, but the session was due to finish soon and she didn't know when Skye and Jason might come back down.

But she didn't have a choice. It wasn't like she could carry a mobile phone around with her.

She had to report to her mistress and she had to report now.

She ran to the front desk and clenched her teeth through the tearing pain of the change into human form. Panting and dripping with sweat, she picked up the phone and dialled.

As the cool air dried the sweat on her skin, she shivered and wished she'd grabbed one of the robes to wrap around her. What if someone walked in the door? She was completely naked. How could she explain that?

She was about to put down the phone to remedy the situation when a cool voice answered. 'Who is this?'

'Mistress ... I mean, Morrigan. It's me. Eloise. It worked.'

There was a pause and then, 'I knew it would.'

'But they know you affected Skye's power somehow.' She held her breath, waiting for the explosion.

'That is unfortunate, but not unexpected.'

The air left Eloise in a great rush. Exhaustion made her vision waver and she leaned on the desk, then winced as pain shot through her shoulder. 'They're going to research in the diaries. Talk to other Pack Witches and find a way to break your link with Skye.'

'They won't find a way. The magic I use is nothing they know about.'

'Oh.' Eloise shivered at her mistress's words, her teeth chattering.

'Why the chattering teeth? Are you frightened by the magic I use, Eloise?'

She stood bolt upright, gripping the phone tightly in her hand. 'No. I'm just cold.'

'You should find some clothes to put on. We don't want you to get sick.'

The caring words should have made Eloise smile, but instead she shivered again.

'Now, tell me what happened after River took the power from the Healer.'

Eloise told her what she'd seen from her hidden perch outside the window. 'She's really powerful.'

'Of course she is. She's full of old power. Twin power. Skye Collins was born with the power of two inside her. Power that should have been mine. But instead, she's shared it with the unworthy Wiccans and the power is now reflecting the soul of them. Bronwyn is a Healer at heart, so the power is transmogrified into Healing power.'

'Then why can't she heal River?'

Morrigan chuckled. 'There is a reason he never ended up with any of the power meant for him.'

Eloise frowned. 'I thought that was because he was a Were and Were don't have any power.'

'That's true, in part. But there's another truth at the heart of it.'

'What?'

'He has some Darkness inside him. You saw the proof of it today. And now we can use that to our advantage.'

'What about Bron?'

'She is key to this too, but not in the way I originally thought. River's feelings for the Healer are just feeding the divide created by the Darkness. I need to use that somehow. I know it.'

'Could the next full moon help? When he next turns into the Beast?'

There was a pause and then, 'No. It falls right at Yule. Rebirth. Fertility. I have other plans for Yule. But if I can bring out the Beast earlier ...'

Her mistress fell silent. Eloise knew well enough not to interrupt Morrigan when she was thinking, so she stayed silent and waited, even though she knew she couldn't stand there for much longer.

Finally she was rewarded. 'There will be sacrifices to make. I'll have to keep asking you to spy for me, even though I know it exhausts you to do what you do.'

'I don't mind. I'd do anything for you, Morrigan.'

'I know you would, my dear. Now, here's what I want you to do.'

Eloise listened, breathless, as her mistress laid out her plans. What she asked would be difficult, painful even, but Eloise hadn't been lying when she said she'd do anything for Morrigan. She meant every word. She'd already learned so much. Since Morrigan had lifted her up, brought her into her confidence, named her friend, not servant, just as Morrigan had done for her brother Cain, she felt special. Loved.

'Now, I've just got to create the right combination of events, and then we will use those keys to unlock my final revenge and break the Were-Witch Pact forever.'

'I'll do as you ask.' There was no answer—Morrigan had already hung up.

Eloise was tired, and it took everything in her to melt her bones again and become the cat. But she gritted her teeth and did as her mistress asked. Then, meowing pathetically, she limped upstairs. Bron and River were both gone, so she had to make Skye take her home. By the time she made it to the top of the stairs, her crippled leg ached horribly, the pain in her shoulder was almost unbearable and her pathetic meows were no longer an act.

She stumbled into the room and fell to the floor. With a cry, Skye ran to her and picked her up. 'Oh, you poor kitty. What have you done to yourself?'

'It looks like she's fallen from the roof,' Jason said, coming close. 'I saw her up there before.'

He reached out to touch her and Eloise had to stop herself from cringing from his hand.

'We need to take her to a vet.'

Jason shook his head. 'She's Bron's Familiar. She'll be able to heal her.'

'But she's in pain and Bron has gone to track River down. We can't distract her from that.'

'Shelley is there. She might be able to help.' Jason brushed his hand through Skye's hair, the gesture human and gentle, far more than Eloise thought animals like him capable of. Then he surprised her further when he leaned down, his fingers stroking gently across her head, and said, 'It's okay, Bluebelle. We'll take care of you until your mistress returns.' He put his hand on Skye's back. 'Come on. Let's get her home.'

Something thick wedged in Eloise's throat as Skye, holding her close to her chest, kissed her mate. 'I love you, Jason McVale.'

'I love you too, Skye Collins.'

As they carried her out and placed her in the car for the trip back to the Packhouse, Eloise tried to ignore that soft, warm feeling inside her and concentrate on her mission. The Were were animals and were rotten to the core. That's what she'd been taught. That's what she believed. One kind action wasn't enough to change that. Nor was the way River brought her treats and talked to her as if she was a confidant.

Guilt stabbed through her at what she'd done today. But no. She couldn't let it affect her decisions. Her mistress had told her how the Were had stolen power from the witches, its natural inheritors. It's why her once great family had been brought to such low straits. They must be stopped.

And Eloise would help to stop them.

17

River knelt next to the garden bed to pull out weeds that had cropped up between the decorative stones. He would need to lift the stones and put in another layer of mulch and newspaper to discourage the growth. He sighed. He'd neglected the place for too long and it was starting to show. Although, why did he bother? When he was gone, it would get worse.

He closed his eyes against that thought and hoisted a heavy slab of concrete onto his shoulder, determined to concentrate only on the task at hand, on the strain of muscles and sinew as he laid a new path.

There was a tentative push of concern through the twin-bond. Fuck! Skye knew where he was. He pushed the concern back, longing for the days when Skye had blocked the bond.

He chuckled at the irony. He'd spent years trying to break through those blocks, but now Skye had accepted her magic and its purpose, the twin-bond was open and he desperately wished it wasn't. She didn't like him being here because of the difficult memories she had of Cantrae House. But what she did not realise was that he didn't share her feelings about their home. He'd been happy here, up until Halloween. Well, as happy as a suppressed and broken Were could be. Unlike Skye, he had always felt the love of both their grandparents.

And he'd had the garden.

It spoke to his heart in ways the house had never done. This garden had calmed his tortured wolf. There was nothing like the warm damp feel of soil on his hands as he laid a plant into its bed, breathing in the rich scents of minerals, the manure and mulch, the sweet exotic perfume of the flowers, the sharp bitterness of the greenery, the cinnamon tang of bark. He could lose himself in those scents, in the rough and silken textures under his hands, the tension leaving his muscles as he dug and patted, lifted and sorted.

In another life—one without the insidious touch of the Beast—he could have found happiness in spending his life as a landscape gardener, working on living projects. The joy of creation and hard, honest, sweaty work was something he could not explain to others. The garden was ever changing, growing, needing him to change and grow with it. It called to him; kept him calm and sane.

He wanted to be buried here, in the garden he loved. The idea of his inevitable death—looming closer now than ever before—wasn't so terrible if he could live on in the plants and trees he had nurtured, his flesh and blood enriching the soil, giving more life to other living things. There was comfort in that.

He lowered the last rough-edged slab into place then straightened, stretching out his back. His gaze roamed over the little Japanese-inspired oasis he had created only a few months before. He'd only been here an hour and already he was more at peace with his world. Warmth roamed in his chest.

'You have a talent, grandson.'

'Grandpa.' River's lips widened further as he faced the direction the voice had come from. But of course, he didn't see his grandpa. Not like he used to. Harrison had used up the power that had remained to him when he'd helped Skye stop Morrigan Cantrae from using Skye's power and killing River. The glow of his spirit was forever depleted and could only be truly seen by a medium like Shelley. He should be gone completely, but somehow Shelley remained as an anchor for him and he could come forth at times with great effort. He'd made that effort during the full moon, his presence a comfort to the ruined, broken half-self he'd been during the days after the nights when he'd transformed into the Beast.

'I didn't thank you for staying with me on the full moon.'

'You don't ever need to thank me, River. I wish I could do more for you.'

'You do enough.'

'It's good to see you back here in the garden. It needed you.'

River's lips twisted as he tried to fight the tightness squeezing his chest, the burning in his eyes. 'I'm so glad you're here, Grandpa.'

'I am, too. And if you need to talk, I'm always here to listen, even if I can't manage to answer back. I'm always here.'

'I know.'

A brush of warmth ran over his head, almost as if his grandpa had stroked his hair, but too soon the sensation was gone and there was only silence. The peaceful silence of a garden; the tinkle of water, the gentle rustle of the warm summer breeze in the giant oak tree above him, and the occasional tweet of a busy bird. He closed his eyes and let the peace of the moment steal into his soul. This is what he'd come for. Solitude. The garden was lover and mother and friend and he would die in its embrace.

Taking in a big lungful of summer-scented air, he let that thought go and turned. There was work to do.

Christmas was near and he always planted poinsettias and Christmas lilies at this time of year. Nobody seemed to be getting ready for Christmas yet, even though it was only a few weeks away. Their time had been too filled with other concerns. But he remembered. His grandmother loved the red and green of the poinsettias and the heavenly smell of the lilies. Even though she wasn't here, he still felt the need to plant them for her. He'd almost missed out on planting the bulbs, but if he did it now, it wouldn't be too late.

Muscles flexing, back arching and stretching, he weeded and replanted, moved rocks and stones, laid down mulch and dug blood and bone into the soil where he planned to plant new vegetation soon. He very quickly built up a sweat and took off his T-shirt, the warmth of the sun a welcome caress.

Returning to his shed, he hoisted another pack of the compacted mulch he'd ordered online and took it out to the garbage bin of water he'd prepared so he could rehydrate it. He'd have to order some more soon at the rate his garden was chewing through it, not to mention those plants he wanted for the northern corner. A new design had begun in his mind and his fingers started to itch for paper and charcoal to mark it out. But he had to finish this first, then he could draw and figure out what he'd need to order and add to it the supplies he was low on.

He dumped the mulch in the water, swishing it around, watching it expand and destroy the reflective surface. His hands stung as the water and mulch clung to the nicks and little tears he'd gained in the last few hours, but it was a stinging he welcomed; as long as he could feel something like that, it meant the rage building inside with insidious stealth hadn't taken over yet.

The sound of the front gates swinging open reached him, followed by the crunching of tires on the gravel of the curved sweep of drive at the front of the house. He stiffened. He didn't need to hear that little hitch in the engine to know who it was. The prickling under his skin as she drew ever closer always told him she was near.

Bronwyn.

His every sense became riveted on the sounds of her arrival. The crunch of tires on gravel. The squeak of the break. The pop of the engine as it cut off. The click and swish of the seatbelt being released. The clunk of the door being opened and closed, the slap of sandalled feet on the stones of the drive. A light tread moving towards him; a voice calling out to Patrick, asking him to stay by the car; the sweet scent of her as she turned the corner and made her way down the path towards him.

He was aware of all of it, the tension of her presence thrumming through him like the sweetest harmony—a harmony with a discordant note at the end.

He should have known she would come after him. She was stubborn, his Bronwyn.

Why did she have to be so stubborn?

He bent to his task, trying to ignore it, to ignore her as she walked over the grass behind him. She'd changed from her uniform; the soft swish of the skirt she now wore brushed against the plants she passed, tangling around her legs. His mouth watered. The scent of the flowers and herbs she used in her work enticed his senses, lingering, caressing. He held back a groan as his cock sprang to life, straining painfully against the denim of his jeans, just like it had earlier in the day when she'd been running that damn oil over his chest.

Sweat broke out on his brow as he clenched his muscles against the rush of desire that fired his veins.

He had to get control of himself before he turned around. He couldn't let her know he was so aware of her. Couldn't let her know she was welcome in a way not even his sister would be. She needed to think he wished her far away.

His hands shook as he grabbed the mulch in the bin and pushed down. More sweat broke out on his skin that had nothing to do with the sun beating on his back or the physical nature of the work. His muscles screeched with the effort of not turning around to face her, to grab her, to run his hands over her body, to enjoy every single petite yet curvy inch of her. He longed to press his hungering lips against hers and drown in the taste and texture of her mouth, the sweet yet spicy scent of her skin.

He wanted.

He couldn't have.

Gritting his teeth so hard his jaw popped, he gave no outward sign that he knew she was there, even though she must know he could hear her, smell her. He hoped she'd think him rude and get peeved, turn around, walk away, forget about him. There was nothing she could do for him and her presence just made everything so much harder because ...

He wanted. He needed. He hungered.

'River.'

He swallowed hard past the gravel in his throat. 'What?'

Undeterred by his rudeness, she stepped closer. 'I've been thinking about what happened today.'

'I'm not going to let you heal me.'

'I'm not talking about that. Well, I am.' She swallowed hard. He could smell her nervousness. 'But I need to clear the air about what happened before my power surged first.'

By the Moon—why did she have to bring that up now? 'I don't know what you're talking about. Nothing happened.'

She edged a step closer, her warmth brushing over him. He squeezed his eyes closed and bent over the bin of mulch, trying to fill his nose and mouth with the wet, musky scent of bark and leaves. It didn't work. He could still smell her. 'River. Talk to me.'

'I'm not in the mood to talk to anyone,' he snarled, stalking away to grab the rake from the ground and drag it across the earth he wanted to mulch.

'River, I'm confused.' She paused, waiting for him to speak, but he wouldn't. If he opened his mouth, he'd say far more than he ever meant for her to know. 'River. I know I shouldn't have touched you like that, but I think your reaction is a little extreme.'

'It's not extreme at all.'

'I think it is. I think you're using the discovery that I take on the pain of the clients I heal as an excuse to cover up your embarrassment about what happened earlier. And believe, me, I get it. I'm embarrassed too—and I have more right to be than you. It was my fault. But you shouldn't stop our sessions because of it.'

'I'm not embarrassed.'

'If that's true, you'll agree to continue our sessions.'

He threw the rake down and swung to face her. The sight of her always squeezed his chest, made fire race through his veins. This time was no exception. He wanted to drag her to him and never let go, but he couldn't. And he was so angry at her for making him feel this way. 'Fuck! Why are you pushing me on this?'

She didn't flinch or step back from him despite his aggression.

Instead, she met his gaze, a small frown marring her smooth brow. 'Because you need me to. Because I affect the Darkness in you and I think that's important. Because I feel your pain and I want to help you.'

'You're mistaken.' He swung away, unable to bear that look of concern in her cinnamon eyes. Kicking the rake out of his way, he stomped over to the bin and yanked out the mulch.

'I'm never mistaken about people being in pain. Especially people I care about.'

He sucked in a breath, her words slicing into his heart. 'Don't care about me, Bronwyn. I'm not worth it.'

'You will always be worth it.'

His fingers clenched in the mulch.

'River?'

He let the mulch fall back into the bin. 'Please, go.'

'No.'

He growled.

'River. Let me in.' She touched his back.

He stilled, the growl catching in his throat, turning into a low hum. His wolf surged out of its hiding place deep inside him and rolled over, delighting in the cool feel of her hand on his too-hot flesh. He delighted in it too, but it wasn't enough. Never enough. He longed to have her hands stroke over him, petting and caressing until his memory of any other touch but hers faded from existence. He wanted—more than he wanted his next breath—to tear her sundress from her body and press against her, equally naked, and revel in the soft silk of her skin against the hard length of his. He longed to carry her down to the soft warmth of the fragrant carpet of grass behind them, her arms and legs wrapped around him as he buried himself deep inside her, his lips on hers, on her throat, her breasts, surrounding himself in her scent and her taste, her heat and her softness, until there was nothing else.

Just him and her.

Combined.

One.

His cock flexed, pressing even more painfully against the hard denim. His balls tingled, tensed. His wolf howled inside him, lunging, begging him to act on the image screaming loud and clear in his mind.

He trembled, trying to fight what instinct pushed him to do.

He lost.

A growl low in his throat, he turned to her, hands reaching to pull her against him. Hands covered in dirt and mulch. He froze. He couldn't touch her and cover her in his filth. He tore himself away and came to a halt at the edge of the grass, half a dozen metres from her.

'River?'

There was worry in her voice, and a quiver of fear, as she met his gaze. He closed his eyes. Fuck! He didn't want to hurt her, but if she didn't leave now, he was afraid he'd do just that. 'Go away.'

'No. You need me.'

His eyes snapped open. 'No. I don't.'

'Yes, you do. And I need to help you.'

Fuck! Why did she have to say that? He could deny himself, deny his needs, but he couldn't deny hers.

'River.' She took a step towards him.

A growl snarled out of him. 'Don't you try to heal me, Bronwyn. I don't want you taking on my darkness, my pain.'

She froze. 'River, I … I should never have told you that. You took it the wrong way. It's not as bad as it sounds.'

'Oh yes it is.'

'But you don't understand. It hurts me more not to heal. I didn't realise how much until I tried to stop after Samhain. I thought I wasn't able … I thought I was weak. But I'm starting to understand that I'm not. I'm strong. But if I'm to keep growing stronger, I need you to let me help you. Please let me help.'

By the Moon! He was making her beg. His beautiful, strong, determined, stubborn, free and joyful Bronwyn shouldn't beg. He wanted to look at her, to give in, to say 'of course you can try to heal me'. But he couldn't. He shook his head. There was too much inside him. He hadn't found enough peace. He wasn't ready for all this emotion. Not yet. If only she'd come a few hours later when he'd had time to calm himself properly. But she hadn't. Gritting his teeth, he glanced up then away. 'Sorry, I ... I'm too close to the edge.'

'I know. I can feel it in you.' Her gaze unfocussed as she took a step closer. 'I can see the Darkness clawing at you.'

'Don't!' He held up his filthy hand, the hand he'd almost touched her with. 'I might hurt you.'

'I don't believe that.' But she stopped where she was. 'You don't want to hurt me.'

'Of course I don't *want* to hurt you. I never *want* to hurt you. Ever. But I might not have a choice.'

'The Beast? It's prowling there, I can feel it, but you've still got control, so it's not the real problem. It's the Darkness. I have a feeling about the Darkness, about how it responds to me.' She reached out to touch his raised hand.

'No. Don't.'

'River. What is it?'

'You don't understand.'

'Then explain it to me.' She took another step closer.

It was one step too far. 'You can't touch me, because if you do, I won't be able to stop myself.'

'Stop yourself from what?'

'From stripping that dress from you, laying you down on that grass and fucking you until you come, screaming my name.'

18

Silence snapped between them.

Bron's mouth dropped open and she trembled to a halt. 'Oh,' she said on a sucked-in breath.

'Shit. I didn't mean ... I just ... Fuck.' He turned and raced away too fast for her to have a chance of catching up.

'Oh,' Bron said on another breath as she tried to take stock of what had just happened. River wanted to fuck her until she came screaming his name. A tingling, trembling blaze raced through her, centring in a pulsing throb low in her stomach. The muscles at her core clenched tight. She pressed her hand low, astonished at the sudden rush of damp in her panties.

River.

The thoughts she'd been having about him, the thoughts she'd been telling herself were wrong and false and stupid, crashed through her. Oh, Goddess. Were her knees actually trembling? Had the air suddenly got thicker, hotter? She needed to sit down. But there was nowhere nearby. She plopped down on the grass, mind spinning.

How had this happened? How had he crawled under her skin and into her heart so quickly, so easily? He was nothing like the man she'd dreamed of ever since she was a little girl. That dream man had never threatened her sense of self like River did. Aside from that, everything about him went against every type of man she'd ever allowed herself to get involved with—his brooding nature and those scars on his face that spoke of terrible pain endured with brave stoicism, while a massive turn-on for most women, were exactly the thing she usually avoided because of the nature of her powers. But this went far deeper than her empathy; far deeper than the need to fix, to heal.

'*... fucking you until you come, screaming my name.*'

She shook her head, trying to rid herself of the impact of those words, the image of him tearing off her dress, his mouth hot on hers making her feel wild and treasured at the same time as he bore her down to the soft grass and thrust into her.

'Oh!' She pressed her palm hard down on her pelvic bone, trying to stop the building wave of orgasm her thoughts had almost brought on. She'd always enjoyed sex; had always been willing to give and take and explore, but never once had she been brought to the point of orgasm by a couple of growled words and a few intense images. Only River had brought her to that point. And given that response, he could easily do it again. Her erotic dreams of the last few weeks featuring him had nothing on this.

'Fucking hell,' she moaned. How had this happened? She was always in charge sexually, never allowing anyone to give or take more than she was willing. How had River got past those defences? How had her control slipped to the point where she didn't have any?

She had no idea. She just wished he hadn't run from her. He might want to fuck her, but his reaction after he said that told her just as clearly that he didn't want to want to give into his urges.

Blowing out a long, shaky breath, she whispered to the air, 'What do I do now?'

'*Look to your roots. Use everything at your command.*'

The voice rang in her head. 'What do you mean?'

'*You already know.*'

She shook her head. She didn't already know. If she did, she wouldn't have just cocked up right royally with River when she needed to win him back. She would have been able to hold back her powers and not channel them into him earlier. She would have truly been able to help him when she'd touched him with her grandma's magically infused oil the only barrier between them.

Oh. My. Goddess.

That was it! She had seen it. Thought it earlier, then cast it aside, not once, but twice, not fully understanding the significance of what it had been.

The Darkness had not only *not* responded to her grandma's magic, it had shied away from it—because it didn't know what it was! 'Look to my roots, indeed.'

She pushed up from the grass, brushing her skirt down, trying to still the trembling of her fingers and put on a face of calm she was in no way close to feeling. She was excited, but she didn't want to give false hope to anyone, let alone herself.

But she had a clue now.

She had to follow old avenues. The family grimoires. She'd mentioned them before but hadn't really thought they'd be of use, because she'd thought of them as lesser. She thought of her original power as lesser. But what if they weren't? What if the answer was truly in what she had always been?

If the avenues she'd pursued so far hadn't worked, then there were other things she could try. It was time she stopped ignoring the ancient avenues of magic tied to her family and use them.

She jumped up and ran to her car.

Patrick emerged from the trees as she came around the corner of the house, forcing her to stop. 'Where are you going in such a hurry?'

'Home. I have an idea.'

He about faced and accompanied her to her car. When they got there, he faced her, his chocolate eyes filled with concern. 'I couldn't help but notice River race out of here. He didn't upset you, did he?'

She touched his cheek; the impact of the touch lit up his aura. 'No. I upset him. Again. It seems I can't get near him without hurting him in some way.'

Patrick opened her car door. 'He'll be fine. Iain is following him. He's fastest of the lieutenants and will be able to catch up and get River to slow down, and if he won't slow down, he's better able to throw his cloak around River as he runs beside him and use its influence to force River back to Packland.'

'Good thinking.'

Patrick's mouth quirked up on one side. 'That's what they pay me the big bucks for. And the fact I'm kind of pretty.'

Bron couldn't help but laugh, the warm bubble of sound breaking through the tension that had been riding her body for weeks. Patrick's low chuckle joined hers, his face breaking into an open smile that warmed her from within. 'Thank you for that, Patrick. I needed a good laugh.'

He pouted. 'Are you saying I'm not pretty?'

Laughter bubbled out of her as she reached up and pulled his head down for a quick kiss. 'You send all of woman-kinds' hearts aflutter with those big, long lashed eyes, and you know it. You don't need me stroking your ego further.'

'Yeah, but it's extra nice when you do it.'

'Flatterer.'

'Milady,' he said with a wide sweep, gesturing towards the driver's seat. 'Your carriage awaits.'

Still chuckling, she hopped into her car, the heat inside enfolding around her like an oppressive blanket. She normally enjoyed that heat, the promise of summer and long lazy days, but right now it made her skin itch. Shifting uncomfortably on her hot seat, she asked, 'Are you coming with me?'

He closed the door with a gentle push and then leaned on the open window. 'I wish. Jason's called me away. I've got all that energy from the power you pushed into me still surging through my veins. Jason wants me to run drills with some of the youngsters. But Gareth is here. He'll shadow you for the rest of the day.'

'Gareth?'

'Oh, I forgot you haven't met him yet. He's come up from the Packlands. He's my cousin. You'll like him.'

'Why do you say that?'

'Well, he's not quite as good looking as me, but he knows his way around a joke and has a special talent you'll appreciate.'

She glanced up at him, about to come back with a quip like she usually would, but the words jammed in her throat as her gaze caught on the faded shadow of the daylight moon high in the sky behind his shoulder. It was three-quarters full.

The full moon was drawing close again; somehow, the reality of that hadn't fully impacted on her. But seeing that three-quarter shadow in the sky, she was suddenly filled with an urgency that had previously only been a whisper in comparison. Instead of witty words, all she managed was, 'That sounds interesting.'

'Is that all you've got for me today?'

'I'm sorry ... It's just, I need to go.' She tore her gaze from the shadow moon and started the car. 'Is Gareth ready?'

'Ready and raring.' He gestured behind him to the young male who emerged from the shadows of the front portico, his sandy hair spiked up, eyes eager. He waved a jaunty salute, then rainbow light surrounded him and a moment later, a large, sandy wolf stood there.

Patrick tapped the roof of the car. 'Right to go.'

'Great. I'll see you later.'

'You sure will, gorgeous,' he said, the cheeky smile full blown on his face. But this time, it didn't make her smile.

She put the car in gear and took off, her mind full of River, the need to find something helpful in the grimoires made even more urgent by the sight of the faded shadow moon, three-quarters full in the sky.

She sped out of the driveway and down the street, heading towards home. A horn blared and there was a screech of brakes. Bron glanced in her rear-vision mirror—crap! She'd just pulled out into the main stream of traffic without checking properly. She waved apologetically at the poor driver but didn't slow down. She had to get home. The closer she got, the more she was certain there was an answer in the grimoires and in the magic of her heritage. She'd been foolish not to see it before.

Adeline had said when she first showed Bron the grimoires, *'The Goddess speaks to us through the words held in these old pages. They hold all the answers to your problems, mo daor, if only you know how to look.'*

She should have remembered that before now.

Well, she might have been an idiot but she wasn't going to be one any longer.

She pulled to a halt in front of the garage and leapt out of the car, vaguely aware of Gareth coming to a stop in the driveway, panting. He had wrapped his aural cloak around him to hide from anyone who wasn't Were or didn't have magic. She waved, gesturing to him so he knew he didn't have to follow her inside, then ran up to the front door.

Her hand trembled as she pushed the key in the lock and it took her a moment, but finally she was through. She dumped her keys and bag on the hall stand, the door slamming behind her as she ran down the hall to her bedroom.

Her grandma's old chest stood in the far corner of the room, the dark wood gleaming in the light coming from the window in such a way it looked like it was lit from within. An omen from the Goddess she was on the right path? She hoped so.

She unhooked the lock and flipped open the lid. It crashed against the wall. Uncaring of the dent in the plaster, she ran her hands over the tomes within while whispering under her breath, 'Goddess, please. I need some help figuring all this out. Please, speak to me. Let me know what to do.'

Nothing buzzed or flickered inside her as she ran her hands over the first layer of books, so she removed them and tried the next, and the next. She was onto the fourth layer when there the buzzing started. She moved to the right. The buzzing lessened. Back to the left. There!

The grimoire with the faded and scratched dark tan leather cover. She passed her hands from left to right and back again just to be sure. As her hands hovered over the dark tan grimoire it shifted, the front cover lifting, the pages inside sifting and rustling.

With a cry, Bron grabbed it up. 'Blessings be, Goddess. Thank you.' She placed the grimoire on the carpet before her and held her hands over it like she'd seen her grandma do. The grimoire trembled then fell still and silent.

'Come on.' Bron clapped her hands with a loud slap and then rubbed them together to awaken the energies. 'You can do this.' She focused her thoughts on the questions she needed answering and held her hands out again. The grimoire flipped open almost immediately. The cover smacked into the carpet and the pages fluttered, falling open on an entry three-quarters of the way through.

Bron picked it up and began to read. It was the story of the Healer and the Moon. Adeline had loved to tell her that story. She said it had helped her find herself when her husband had left. Bron hadn't understood back then, but now she did. The Healer in the story had used the power of the moon at Yule, a moon of rebirth and redemption—a true Healer Moon—to find her essence in her darkest time and save her people. She'd used a new version of an old kind of magic to infuse into her spell and that was what had helped her win the day. But she had only known to do it because of the information given to her in a vision quest.

Her grandma had mentioned that a version of the story was written in every grimoire, but each version held the same spell. Adeline had recited the story so often, Bron knew the spell by heart.

A sleep spell for vision questing. She chewed on her lip. She wasn't certain how that would help her with her problems, but if that was what the grimoire said she had to do, then she had to trust it. Vision or vision quests were by no means a straightforward means to an answer. But then again, Adeline had always said that all answers could be found in your dreams.

Bron had to trust that was true.

The spell had to be performed at dusk—so she still had time to gather the ingredients in her garden and settle herself with some meditation. Getting up, she placed the grimoire reverently on her dressing table and then went out into the garden with a basket and shears.

If it hadn't been obvious before, it was obvious now—the garden had been designed for her. Everything she needed was here; lemongrass for its uplifting properties, not to mention its great claritive scent; lavender to calm, and to enhance the lemongrass; rosemary with its dark green spiky leaves and spicy smell was one of those super herbs that was good for so many things, including its memory-enhancing properties. It was also wonderful for de-stressing and to help cure headaches, one of which had been crawling in her head ever since she'd woken that morning.

She put the rosemary in the basket and continued picking the herbs and flowers she needed for the spell. She stayed focused on the task until she walked past the quaint log seat River had placed near the water feature. The faint scent of chilli and chocolate tantalised her. She stopped, bending down to breathe in the richness of the fragile, fading blooms. They should have died by now, but River had managed to keep them alive. Why would he bother when the only person who would truly appreciate that scent here was her? It didn't make sense. He couldn't seem to stand being around her for long, despite the fact that he wanted to fuck her and make her scream his name.

But there were the blooms, kept alive, for nobody to enjoy but her.

As she breathed in the delicious aroma, thoughts spilled through her mind that just couldn't be true. She shook her head. He didn't like her. And she couldn't stand here wishing that he did. She had things to do. Problems to solve. Answers to find. Her true identity to uncover. Any other issues would have to wait until after she figured out who she was and what she was supposed to do.

She returned to the house, closing the sliding door behind her, but the scent of chilli and chocolate lingered, haunting her, teasing her, reminding her of something she could never have. She tried to ignore it as she fetched the grimoire and went about the preparations. But the insidious thoughts kept poking into her consciousness every time she breathed in the whisper of luxurious scent.

Finally, she slapped her hands on the bench top in the kitchen and said, 'Enough! Just because you want something doesn't mean you can or should have it.' Closing her eyes, she concentrated hard.

A flame leapt to life in every wick in every candle in the kitchen and lounge room. A multitude of scents filled the air, drowning out the exotic, erotic smell of chilli and chocolate that would always remind her of River. She took in a deep breath, taking the other scents inside her body and waited for the relief to take over and the tension to slide away.

It didn't.

Cursing, added a sprig of rosemary to her mortar and pestle, grinding it down to release the oils before sprinkling in the chopped lemongrass, lavender and chamomile.

As she worked, she began to hum under her breath, an old Muse song that always made her smile.

This time, she couldn't find her smile. Instead, the tension carved a groove between her brows.

'Bronwyn, grief is not forever. Stop acting like it is the only thing that matters.'

Her mother's words echoed in her head—words said after Adeline Kincaid's funeral all those years ago. Words that Bron had thought horribly cruel and heartless then. But now, she wondered if maybe her mother had a point. She wasn't the centre of anyone's universe—she wasn't even the centre of her own right now. That's what she needed to work on. Find herself. Be true to who she was. A Healer who would find a way to help the man she loved.

She sucked in a breath. Held it. Then let it out with a wild rush as the truth washed over her.

She loved him. She loved River.

She couldn't hide from it any longer. She was seeking truths and to do that, she had to be truthful to herself.

But oh ... it hurt, knowing he would never return her love. However, she wouldn't let it stop her from helping him.

Nothing could do that.

'Do the spell, Bron,' she muttered. 'Just do the damned spell.'

19

Hours later, Bron lay down on her bed. The jasmine she'd picked was in a bowl on her bedside table. The fresh oils she'd decanted were mixed and had been dabbed on her pulse points and at the point of her third eye. Candles had been set on all surfaces and lit; they flickered softly, a golden glow in the otherwise dark room.

Clouds obscured the three-quarter moon, so even though her curtains were open, she couldn't see the garden outside. She wished she could open her windows so she could at least smell those wonderful scents that lingered out there, blown on the still warm night air; however, if she smelled the chilli and chocolate bloom again, she wouldn't be able to concentrate on what mattered as she put herself into the dream state, so the windows remained closed.

Canting the spell three times in her head, three times in a whisper and three times out loud, she closed her eyes and began the meditation cantrip her grandma had taught her years ago when she couldn't quiet her mind. She breathed in deeply of the chamomile, lavender, rosemary and lemongrass from the burner near her bed, the faint sweetness of jasmine lingering on the edges of the key notes. The combination smelled like her grandma.

She smiled. Her body became heavy and her hands fell to her sides. The flicker of the candlelight shone through her eyelids, a golden glow that grew and filled the blackness in her mind.

Grandma. Everything always went back to her grandma.

Adeline had been so wise. She'd understood Bron before she'd understood herself. She'd introduced her to her heritage, opened up a world of possibilities for her, been there when Bron's parents had been too wrapped up in themselves and their work to care for their sensitive, magical daughter. She'd even helped Bron understand about the man who kept coming to her in dreams, laying claim to her in a way that was completely incomprehensible and not a little frightening to a young girl.

She'd always wanted to be like her grandma. To follow in her footsteps. To be loved and adored by her coven, by her customers, by her friends. When she'd watched her grandma work, she'd thought *this is the life I want*, if only she could stand up to her mother and father and tell them, 'I want to follow in Grandma's footsteps, not yours.' She'd thought she'd done Adeline proud—but now she wasn't so certain.

'You are not your grandma, daughter. You never were.'

The beautiful, lyrical voice wove around her, the words stabbing at her. Her heart pounded in her chest. Her breath rasped in her throat as she grasped at the courage to speak. 'You mean ... I'm not good enough to be her.'

'That is not what I said, Bronwyn Kincaid. You must make your own footsteps now, my moon daughter.'

'But I don't have my own footsteps. There are only my grandma's.'

'You are not your grandma,' the voice repeated.

Tears burned in her eyes as she stared into the oppressive dark that was the beginnings of the vision quest; the dark surrounded her, pressing in on her, making her shiver. 'Please ... what do you mean? Am I not meant to be a Healer? Are you saying I'm not good enough?'

Silence greeted her.

Moonlight suddenly pierced the dark; the vision quest had taken her outside and into a strange wood. Clouds skittered overhead in the night sky, the two-thirds moon bright and clear behind them. Silver shadows glinted strangely on the twisted old trees that surrounded her. The wind rustling the leaves above her head wasn't a friendly, whispering wind. It whistled, taunting her, as the words in her mind echoed back to her.

'You are not your grandma.'

Anger started to build inside her as those words wound around her again.

What right did some voiceless presence have to make her feel less than she was? 'You are wrong,' she shouted into the night. 'I am a Wiccan Healer, like my grandma was before me as Fate intended. I followed the path, the message left for me after she died.'

'That wasn't your path. You didn't listen to the whole message.'

The roar of her anger stuttered inside her, allowing doubt to shove its way back in. 'But, she left me everything—her shop, her house, the grimoires. I didn't mistake that message. I know I didn't. I picked up the thread Fate handed me and followed it. You can't tell me I wasn't supposed to do that?'

The odd, whistling wind rustled louder through the silvered leaves overhead. *'You didn't pick up the whole thread. Just as you are not picking up the whole thread now.'*

She jumped as the voice sounded around her, no longer just in her head. 'What th-thread?' Her voice was a dry husk. 'Wh-what are you talking about?'

'You are not only a Wiccan Healer. Nor are you only a witch.'

'Then what am I?' she asked the wind.

'The answer is in your heart.'

Anger rose again past the doubt; anger that had risen the day she realised she was tired of being told by her parents who she was meant to be, what she was supposed to do. The anger bubbled in her chest, making her breath come in short, sharp gasps as she spun in a circle and shouted to the sky. 'Who are you to tell me that? I'm leading a perfectly happy life—so what's wrong with that? Who are you to question that?'

'I am your Goddess. And you are not perfectly happy, Bronwyn daor.

And you won't be. Not until you have accepted who it is you are meant to be. The strength inside you must become the strength without. When you have embraced your true Fate, listened to the truth in your heart, then you will be perfectly happy. Then and only then will the man you dreamed of step out of the shadows and join you, hand in hand, to forever be a reflection of your strength at your side.'

'I don't know what you are talking about.'

'Yes you do. You saw it in a dream when you were a child, but with only the half thread of Fate in your hand, you forgot the important parts. Follow the thread. Pick it up from where it broke in two. Be who you are meant to be and trust in yourself. Listen to your heart, it will help you find the other part of your soul. Because when you do that, you will truly be whole and happiness will glow from within, not just be a face you put on to please others.'

'No, no!' she cried. 'I am happy. I want to be who I am.'

The voice didn't answer. There was only the echoing of the whistling wind saying over and over, *'Find the other part of your soul. Your happiness is there.'*

The wind disappeared and in its place a fog began to creep through the trees surrounding her, its fingers crawling along the ground, reaching towards her with a cold, grey, wet grip.

Ice skated along her skin, fear tightened in her chest as the fog began to swirl around her feet, pulling at her, grabbing at her clothes, soaking through the material until they were a heavy weight on her skin. She tried to brush off the fingers of fog, but it just swirled around her, a silver grey that held its own eerie light.

The world swam around her. She began to hyperventilate. Her heartbeat was a drum in her chest, its painful beat throbbing in her head. She lifted her hands towards the sky as the fog crawled up her body, pulling, pulling. 'Wake up. I want to wake up now.' She clicked her heels together three times, like Dorothy in *The Wizard of Oz*, using her "safe word" that was supposed to pull her out of the vision casting if it got too nasty for her to withstand.

Nothing happened.

'I want to go home, I want to go home, I want to go home,' she cried, her voice a piercing wail in the fog as her heels clicked together over and over. The fog sparked and swirled, pulling her further into the land of vision-dreams. She struggled and fought it until the breath squeezed her lungs and her cries died on her lips, heart a thunder in her chest.

'You cannot go home yet. There are still secrets to be found in the past. Things you must know if you are to conquer what must be conquered.'

A wolf's howl sounded out of the darkness.

'Go. Go see what the past has to tell you. You have ignored it for too long.'

Bron tumbled out of the whirling dark fog and landed in a crinkle of dried leaves. The scent of moss and damp earth filled her nose as she took in a sobbing breath. A wolf's howl sounded again—an aching, lonely heart. Pulled towards it, Bron stumbled to her feet, dead leaves clinging to her bare knees and hands. Not stopping to brush them off, she ran through the trees towards the sound tearing at her heart, squeezing her chest.

The wolf. It sounded so sad. So sorry. So full of grief and pain. She had to do something to stop the pain. To help.

The dark woods opened up onto a clearing. A witch stood in the middle of the clearing, sky clad, deep red hair a lick of blood on her pale skin which shone silver in the glow of the three-quarter moon above her. An ancient stone Dance, crumbled into disarray, stood sorry sentinel around her.

In the shadows of those stones, shapes crept towards her.

At first, the way they moved made Bron think they were animals, but then she realised they were people; men and women, clothed in animal skins sewn together with rags. They were thin and dirty, yet despite their unkempt state and the hesitant way they moved through the shadows, there was a certain fluid beauty in their forms.

One turned to look behind him, his eyes glowing eerily blue in the dark. Another looked back, and another—amber and silver orbs glowing in the night, seeing beyond the light and into the dark places where only shadows hid.

Were.

Except these Were, in their human forms, were more animalistic and wilder than any Were she'd ever met.

One of the Were lifted his head to the sky and howled. The female to his left picked up his howl. Shivers skated over Bron's skin as she saw more and more male and female Were—adults and children—slip from the shadows of the trees, walking towards the Dance and the witch standing naked at its centre.

The witch, seemingly oblivious to her audience, raised her arms to the moon, and in a voice as clear and enthralling as a nightingale's song, called out, 'Moondust, come to me.'

Shivers traced fingers of excitement across Bron's skin and up and down her spine as moondust fell from the sky at the witch's command, covering her in sparkling glitter that swirled and reshaped itself as she moved her hands in the moonlight.

The Were stopped as one, their bodies vibrating as if they fought to move; a rising sea held at bay by some mysterious, unseen, yet turbulent force. Then as one they howled, the sound piercing the night with their fear-tinged, grief-stricken song.

The witch's lips moved, her voice a mere whisper among the howls, but a whisper full of magic that made it resonate above the noise around her. 'Have faith, my friends.'

A male stepped forward, taller and broader of shoulder than the rest, with the bearing of a King—confident and yet weighed down with more worries than one person should ever hold.

The Alpha.

Three others—two male and one female—leapt to stop him, but he turned to them, holding up his hands. 'Be still. I will not come to harm. The witch has promised and she has bound herself to that promise. Her spell binds her far tighter than it binds us.' He continued walking towards the Dance, those behind him clearly on guard despite his words of reassurance.

Bron edged towards the Dance, mesmerised, an invisible watcher, an astral traveller, brought to this place by the vision quest.

The Alpha stopped just outside the Dance where the moondust

swirled and sparkled in the ever-brightening glow of the three-quarter moon.

'I am so very glad you have come,' the witch said, her lips curved in a gentle smile.

Fists two rocks at his sides, the Alpha's gaze darted from her to the Dance and the moondust and then back to her. His chest heaved, nostrils flaring as he breathed heavily. He seemed to be fighting against something. Tendons stood out in his neck and shoulders as he fought against whatever fear held the others at bay one hundred paces from the Dance. Yet he didn't run. He stood firm, his gaze intense, his stubborn form of bravery stamped in the jut of his jaw and the steel in his blue eyes.

'Are you so certain of this, Healer?' His voice was gruff, hidden pain and an edge of violence bringing a rawness that made Bron flinch.

Yet the witch was serene as she said, 'I am. This is the answer to all of our problems. But you must trust me.'

'And if this trial tonight works?'

'Then we will go forward with the Pact.' The light from the moondust brightened and lit the entire Dance.

A low growl rumbled in the Alpha's throat, then lifting his head, he howled, the saddest, most grief-filled sound Bron had ever heard. With the sound still echoing in the silence around them, he lowered his head and looked at the witch, his ice-blue eyes burning almost white hot with a glow of reddened coal at their centre. In a voice rough with bloodlust, he growled, 'I cannot hold the wolf at bay if you keep up with your magics.'

'I do not wish you to. Let it loose, Ioan. Only then will the McVales be free.' The witch gestured to him to enter the Dance, her long red hair blown in wild tangles away from her face by an ethereal wind that had no earthly home.

She held her hand out to the Alpha. 'Come. From this time we will be brother and sister. Joined by blood and magic, by friendship and love. Tonight I give you the gift of choice. Turn tonight, on this three-quarter moon, and allow your wolf to feel the freedom of its change and know that neither of you is a slave. When you see what I say is true, you and yours will join me and give me and mine the gift of your strength. Come. Mark my flesh and we will be one.'

'My wolf will kill you.'

She held his gaze. 'No. I trust you and your wolf. The question is, do you trust yourself to shake off the Darkness?'

The Alpha, his bare chest glistening with sweat, his breath a heavy rattle in his throat, held still for one, interminable second.

Then he moved into the light of the Dance.

The moment he stepped past the edge of the stones and into the moonlit-drenched space in its centre, he came to a shuddering halt. Stiffening, his teeth gritted together with snapping force. Tendons stood out on his neck, shoulders, arms. His feet curled into the green grass, his back arched. Something writhed under his skin, black and oily. The sight of it made Bron shiver. The blackness seemed to be fighting something, to be trying to sink back into hiding, but it wasn't winning. The Alpha's eyes widened, and on a terrible, agonised roar, his head tipped back and the blackness flew out of his mouth, nose and eyes. The moment it left him, he fell to the ground, sweat-covered and shaking. The black, amorphous blackness—similar to what she'd seen in River—hovered above him, swirling and pulsing as if it was trying to get back to him, but the light glowing down on the Dance held it contained.

'By my Goddess's will, be gone,' the witch cried. She made a shoving motion with her hands. Golden light hit the dark, swirling shape. It screeched, a sound akin to tearing metal, then the Darkness surged and split in half. Both halves moved in different directions then swooped down, back towards the home it had dwelled in for aeons beyond counting.

But the witch lashed out with the golden light again before it got close to its target. Fingers of light grasped the two halves, lifted it up away from the Alpha, and pushed it together. Hands outstretched, sweat on her brow, she pushed her hands together, shaking with effort. 'Be gone, I say,' she cried again.

A high-pitched wail split the night sky, lashing at all those below with a desperate threat-laced plea, and then the dark mass that was the Darkness was gone.

Trembling, the witch lowered her hands and wiped her brow. A relieved smile blossomed on her face and she turned to the Alpha as he slowly pushed to his feet. 'Now it is time to take back control of your birthright as it was always meant to be.' She made a sweeping gesture and the moondust she'd held aloft with her will fell on him.

A cry exploded from his throat as the silver of moondust landed on him, his back stiffening, arms thrown out—but this time, it was like he received a benediction. The light of the moondust paled in comparison to the burst of golden-rainbow light that swept over his body. He began to shake, then his form shattered outwards.

Bron threw up her hand in front of her eyes, blinded by the throb of light that surrounded him.

'Come. Witness this.' Bron looked up to see the witch hold her hand out to her. 'Witness how the moondust can be a cure, not a curse.'

Bron held out her hand—she couldn't stop herself—but as she touched the witch, something shifted inside her, melding, flowing. Coolness touched her skin and she looked down—she was sky clad! Not only that, she stood where the witch had been standing in the Dance.

She spun around. The witch was gone. She looked down again; her skin glistened like diamonds as thousands of sparkles of moondust fell on her.

The witch hadn't disappeared—she'd become the witch.

A howl tore the air just metres from her, almost deafening in its ferocity. The largest silver- and gold-coloured wolf she'd ever seen stood in place of the Alpha, its lips pulled back in a snarl, its blue eyes subsumed by the glowing red of bloodlust.

She whimpered, fear a terrible pain in her chest.

Run.

She knew she should run.

Yet she didn't. Instead, against her will, she held out her hands to the snarling, vicious animal before her as it crouched, ready to spring, its lips pulled back over sharp white teeth.

Run.

But the witch that she was now a part of didn't run. She turned her head to expose her neck, and said, 'Blood me. I trust you to keep us both alive because you are now free.'

As the moondust settled on the Alpha wolf, making his fur look like it sparkled with a thousand diamonds, he leapt at her exposed throat, his snarl snapping through the air just before his teeth sank into her skin.

20

ron screamed, sure that her jugular was about to be torn open, but the witch simply lifted her hands and the moon-dust rose into the air. Rainbow light streamed around her. Sharp canines withdrew from her throat in a sharp, slice of pain, and then before her stood a Were male.

But not the Were male from the vision quest. This was a male who came straight out of her dreams. His hazel eyes glowed as he looked down on her. The white twist of scars across his handsome face were visible in the moonlit dark of the room. As was the shag of auburn hair.

All precious to her.

'River?' she asked, unsure if he was really there or if she was still in the middle of her vision quest.

'Bronwyn. Are you okay?' He sat on the edge of her bed.

She nodded, unable to speak as his deep voice melted the fear and uncertainty inside her. He reached out as if to touch her, but then drew back.

She sat up, reaching for him before he could stand, her hands colliding with his hard, T-shirt covered chest. She gripped the material, pulling him back down to sit on the bed, and burrowed into his chest.

'River.' She breathed out his name like it was a balm. 'River.' She didn't care why he was here. He was here. That was all that mattered. 'River,' she whispered as his arms went around her.

His hand was in her hair, holding her against his chest, his other rubbing up and down her back, only a thin swathe of the cotton singlet and yoga pants she wore between his hand and her skin. She pressed harder against him, burrowing her face into him, clutching at his back as if she were afraid he would pull away at any moment. 'River.' His name trembled from her on a sigh of relief.

He didn't say anything, but a long soft growl hummed in his throat. That growl soothed her as soft words from him never could. His lips were against her brow, pressing to her hair. She lifted her face, needing to feel those lips on hers, reaching for him. He stilled, his lips a bare centimetre from hers.

'River?' He began to draw away. 'No!' She clutched him to her even though if he wanted to break her hold, he could. Easily. He didn't move further away, but the liquid warmth of before was gone. He was tense now. That tension thrummed against her nerves like an off-tune guitar string. 'River. Don't go. I need you.'

'No. You don't.' His voice was gruff, but not unkind. Not to her. Even when he'd spat out that he wanted to fuck her, it hadn't been unkind. It had been full of wanting. Why hadn't she noticed?

He shifted back. Panic enveloped her and she cried, 'Don't leave me.' She grabbed his arm, hauling herself back against his chest, face buried in the warmth there, hands gripping the T-shirt, knuckles pressing into his back.

The vision quest's message had been clear. Be true to herself.

And the truth was, she loved River. She wanted to be with him.

There was nothing wrong with that. There never had been. Maybe he didn't want her in the same way, but he did want her. And for now, after the confusion and violence of all she'd seen in the vision quest, she needed his solid warmth, the certainty of the desire he caused to race through her system. She needed him against her, skin to skin. She wanted to share her love with him. There could never be anything wrong with that. 'Don't go,' she whispered against his chest.

A sigh brushed over her hair as he trembled against her. Was he still undecided or was he waiting for her to make the first move?

Her fingers found the edge of his T-shirt, slipped underneath to touch the warm, firm skin. He sucked in a harsh breath. But he didn't move away.

Taking courage, she shifted closer, practically sitting in his lap, her hip brushing against his erection. His breath hitched again and he tried to push her back. But he didn't mean the repudiation; she could feel that clearly enough with how his fingers clutched her clothing, holding her even as he tried to pull away.

She gripped him tighter and pressed her lips to the pulse point in his neck, nipped at his skin. He jerked, a low groan sounding under her lips.

She licked at the hurt her teeth had caused.

'Bronwyn.' The harsh sound was a caress—a rough, desire-tinged caress. Encouraged, her lips moved against his throat as she moved so she could swing her leg over him to straddle his lap. His hands gripped her hips, tight, before she could settle down onto him, almost as if he was about to push her away. But he didn't. He just held her there, hovering over him, not allowing her to press herself against the rigid length of him.

'Bronwyn. Stop.' His fingers tightened, sinking into her skin. 'You don't know what you're doing.'

'Does this feel like I don't know?' She kissed up his neck, her hands on his shoulders now, moving up into his thick, silky hair.

'You're half asleep.' His voice, a tight husk of sound, thrilled through her, pulsing into her core.

'I can promise you,' she said between kisses, 'I'm not even close to being asleep.'

His hands, gentle yet strong, grasped her shoulders and pulled her away from his neck in such a way that she was still unable to sink onto his lap—he was so much taller than she was. 'Bronwyn. You have to stop. This isn't right. This isn't what I came here for.'

'What did you come for?'

His gaze searched hers for a long moment, his breath coming fast. 'I was at the Packhouse looking after Bluebelle.'

'Bluebelle?' she sat back. 'What happened?'

'She hurt herself. Skye and Jason brought her back to the Packhouse to be patched up, but you never arrived there and she would only let me and Shelley and Skye touch her. So I helped.'

Bron nodded, relieved to hear her Familiar was in good hands. She'd go over and check on her later. After she dealt with these feelings for River. 'But that doesn't explain why you are here,' she said, watching him carefully.

'You were distressed.'

'How did you know that?'

'I ...' His gaze slid from hers. 'Through Skye. Her link with you.'

She swallowed hard against the sudden cold that swept through her. 'You're lying. Why?'

His lips pressed together and he shook his head.

'There's a connection.' She put her hand on his chest over his heart. 'Here. Between us. I know you feel it. Why are you denying it?'

His jaw was clenched so tight now, she thought it would break, but his hands were gentle on her shoulders, his thumbs moving across her skin in a silken glide that sent molten shivers chasing straight to her core. 'I don't ... want the connection,' he bit out.

Ice shivered down her spine, sunk into her skin and froze her desire. She swallowed hard, but knew she had to face up to this. It was part of her truth. 'You mean you don't want me. I'm not enough for you. I push you and annoy you and hurt you and have forced you to accept my attempts at helping you and all for nothing. I get it. I understand. But River, I want you to know, it's not like that for me.' The words spilled out of her, necessary but painful. 'I know I should see you as my best friend's brother, my client. And I've tried. I've tried so hard to do the right thing. But I can't. I just can't.' Her fingers clutched against her heart, her body trembling. 'I want you, River. I need you so badly it hurts.'

'Fuck.' One hand dropped to her waist, his fingers clenching on the soft material of her singlet top, his intense gaze burning into her.

She squeezed her eyes closed. *Oh, Goddess! He hates me. And it's all my fault. All my stupid, idiotic fault.* 'I'm so sorry. Let me get off and then you better leave.' She shifted, making her fingers unclench and let go of his hair.

'Don't move.'

'But River, I know you don't want this. You couldn't have made it clearer.'

'You've got no idea what I want.'

Then his mouth was on hers. Hot. Hard. Wet. Wild. The taste of him was in her mouth before she had a chance to breathe, to think, to feel, his tongue tangling with hers in an open-mouthed kiss that was all want and possession. He twisted, lifting her, and laid her down on the bed, the hard heat of his erection pushing against her core.

Something tore. The cool of night air caressed her skin, then heat as his chest pressed against her breasts, his legs, still encased in jeans, falling between her parted ones, pushing him more firmly against her core. She sobbed with the joy of the sensation; of being weighted down, pushed into the soft give of the mattress by him. By this man she had longed for, for so long, without even realising it.

His lips left hers and she whimpered a protest, but then bit back on a cry as his hot, firm mouth pressed just under her jaw then chased down her neck, nipping, sucking, licking her heated, desire-slicked skin.

'Bronwyn.' Her name was a ragged breath against her neck. 'So beautiful.' His hand moved, fingers tracing down her neck, across her chest to cup her breast. She pushed up into his palm, grinding her core against the erection bursting at the seam of his jeans while her hands traced over the muscles of his shoulders and down his back. The hand in her hair tightened, almost painfully, but then it moved, gentled, his thumb sweeping her cheek, touching her mouth. She rolled her head to take it into her mouth, sucking. 'Ah, by the

Moon,' he groaned. 'You are going to be the death of me, Bronwyn-mine.'

'Kiss me, River.' It sounded more like begging than a demand, but she didn't care. Right now she was a slave to him, to the sensation of him lying on top of her, pressing her into the bed.

'Not a good idea. This has already gone too far.' He stared down at her, eyes burning coals of amber in the semi-dark room, a gaze that seared into her soul, shattering her open.

'River,' she pleaded. 'Don't let go. I don't care why you're doing this right now, but please, don't stop. If you stop I'll fall apart and never be able to pull myself back together.'

His hand brushed back and forth across her breast, fingers circling the nipple as the other hand moved back up to her throat, holding her still in a way that was pure predatory male. She moaned and pressed into him. His burning, liquid hazel eyes with their amber centre bore into hers. 'If we do this, it means you are mine.'

'I'm already yours.'

He hissed out something that sounded like, 'you have no idea', but she didn't have time to process it, because his lips were on hers again, his tongue brushing the seam. She opened, welcomed him inside.

Welcomed him home.

Fire leapt inside her, racing through her veins, searing her as he deepened the kiss. She gasped for breath but didn't break away as his lips ravaged hers, his tongue doing things inside her mouth that she never remembered experiencing before. It was a new dance.

The last dance.

The thought flamed through her mind and then was gone as his hand shifted on her throat, his thumb stroking over the pulse point at her neck. 'I want to bite you, right here.'

An image from the vision quest, of the wolf leaping at her neck, had panic rising for a moment, but when she opened her eyes there was something more than lust in his gaze. He cherished her. In his eyes, she was a treasure waiting to be found, opened up, explored, loved.

Nobody had ever looked at her like that.

She turned her head to the side, exposing the pulse that visibly thumped under her skin. 'Take whatever you want,' she murmured. 'Whatever you need.'

'Do you know what you're agreeing to?' he growled.

She nodded. She'd studied the nuances of Were social interactions—it was her job as Pack Healer to know. This was an act of trust between lovers. She was more than willing to give him her trust. In fact, if he wanted it, she would give him her love.

But that was for another time. He was here with her. It was what she'd longed for. What she'd dreamed about ever since that first day of treatment when he'd taken his top off in front of her. No. This was something she'd dreamed about far longer than that. This sense of rightness. She'd been so wrong about her dream man. It was River. It had always been River. She needed him, to chase away the nightmares, to fill the empty part of her that had always been there. She had to make him see what could be between them if he only allowed it to be so. And this lesson in trust was the first step.

He hesitated.

'River. I need to feel you. Everywhere.'

His growl turned into a moan and then his mouth and teeth were on her neck. She bit back a gasp as his teeth sunk in, surrounding her pulse point, not breaking the skin, but marking it deeply. She would have a bruise there for all to see. He licked across the spot then bit down a little harder, a low hum sounding in his throat.

'Oh, Goddess!' she gasped. It should be painful, but it wasn't. Her skin tingled where his lips touched. Warmth expanded out from the pressure of his teeth on her skin, a corresponding warmth growing at her centre and around her heart. His fingers circled her nipple, lightly pinching the bud so that it ached with wanting more. She sobbed as his hand left her nipple, travelling down her stomach, her muscles jumping under his touch. She writhed on the bed, pushing her core harder against his erection still firmly encased in his jeans.

'Take your jeans off. I need you inside me now.'

'Not yet,' he growled against her skin, the vibration of sound creating a new sensation that made her want to scream. He was creating a storm inside her with not much more than his teeth and tongue and the weight of him on top of her. What would it be like when he was actually inside her?

The thought exploded in her mind like mini-fireworks. Her fingernails dug into his back as she struggled to get closer, to shift her head. But he wouldn't let her move. He had her pinned, teeth at her neck, hips pushing her into the bed, legs wound around hers. Even his hands—one on her throat, the other on her stomach—were keeping her in place.

She vibrated with the urgency of her need. An urgency he seemed determined to ignore.

Whimpers puffed out of her lips as he stroked along her stomach, his fingers making little whirling patterns on her skin, dipping into her belly button, moving lower and then back up again. Teasing. Tormenting. 'You're driving me insane.'

His lips curled against her neck as he made soothing noises in his throat. But still he held her captive with his hand, his mouth, his teeth still gripping her, surrounding the pulse of life force in her neck, as his other hand continued its languorous path down her stomach.

His fingers ran along the top of her light cotton yoga pants. 'These have to come off,' he whispered.

He shifted enough so that she could lift her hips, but before she could reach to help him remove her pants, he'd torn them off, the material making a short, sharp ripping sound in the quiet of the room. 'Hey!' She protested weakly as his hand ran up her leg, soothing any hurt. 'They were my favourite thing to sleep in.'

He lifted his head as his fingers trailed up her thigh. 'You don't need them.' His finger brushed over the curls at the apex of her legs. 'When you sleep with me, you'll sleep with only me wrapped around you.' He nudged her legs further apart with his thigh and then brushed his fingers back and forth over the seam of lips protecting her core. She whimpered as the ache increased. 'When you sleep with me, you'll sleep with only me this close.' He pushed his fingers between those lips, slipping through the slickness of her desire.

She jerked, her breath caught in her throat as the sensation of his finger sliding across her labia and circling her clit, tore through her. 'R ... River.'

'When you sleep with me, you'll sleep with only me inside you.' He rubbed his thumb over her clit, pushed his finger inside her and bit down on the pulse point in her neck.

Something in her brain exploded. Behind her eyes she saw black and then the brightest light as her body arched up with the orgasm that had her, sudden and hard, in its grip. 'River!' His name was a scream, cut off by his mouth on hers. His thumb worked her as his finger was joined inside her by another, pumping in and out, as the pulses of orgasm clenched harder and higher and tighter; until she thought she might pass out from the pleasure of it. She'd never had an orgasm like it. It went on and on.

He shifted; his hand left her throat, his lips and teeth left her skin —not that their absence freed her to move because his thumb and fingers on her clit and inside her made that an impossibility—and then he was back and she sighed as the skin of his legs nudged hers further apart.

He pulled his fingers out of her, but before she could protest, the tip of his impressive erection slid through her wetness to hover over the entrance to her core.

There he halted.

She whimpered again, the orgasm still pulsing inside her. She tried to lift her pelvis, to join them, but he grasped her hip in one hand and held her still. His eyes blazed with a fire of desire that threatened to burn her to cinders. It sent a little frisson of fear through her, alongside soul-baring longing. Incredible though it seemed, that look was for her. It might not last, but it was hers and hers alone for now. Reaching up, she cupped his face in her hands, her fingers tracing over the stubble of his unshaven chin, the firm perfection of lips that had tortured her with his kisses alone, tracing the cool lines of the twisting scars on one side and the smooth, warm skin on the other.

'River. Now.'

He shook his head. 'If I do this, there'll be no turning back.'

'I don't want to turn back. I want this.'

'You will be bound to me. You can't want that.'

Bound? Of course she wanted that. But he didn't mean it. He didn't want her. This was just her desire speaking. And given it was speaking so loudly, she decided not to question it, but let it scream out its ultimate need. Holding his face in her hands, she looked into his blazing eyes and said words that seemed torn out of her. 'I want it more than I want to breathe. Only you can give me what I need. But please, you have to give it now.' She pushed her pelvis up again as his grip on her hip loosened and the tip of his erection slipped inside her.

The burning increased. 'Oh, Goddess, River. I'm burning. Make it stop. Make it stop.'

With a growl, he dropped his head to her neck, bit and pushed inside her, the long thick length of him almost more than she could stand. Her scream of pleasure tore through the air, ringing around her.

He held still. Lifted his head. 'Bronwyn?' His voice was filled with worry.

'Please,' she sobbed. 'Don't stop. I need you, River. I need you.'

He peeled her hands from his shoulders and held them against the pillow as he began a slow, long, rocking motion.

'Oh, Goddess!' she cried out again.

He kept up the motion, slow at first, then increasing in speed, his lips on hers, on her neck, sucking on her nipples, and all the time he held her hands, their fingers twined.

The fire inside her built higher and higher, remorseless, burning every thought and feeling in its passion-fuelled wake until she was nothing but muscles tightening and pulsing in a wave that caught her and took her, crashing over to tumble and spin in a wild vortex of ecstasy.

River cried out at the same time as the orgasm fully took her, his energy filling her with so much light, she thought she might be seared by it from the inside out. But even through the searing, blinding lights, one colour always held steady—burning hazel tipped with amber and gold, staring into her eyes, into her soul, owning her, claiming her, tearing her apart and putting her back together in a new body that would never be able to forget this moment it was born anew.

Wrapped together, they spiralled into the warm, welcoming dark.

21

Bron awoke slowly, aware she was hot. And full of a sensation of heavy lethargy. The red flare of daylight danced across her closed eyelids—the day had obviously well and truly started.

Why on earth was she still in bed? Was she sick? Apart from the heat and the lethargy—not to mention muscles that were a little sore—she didn't feel sick. Then why was she still in bed? She never slept this late. She usually got up at the crack of dawn.

She tried to sit up.

A hard, warm band across her chest prevented her, as did the growl next to her ear.

'You're not going anywhere.'

'River.' Memories of the night before cascaded through her mind. 'You're still here.'

'I'm not finished with you yet.'

She shifted, smiling as his erection pressed against her bottom. 'I'll never be finished with you.'

Muscled, hair-roughened legs nudged her thighs apart and then he was inside her, hot and hard and long, filling her, as his hand cupped her breast and his mouth moved to press a hard, wet kiss to the juncture of her neck and shoulder.

For long, silent minutes, she did nothing but let him ride her from behind, moving with him to increase the pleasure, arcing her neck and turning her head so that she could meet his mouth for a hard, tongue-tangling kiss, before giving herself over completely to the sensation of him inside her, his hand on her breast, his other skating along her stomach to bury his fingers in her curls and slide his index finger over her clit until her body tensed. Lights exploded behind her eyes and she was carried away again on waves of sensation more intense than anything she'd ever felt before.

He tensed, crying out her name as he spilled his seed inside her before biting down on the tender spot on her neck he'd marked the night before.

She gasped, pleasure more intense than before shuddering through her.

Then his thumb pressed into just the right spot, circling. The wave of orgasm expanded, pulling him into her and along with her. They rode it together, lost to anything but each other for what seemed a blissful eternity.

She resurfaced from her pleasure-induced fugue state, a smile on her lips. River still had his arms wrapped around her, his muscled stomach and chest against her back, his cock still inside her, filling her.

She couldn't help but smile in utter contentment. She had given herself to him, loved him with everything in her, and yet it was deeper than anything she'd ever imagined. She almost purred as she whispered, 'Is this a dream?'

'I don't know,' he said gruffly. 'You tell me.'

She frowned. His arms were no longer loose around her; they were stiff with tension. He also sounded uncertain. So unlike the man who'd just told her he wasn't finished with her and then loved her like she'd never been loved before. Then it dawned on her. Of course he was worried. Being with her was his first time. But how could he not know it had been good for her? More than good. Extraordinary. Mind blowing. World changing. She had to find the words to explain it to him.

'River,' she said, trying to turn around, but he was still inside her, his arms banded around her waist, one hand cupped possessively over her breast. She liked the feeling of his hand there. She wanted to make sure it stayed there. That there was the possibility of a repeat.

Tentatively, she reached up and stroked his cheek and tried to let her heart speak the right words. 'Last night ...' Her throat cracked and she took a deep breath, started again. 'Last night was the most incredible experience of my life. I've never felt so close to anyone. It has never been like this for me before. So ... so ... intense. So ... fulfilling. I don't want this to ever end.'

'Fuck.' He tensed even more. 'What have I done?'

Ice punched into Bron's chest at his words. The bliss of a moment ago was instantly torn apart by the ravaging grief in his voice. An arctic chill chased over her skin as his arms loosened their hold on her and he pulled out of her, edging away.

No. She wouldn't let him pull away. Not this time. Not after what they'd shared, after what she'd learned about herself last night in the vision quest. She still wasn't sure what it all meant, but she was sure about the message it told her about her heart. She had to follow her heart. Believe in what it told her. And it was telling her this man was hers.

She wrapped her arms around his broad chest before he was able to roll out of the bed. 'Don't turn away from me, River. Talk to me. Tell me what's going on here.'

He stared at her, his mouth a grim tight line. 'I should never have done this.'

Tears burned, his words acid on her heart, but she wouldn't let them spill. She could not let him tear them apart without telling her why. 'Why shouldn't you have done this?' Her voice was almost too thick with tears to be understood, but she held on tighter. 'We are two consenting adults who decided to make love. There could never be anything wrong with that. Not with what happened between us. Not when it felt so right. And I know I wasn't the only one to feel that. Was I?'

River almost swore as her words tore at his heart. He'd fucking made her cry. What kind of an arsehole was he? 'No. You're not wrong.' But he was. What he'd done was. 'But it still doesn't change the fact I shouldn't have done this. I shouldn't have let things go this far.'

'But why?'

Her hands were fists against her chest as if she was holding in something bursting to get out. No. Not bursting to get out. Tearing her up inside by the look on her face, in her eyes.

Fuck! He raked his hand through his hair, wishing he didn't have to look into those beautiful, tear-drenched eyes, but if he didn't, he wasn't much of a man or Were. Nostrils flaring, breath coming too fast for comfort, he met her pained gaze and said, 'Because I forced this on you. I gave you no choice.'

'W-what?' She blinked. A tear spilled down her cheek. 'This was my choice. I chose this. If anyone forced anyone here, it was me forcing you.'

He almost laughed at that. But there was nothing funny about this. 'You don't understand.'

'Then explain it to me, River.'

He stared at her, words not coming. How could he explain it to her? How could he tell her that she was his entire world? That she would always be his choice. That she was his mate, yet he couldn't accept her as such. He had never wanted her to know. Never wanted to make the bond take hold. Yet, despite all that, he'd just gone and mated with her, starting the bond in a way that would be hard to undo, and all without her knowledge or consent.

She thought they'd had sex. A possible one-night stand as far as she was concerned. And yet he'd started the process that would tie her to him for life simply because he was too weak to stand strong. The Beast had torn down nearly every avenue of strength he had in him, and what he had left he was putting into fighting what the Beast was doing to him.

He'd had no more to fight the inexorable pull of Bronwyn. And so he'd given in and experienced ... heaven.

She watched him, her beautiful eyes filling with despair with every moment that passed in silence. 'Why don't you want me?'

Her voice sounded so small. It tore at him, tore at his last shred of self-respect. Reaching for her, he pulled her to him, holding tight. 'I want you, Bronwyn. I've never wanted anything the way I want you. But I can't have you.' She jerked in his arms, but he didn't let go, just held tighter, his lips against her hair. 'I shouldn't have let last night happen. Not because I didn't want it with every shred of my being, but because it wasn't right. Not for you.'

She pulled away and this time he let her go. 'Why would you say that? If I wanted to be with you, then that is right for me, and nothing you say can make me believe otherwise.'

He held her face in his hands, stroking a single tear from her silken skin. 'You gave me a precious gift last night, but it's a gift I don't deserve because you don't understand why you gave it to me.'

She hiccoughed out a laugh. 'I gave myself to you because I needed to. Because I wanted to. What's not to understand about that?'

He stilled. Now. He had to tell her now. 'You've said during our sessions together that something is blocking you. You've assumed it was the Darkness and I've let you believe that, because it seemed the right thing to do. But it's only partially true. *I* was blocking you too.'

'What? Why?'

'I blocked you because you are an empath and I was afraid you'd find out how I feel and that it would influence you. I couldn't have that.'

'But ... but that could have affected the treatment. Why ...' She stopped, took in a deep breath and said on a whisper. 'Why couldn't I feel you blocking me? And for that matter, how were you able to block me?'

Here it was. The truth he couldn't escape. He touched her lip with his thumb, the warmth of her a delight even as the knowledge shivered through him that this might be the last time she'd let him touch her in this way. 'I used the bond that ties us together. Just like Jason did to Skye when he was trying to protect her from her powers and how they'd react to the truth of him.'

'But they're mates.'

He nodded.

Her eyes widened as she finally came to understand what he was trying to say to her. 'You're my mate?'

He shook his head. 'I can't speak for that. All I know is that from the first moment I laid eyes on you, I knew you were *my* mate.'

Her eyes wide with wonder, she slowly—so slowly, as if she was afraid he'd shy away—lifted her hand to touch his face. 'Why didn't you say anything?'

He swallowed, tried to look away, but couldn't. His entire being was pinned by her gaze, her touch, her trust and desire. 'I'm broken, Bronwyn. I don't deserve you.'

A tear trembled out of her eye. 'So, you mean to deny me?'

The pain in her voice slashed across his heart. Yet, he couldn't lie to her. Not now. 'I did. I wanted to deny you. I never meant to burden you with my existence, but I wasn't strong enough. I couldn't stay away. I couldn't deny the need to be with you. I couldn't deny you when you sought me out. The Healing sessions were exquisite torture.'

A little burbling laugh escaped her as she whispered, 'They were for me too. I wanted to touch you in ways a Healer just shouldn't want to touch a patient.'

'I'm sorry. Those desires were probably driven into you from me.'

She shook her head, the pain in her eyes dissolving as joy lit their depths. 'No. My desires are my own.' And as if to prove it, she nuzzled up his throat, over his chin and then pressed her lips over his.

'Bronwyn. This isn't—'

'Shh.' She put her fingers over his lips, cupping his face, holding him there with a strength that surprised him. 'Don't say this is a bad idea. It's not a bad idea. It's the best idea. I want you. So much it hurts. I've never felt something this strong. It's like if you're not there, I'm only half of who I am meant to be.' She frowned. 'I dreamed you when I was little and held onto an idea of you that was only half formed. Until last night, I didn't realise the meaning of what I felt for you.' She leaned up, pressed her lips to his then leaned back enough to whisper, 'But I know now. I see you and only you and I can't imagine a time when I'll see any different. And if I understand this mating thing, it only works if both parties are involved and are in total agreement with how they feel for the other. So, if I am your mate, that makes you mine.'

'That only works for Were.'

She shook her head. 'No. It works for humans and witches too. I know it does.'

'How can you know?'

She brushed her fingers over his frown, smoothing over his skin, wiping away his concern with the soft caring touch that came from the heart of her. 'Look at your parents. At Skye and Jason. Skye always felt drawn to Jason in a way that was inexplicable to her until she realised what it meant. She says it's deeper than love. That she feels what he feels and he feels what she feels and that it feeds on itself until their emotions are intertwined and entangled.' She smiled, her eyes misting over with some memory he knew was of his sister. 'Shelley was worried it was like an addiction. That Skye wasn't seeing clearly. I mean, for her to say she could only be whole with Jason ...' She shook her head. 'It sounded preposterous. She'd always tried so hard to be her own person after the way your grandmother tried to rule her life. I have to admit, I was a little worried too.' Her gaze cleared and she looked up at him. 'But now, I understand. I am myself, but I'm also part of you, as you are part of me. You are the part of my soul I never knew was missing, but now I have it, I never want to do without it.'

Her words were like claws tearing at his heart, making his wolf whimper and the Beast growl in triumph. He'd allowed himself to forget about the Beast, about what was happening to him in the bliss of holding her, of believing for one passion-fuelled night that she could be his. But he should never have forgotten. He was going to hurt her in the worst way and it killed something deep inside.

He pulled away before she could see the pain reflected in his eyes. 'River?'

Her hand on his back stopped him from leaving the bed entirely.

By the Moon, he was so tied to her already, even though the mating wasn't fully completed, he couldn't bring himself to pull away.

The bed shifted behind him and then her arms wrapped around him, her lips pressed to his shoulder. 'River? What is it?'

He closed his eyes, wanting to savour the feel of her, knowing he shouldn't. This had already gone too far. If he'd known the second part of the mating would start so quickly, he would never have made love to her again this morning. But having lived outside of the pack for so long, he didn't know the ins and outs of mating other than the basics.

He'd never watched anyone but his sister go through it, and even then, it was through a drug-infused haze. He'd had no idea so much of it was driven by instinct.

He would never forget sharing what he shared with Bronwyn, and there was a part of him that couldn't regret it, but he couldn't let her tie herself to him inexorably. It wasn't right and it wasn't fair to her. Not when she would be the one left behind.

Her small hand cupped his scarred cheek, shifting around to face him. He hated when people touched his scars, but not when she did. Opening his eyes, he drank in the sight of her. Her dark pixie haircut in disarray, her lips swollen from his kisses, her pink-tipped breasts swollen with her desire; the scent of that desire drifting on the air around him, tormenting him in ways he thought impossible.

'River? What did I say? You seemed so happy and now ...' She bit her lip. 'Are you regretting last night?'

He gathered her into him, acceptance tearing him in half. The full moon was only a week away. The Beast was growing stronger and stronger inside him. He couldn't wait until it burst out of him at the next full moon.

This was the last time he could hold her.

Pressing his lips to her temple, he kissed her gently and whispered, 'No. I will never regret last night—it was a gift I will never forget. But I can't, in all good conscience, allow this to go any further.'

She stiffened, her fingernails digging into his chest. 'What do you mean? We're mates. You can't possibly deny that now?'

'The mating isn't complete. What we shared this morning—that was the second step. But for it to be fully functioning, there are still a couple more steps.'

'The bond wine and declaration before the pack—I know. Let's do them. I want to belong to you. I want you to belong to me.'

'No.'

She shot off his lap to stand before him, and even though she was gloriously naked, she still managed to have the bearing of a queen. His queen. She looked deep into his eyes even as she asked, 'You mean that?'

He nodded. 'I can't cause you this pain.'

'If you didn't want to cause me pain, you shouldn't have come to me last night.'

'I know. It won't happen again.' Unable to stand the way she looked at him, he rolled over the other side of the bed and stood up. Where were his jeans? Finding them, he tugged them on, wincing as he pulled them over his still erect cock, aware every second that she watched him. He turned to face her, then seeing her expression, looked away again. Fuck. He was such a coward. 'Where's my T-shirt?'

She pointed to the end of the bed. 'I think it's torn.'

The rawness in her voice made him wince inside. But he couldn't show that pain, not to her. He shrugged. 'It's warm outside. I won't need it.' He wanted to leave, but she was standing between him and the door. He turned to the open window that led out to the garden he'd created just for her.

'No!' she yelled, seeming to read his mind. 'I won't let you do this, River. You can't make love to me like you did last night, tell me we're mates this morning and then run away. It doesn't work like that.'

'It has to,' he bit out through clenched teeth.

'Tell me why?'

He threw his hands up, exasperated with her, with himself. Why couldn't she understand? Why couldn't he say the words that would release her?

I don't want you.

But he couldn't do it. They'd be a lie, and because they were mates and because she was so goddamned intuitive, she would know it. 'I can't let the mating continue because I can't be responsible for hurting you.'

'But you are hurting me. Right now in fact.'

'Not as much as if I let the mating finish.'

'What do you mean, River?' She walked slowly towards him, bare feet brushing softly against the floorboards.

He stood still, trying to radiate a 'don't fucking touch me' attitude, because if she touched him one more time, all his good intentions would be undone. It seemed to work. She stopped. Fists clenched, seemingly unaware of what she was doing to him. He couldn't make himself look away. Her skin flushed under his regard. Her nipples hardened. He swallowed and pushed his hands into his sides. He couldn't touch her. He wouldn't.

'Is this about you being scarred? About not being able to turn into a wolf? Because if it is, I don't care about that. And if you think I do, then you don't know me very well.'

He made a sound of annoyance. 'I know none of that matters to you. I know you see my scars but don't pity me because of them. For the first time in a long time, they don't matter to me like they always have because of how you see them. But I wish you didn't look at me like that. I wish the reason I have them frightened you. It would make this so much easier. Because it *does* matter. I *am* broken, Bronwyn, and you deserve so much better.'

She shook her head. 'No. No. You don't have to be broken. I can help you. I'm so close.'

'Not close enough.'

'Okay, so, maybe I won't have helped you by this next moon, but we can try again after. Jason will keep you locked up—'

'It won't be enough.'

She blanched. 'What aren't you telling me?'

Her cinnamon eyes, full of unshed tears again, implored him. He tried to hold it back, the words that would destroy them, but he couldn't. Not when she looked at him like that.

'I'm dying, Bronwyn.'

'No.' She shook her head, vehement. 'No. I would have seen that. In your aura. I would have felt it in your soul.'

He squared his jaw against the fear, the tears in her voice. 'No. You wouldn't. Not this. I've been dying for years.' He glanced away. He couldn't watch the anguish crumbling her certainty. 'Maybe, if the Were had found us earlier and released Skye's powers, things might not be so bad for me now. Maybe it would never have made any difference.' He shook his head, delving deep to find the strength to say what he'd tried never to think about. 'Something happened to me the night my parents were murdered.' The words were barely a harsh whisper. 'I've never felt right since.'

'But you weren't truly affected by the Curse because you are Skye's twin and you were always with her.'

'This has nothing to do with the Curse.'

'You're talking about what the rogue coven did to you? But I've been working on that. The schism between you and your wolf, the Darkness I can see in between. I think I can …'

He slashed the air between them with his hand. 'No. It's too late. There's nothing you can do. There never was. The Darkness isn't just in me, it's a part of me. It's been there for too long and there's nothing you can do to stop it from taking over. The Beast is growing in strength all the time and very soon, he is all I will be.'

'River, no!'

'That's why I never wanted you to try to heal me, because I knew it was useless. Because I knew the failure would hurt you. I didn't want to be responsible for that. My death will tear a hole in the pack as it is, and I was trying to make that hole as small as possible. That's why I pulled away. Why I couldn't let myself be a part of anything. Why I should never have touched you and started this.' He took a step back, the motion agony. 'But what is done is done and all I can do now is to stop it from going any further.'

'I don't believe that.' She stepped forward, reached for him.

He darted away. 'Please, Bronwyn, don't touch me. It will just make this harder.'

'Nothing will make this harder. You're saying you don't want to be a part of my life, that you don't want me to be a part of yours. How can that be anything but soul tearing?'

River tipped his head and stared at the ceiling, the strength of his wants, his needs, pushing him to reach for her. He fought them with every last ounce of his control. 'It would be so much worse if our mating completed. I am degenerating. I can feel it in every fibre of my being. And I can't make you feel the pain of that with me. I can't have you becoming a target when I turn rabid. I can't make Jason responsible for taking me down. I'll kill myself first.'

'No!' Her scream shattered the air and her hands were on him, holding his face as she pressed her body against his. 'No. I won't let you.'

The warmth of her Healing power in her hands tingled over his skin.

The thing that was wrong inside him—the dark, insidious thing tearing him in two, the thing that would kill everything he was—slashed out at her.

She flew backward, like she'd been kicked, a ravaged cry torn from her lips as she landed hard against the bed and slumped to the floor.

'Bronwyn.' He wanted to go to her but couldn't allow himself to move. The thing inside him writhed and pulsed under his skin, pushing forward. His vision began to darken, his skin to itch and stretch as the room was drenched in the red of rage. His hands reached out to hurt, to squeeze the breath from her little, insignificant body.

'River?' Fear filled her eyes as she scrambled to her knees, gaze locked on him.

Her fear made the Darkness inside pulse in joyful expectation.

The sensation snapped him from the rage that always seemed at the heart of him. Swallowing hard, he took a stumbling step away from her. 'It's good you fear me. You should.'

'I don't fear you. I fear *for* you. River, please listen to reason—'

'No. You need to listen.' He wanted to touch her, soothe her, tell her everything would be okay. But he couldn't. 'I have to leave,' he snarled. 'I'm so sorry. I shouldn't have let it go this far. But it won't go any further. I'll free you from me. I promise.'

'No!' She began to scramble to her feet.

He turned, leapt through the window and ran.

'River, no!'

Her scream followed him as he raced through the garden, along the side of the house and out to the front. He intended to run as far from her as possible, as far away from the pack as he could get. Then he would do what he should have done the night after Halloween when he realised what was happening to him. Only then would Bronwyn be safe. Only then would she be free to be who she was always meant to be. It was his presence holding her back.

He would kill himself. It was the only way.

There was a pop of sound to his right. Something hit his shoulder, a slapping sting like a mosquito bite with the impact of a punch. He lost his stride and stumbled onto his hands and knees, dirt and pebbles tearing his palms. Dizziness swam through his head. Air screamed in and out of his lungs like he was trying to breathe through soup. He crashed onto his shoulder, rolled over onto his back to stare at the bright sun overhead.

'River!' Iain's cry, somewhere close, was followed by another pop, a grunt of surprise, a sharp exclamation followed by the crash of something heavy hitting the ground a few metres away.

The sound of laboured breathing—his and Iain's—wasn't enough to cover up the thump of footsteps closing in, crunching over gravel. They stopped. Through swimming vision, River saw the outline of someone standing over him, the sun creating a glowing nimbus behind them, their face obscured in the shadows.

'No,' River managed to whisper. 'Don't stop me.'

'Oh, I don't intend to stop you. I intend to hurry you along.'

Shock shivered through River, his breath hitched as he mumbled, 'Morrigan.'

Morrigan didn't answer. She just turned and gestured behind her. Others—two large men—appeared beside her. 'Bring him. He won't hurt you. He's going to help us now.' She bent closer so that he saw her face—the face of his grandmother, yet younger. 'You and I are going to break the Pact and destroy those who should have been destroyed centuries ago.'

'No,' River said, struggling to get away. But he couldn't move. Could barely breathe. His heart beat a loud, fast drum in his chest, echoing in his head. He tried to fight the effect of whatever drug had been shot into him, but it was no use. As the men bent over him, he saw Morrigan turn, saw her cold smile.

Everything went dark.

22

Eloise—in cat form—yawned and stretched in the patch of sun coming through the window behind her. Her sore shoulder twinged, but it was much better than it had been the day before, thanks to River and Shelley's ministrations. Skye had made her such a comfy bed and had fed her some yummy smoked salmon for breakfast and then roast chicken for lunch. She was very tempted to sleep again. But that wasn't what she was here for. She was supposed to be watching the Were and their witches, to report back to Morrigan anything useful they might be able to use against them.

An uncomfortable twinge tightened around her heart and jagged low in her belly. Guilt? No. It couldn't be. River and Skye and Shelley's kindness yesterday in taking care of her didn't change anything. The Were were evil at heart. They enslaved witches. Used them.

But do they?

The insidious question had been growing louder and louder in her mind. The more she observed, the more difficult it was becoming to equate what Morrigan had told her with what she saw.

But no. Morrigan wouldn't lie. She had the best interests of the coven and all witches and Wiccans at heart.

So, she just needed to forget that doubting voice and get on with her job.

She stood and walked in a circle the way cats did, observing the room as she did.

The air was filled with scents of baking mince pies, pine needles and dust from the boxes of Christmas decorations on the floor and the kitchen island bench. Jason and Skye were standing by the kitchen island, Jason behind Skye, his arms around her, his face buried in the curve of her neck, nuzzling, as she sorted through the decorations. She giggled.

Eloise stopped in place, unable to make herself look away. How could the witch stand to be that close to him? Wasn't she afraid he'd bite her? Tear out her jugular? He was a wild animal after all. That's what Morrigan called them. Yet she seemed to like it.

Morrigan is wrong.

She shook her head against the whisper in her head. What the hell was wrong with her? Perhaps being a cat so long was making her lose her mind. Although she felt as sane as she ever did.

She'd just have to try to hold steady against whatever it was. She probably wasn't reading their relationships right. She jumped onto the couch to get a better view and wake herself up, nestling between strings of green, gold and red tinsel draped there. Kneading the tinsel and couch cushions with her paws, she watched them.

There was no fear between them. No subservience. Only friendship and trust. And love. Perhaps these Were were different from the Were Morrigan knew? Or they were just extremely good at subterfuge.

That explains the Were but not the witch's reaction to him.

Goddess, she had to stop thinking like this. She simply had to listen. And report. That's what she was here for. Not to go soft. Alfrere had been too soft and look what happened to him. She really had to finish her task and get out of here. The longer she spent in this house, the more she found herself questioning things she'd never questioned before. Perhaps that was the true danger—the charm of the Were.

Shelley ran into the room a book clutched against her chest. Adam sauntered in after her. Eloise forced herself to stay where she was, but it was difficult with two Were so close.

Shelley slammed a diary down on the bench in front of Skye and Jason, the sound making Eloise jump and almost fall off her perch. 'We have a problem.'

Eloise stilled—had Shelley discovered what Morrigan was up to?

'What? More than the problem of a homicidal ancient witch out for revenge against all Were-kind?' Adam said as he leaned against the edge of the table behind her.

Shelley shot him a look that would have withered a lesser man. He just flashed her a smile, which seemed to aggravate her further. 'Can you please be serious?'

'I'm not sure. I've never really tried. But for you, Kitten ...'

'Adam!' The Alpha in Jason's tone made Adam snap to attention and Eloise's fur ruffle. He was so ... commanding. He could so easily make others subservient to him. Yet, despite the fact that Adam stopped making wisecracks, he didn't stop smiling. He wasn't cowed at all.

Eloise pulled her attention back to the conversation as Skye reached out a hand and touched Shelley's wrist. 'What is it?'

'This.' Shelley opened the diary and pointed to a long passage on one page.

Skye turned the diary around and frowned. 'This seems much older than the ones I've been reading.'

Shelley nodded. 'We've all been mostly reading from the latest ones—your aunt's, your father's. Which makes sense, seeing he was the one who was training you and if there's any help to be had, you'd find it in his diaries. But after finding that information about body shifting in some of the older diaries, I decided to go even further back. This is one of Bridgette Colliere's diaries.'

'What?' Skye's hand moved over the diary reverently. 'Where did you find it?'

'Jason brought it down from the main Packlands last week for me.'

Skye glanced up at him. 'You didn't tell me?'

He frowned. 'Shelley said she was doing some personal research into her ghost problem and you've been so busy with your own study, I didn't even think about it. I wasn't keeping it from you.'

Skye touched the centuries-old paper reverently. 'It's so well preserved.'

'It's coated in a spell of preservation,' Shelley said.

Skye met her friend's gaze. 'Did you find out something about how to control the ghosts?'

Shelley grimaced. 'I actually lied about that. But I didn't want to say anything just in case I was barking up the wrong tree. I didn't want to worry any of you.'

Skye snorted. 'Well, now you've got me worried.' She bent over the passage. 'It's hard to read.'

'It's the ancient form of English it's written in. It takes a little getting used to.'

'Why don't you give us the crib notes?' Adam suggested.

Shelley pulled the diary back to her, hands shaking. Eloise edged closer, wishing she could read what was there—but a cat jumping onto the bench and looking at the page would draw too much attention.

'Here.' Shelley pointed. 'It says you are related to the ancient witch, Morghanna Cantrae.'

A roaring sounded in Eloise's ears at that information. She jerked to her feet so suddenly, she fell off the couch in a sliver of tinsel wreaths. Unlike a cat, she did not land on her feet. A yowl of pain punched out of her as she smacked into the ground.

Despite the noise she'd made, everyone's attention was still on Shelley, their shocked silence holding them still.

Not wanting to miss anything once the conversation started up again, she tried to extricate herself from the tinsel, but just slipped and slid, the wreaths knotting around her legs and body.

Adam, who was closest, turned to look at her, then bent to help. With a few deft swipes, he managed to untie her from the shiny, dusty mess and plopped her on the back of the couch. 'Bad timing with the comic slapstick, little kitty-cat,' he whispered, ruffling the fur on her head with a rough pat. 'Do it again later and you might get more attention.'

Surprised by his actions, she didn't even think to lash out at him as Skye's harsh whisper broke the silence. 'What? We're related to Morghanna Cantrae? No. That's impossible.'

'It's not impossible.'

'But Morrigan and Morghanna were the last of their line,' Jason said.

Shelley shook her head again. 'That's what everyone was led to believe, because Bridgette Colliere thought it was the only way to keep him safe from the others.'

'Keep who safe?'

'Morghanna's son.'

Eloise's hair stood up on end. Morghanna's son! Morghanna's son had died with her.

At least, that's what family lore stated.

'But Morghanna didn't have a son.' Jason's words ricocheted through her. 'She didn't have any children. There's no record of that.'

Goddess! Was that true? He sounded like he was telling the truth. But Morrigan told a different story. Which one was right?

Shelley's next words rode over her thoughts. 'There is a record. In Bridgette Colliere's diary. She and Morghanna had been best friends. They met after their respective covens were almost decimated and joined together to stay safe. Morghanna helped Bridgette bind the packs and covens to the Pact.'

'Why don't we know that?' Adam asked.

'I don't know. But Morghanna was tied to the MacCraes, so they were separated by distance, but they maintained their friendship. In fact, Bridgette was there for the early birth of Morghanna's son, and when Morghanna left to try and find Morrigan again after Alistair, her husband, had a vision, she left their son in Bridgette's care. She didn't want to take him on the journey because she knew it could be dangerous, not to mention he was very small. Bridgette had only kept him alive by using a combination of magic and herbal lore to help him breathe.'

'Why would she leave her son to court such danger? I mean, even though Morrigan was her sister, she was still evil,' Skye said.

'The danger wasn't Morrigan. In fact, Morghanna was worried about her safety apparently, not her. It was the time of the Witch Hunters. Many witches and warlocks had exposed themselves due to their powers getting out of control. People had been hurt and killed and it was too easy for simple peasants who had once relied on the witches and warlocks to care for them when they were sick, to make it rain when they needed it, to help with failing crops, to believe the evil being said about the covens who had once lived openly among them. Many were captured, tortured, burned at the stake; many who weren't even witches, just simple herbalists and midwives. Strangers too. If you weren't known by anyone in a village, you were under suspicion. Morghanna knew by leaving the safety of Packlands, she could be exposing herself to all of that.'

'But she went anyway?'

Shelley nodded. 'With her husband. She loved her sister and couldn't let whatever the vision was about happen to her.'

'Hard to believe she and Morrigan are sisters then.'

Shelley shook her head at Adam. 'Morrigan wasn't evil back then. It was what happened to her sister that changed her. But the journey to find Morrigan started a sequence of events that led to Alistair's death at the hand of Lachlan MacCrae, the son of the Alpha Morghanna was tied to. And due to what Morghanna did to stop Lachlan from rampaging through a nearby village, and the Healing she did to save those he'd injured—even though she couldn't save Alistair—she was exposed to the Witch Catchers. They captured her and she was tried, tortured and burned at the stake for witchcraft. It's why Morghanna canted the Curse—to take her revenge on the MacCraes, but also to ensure the Were would never let such a thing occur again—and to make sure they looked after her orphan son. At least, that's the assumption somebody wrote.'

'Somebody? Bridgette didn't write it?'

Shelley shook her head. 'The writing changes at this point. I'm not sure why. The writer doesn't identify themself and there's only a few more entries after that.'

Eloise couldn't believe what she was hearing. Morrigan couldn't know any of this. What was she going to say when she found out?

'So, Bridgette adopted Morghanna's son?' Jason asked.

'Of course she did. He was a little baby. The son of her friend. What else could she do?' Skye said.

Shelley shook her head. 'Nothing as simple as that. With the death of the MacCraes, there was nobody to claim him. Except for Morrigan.'

'But Morrigan doesn't know of his existence, does she?' Skye said slowly.

'No. And she never can.'

Wrong. She was going to find out this very night.

'But if she knew I was the direct descendant of her sister, surely that might change her mind about trying to destroy me? We could use this to our advantage.' Skye's gaze skated between Jason, Shelley and Adam, the light of desperate hope in her eyes. 'I mean, it's her grief over the loss of her sister that's fuelling her rage. If she knows she hasn't truly lost the last of her blood, then surely that might change things?'

'She doesn't want to destroy you, love,' Jason said, grasping her hand. 'She wants to use your power to fuel her own so she can break the Pact and kill all Were.'

'But that would destroy me, don't you see? Surely she wouldn't want to do that to her blood, if her blood is so important to her.'

Jason brushed her hair back from her face. 'The fact you will eventually die when she takes your powers is just collateral damage to her. She's too far gone to think otherwise.'

'But we could try.'

Eloise's mind whirled. Could Skye be right? Would Morrigan change her mind? Skye was her blood. As was River. And Morrigan was always saying that blood mattered. Goddess! She needed to get this information to her Mistress as soon as possible. She leapt off the couch and padded to where the doggy door for Tom's puppy had been installed. But just as she was about to step through, Shelley spoke and Eloise halted in mid-stride.

'No. We can't tell Morrigan. She can't ever know.'

'Why not?'

'Because if she did, it wouldn't be you she'd come after, it would be River.'

'What? Why? He has no power. Without me, he is useless to her.'

'No, he's not. You see, Alistair had a little secret.'

'What secret?'

'He was at least half-Were,' Jason said, understanding suddenly coming to his eyes.

'No!' Skye breathed. 'How could that have been a secret? And why would he need to keep it a secret? I mean, what was wrong with a witch and a Were mating? Bridgette was mated, wasn't she?'

'It doesn't say,' Shelley said, looking down at the diary, flipping back a few pages. 'All Bridgette says is that they were shocked when one night, not long after Morghanna and Alistair left, the baby's eyes changed. He grew fangs and howled at the moon. She meant to ask Morghanna about it the next time they scried, but Morghanna died before she could.'

'Why did they still keep his birth a secret though?'

Shelley pointed to a section and read, 'Because of the Curse, not a single person, Were, witch or human, can ever find out the child is Morghanna and Alistair's son. Nobody can discover he is part Were. Especially not Morrigan.'

'But why? At that time, there must have been other part Were children born,' Jason said. 'He couldn't have been the first.'

'He wasn't. But his heritage wasn't like the others. The curse Morghanna invoked was especially tied to her own blood to help keep those like her with power in their veins safe, and yet, the curse she invoked had the power to destroy her own son because he was half Were. The writer actually posits that she couldn't have known of Alistair's Were heritage because if she had, she would never have canted the Curse as she did. 'Until the night his eyes changed and fangs grew,' she read again, 'the babe has shown no signs of his Were heritage. So she must not have known. She could not have known. For if she had, she would not have brought this danger upon him.'

'But he was a baby. How would they know?' Skye asked.

'Regardless of whether a baby is full Were or half,' Jason said, his arms crossed over his chest, his expression worried, 'their first change is a few hours after their birth. It's not always a full change, but it always happens. It's like our genes need to do a function test or something. Nobody has ever been able to figure out exactly why we're always born in our human form and then change into our wolf form soon after. But one thing we are certain of is that it always happens, regardless of if you are full, half or quarter. The fact Morghanna's child didn't do that would be enough to make everyone believe he carried no Were in his genes and was wholly witch—like you,' he said to his mate.

'What if Alistair was less than quarter?' Skye said. 'That would explain why nobody knew he was Were.'

Jason sighed. 'No. If he was less, he wouldn't change at all. The fact he did change suggests that Alistair had to know he was Were and was keeping it a secret. The question is, did Morghanna know?'

'I'm with whoever wrote those last entries,' Adam said. 'She couldn't have known, given she canted the Curse.'

Skye made a frustrated sound and waved her hand. 'We've kind of got off topic here. What does any of this have to do with Morrigan not finding out about River?'

Eloise wanted to know the answer to that question, too. She watched, impatient, as Shelley paced away, running her fingers through her hair.

'There was strong opposition to the Were-Witch Pact from certain sects of the witch and warlock community, but Bridgette was the most powerful witch that had ever been seen and there was no way they could undo what she had canted. However, Morghanna's curse found a way around that for the few that were tied to the MacCraes, and obviously Morrigan decided to try to use it. But she didn't know there was an easier way.' Shelley's fingers clenched around the edges of the bench as she looked her friend in the eye. 'Morghanna's son is key to the Pact's survival or destruction. As are his direct descendants. If any of them are hurt or killed by Were or by magical means, the Curse would immediately come into effect and because Alistair, and therefore his bloodline, wasn't tied into a particular pack, it would affect them all.'

'Oh, God.'

Eloise felt like she'd been struck by lightning. She'd been given the knowledge her mistress had been searching centuries for, but it wasn't the salvation they needed. If River was killed, then the Curse would unfold. But if River was killed, then Morrigan would lose one of the last connections to her sister.

What should she do?

Blood mattered.

The words rang in her head and there was no escaping from them. Morrigan had made all of the coven know how important blood ties were. They mattered over everything else. It's why she tied all those closest to her with a spell fuelled by blood magic.

So, there was only one thing she could do.

She had to tell Morrigan before her mistress did anything she would forever regret.

She took a step but hesitated. If she went back not having heard everything there was to hear, Morrigan would be angry.

Turning back around, she retuned into what Shelley was now saying.

'... writer, Morghanna's son's safety was paramount. If those who opposed the Were-Witch Pact were to find out about him, then everything Bridgette had worked so hard and long for could be destroyed. They had to make certain he survived; that his progeny survived. So the writer somehow had him adopted by the Alpha of Pack McVale and bound him to one of Bridgette's daughters. When they were old enough, they were married and had children of their own, thus securing Morghanna and Alistair's line and entwining it not only with the power of the coven but with the power of the Werebond, the Packbond and the magic of the Pact.'

'But then, doesn't that mean both of us are at risk if she finds out about our heritage?' Skye asked.

'No. You don't understand. The blood isn't as strong in you.'

'How do you know?'

'Because you're a witch and River is a Were.'

'That's because my mum was a Were.'

Shelley's eyes were full of regret as she shook her head. 'No. It's not. The Were gene is passed down through both male and female lines, but the colour of the wolf is very specific to their bloodlines. Jason is a silver and gold wolf because his father was silver and gold. Adam is black because their mother was black.'

'My mother was silver and white. And River is ...'

'He's russet-coloured,' Jason said quietly.

'Yes. And if the family trees in the diaries are anything to go by, Ivy's parents were silver and white and black and white, and those colours feature heavily in her lineage. There is no record of a russet-coloured wolf in your mother's background.'

'River is Were because he got the gene from my father?'

Shelley nodded. 'I have no idea why the gene was recessive for so long that there's no record of a Were born to the Colliere line before. It's even more puzzling given what Jason just said about Were genes. Maybe when your father mated with your mother, it was the first time a Colliere had mated with a wolf for centuries, bringing the recessive gene to the fore. But the point is, River is a Colliere/Cantrae Were, not a Fergusson Were; his Were genes passed down from his ancient grandpa. Which means,' Shelley swallowed hard, her eyes filled with worry, 'River is the last male of Alistair's line. The danger that was attached to Morghanna's son is now River's, a blood spell inherited through generations. If he dies without progeny, without having experienced life and love and all the things Morghanna wanted for her son, then the Curse will be enacted again, and in full this time.'

Eloise wanted to change, to tell them they didn't need to worry, that it would never happen. Because to Morrigan, blood mattered. And once she found out, she would protect River and Skye, not try to use them and kill them to break the Pact, no matter how much she hated the rest of the Were for what they'd done to her sister.

'So we're back to where we started when Skye was taken,' Adam said into the stunned silence.

'We can't let anyone know this. Ever.'

They all nodded at Skye's statement.

'The diary needs to be protected. It can't fall into the wrong hands.' Shelley picked the diary up, clutching it to her chest. 'Imagine what could happen if—'

Her words were cut off by the sound of the front door slamming. 'Skye? Shelley? Jason?'

'In here, Bron.'

The icy touch of premonition curled along Eloise's spine, ruffling her fur and making her arch. She knew what had happened. Morrigan had taken River. She planned to do something horrible to him to break the Pact.

Hissing, she flew out of the doggy door, not waiting to hear the details of what had happened.

She had to get to Morrigan. She had to tell her what she'd heard before her mistress did something she might regret. Forever.

23

B ron flew around the entrance to the kitchen, gasping for breath, her face white, eyes wild and full of tears. 'Thank the Goddess you're all here.'

'What's happened, Bron?' Jason asked, rushing to her.

'River?' Skye asked.

'I can't feel him. I can't sense him. Oh Goddess! My head.' Bron doubled over, clutching her head.

'Bron!' Jason wrapped his arms around her, holding her upright, while the others flocked around her.

'Bron, where are you hurt?'

She peered up at them, at the sea of familiar faces in front of her, but at the same time, she saw something else shadowed around them. A room. No. Not a room. It looked more like a cellar; racks of wine lined up against bare rock walls. She shivered at the damp cold air.

'Bron?' Fingers pressed at her head. She looked up to see Shelley peering at her. 'Where does it hurt?'

'I'm not hurt,' she gasped. 'River. It's River. He's been taken.' The shock of her statement slammed into them; Skye and Shelley took a step back, Jason's fingers tightened on her arms, and Adam ... Adam just stared at her with a look that made her shudder.

'No. No,' Skye said, desperation in her eyes.

'No,' Jason said, echoing his mate. 'That's not possible. He's guarded. Iain would have let me know if anything had happened.'

The front door slammed and Patrick ran into the room. 'Iain's missing, and Gareth too.'

'What?'

'How can they be missing?'

'Does this mean Morrigan's got River?'

'Shut up everyone. I have to concentrate. Adam, can you take Bron?'

Hands shifted on her and she was pulled against a warm, strong chest—the wrong chest, her soul and heart cried. Adam lowered her into a seat then stood beside her as if on guard. But he wasn't looking at her. Nobody was looking at her. Their gazes were all pinned on Jason.

She tried to focus her gaze on him too. He closed his eyes, his brow furrowed. Everyone held their breaths, waiting for him to use his Alpha link. His shoulders slumped after a moment and she knew —she knew—before he said the words she didn't want to hear.

'I can't contact any of them.'

The room erupted around her; shouting, pacing, Jason demanding calm, calling others to him, people moving into the room as he took control.

'But why would Morrigan take him now? She can't do anything until Yule.'

'Skye's right,' Shelley said. 'She'd need the power of the cross-quarter days and a full moon to make a grab at Skye's powers again.'

'I won't let her anywhere near her. Or any of you,' Jason growled.

'But if she is somehow still connected to me by what she did at Halloween ... Oh God! If she's got him ...'

Skye's confused, pained voice disappeared in the roar in Bron's ears. A fist had clenched around her heart and squeezed at this confirmation of her fears. A small part of her had hoped she was wrong about River, even though she knew she wasn't. She'd felt him being taken. Had been knocked unconscious by it. When she'd woken, hours later, it had been to a feeling of such emptiness that for a moment she thought someone had died and she just wasn't remembering. Then she'd felt it.

The loss of River in her subconscious. She'd barely been aware of him being there before last night. He'd become a part of her so slowly that she hadn't realised how inexorably woven into her psyche he was. And now there was an empty place where he had been.

'Bronwyn. Please don't cry. Not for me.'

Bron sucked in a breath at the sound of his deep voice in her mind. 'River?'

Silence fell around her as everyone spun to look at her. But she didn't really notice them. All she noticed, as she wrapped her arms around her chest as if to hold her aching heart in, was that she wasn't empty. The space where River had been wasn't empty. It had just been silent. So silent, she'd thought he was gone. But he wasn't.

'He's here,' she said, grinning like an idiot as the tears poured down her face. 'He's still here.'

'What is she talking about?' Shelley asked.

'I can feel him. He's here, with me. He's not gone.'

'How could she know that when you don't?' Skye asked her mate, desperation seeding her tone.

'She couldn't unless ...'

A face swam before Bron's eyes as large hands grasped her shoulders. She tried to focus on the face, but it was hard to see through the tears and the strange shadow image of the cellar.

'Bron? Did you and River start the mating last night?'

Bron nodded.

'Bloody hell,' Adam said. 'How did that happen without you knowing, J? The Alpha always knows.'

'Not when the Were is almost a lone wolf.' Jason's lips pressed against Bron's forehead as his fingers tightened on her shoulders in an encouraging squeeze. 'I knew it was a possibility, but I wasn't certain he'd let it happen. This is more than I could have hoped for. It's wonderful news.'

'How can you say that?' Skye asked. 'River has been taken. And Iain and Gareth. We have no way of knowing where they've been taken or what's happened to them.'

Shelley nodded. 'Skye's right. How can Bron being River's mate be a good thing? It's horrifying. For them; for us.'

'There you're wrong. It makes all the difference.'

As Jason shifted, Skye came into view, her eyes wide and glistening as fear and worry tinged their green depths, her face paler than she'd ever seen it. Her heart lurched in her chest, a desperate need to allay some of that fear overtook her. With no further thought, she whispered, 'I can find him. I can see where he is.'

'What?' Skye whipped to face Jason. 'Can she? Is that possible? I thought the mating had to be complete to have what we share?'

'It's unusual for it to occur so soon, yes, but not impossible.'

'How?'

Jason's smile widened. 'Because of the Healing. They don't need the Bond Wine or anything else. Bron is already in his veins. Her essence has been in him since that first night. It's what the dark thing marring his soul has been fighting against. Huh.' He shook his head. 'I didn't see it.' He looked up, wonderingly, at Bron. 'But you started the mating the moment your Healing power touched him that first night.' He gripped Skye's hand. 'This will save him. It's the only thing that ever could.'

'He won't let it go any further,' Bron muttered.

Jason's smile widened as he pulled Skye into his side, his electric blue eyes glowing with what he felt for his mate. 'It's not only up to him. And if you can see where he is in your mind, if you can hear him in your head, it is already too late. He can't pull back now, no matter how hard he tries.'

'I don't want him to try. I love him. I need him in my life.'

Jason nodded. 'Then let's save him and the others and you can make him see the truth of that.'

Bron took in a shaky breath, her hands gripped tight in her lap. 'Okay. What do I have to do?'

'Close your eyes and concentrate on him. Find the essence of him in your soul and follow that down the mating link to its source. Fill your mind with him. You're already seeing a little of what he can see, but if you concentrate on him and only him, it will become clearer. And maybe you will see something that can help us figure out where Morrigan has taken all of them and what she plans to do.'

Skye sat beside her and took her clenched fist into her warm hands. 'You can do this, Bron.'

'I know.' A few days earlier she might have questioned it, even the day before she might have questioned it, but something had changed in the last twenty-four hours. The full meaning of the vision quest wasn't quite apparent to her, but she had grasped the bit that had been clear. She'd shared something with River the night before, something she never imagined could be possible. And all because she'd seen herself as she truly was and managed to grasp the courage to explore that. To hold what she wanted in her hands for the first time in her life and own it. Enjoy it.

Her grandma had tried to tell her weeks earlier, but she hadn't been ready to truly listen. She had listened to someone else. River. Like her love for him, how much she trusted him, the depth of it, had crept up on her. She had listened to him when she hadn't even listened to herself. She'd healed Tom because he knew she could; she'd tried other ways of using her knowledge about healing to reopen her business with great success; she'd looked deep into herself, past the hurt and abandoned little girl she'd always felt like, to the Goddess-struck brilliance he saw every time he looked at her, and she'd seen her worth.

She wasn't just able to heal. She was a Healer. She was a friend, a Pack Witch, a businesswoman, a faithful granddaughter and a loving daughter to parents who didn't deserve her love but still got it anyway.

And best of all, she was bound to the kindest, most artistic and wonderful Were she'd ever met and was ever likely to meet.

She was River's mate. And he was hers. The part of her soul she had never known was missing but that now made her complete. She'd felt the truth of it before, but now she knew with no doubt, that he was as essential to her as breathing.

She couldn't lose him.

Bron's mouth twisted as fear gripped her and whispered insidious thoughts in her head.

You failed to help him.

He's in danger.

He's all alone.

What makes you think you can help him now?

She shook her head. *Because I can. Because I will.*

With that mantra in her mind, she banished the old voice of creeping doubt. It had no place in her life anymore. River wasn't alone. He had her. He would always have her. And she would make bloody certain they all survived this so she could force him to understand the importance of that.

Skye squeezed her hand again. 'I don't want to rush you, Bron, but we have to save River. Now. Shelley, tell her.' Skye nodded at Shelley.

Looking graver than Bron had ever seen her, Shelley told her about what she'd read in Bridgette Colliere's diary.

'Goddess, no.' Bron's fingers closed tight around Shelley's. 'She couldn't know that, could she?' She looked up at Jason.

'The diaries have always been kept safe. No one but the McVale Coven members are allowed to read them and given I've never heard a rumour about Morghanna's son from any other source, I think we're safe to say nobody else knows. I think he's safe for now.'

She met his steady gaze. 'He's not safe. Morrigan is insane. She can and will hurt him. And the others too.'

Determined not to fail, she closed her eyes, conjuring up an image of River. His beloved face, his gold-flecked hazel eyes burning, searing into her with a look that made her feel like she was the only thing that could assuage his hunger. She sank into that look, gave herself up to it as she'd given herself up to him last night. Light flared in her mind's eye, then she was soaring, flying along a twisting path of fiery gold and deepest russet with flecks of green.

She gasped as the twisting path ended and an image of a cellar swam into her mind. 'I can see where he is.' She'd seen this cellar before, but the image this time was far clearer as Jason had said it would be.

The room was cool and smelled of the thick scent of clay in the carved-out walls, touched with the scent of salt. 'He's underground. In a cellar ... but there's nothing to tell me where it is.'

'Ask River if he knows.'

She took in a shaky breath, her chest tight and hurting, and thought to that part in her she now knew was River. 'He's groggy. Morrigan injected him with something. It's why it's all so hazy.'

'Ask him if he knows where they took him.'

'River. Do you know where you are?'

'Bron?'

'Yes, it's me, my love.'

'How? How are you in my head?'

'The mating.'

'It's not complete.'

Bron trembled at the pained rejection in his tone but kept her voice steady as she answered him. 'Complete enough to help me find you. I know Morrigan's got you. Can you tell me anything?'

'A cellar. I'm tied down to a table. There's light, but it's not much. I can't tell you anything else.'

She told them what he said.

'Okay.' Jason's thumbs rubbed in soothing circles over the back of her palm. 'Close your eyes and concentrate on not only what he sees, but what he smells, what he hears. Any of those could give us a clue.'

Lips pressed together, she bit the inside of her cheek as she tried to go deeper, tried to find some clue to let them know where he was. Hot tears ran down her face, cold sweat pricked her skin; her heart thumped loudly in her ears, her breath a harsh rattle in her throat as she tried, tried, tried so hard to see or hear something. Anything.

'Are you okay, Bron?' Shelley's voice near her ear. 'She looks like she's going to be sick.'

'Are you sure she can do this?'

'She has to.'

'Shh, let her concentrate.'

Bron cut out the distractions around her and sank into her mind, concentrating with everything in her on River, on where he was. 'I can smell damp, like mould. And dust. And salt.'

'That could be anywhere.'

'Shh.'

She took in a deeper breath. 'Pine. I can smell pine.'

'Like disinfectant?'

She shook her head slowly, breathing in again. 'No. It's not strong like disinfectant. It's softer. Fresher. Pine trees maybe?' She cocked her head. 'And there's a low rumbling sound.' What was that sound? She knew it. Had heard it many times before.

Her eyes snapped open. 'I can hear the ocean. Waves smashing into a beach.'

'Pine trees and a beach nearby. That could be most of the Peninsula and a great deal of the forested areas near the Great Ocean Road.'

'No. She couldn't have taken him that far. She's only had him a couple of hours, so we have to guess she's taken him somewhere with a cellar on the Peninsula.'

'But we still don't know exactly where,' Skye said, her breathless plea full of worry.

'See if you can find anything else, Bron. Anything to pinpoint a place.'

Bron was shaking with the effort, but she nodded and closed her eyes, seeking deep inside herself, deep inside River. Tears fell faster down her cheeks as she pushed outward, trying to feel or sense anything. But there was nothing other than what she'd already sensed. She pushed harder, grasping onto her determination of before. Pain stung her palms as her fingernails drove into her skin.

'*Don't hurt yourself, Bronwyn. Not for me.*'

'What about for Iain and Gareth. She's got them too.'

'They wouldn't want you to hurt yourself to find them any more than I do.'

'I don't believe that. I'm not more important than any of you. Especially you.'

'That's not true.'

He began to pull away from her. She held on tighter. 'Don't, River. I won't let you refute me. I'm going to hold on no matter what you say. So help me. Please help me find you. I can't live without you.'

'Don't say that, Bronwyn. I've already told you, I'm dying anyway.'

'No. I won't let you.'

'There's nothing you can do.'

His words were like a spark inside her mind, her Healer magic aligning with the new power to deny the truth in them. Knowledge gushed into her, through her, all the pieces and clues falling into place.

All she had to do was believe. That's what her grandma had been trying to tell her. Where River's trust had stemmed from. What the vision quest from the Goddess meant. If you believed and you had the ability, you could make it true.

At one, finally, with who she was, she stared down the face of the mating bond and knew what she had to do.

'You're wrong,' she said, voice resonating with the strength glimmering inside her. 'When it comes to Healing, there's nothing I can't do.' And saying that, she reached right down inside her and wound as much of her magic and herself around the mating bond as she could.

'Bronwyn. What are you doing?'

'I am creating a beacon to light my way. I will find you, River. And then I will rid you of the Darkness and heal you and we will finish this mating. I'm not letting you go. Ever.' She flooded all the love and joy she felt for him through the mating bond, creating a light so intense, even in her mind she almost had to look away.

But it wasn't enough. She needed more power.

She pulled it from her friends, from Jason, from the pack.

Shelley and Skye gasped; Jason's hands tightened on her fists;

Adam jerked beside her and muttered, 'What the fuck?' But she ignored their sounds of surprise and used the power she could syphon from them to pour into the beacon she was creating.

Finally done, she opened her eyes. Strength poured through her, from her. If she wished it, she was sure she could fly.

Jason knelt in front of her, his face pale, blue eyes glowing with awe-filled apprehension. 'What just happened? What did you do?'

'River is convinced the Darkness inside him is going to kill him. I poured my love into him, and all my Healing light to chase away his hopelessness. As I did it, I realised I could use that light to create a beacon that would allow me to find him. But I needed more power, so I took it. I hope you don't mind?'

'Mind?' Skye plonked down hard on the couch beside her. 'You are a genius.'

A smile broke out on Bron's face, a true smile, one she hadn't felt for too long. 'You can feel it too, can't you?'

Skye nodded.

'It's so bright,' Shelley whispered.

'What's bright?' Adam asked.

Bron looked at him and then back to Jason. 'It doesn't matter if I can't see or smell or hear where River is. The beacon I've created will show us the way.'

<h1 style="text-align:center">24</h1>

Morrigan's athamé sliced down, the glinting silver now dripping with blood.

River bit back a scream as the knife cut into his chest again. His wolf, brought forward by what Bronwyn had done, lunged inside him, snarling. The Beast—which had gone quiet when Bronwyn had slammed her love into the mating bond—stirred, interested in the pain. 'No,' he gritted out between clenched teeth.

'No?' Morrigan laughed. 'That's all you've got to say?' She grinned down at him, eyes swirling blackness. 'Let's see if I can elicit more than a "no" from you.'

The knife sliced across his chest once more, a line of hot fire. River jerked against the bindings holding him down.

The Beast growled.

River grasped at the golden wash of love Bronwyn had flooded him with—what seemed like an aeon ago but was possibly only an hour or so—and wrapped it around himself. The Beast slashed at it, its claws leaving a smear of Darkness through the gold.

River cried out, 'No!'

'Still no? Maybe this will make you scream.'

The point of the knife dug into his pectoral muscle, scraping along bone. He clenched his teeth, the strangled scream of anguish becoming a moan as the Beast snarled inside him.

The knife lifted again, his blood dripping from the tip. He braced himself.

'No, Mistress. You can't kill him.'

Morrigan's raised hand stilled, her knuckles whitening, the athamé shaking as she turned to glare at the bedraggled girl who stood in the doorway. 'You dare to stop me?'

'You can't kill him,' the girl said again as she limped towards Morrigan, her hands held out in appeal before her.

River's nostrils flared. That scent. He knew that scent. It had entered the room with the girl. Her scent but faintly tangled with another one he knew intimately: Bronwyn!

What the hell? Who was she?

'Please ... Mistress. Just listen ... to me.' She panted heavily, the words coming in gulps. 'He's related to you. He's a direct ... descendant ... of Morghanna's son.'

'My sister's child died with her.' Morrigan's voice was low, but so full of suffering and grief it took River by surprise.

'No. He didn't. Please ... you have to ... stop and listen.'

'You should be at your post. Why did you leave it?'

'You said to tell you ... if I found out something important. And I did.'

'Why didn't you contact me by phone as agreed?'

The girl took in a big, shuddering breath, steadied herself and said, 'I tried, but Cain refused to pass on my call. He said you were busy.' She waved her hand at River—her palm was scraped raw, as was the one she held by her side. 'He wouldn't listen when I tried to tell him. So I stole some clothes and one of their cars. I got here as fast as I could.' The girl moved, her left foot dragging across the dirt floor, bruises showing on the pale skin where the oversized T-shirt hung off her shoulder.

Bronwyn's T-shirt. The one she often changed into after work.

Where had she gotten it from? Had Bronwyn sent her here?

The girl's gaze flickered to Morrigan, then back down again as she clasped her hands in front of her. 'Please, Mistress ... Morrigan. You have to listen. You've always told us blood matters.'

'What does that have to do with this?'

The girl swallowed hard, her face paling at the venom in Morrigan's tone, but she stood steadfast even with her gaze lowered. 'Shelley found something in the diaries, in Bridgette Colliere's diary specifically.'

Morrigan hissed and stiffened. The girl's gaze flickered up to Morrigan, but when her mistress said nothing more, she continued on. 'Sh-she said Morghanna birthed her son early. Bridgette Colliere kept him hidden from you and then mated him to one of her daughters.' She pointed at River. 'He is the direct descendant.'

River jerked as if he'd been hit. The girl's words roared in his head, swirling around sickeningly, making it impossible to take them in.

Morrigan's sharp bark of laughter cut into the swirling mayhem of his thoughts. 'That's impossible. I'd feel it if he bore my blood. He is nothing but a filthy Were.'

'Who are you calling filthy, bitch?' River snarled.

With murder in her eyes Morrigan swung to him, the Athamé slashing down. The girl cried out, flinging herself forward and across his chest. The knife scored across her back.

She jerked and screamed. Blood sprayed across his face.

Shocked silence followed her scream. River stared up at Morrigan —her face was filled with rage-tinged surprise—then down at the limp form on his chest. Was she dead? Had she died trying to protect him? Why would she do such a thing? Who was she? 'Don't die, little one. Don't die,' he whispered. 'Not for me.'

She stirred, groaning. River let out his breath in a gush of relief that stirred the tawny hair spread across his blood-stained chest. She shifted, lifted her head to look at him so he saw her eyes clearly for the first time. Peridot eyes with a cat-like slant. Eyes that had stared at him in just that way before, but he couldn't for the life of him remember when. 'Who are you?'

She shook her head and pushed up from her prone position,

blood dripping from the cut that ran across her arm and back, a red stain on Bronwyn's favourite T-shirt. But she didn't seem to notice the blood, or the pain. Instead, she stood awkwardly, those big, pleading eyes turned on Morrigan. 'You can't kill him. He's your family. And you always say blood matters.'

Morrigan's lips curled. 'I'm not related to the Were.'

'You are. Through your sister. I heard.'

Morrigan paused, eyes unfocused as if listening to something and then nodded. 'Yes. You're right. They lied to her. It's a trick.' Her eyes focused on the girl again. 'They must have figured out you're a shapeshifter. That you were playing at being the Healer's cat. You must have given yourself away.'

'No. No Mistress. I didn't. I promise, they had no idea.'

'Bluebelle?' The word left his lips before he could stop it.

The girl turned, pinning him with those familiar peridot eyes, and nodded. 'See. He got the closest to me and he didn't know. I'm telling you the truth, Mistress. The witch, Shelley, read it out of Bridgette Colliere's diary. Morghanna bore a son before she left with Alistair to find you. They thought you were in danger. After she died, the McVale Pack and Coven hid him from you. He was mated to Bridgette's daughter. River and Skye are the direct descendants of that match.' She pointed at River. 'He's your family. Your blood.'

Morrigan stood, poised, looking like she might strike again. Then she swore and began to pace to the door and back, muttering to herself.

Nausea roiled inside River as he stared up at the girl standing beside him. The eyes, the colour of her hair, the limp ... all things she shared with Bronwyn's cat. She must be a shifter for him to never have guessed. The entire pack would have smelled the magic if it had been a transformation. 'Bronwyn helped you. Looked after you. And you're betraying her?'

She shook her head, eyes wide, pleading. 'No. I'm trying to help.' She laid her hand on his chest. The sticky warmth of her blood felt almost soothing as it mixed with his. 'I'm sorry you've been hurt.' She bunched up the hem of the oversized T-shirt and dabbed at one of his cuts. 'You were kind to me. I never meant for you to get hurt.'

She hadn't. He could see that in her eyes. But she'd seen so much and told Morrigan about all of it. Even the private things he wished nobody knew about. Morrigan had been torturing him with that information—the sting of her knowing such private things a greater pain than the slashes of the athamé. This girl was the reason he was here. The reason Bronwyn and Skye and Jason and the pack were still in so much danger. She was the enemy.

So why should he believe her?

Because she had just taken a knife blow meant for him. And now she stood between her mistress and him, trying to save him.

Brave. So brave. Despite everything else she'd done, it meant there was something good in her, unlike the rest of the rogue coven.

He moved his hand, managing to grasp the edge of the T-shirt. She stopped dabbing, stared down at him with those incredible eyes. He swallowed hard, then whispered, 'Don't. Don't tell her our secrets. She's not what you think she is.'

Her eyes clouded over with doubt, but still she said, 'She's not what you think she is, either. If I tell her this, you'll live.'

He shook his head. 'She's insane.'

'She's not. She's just grieving.' She stroked his cheek. 'I'm sorry. But I have to tell her. It's the only way forward. The only way to make certain another, bigger mistake isn't made. Trust me.'

He let go of her sleeve. 'You're wrong. She's well past listening.'

'Let me save you.'

'What are you saying to that Were? Why are you talking to it at all?'

The girl spun around at Morrigan's question. 'He ... he grabbed my sleeve. I was asking him to let go.'

Morrigan's lip curled. 'You don't ask the Were. You just make him.'

She waved her hand and River gasped as pain clenched around his throat, his chest. He tried to suck in a breath but couldn't. He couldn't breathe!

'No. Mistress. Please, stop. You don't want to do that.'

'Why not? Why don't I want to do that?'

'Because he *is* your blood. He's a direct link to your sister. You would never forgive yourself if you hurt him.'

Morrigan stared at the cat-girl, her chest heaving, fingers clenching and unclenching at her sides. Then she flicked her fingers and River was able to gasp in a breath, and another.

'Thank you, Mistress.'

Morrigan's lips curled into a smile as her gaze swept past the girl towards River. 'I wasn't going to kill him, yet, anyway. That's something he's going to do to himself.'

'No.' The girl shook her head. 'No. He wouldn't do that. He's got the pack. He's started mating with Bronwyn. He's got too much to live for.'

Morrigan's eyes glinted with something that made River feel like Death had just stepped into the room, waving his scythe. 'I know. I felt a connection when it happened. It will be useful, but it can't be allowed to fully form—it will stop the Darkness from sinking in its claws.'

'The Darkness? What are you talking about?'

'I'm talking about the thing that's going to help push him over the edge and make him destroy himself and everything he loves.'

'No. I won't. I'll kill myself first,' River said, breath still sawing in his lungs.

Morrigan chuckled. 'You won't. Not until after the Beast has its way.'

The girl took a stumbling step forward. 'Mistress, you can't hurt him. He's your blood.'

'No! He's a Were. He is one of the things that killed my sister and enslaved our kind. He and every single last one of them must pay for their crimes.'

'But Mistress ...'

Morrigan waved her hand. The girl clutched her head. Crying out, she fell to the hard, stone floor, and curled into a writhing, whimpering ball.

'Stop it!' River yelled. 'She's one of yours. Stop.'

Morrigan laughed, ignoring him to focus on the girl. 'You think the Were cares for you? You silly girl. Did he fool you into thinking he was kind? Human?' She jerked her hands and the shifter-girl's whimpers turned into sobs as she stopped writhing. Morrigan walked towards her. The girl looked up at her with a tear-stained face. 'You will learn to do as you are told, Eloise. Now, get up and clean the Were down. I have plans for him. What you have told me just means those plans will work even faster than I thought.' She jabbed Eloise in the side with her booted foot hard enough to make the girl grunt and curl around the hurt. 'Get up. I'm going to play with our other captives, prime them for the sacrifice. Once I'm done, I'll be back to torture this one further. He must be tipped over the edge, and given what you've told me, I think I know exactly how to do force him to it.'

Eloise stared at her. 'You lied to me.' She tried to push to her feet, groaned and vomited at Morrigan's feet.

Morrigan leaped back. 'Filthy whore. You better clean up that mess. I don't want this place smelling of vomit when I get back.'

'Leave her alone,' River snarled.

A nasty smile plastered across the face that had once belonged to his grandmother. 'She's mine to do with as I will.' She pulled Eloise up by the hair. The shifter shrieked, the sound cutting off when Morrigan slapped her, hard.

'I'll kill you for that,' River shouted, a fury inside him that had nothing to do with the Beast.

'I'd like to see you try.' She dropped the girl to the floor and kicked her so hard River heard the snap of a rib.

'Leave her alone, you bitch.' He lurched against his bindings, the table shaking with his efforts to get free.

Morrigan laughed, the sound a venomous strike. 'You'll never get free of those bindings, River, dear. You are nothing but a scarred, broken, miserable excuse for a Were. You can't even change in full. You're a monster, trapped inside a monster.'

'A monster you don't want to unleash,' River grated out, trying not to let her words poison his soul.

Morrigan's chuckle rumbled in her chest. 'Oh, you have no idea how much I want to unleash your Beast. Your Beast and I are going to have so much fun. Together, we are going to destroy the Were.' She clapped her hands together.

'I would die first.'

'Yes. You will. Although, not first.' She tipped her head to the side and breathed in deeply, eyes closed. 'Yule is only a few days away, but with this news, I no longer have to wait until then. By the end of the full moon, you will die, the Were will be destroyed, the Pact will be broken and all my lovely brothers and sisters will finally be free to join me and glory in the strength the Darkness has shown me. We have been subservient for too long. Glory days are coming. Glory days.' She spun, and still chuckling, left the room.

A shuffling noise caught his attention. He craned his neck in time to see Eloise trying to push to her knees. She was covered in blood and vomit and dirt, the pain on her tear-stained face showing something that went deeper than physical hurt. He felt so sorry for her, but still, he had to say, 'You can't let her do this. You can't let her destroy an entire people in the name of revenge.'

She shook her head, not looking at him. 'I meant to help. I thought she'd listen. Thought she'd understand. She always said—'

Yelling echoed down the hall—Iain's voice—cut off with a sharp grunt. River twisted against his bindings again, but it was futile. There was a shout and a loud slap, like a whip hitting flesh, a short, sharp, pained cry. Violent images of what Morrigan could be doing to his Shadow and the younger Were, Gareth, flashed in his mind's eye. He pulled again, desperate, but it was useless. He needed help.

He turned to Eloise. She was muttering to herself as she made it to her feet, clinging to a set of drawers against the wall. She trembled so hard, River thought she might collapse again despite the support of the furniture.

He wanted to give her time to pull herself together, but there was none. 'Eloise.' She stopped muttering but didn't look at him. 'That's your name isn't it? You're a good person. I can see that. And I'm not saying this so you will free me, because it doesn't matter what happens to me.' A scream tore through the air, echoing through the caves from another room. River flinched and pulled against the restraints again, to no avail.

He looked back at Eloise. She paled, as if the scream had torn at something inside her. 'Eloise.' She jumped and turned to face him.

'Yes?'

'She's hurting my friends. They've done nothing to you or any of your coven. They don't deserve this. Please help them. Don't let them suffer for the revenge of a mad woman.'

She looked pitiful, her expression desolate. 'How do you know I'm not like Morrigan?'

'Because of what you just tried to do. Because I could sense the goodness in you when you were the cat. You thought you were doing right. Now you know that was wrong. Right that wrong, Eloise. Help my packmates. Don't let them die.'

'What about you?'

He turned his head, staring up at the ceiling. 'My time was up long ago. I'm dying already. It doesn't matter what Morrigan does to me.'

'No.' Eloise gasped, took a stumbling step towards him.

He stared at her, confused. 'Why does that worry you? I'm nothing but a filthy, broken Were.'

'No, you're not. I've seen who you are over the last few weeks. You were kind to me when you didn't have to be. There's not many who would have done that.'

'You don't know the right people.'

'Maybe.' She reached out, touched him, her fingers still sticky with blood. Hers. And his. 'You can't die. You're good. Important. Special. Whatever it is, whatever you think is killing you, you have to fight it.'

Breath shuddered out of River's lips as a tear spilled from his eye. 'Don't you think I've been doing that? I'm not that strong.'

'I know you can be.' She shifted, gripped his hand. 'You have to try. If you don't, they'll all die.'

'What are you talking about?'

25

The little shifter glanced behind her, edged closer and whispered, her voice desperate. 'Alistair, Morghanna's husband, he was part Were. Morghanna didn't know, or Bridgette thinks she would never have canted the Curse.'

'What difference does that make?' His eyes widened as she told him what she'd heard.

'... And because you have the DNA of her son in your veins, if you die, the Curse will be enacted, but not just on the Were. It will be enacted on anyone responsible for not keeping you safe, and that includes your pack's coven.'

'Bronwyn!'

She nodded. 'You have to live, River. You and Bronwyn have something special and you can't allow that to be destroyed. Don't give in. I'll try to help your friends as long as you promise not to give in.'

Another scream shattered the air. Gareth. Morrigan was torturing Gareth. River gripped Eloise's hand, squeezed. 'I promise. But please. Help them.'

'I have to get you free first.' She reached out to touch his bindings, but a spark of flame snapped at her, burning her fingers. She tried again, but flame sparked out. Tears glistened in her eyes as she tried a third time, but she couldn't get anywhere close to touching the bindings without getting burned.

'Stop it, Eloise. Don't hurt yourself. The bitch has obviously done something to the bindings to stop anyone bar her from touching them. Just save my packmates.'

'But Morrigan ... she'll be back, and I'm so afraid of what she plans to do.'

'She won't kill me. She said so.'

'She can hurt you. She wants to unleash your Beast.'

'It'll kill her if she does.' There was another harsh cry, another voice yelling, then silence. 'Please. You have to do something to help them. Now.'

She shuddered but didn't look away. 'Remember your promise.'

'I won't forget,' he growled. 'Now, go. Help the others. Leave Morrigan to me.'

Nodding, Eloise backed out of the room. 'I'll be right back to help you.'

'I don't think so, Little Bit.'

Eloise swung around. 'Cain!' She backed away from the door, from the man standing there. He had to be Eloise's brother—they had the same hair and eyes—but there the resemblance ended. Where there was innocence and goodness in her, there was none in Cain. His expression was harsh with hatred as he marched into the room and dumped the body he had slung over his shoulder on the floor near the far wall.

Iain.

His T-shirt was shredded on his back, the long slashes sticking to his skin, coated in blood. For a moment, River thought his Shadow was dead, but then the Lone Wolf groaned and rolled over. His face was bruised, swollen, and blood oozed from a cut above his eye, covering half his face with rivulets of deep, vivid crimson.

'Cain! What have you done?' Eloise asked, her eyes pinned on the injured Were.

'I wouldn't be worrying your head about him, Little Bit, after what I just heard.'

'I don't know what you mean.' Fingers clenched and unclenched by her side, her gaze darting between him and the door.

'Oh, I think you do. Traitor.'

'Leave her alone,' River spat, pulling once again against the restraints. But he couldn't budge them. He had to watch, helpless, as the bigger man stalked towards his sister.

Eloise held her hands out. 'I'm not a traitor. You heard only part ... you don't understand. I found out something that changes everything.'

'It doesn't matter what you found out, Were-lover. They've pulled the wool over your eyes; done exactly what Morrigan said they do to our enslaved brethren.' He shook his head slowly as he came to stand before her. He'd backed her up against a wall. 'What I can't believe is my little sister fell for it too.'

'No, Cain, you don't know. You didn't hear.'

'Enough!' He slapped her, the impact making her head snap back, thumping against the wall.

'Leave her alone,' River snarled as he pulled harder against the restraints, but only succeeded in cutting his wrists open on the harsh leather.

Eloise turned slowly to stare at her brother, eyes wide with shock, the red imprint of his hand blooming on her cheek. 'Why are you doing this? You know I love our mistress, but she's mistaken about—'

'Our mistress is never wrong,' he roared. Then slapped her again, so hard this time that when her head hit the wall, she slivered down it to the floor.

'You bastard!' River yelled. Oh Gods. Was she unconscious?

Eloise moaned, then moved to curl into a ball.

Cain stared down at her, not an ounce of remorse on his face as he said, 'Morrigan is sacred. A Goddess. And you have fallen, Little Bit. You are tainted.' He spat at her and then stalked back over to where he'd dumped Iain on the floor. River struggled harder, snarling, but Cain didn't even look his way as he kicked Iain.

Iain groaned and rolled away. 'Not dead yet. Let's see what my mistress can do about that.'

'Cain. Stop. This isn't like you.'

He spun around. Eloise had uncurled herself, was trying to stand.

Cain's eyes widened at the sight, then narrowed, filling with hate. 'You have no idea who I am or what I can do. While you've been playing pet, I've been training with our mistress. She's shown me things you could never imagine. And you never will.' He laughed, the sound empty, remorseless. 'You know, the pity of it is, we were both adopted into this family to stand at her right hand. But now ...' He shook his head. 'I wonder what she will say when she finds out you're a traitor.'

'I'll want her put in chains with the others,' Morrigan said, sweeping into the room. Another man, slightly older than Cain, followed her, Gareth slung across his shoulders. The young Were was even more battered than Iain.

'You bitch! What have you done to him?'

'Ben here has tenderised them both in preparation for the Beast.' Morrigan gestured at the older man then turned a sickly smile on River. 'And despite being Eloise's adoptive cousin, I know he'll enjoy doing the same to her to get her ready for the Beast. He's always been jealous of her talents.'

'You'd kill one of your own?'

'Your kind killed the only person I ever called my own!' She jabbed her finger at Eloise. 'She is simply a tool. One that you and yours has ruined.' She turned to Cain. 'Tie them all up and then get him ready.'

'No,' Eloise said, finally gaining her feet. 'No. You can't. I didn't—'

'You've gone soft, my lovely one.' Morrigan was suddenly in front of her.

Eloise flinched but met Morrigan's gaze. 'I'm not weak. I'm seeing clearly for the first time. They're not the monsters. *You* are.'

'How dare you talk to the mistress like that,' Cain roared, grabbing her arms and pulling them up behind her.

'Leave her alone!' River's struggles to get free intensified.

'River. Don't. Don't hurt yourself. It's what she wants.'

Cain shook her again. 'Don't talk to it.' Spittle flew from his mouth as he ground out those words next to her ear.

'River's a person, not an "it".'

'He's an animal,' Morrigan snarled. 'A misbehaving one at that. He needs to be taught how to behave.' An arc of power surged from her fingers, hitting River square in the chest. His mouth opened on a silent scream as his body began to vibrate and arc up off the table. His head whacked against the wood, frothy saliva foaming on his lips, as his breath rattled in his chest.

Eloise shrieked, 'No.' Her cry was cut off by a loud slap, but still she didn't stay silent. 'Please. Please, don't hurt him. He hasn't done anything to you.'

'Yes, he did. He and his kind took my sister from me. They took my family. They took half my power. I want it all back.'

'But he's your family,' Eloise said. 'He's your blood.'

'You lie,' Cain hissed in her ear, pulling her arms up tighter.

'It's the truth,' she managed to gasp.

Morrigan slapped her again. Eloise's head snapped back, her temple smacking Cain's chin. Cain's grip on her arms slackened. Eloise lunged, twisting out of his grip. He made to grab her, but she ducked to the side and slammed right into Ben, who shoved her back into Cain. Cain's arm bounded around her middle, holding her arms tight to her sides so she couldn't reach back and scratch his face. She kicked at his shins—even in his crazed-by-pain state, River had to admire the fight in her.

Cain swore and visibly tightened his grip around her chest, his other hand coming up to grab her around the throat. 'I'll break your neck.'

River tried to move, tried to tell her to stop fighting for him, to just escape, but he couldn't make more than a strangled sound, his body vibrating and jerking with the lightning-sharp pain that arced through him. He watched, helpless as she struggled.

'Please ... can't breathe.'

'Perhaps you don't deserve to.'

A tear slid down her cheek. 'You're my brother.'

'I'm not the brother to a traitor.' Cain's fingers tightened.

She made a choking sound. River was sure she was about to die. But then all of a sudden, light flared around her and her outline shifted, dissolved. Cain cried out, stumbled back and then with a roar, lunged at the cat that had suddenly appeared at his feet. The cat took off for the door and he crashed heavily to the ground, his arms full of nothing but air.

'Stop her!' Morrigan shrieked.

The pain screaming through River's nerves evaporated and he fell, panting and sweaty, back to the table just as Eloise darted around the door, the power bolt Morrigan threw at her barely missing. It hit the doorway with an explosion of wood and plaster. Chunks of dirt fell from the ceiling.

When the dust cleared, there was no sign of the cat.

She'd got away.

With a roar, Cain took off after her. River could hear more power bolts going off, getting fainter with distance. He prayed to whatever god would listen that the little shifter got away to safety.

Morrigan, fists clenched at her sides, stared at the rubble in the doorway.

Chuckling, his voice barely a rasp, River said, 'She really got one up on you.'

'Shut up.' She slashed her hand and his body bowed up from the table as pain arced through him again.

'Mistress, stop. He won't be strong enough for the ritual.'

She let out a cry of frustrated rage, but the pain disappeared, leaving River trembling and weak. But thanks to Eloise, he was no longer hopeless. 'She'll get my pack. If you're here, they'll kill you.'

'What? And kill your grandmother with me? I don't think so.' She leaned over him, smiling.

Even though it was his grandmother's face, River could see no resemblance between the woman who had loved him and tried to protect him, and this revenge-driven witch. No scent of his grandmother remained. 'My grandmother is gone. You're nothing but her shell.'

Morrigan's smile widened and she chuckled. 'That might be true, but then, I'm not planning to be around when they get here.'

'Then how will you exact your revenge?'

'Oh, you will do it for me.'

'No. I won't.'

'You'll have no choice. You're going to change into your Beast and you'll kill them.' She pointed to Iain and Gareth, who now hung from shackles bolted into the wall. 'I've bloodied them for you. Made certain they're nice and tasty. The Beast won't be able to resist. It will tear these two apart without blinking. Then, wild and rabid, it'll go after the others. It will hunt down and kill your Bronwyn, your sister, Shelley, because that's what rabid animals always do—go after those they love the most. And the moment that happens, the Curse will be enacted and I will use the power of that to tear the Pact apart.'

Bile rose in his throat, but he swallowed it down. 'I won't change. I haven't changed with all the torture, and I'm not about to do it now. Not without the full moon. Whatever combination of magic and drugs you shot into me years ago made certain of that.'

She smiled at him, ran her finger down his cheek, over the burn scars, her touch making him aware of how ugly they were. 'There was no magic. That was just a tranquilliser. Your rage that night let an ancient part of yourself surface that had long been denied, and with it, the Darkness was granted entry. Your grandmother and grandfather's meddling kept the Darkness that was once a part of the Were sleeping, but as with all sleeping things, it dreamed. Such delicious dreams of rage and revenge. Those dreams became your reality because you were so angry with the world.' She laughed. 'You're broken, but not because of anything I did to you. That animal was already inside you. You're the one who let it out, let it take over. You did that to yourself.'

'You're a lying bitch.' But as he said it, dread rose up and he couldn't look in her too knowing eyes.

She brushed her fingers through his hair, just like his grandmother used to do to soothe him. But after two strokes, she gripped his hair tight and yanked, forcing his head back so he couldn't help but meet her gaze. 'I might lie about plenty of things, but this isn't one of them.' She let go and his head thumped back against the table. 'But believe what you will. The whys and wherefores matter nothing to me. You are a tool, and I will use that tool.'

His head throbbed, his entire body ached. The cuts on his chest burned. But he gritted his teeth against the pain and said through clenched lips. 'I won't change. Nothing you can do will force me to. Only the full moon can do that. And that is days away. My pack will be here within the hour.'

'Oh, I am counting on it.'

He shuddered as icy foreboding chased along his skin and down his spine at her words. Her smile was so icy, it was like being hit by an avalanche of snow. She gestured at the ceiling of the cave and he looked up, seeing a depression there that he hadn't noticed before.

'Ben, now that Cain is chasing his traitor sister around, I will need you to assist me.'

Whatever I can do, Mistress.'

'Open the moon door,' she said.

26

en walked to the other side of the room and pushed on a rocky protrusion. There was a grinding sound above River's head and a scattering of dirt fell on him as the indentation in the roof pushed upward then slid to the side.

Through the perfect two-metre-wide circular opening, he could see a scatter of stars and the three-quarter moon. His hands twitched at his sides. Deep inside, his wolf howled.

No. Not just his wolf. The Beast's hunger swept through him at the sight of the almost full moon. Almost a week off the three-day full moon cycle, it didn't have the power to force the change, but the moon's magic called to the Beast none the less. It sat up and howled a song of near freedom.

River clenched his teeth, not wanting to allow that sound to rip from his throat. It wasn't a song of joy or relief—it was one of violence and blood. The Beast wanted to sink its teeth into warm flesh, to rend and tear, to taste the saltiness of blood on its tongue, the warm thickness of it as it drenched a throat parched and dry and sore. It wanted to feast of the flesh, like his full-wolf brethren had done for years beyond counting before the Pact was drawn. But unlike those long-ago brethren, the Beast didn't feel sorrow for the death and destruction it wrought. It longed for it. Wanted to lose itself in an insanity beyond stopping—to drown in an ecstasy of blood and gore and death.

River shook against the madness inside him. He couldn't bring himself to believe what Morrigan had told him—that he was responsible for creating the Beast. And yet ...

Images, like an old movie, flickered into River's mind. A car, swerving to miss a bolt of lightning that came from another car. Another bolt. Then another. Too many, too close. The car was hit. Its wheels squealing on the dark bitumen, it hit the dirt on the side of the road, spun wildly and smashed through a fence, across a paddock straight towards a huge ghost gum.

'No,' River whispered, as the memory-images careened wildly, flashing sickeningly with what he could see in the present—Morrigan lifting her arms as Ben reverently removed her gown, leaving her naked, her pale skin glowing silver and pearlescent in the light of the moon. She flung her arms up to the moon door above him. Ancient words, dark and full of a power that had his hair standing on end, erupted from lips painted as red as blood.

In the other part of his mind, he was looking through the eyes of a terrified and angry boy as the car he was in spun off the road. Metal screeched with a high-pitched, torturous groan as the tinkling smash of shattering glass erupted back on him. He dived sideways, trying to cover his twin, the glass cutting through his clothes, embedding in his skin in sharp little flares of pain.

Then silence.

The scent of blood and fear, excreta and death, rose around him.

He looked up from where he had thrown himself. His mama was impaled on a branch that had been driven through the windscreen, her head flung back at an odd angle, her brown eyes staring out lifelessly at the tree above them.

His papa moaned—a sound filled with so much grief it shivered into his soul—his tear-filled gaze pinned to Mama's face.

Numb with shock, he watched, unable to move, as Papa strained forward, trying to reach his mate. But his legs were pinned under the steering wheel and his fingers barely scrabbled along her shoulder. His mouth twisted in a grimace of pain. Blood ran from his temple, darkly, thickly red against his too-pale skin.

'Mama?'

Skye! He was still lying on top of her. He pushed back off her as she began to scrabble wildly at her seatbelt. He knocked her hands aside and pushed the button.

Skye sprang forward like an arrow loosed from a bow. 'Mama?'

Papa turned, holding her back, his lips twisted horribly as he tried to force down a cry of pain. His gaze skated over River and Skye then flickered past them. Panic flared in his eyes, obscuring the pain and the grief. 'Skye. River. Get out of the car. Go. Find the pack. They're on their way … I can feel them.'

Skye began to shake, and whimper a denial, but Papa pinned her with his gaze and said, 'Run. NOW!'

Skye began to scream, 'No. No. I'm not leaving you Papa. Mama!'

She wasn't going to move. But River was part animal, used to obeying the pack hierarchy at a cellular level and their Coven Leader had given them an order. He grabbed her hand and jerked her to face him. 'Skye. We have to go.'

'But what about Papa? And Mama.'

'There's nothing you can do for us now except to run,' Papa said. 'Run to the safety of the pack. David McVale will look after you. Run and don't look back.'

'I can't.' She threw herself forward, wrapped her arms around him from behind.

He patted her arms, his gaze capturing River with something more than a simple caress. 'Take care of her.'

'I promise.'

'I'll take care of River, too,' Skye said, tears pouring down her face.

'I know you will. Now go. They're coming. I only hope the wolves find you first.' He shifted, winced. 'I tried to change what I saw. I tried.' He clutched at her hand. 'Trust Jason. He'll find you. You are bonded already.'

'Papa. I don't understand. Papa?' Her lips trembled and River felt her turmoil inside him, a twin to his own.

'This is not for you to understand right now. But you will. I promise.' He shifted again, even though the pain it caused him made his face pale further, his features pull tight. River lunged forward, hugged him tight, pulling his sister around so that their father could wrap one arm around them. A kiss was pressed to his head, then to Skye's before their Papa could hold himself in that position no longer and fell back with a groan. 'Go,' he whispered, his voice a wheeze now as he struggled for breath.

River took her hand and reached to open the door.

It was yanked outward before his fingers touched the handle. Hands grabbed him. Skye was torn from his grasp, pulled out the other door. Papa's cry, a sound of grief and rage, echoed in the night around them as he was dragged from the car, kicking, snapping.

Skye was screaming.

'Skye!' he yelled. 'Skye!' He began to tremble, his body heating from the inside out in waves that became a sparking golden-rainbow glow that covered his form. The men holding him cried out and dropped him.

There was a loud snap of sound behind him; the sharp jerk of a dart hit him in the back. He screamed as the change jerked to a halt. He tried to push through, to become the wolf, to help Papa and Skye —whose screams had turned into shrieks of rage as she yelled at someone not to hurt him—but everything was swimming. The soil beneath him rocked and roiled, rising up to smack him in the face.

A female voice—a stranger's voice, yet somehow familiar— snapped out a command he couldn't seem to make himself understand. Hands grabbed him, fingers digging into his upper arms in a bruising hold. He was pulled from the ground. His head lolled. But even though he could barely see past the swirling blackness that began to cover him, he saw his sister, outlined in the moonlight, a stream of bright red blood running from a gash on her temple, dripping off her chin.

Two forms lay slumped at her feet. Her hands were outstretched, blue fire arcing from them in an uncontrolled display of power that was at once awesome and terrifying.

She was trying to stop the men from reaching the car. But it didn't matter if they got there or not. The scent of petrol was heavy in the air.

A bright flare to his right. The car exploded.

The explosion blew him, and the men holding him, backwards. Heat rushed over them, so hot it burned. He struggled, futilely, to gain his feet as Skye's grief-filled screams rang in his ears. Blue lightning struck the shadowy shapes of men and women around him, lighting them up in blazes brighter and hotter than the sun. Her rage blended with his in a wash of red darkened on the edges with a creeping black.

He stumbled forward, slashed out at the men near him with half-changed claws. His parents were gone, but he had to save Skye. Had to protect her. But he couldn't get near her. She was lit up so bright it looked like she was going to explode. Helpless fury burned cold and dark through him, into his chest, burrowing deep.

'This is ridiculous,' the mellifluous female voice snarled. He swung around, determined to kill her first. She was holding a gun. He leapt towards her. Three darts punched into his chest. He flew backwards, rolled, tried to get up. Darkness swam into his vision and he fell, face to the side in time to watch the witch drop the gun and extend her hands. Lightning shot out and hit Skye in the back. She jerked as the energy bolt zapped through her system, her lips pulled back on a voiceless cry.

River tried to call out her name, tried to move, but the black of unconsciousness had almost taken him.

'Let me in and I will give you your revenge.'

The voice—echoing and wrong, so wrong—sang a song that reverberated in his desperate heart.

'Let me in and I will help you to save her.'

'Yes. Yes.' A vicious howl echoed inside his mind; a howl that sang of violent revenge; of justice taken.

'Yes, that's it. Let the animal free.' That familiar, mellifluous voice pulled him out of the vision and he looked up to see Morrigan in the present, standing over him, her smile a red slash in her face. 'Remember all the terror. Remember your reasons for inviting in the Darkness and allowing it to create the Beast. Remember what you wanted to do to those who threatened you; to those who wanted to stop you from reaching your goal.'

She began to cant a spell, the notes around the words a discordant harmony that twanged against his nerve-endings. His skin twitched, his heart pounded, his breath a raw rub of heat in his chest.

He tried to fight, tried to stop it, but the Beast surged forward, tearing through the bonds that held him in place.

River screamed as he fought against it.

Morrigan lifted a knife high, chanting. The silver blade gleamed in the moonlight, shining down from the moon door above him. Oh God, yes. Kill the Beast. Don't let it out.

'Do it. Do it,' he pleaded.

'No! River no. You can't die.' A voice, a dear, love-filled voice, shrieked a denial in his head, pushing the Beast back, stopping it from bursting through, from taking him over.

'Bronwyn,' he croaked through a voice turned raw with screaming. He remembered what Eloise had told him, remembered how important it was for the pack, for Bronwyn, that he stay alive, but, 'I don't think ... it's an option.'

'River. Stay alive. You have to stay alive for the pack. And for me. I can't live without you.'

'Bronwyn,' he said, more loudly this time.

'We're coming. Hold on.'

At her words, adrenaline-fuelled strength coursed through his veins, pushing through his muscles. He pulled against the bindings, every sinew straining, ignoring the pain that lashed and burned the tortured skin of his wrists. Sweat dripped from his brow, stinging his eyes, but still he pulled and struggled, his gaze on the evil-looking blade that hovered above him. He didn't look at Morrigan—in her eyes he'd see his death.

He no longer wanted to see his death. He wanted to see hers.

Morrigan's incantation stopped on a long, ululating cry. The knife slashed down. River fought to raise his hands, to knock the knife away as it came down towards his chest but it was useless. *'I'm sorry, Bronwyn. I love you.'*

They were the most selfish words he could have said at that moment, but for the life of him, he couldn't stop himself from saying them, just once, before he died. They were the sweetest words he'd ever said.

The knife bit into his skin and he grunted at the sharpness of the pain.

The grunt turned into a gasp of surprise, because instead of plunging into his chest, puncturing his lungs and stopping his heart, the knife swept across his chest, biting into the skin, but going no deeper than a couple of layers.

Morrigan made another sweeping slice across his skin. Five carving swipes. Each swipe a burning throb of pain. Hot blood dribbled down his sides as his lungs heaved, his heart a hurtful hummingbird banging against his ribs.

The sigil she carved in his skin—there was something terribly wrong with it. The Beast stopped howling, stopped pushing and lunging to get out. It sat back, a satisfied hum in its throat. 'What are you doing?'

She didn't answer, just put the knife down then held her hand high above him again. A fine sprinkle of something fell from her fingers. He hissed, jerking against his restraints as it fell on his wounds. Fuck. It was like she'd rubbed salt in his wound, except worse. It sizzled, burned. He looked down at his chest; the symbol she'd carved glowed like coal. He clenched his teeth against the pain as the glow brightened but couldn't help the groan that escaped as every sinew tightened, vibrating with the stress of the burning.

Black edged his mind.

'*Yes. Yes.*' The whisper was filled with such emotionless cold it made him wish he could die rather than hear it again.

Morrigan cried out another word. Orange light shot out of his chest, up and through the moon door. River's back came off the table, his restraints the only thing holding him down as the light lifted him, higher, higher. His wolf whimpered from that blocked-away part of his mind it had retreated to. But River clenched his teeth against the scream tearing at his throat.

As suddenly as it had come, the burning light cut off and River slammed back onto the table, panting, muscles twitching, rivulets of sweat pouring from his body and face.

Morrigan laughed softly and lifted her arms again as she looked up, her face bathed in moonlight. 'Thank you, Dark God, for the blessings you give.' She looked back down at him. 'Are you ready?'

His muscles trembling and twitching, he managed to say, 'Go to hell.'

She smiled, ran a soft finger along his brow, across his scars, down his throat to his chest. 'You first.' She ground her finger into the symbol she'd carved.

River tensed as the sensation tore through him.

'So strong. So stubborn. But it won't help you in the least when I call the moon.' She scribed a symbol between her bare breasts with his blood.

He shuddered and looked away from her.

'Oh, Dark One, please grant this supplicant her wish and send me the moondust so that I might cleanse this sinner before me.'

River couldn't help but look up, in time to see something sparkling and silver separate itself from the moonlight.

A memory sparked in his mind. Of Skye calling to the moondust, bringing it into the car as they drove to pick up their mama from the Harvest Moon festival. She'd brought it into the car, dancing it across her fingers, had turned to show him. His wolf had almost busted out of his skin.

Moondust.

They'd played games with moondust as children. He'd tried to remind her of it months earlier when he'd been in a drugged trance, thinking it might be the thing that could help him to turn; that could save him from madness. He'd been glad that she hadn't understood because he knew now if he'd turned that night, it would have been into the Beast. He'd not brought up moondust again. Hadn't thought anyone else knew how to call it. Papa hadn't been able to do it. It was part of Skye's special gift; something only one in a million witches could manage.

A talent Bridgette Colliere was said to have.

And apparently Morrigan Cantrae.

The moondust glittered in the air, hovering above him, so pretty, like the fairy dust he remembered. But this wasn't fairy dust. If it touched him, he wouldn't be able to stop the Beast from tearing its way out. The hammering thump of his heartbeat was loud in his ears as he struggled frantically to get out of his bindings. He had to do something. Had to stop her.

Morrigan dropped her hand. The moondust fell on him.

A scream ripped from his throat as the moondust glimmered on his skin, sinking into the symbol on his chest, disappeared. It was cool, the tingle it left in its wake familiar, soothing. But nothing could sooth him as he made one, final, terrified grab for control.

It wasn't enough.

He wasn't strong enough to fight the power of the moon that surged through him.

'No! River, don't let go. River!' The panicked scream in his mind was lost in the Beast's roar of triumph as it tore control of their fractured psyche from River and burst free.

It was almost as if he floated above himself, seeing the horror of what his body was becoming.

The glow of the Beast's change was cast in the fires of hell, tinged in red and mottled with black. Claws tore out of elongated fingers, razor-like teeth sprang from the muzzle now protruding from his face. Ears shifted, growing, as hair pushed through its skin. Ribs popped out, its spine cracking and twisting in painful, vicious breaks before snapping back together, newly formed.

Then he was pulled back down, inside, his mind subsumed by the Beast and its madness until he was it and it was him.

He snarled. It snarled. And they were one.

Something held it down. The Beast bellowed and pulled against the restraints, tearing free easily, its strength amplified by the symbol carved into its chest and the moondust sunk deep into its skin. It leapt from the table to land in a crouch by the wall.

It sniffed the air. Spotted a victim.

She stood at the other side of the table, her breasts globes of milky silver shining in the moonlight, her hair a lick of dark red blood on palest skin. She smiled, seemingly unafraid, although it could hear the fast beat of her heart.

She was excited. And aroused. The sweet musk of her sex filled the air, but it wasn't interested in her sex. The scent that truly sang to it was the warm salt of her blood. It wanted it. Now.

It snarled and lunged.

She raised a hand.

The Beast hit the floor. Rage pulsed through it and it leapt again only to be slammed to the floor again.

A sound was torn from it, ravaged, angry.

She laughed.

Limbs shaking with red-hot fury, it gathered to leap again—no prey ever got away. This time, before it leapt, something heaving gripped it and shoved it down, limbs sprawling on the cold rock floor.

'You can't hurt me. I have bound you with my blood.'

The Beast lifted its head, pulled its lips back in a snarl. Spittle dripped from its elongated eye-teeth and onto its chest. It wanted to sink those teeth into the flesh of her neck, tear out her jugular and bathe in the spray of blood, but it couldn't move off the floor.

The naked prey smiled as the Beast thrashed against the invisible bond holding it down.

'You can't hurt me, but ...' She gestured behind it. 'Turn your intent to one of them and you'll be able to move.'

It snarled. It didn't want anyone else. It wanted to kill her. The

Beast wasn't exactly certain why that was so important, but a soft voice whispered that it was.

The witch's laughter lit the air. 'I understand your need to kill the one holding your leash, but I am not your prey. Not tonight.' She moved her hand.

Pressure pushed on its head, turning it against its will. Its muscles strained against the magical hold, but it couldn't stop the turning of its head. Then it didn't matter. Standing by the far wall in between two semi-conscious Were who were strung up by chains, was a man.

Prey.

The man's supercilious smile faded as its attention snapped to him and the chained Were. 'M ... Mistress?' he stuttered. Eyes wide, he glanced past the Beast, his expression beseeching. 'Mistress, please. Protect me.'

She laughed. 'You must protect yourself, Ben. If you can do that, you are truly worthy to be by my side.'

'But Mistress, my magic is not that strong.'

'Pity. But take comfort. Your sacrifice will not be in vain.'

'Mistress, no. Mistress, please,' the prey blubbered.

The Beast found its feet and pushed upright, its gaze fixed entirely on the new prey. Nostrils flared as it breathed in the sweet scent of fear. It growled, a low rumble of satisfaction. The prey was trembling and blubbering. There would be no stalking. No hunt. Just the kill.

The kill would be enough. For now.

The Beast leapt. The prey shrieked and pushed behind one of the chained Were, using the injured male as a shield. The Beast swiped out with a claw at the chains in the walls. Metal shrieked and sparked, but the chains didn't break. It grabbed the chains and pulled, yanking them out of the wall with a groan of protesting rock and metal. Flinging the chains—and the Were attached to them— aside, the Beast turned back to the prey.

The prey tried to protect itself by muttering a spell. The Beast darted forward, grabbed the prey and sank its teeth into his jugular before the spell became more than words in the air.

Hot, salty blood gushed into its mouth and it groaned in satisfaction.

The prey thrashed, but the Beast held him tight. Bones popped and crunched. The prey's cries became a high-pitched scream. It hurt the Beast's sensitive ears.

The Beast reached up and crushed the windpipe. The sound cut off.

The Beast smiled. It could feast in silence.

27

'No.' Bron clutched her head as the world tilted and then was washed with a red haze. 'No,' she breathed.

'Bron? What is it?'

'Adam. Is she okay? What's wrong?'

Strong fingers gripped Bron's arms, holding her upright when she would have fallen to the ground. But she didn't see who it was, her sight filled with red images of a cavern that flickered and then blinked out. 'River. No!'

'River? What about River? Bron?'

She looked up at the faces surrounding her, the red haze gone, an emptiness taking its place. 'He's gone.' Was that her voice? It didn't sound like her voice. It sounded like an animal in pain.

Oh, Goddess!

River. He'd been in so much pain. Yet he'd struggled to hold on. But now ... 'He's gone.'

'What do you mean, "he's gone"?'

She looked blindly out into the night beyond the ring of faces surrounding her. 'I can't feel him anymore. The Beast. It's taken over.'

Skye glanced up at the moon hanging in the sky and then back down at Bron. 'But how is that possible? The full moon is days away.'

Bron shook her head. 'Morrigan called moondust and the Beast tore free.' She clutched her head, the echoes of pain stabbing through her mind. 'River fought, but it wasn't any good. The fury seemed to make it worse. There was a rush of such violent anger ... It tore me apart.' She blinked back the tears. The taste of blood rushed into her mouth. 'Oh Goddess, it's killing someone. River's gone. He's gone.'

Skye gripped her hands tight. 'If he's gone, how do you know he's killing someone?'

Jason nodded. 'He's still in there, Bron, or you wouldn't feel what he's doing.'

'But the light I was following, it's almost gone. It's not clear.'

Adam nodded. 'Jase is right, Bron. Don't give up now.'

The words slapped the numbing fear from her and she snapped, 'I'm not giving up.'

'Good. Use what you know, what you feel, to help strengthen the bond,' Jason said.

Sucking in a shaky breath, she held out her hands to Jason and Skye. 'Give me your hands. You both have bonds with him. Maybe if I tap into yours, the triple bond will help. Threes are always the charm in magic.'

They took her hands. Swallowing hard against the bile rising in her throat, the taste of blood in her mouth, she gripped their offered hands tight and closed her eyes, seeking their bonds—one Alpha, one twin, both filled with love—and bound them into hers.

The strength of them, of their bonds, vibrated through her, making her gasp as the pack's strength rode alongside her bond with River. Through it she felt their friendships, their loves, their bonds to pack and each other, all strengthened by their Alpha and his mate.

And inside them was the determination and desperate need to find the one who belonged to them all.

Bron's lips trembled as the joy of that knowledge thrilled through her. 'Feel this, River. Come back to us.' She grabbed all that they'd given her and pushed it into her bond with him.

For long moments there was nothing but the pack, then, like a warm breeze, the presence of him flowed back into her mind. A mere echo of who he was at first; but an echo that grew louder, stronger.

His presence was almost tangible in her mind now, and she could once again see through his eyes, feel what he felt, taste and smell and hear what he could.

Blood was hot and salty in his mouth, quenching a terrible thirst in the Beast. River fought against the thirst. He reached towards her, trying to find some way to push through. She had to help him. The pack had to help him. But how could they do more than they already were?

He turned his head and she saw Iain on the wall.

He was unconscious. But his presence lit an idea in her. If only she could wake him up, then he might be able to help her. It was worth a try.

Digging back down through the pack link, she made her way to Iain, desperation a hot claw in her throat.

She could do this. She had to do this. 'Iain, wake up. I'm here to help you, but you have to wake up.'

THE BEAST GROWLED as an unwanted presence fluttered in its head. It bit down harder on the prey, unwilling to allow that presence any leverage.

A groan sounded close by.

The Were still strung up on the wall made the noise.

The Beast glanced over at him.

The Were's eyes fluttered open, and despite being bloody and broken, he lifted his head and looked at the Beast. Began talking to it.

No. Not to the Beast. To the male it had once been.

'River ... man. Stop. You don't want to do this. You won't ever forgive yourself.'

The Were didn't know what it was talking about. The Beast *did* want to do this. What did it care of forgiveness? It had no feelings other than rage and hunger. It snarled and bit deeper into the warm flesh of the prey.

'River. I know you're in there somewhere. Your Bronwyn says she can still feel you. You have to listen.'

The Beast growled and held the prey tighter.

'River. The Beast isn't you. Don't let it be in control.'

The presence fluttered inside the Beast's mind; a presence it hated. A presence that found the delicious blood nauseating, that wanted to stop feasting, that wanted to plead for forgiveness from the lump of meat in the Beast's arms. That presence disturbed its feasting.

Rage rose up, and with a howl, it flung the rag-like, cooling prey across the room and swung to face the talking tormentor.

The Were needed to stop talking. While he spoke, the River-presence inside pushed up, started fighting, wanted to take control again.

No! This body belonged to it. To the Beast.

It licked at the blood dripping from its fangs, and snapped at the Were who hadn't shut up, even when the Beast swung to face him. The Were, chained though he was, met the Beast's glare, unafraid.

It was impressed. This one would make challenging prey if he weren't chained to the wall.

'Iain,' a weak voice muttered from behind, almost drowned out by the sound of chains dragging across the concrete floor. 'Don't upset him.'

'Oh, Iain, yes, please. Do upset him.' The witch laughed again. 'Please, keep upsetting him.'

The one called Iain didn't seem to hear them. He just kept his eyes on the Beast as he continued to speak to the River-presence. Even bruised and battered and bleeding like he was, he exuded strength. And determination. They were both things the Beast could appreciate. Not that they would stop it from killing the Were. Especially if it would shut him up.

It crouched to spring.

Something hard and sharp smashed into his head, knocking the Beast sideways. Head ringing, it shook the pain off and turned.

The other Were, the one thrown aside before, stood there, gaze unfocused, one arm held across his body at an odd angle, the other holding onto the chain still attached to his wrist, swinging it in front of him.

More prey. And this one *would* put up a fight.

On a snarling roar of excitement, the Beast prowled forward.

'Gareth. No. You can't fight it.'

'I don't think I have a choice about that,' the Gareth-Were said, swinging the heavy chain at the Beast as it darted forward.

The chain smashed against its side; the sharp end torn from the wall cut a gouge along its ribs. The Beast howled as the pain snapped through its mind, pushing the River-presence further down as the heat of burning rage consumed it. It bared its teeth at the Gareth-Were, but didn't leap forward, now more wary of the chain.

'River. Listen. You know me,' Iain said from behind it. 'We're friends. I know you have more control than this. Don't let the Beast win. Don't let Morrigan win.'

The River-presence in the Beast's mind cried out his protest, tried to exert himself. The Beast trembled. Its claws retracted. The burning rage in its chest lessened a degree, then another as the River-presence clambered up, out of the dark hole he had been pushed into when the moondust had forced the change and the Beast had surged to the fore.

'That's it, River. Don't let it win. You are strong, man. One of the strongest Were I've seen. You survived twenty years without pack. Without changing. If anyone can fight the Beast, it's you. And if you can't, then think of your Bronwyn. Fight for your mate.'

Iain's voice droned in the Beast's head. It tried to shake the words out, but they wouldn't go. Just echoed louder and louder as River pushed into the shared mind, trying to take back the body, one word chanting over and over in his mind: Bronwyn.

'No! No. You're ruining my plans.' Lightning lashed across the room, the fork darting out to hit the wall above Iain. Large chunks tumbled down, loosing the chains, hitting the Were. He disappeared under dirt and rubble.

A memory sparked in the Beast. It had seen lightning like that before. It had created a similar avalanche of rock before; rocks that had hit it; hurt it.

'Iain!' Gareth ran past the Beast, the chain dragging on the floor with a screech of metal on rock.

Rage a red torrent of heated blood in its mind, shoved back the River-presence. The Beast grabbed Gareth, its retracted claws springing out and piercing skin, shredding muscle, and threw him and the chain at the wall towards the other Were lying, boneless and bleeding amid the rock and rubble.

Lifting its head, the Beast glared at the moon. It tormented him, held him in its sway. Lifting its arms, sharp claws glinting with blood in the moonlight, it howled.

'Yes. Yes. That's my Beast.' The crooning of the witch broke through the tortured howl. It turned, chest heaving, a low rumble of hatred vibrating through its chest and up its throat.

It wasn't *her* Beast. It belonged to nobody. Except the moon. And if it could change that, it would.

She walked out from behind the table, edging closer. Foolish bitch. It snapped its teeth at her and swung out with a claw. Power, hot and hard, shoved it back.

The witch smiled. 'You can't hurt me, my Beast. We are blood bound. But there are others out there you could hurt.' She pointed at the open door. 'Others who would want to see you caged; to never see the light of the moon and bathe in the blood that is rightfully yours.' Her green eyes glinted, something dark and oily shining from their depths. It was a darkness that sang to the Beast. It knew that darkness. It filled the Beast too.

'Yes. I am the Darkness. And we are one. Now my Beast. Do as she suggests. Roam free and do what you will on those who seek to stand in your way. Take the prey that is yours to take; kill the witch-Healer seeking to destroy you and become stronger. Become my unstoppable force.'

Prey.

Its lip curled on a snarl, as it glanced towards the door, nostrils twitching. Yes. There were more prey out there like the one it had just blooded itself on. Humans so close it could taste the scent of them; flesh and blood and sinew, warm and delicious, calling to it.

And behind that scent was something else. Something wilder. Stronger. Were! They were nearby. And witches too.

The River-presence fluttered in its mind, sparked to life by hope. They were coming for him. For the others. To save them.

'Yes. You can feel them, can't you? River's mate, Bronwyn, is coming for you. You know what she wants to do to you. She wants to kill you. She wants River back. You need to kill her. Make sure she never gets that snivelling half man back.'

The Beast roared and leapt towards the door.

Yes. The witch was right. The Darkness was right.

It must kill River's mate.

The presence inside cried out, tried to struggle free again, but the Beast had full control now. It filled itself with fury and hate and swiped out, tearing into the presence, ripping at him with one image that tore hope and happiness from his heart:

Bronwyn on the ground, her throat an angry red wound, her eyes staring blankly at the moon riding high in the night sky.

28

'River, no!' The red haze swept through Bron's mind and then she was pushed out with such force she flew backwards, bowling over those who stood behind her. They landed hard, a pile of twisting, groaning bodies. 'What happened?'

Adam's question barely registered, her mind still caught on the image of her death.

River had tried to save her from that image—shoving her out with vicious force. But not before she'd felt his love. A love that would kill him if anything ever happened to her.

'No.' She shook her head, pushing to her feet. 'No.' She began to run. 'It's not going to happen.'

'Bron, stop.'

A hand grabbed her but she shook it off. 'I'm not losing him. Not again.' She headed towards the trees at the side of the road—River was in that direction. She was certain of it. But before she got more than a few metres, something streaked out of the undergrowth that bordered the field next to the road, making her jump. Hands grabbed at her, firmer this time, stopping her headlong flight.

'What the hell?' Jason turned to protect Skye.

Bron looked down at the shape as it darted through patches of moonlight towards her; it was a tawny cat. A cat with a pronounced limp. 'Bluebelle?' The cat meowed up at her, its peridot eyes oddly intelligent, even for a Familiar.

'How did your cat get here?'

Bron shook her head slowly as she bent down to fondle Bluebelle's ears. 'She must have been in one of the cars.' Her fingers caught in something wet and warm just behind Bluebelle's ears. 'She's been injured again.' Bluebelle skittered backwards as she reached for her. 'It's okay, Blue, I won't hurt you.'

Bron spread her hands. Bluebelle took a cautious step towards her, then another. Just as Bron was about to gather the injured cat into her arms, a man emerged from the bushes the cat had run out of.

He stopped as he saw the group of people standing on the edge of the road. It was difficult to make out his features in the shifting shadows of the trees, but it was clear when his attention turned to Bluebelle. 'Give that cat to me,' he snarled.

Bron snatched up Bluebelle, holding her close. The cat was trembling violently. 'No. This cat is mine.'

The man snorted. 'That's not a cat.' He took a step towards Bron. Jason and Adam moved in front of her, the warning in their stance more than enough to have the man coming to an abrupt halt.

His eyes darted between them and the cat, a light of understanding dawning in his expression. 'You're them, aren't you?' He curled his fists at his sides, lips drawing back as he glared at the cat. 'You traitorous bitch. You would betray our mistress and your own family to them?' He flung out his hands. A wave of heat erupted from them.

Skye threw up her hands to block the brunt of the magic coming their way. The force of the two magics hitting each other was an explosion, throwing them back. Bluebelle hissed and jumped out of Bron's arms, racing towards the man.

Bron scrambled to her feet. 'Bluebelle, no—' The sound cut off as her Familiar shimmered in the moonlight, its form melting, expanding out and up until in its place stood a naked woman, her pale skin glowing in the moonlight. Deep bruises and drying blood showed on her shoulders, arms, ribs and legs. She faced the man, her arms held out. 'Cain, stop.'

Adam growled, Jason's stance changed from defensive to attack. Bron felt the pull through the Alpha bond as he called the pack to him but was too stunned by the fact that her cat had turned into a woman to say anything.

'They are the enemy, Eloise. Are you too far gone to see that?'

'They're not our enemy. Morrigan is wrong.'

'Morrigan is a Goddess.' Eyes wild, Cain slashed his hand down.

Eloise grunted and staggered as a new line of blood erupted across her shoulder. But she didn't collapse. She sucked in a deep breath and said, 'If she was, would she have sent a brother to kill his sibling?'

'You are not my sibling. You are but a traitor. You deserve death.'

'I deserve to be told the truth, as do you.'

He shook his head. 'I know the truth. You've allowed your beliefs to be twisted. By *them*.'

'No. Morrigan has filled you with lies. She's taught you dark magic. She's deceived us.'

He jerked his head towards the group standing behind her. '*They* are the deceivers. How can you not know that? How can you, who have been chosen to stand at our mistress's right hand with me, turn on her? She found us, took us in when we were discarded by our own blood kin. I thought you understood the work. How important it is.' He shook his head, eyes pools of darkness. 'You are an endless disappointment, Eloise. It will be my pleasure to put you out of our family's misery.'

He swiped his hands and Eloise staggered, blood blooming across her stomach. He lifted his hands again.

'No!' Bron surged forward. Out of the corner of her eye she saw Adam and Jason move, their forms shimmering as they leapt, one towards Eloise, and one towards Cain.

Eloise staggered as whatever magic her brother had cast hit her. Blood a bright spray in the silvery moonlight, she fell backwards. Bron reached her just after she hit the dirt, her senses aware of Skye casting defensive magic to protect Jason as he attacked the warlock who was obviously part of Morrigan's rogue coven. Adam's bristling black wolf stood protectively in front of Bron, lips pulled back in a warning snarl as he stared at the battle raging. Howls sounded in the night air as the pack turned as one to return to their Alpha, to help protect their Pack Witches.

There was a startled cry as Jason attacked, the snap of bone, the shout of pain, the acrid scent of magic in the air as the warlock tried to defend himself.

She ignored it all. She had to concentrate on doing a Healing on the woman who had been masquerading as her cat over the last few months.

How could she have gotten away with it? Surely the Were would have scented she wasn't truly a cat? None of it made sense. But that didn't matter. She shoved the questions aside. All that mattered was that this woman was injured, her blood seeping into the dirt road in a dangerous flow that meant death was only minutes away. And she had to help her.

Peridot eyes opened, beseeching. 'I didn't tell her. About River. I didn't tell.'

'Don't talk Blu—' No, that wasn't her name. What had the man called her? 'Eloise. Don't talk.' There was blood everywhere.

'Bron ...' She coughed, a bloody, gurgling sound, dark red speckling her lips. 'Please, don't let them hurt the others. Don't hurt my brother ...' She grasped Bron's arms, her fingers like ice. 'She lied to us and ... he doesn't ... know. He doesn't ...' She gasped, her eyelids fluttered and she passed out.

Bron stared at her as zaps of magic and the snapping of teeth, the tight, wet, ripping sounds followed by shrieks of pain, filled the air behind her.

A lightning bolt hit the ground a few feet away from them. Adam snarled and in a flare of bright, rainbow light, turned from wolf to man. Before she could blink the halo of light from her eyes, he scooped her into his arms and began to back away from the fight.

'Adam! Put me down. I have to help Blu— Eloise. She's badly injured.'

'Will she die?'

'If I don't help her, yes.'

'Good.'

'Adam!'

'She's a spy. She's been reporting back to Morrigan all these weeks.'

'Not everything, or River would already be dead. She tried to help him, Adam. You have to let me help her.'

He didn't answer, just gave a tight shake of his head, the pain flashing in his eyes stabbing at her. 'I'm trying to protect you.'

'I know.' She laid her palm on his chest, the fast beat of his heart thumping hard, his muscles tense. 'But I am the Pack Healer.' She sent calming warmth through her hand into him.

His heart stopped thudding, his muscles loosened, his pace slowed.

'Let me do my job.'

'She's not pack.'

Bron shook her head and sent more warmth through her hand. 'That's not how it works, and you know it. I have to help. It's who I am. Please don't take that away from me.'

He stopped, his mouth screwed up as if he were arguing with himself, but then he closed his eyes and sighed. 'Okay.' He turned and jogged back towards the woman.

The fight had been pushed up the road with the arrival of more of the pack. They were ringed around Cain now, some in their wolf form, some still human. Skye stood among them, protected behind Jason; his fur looked a little singed, but not seriously.

Cain, on the other hand, looked like he was about to collapse. Blood streamed from multiple wounds—none of them killing bites, but enough that it must be depleting his strength. He swung his hands up wildly as the pack circled closer, a bolt of lightning going wide, exploding on a tree on the other side of the road, lighting it up with a flare of green and orange and blue flames. He staggered.

The pack growled as one, tasting their victory.

'Adam, please don't let them kill him. Morrigan has used him like she's used all the others in her rogue coven. They need our help. All of them.'

He let out an annoyed breath. 'I'll tell Jason.' He closed his eyes, that look on his face she knew meant he communicated with his Alpha.

She turned back to Eloise and put her hands out, bare inches over cold, cold skin, closed her eyes and tapped into her powers. They flared to life quickly, seeking to do her bidding in a way they never had before. She didn't have time to marvel or question. If she didn't do something now, Eloise would die.

Quickly, she assessed the injuries. The external ones were not the most dangerous. There was internal bleeding. Eloise's lungs were filling up with blood and if Bron didn't do something, she would drown.

She'd never done anything like this before—pulling someone back from the precipice—but deep inside, she knew she could. She'd finally tapped into the heart of who she was and this was what she was meant to do. Wrapping the truth of that around herself, she pulled on that ancient well of power that had always been inside her and let it flow, not just out of her hands, but out of her entire being. She opened her eyes to see the golden nimbus of it expanding past her aura to encompass the injured woman lying before her. The light sank into Eloise, surrounded her, lifted her, encasing her in a golden glow that lit the surrounds as if it were day.

Wind rustled in the trees, a song of benediction; the grass in the nearby fields glowed greenly. Sweet, floral scents twined with rosemary, lemongrass and lavender, wrapped around her; scents that couldn't be there because none of those flowers grew nearby, but seemed to be called from the aether to enhance her Healing spell.

Mother Nature seemed to answer her call, allowing her to draw more power from the earth, the wind, the water and the fire until she *was* the four elements with aether making five.

They sang inside her, rejoicing in coming together in the body of a true Healer. It was something else she'd inherited from Skye—an unusual occurrence for a witch or Wiccan. Normally power was bound by and into only one or two elements, but Skye had access to all of them. And so, it seemed, did Bron.

They filled her now, their strength and joy streaming through her, bringing a fulfilment she'd never before experienced in her work.

This was how it was always meant to be. Bron embraced the sensation, revelling in the freedom it offered, the excitement of discovery, of a future unbound by the past or present. The glow filled her, expanding out, and then she sighed and smiled as the whisper of her powers told her the Healing was complete.

More Healing would be needed over the days and weeks ahead, but Eloise was out of danger.

Pulling the power back to her, she lowered Eloise to the ground slowly, gently depositing her on a soft patch of grass and then turned. The pack surrounded her, their gazes riveted on her, a low hum sounding deep in their throats. As she glanced around the circle, she noticed that not one of them was injured.

'Bron. What did you do?' Adam's incredulous voice sounded next to her.

'She just became what she was always meant to become.' Jason came to stand before her, his hands stretched out to grip hers. 'She is a true Healer. Our pack is incredibly blessed to have her as one of us.'

Bron smiled.

'That was astonishing.'

She turned to embrace her friend as Skye moved to her side but the world span and she staggered.

'Whoa.' Hands caught her.

She looked up to see it was Adam. 'Thanks. I'm a little tired.'

'You look more than tired. I think you used up a bit too much juice.'

Bron swallowed hard. Her throat was raw and dry, her mouth parched, with a strange acidic taste on her tongue. 'You might be right. I don't think I can do that again anytime soon.'

Jason and Skye cupped her face, stroking her hair. Members of the pack followed their lead, coming forward to touch her with a hand, a kiss, a brush of knuckles on her cheek, a squeeze of her hand, a cold wet nose pressed against her arm, her fingers, a furry head bumped against her thigh.

Acceptance.

Love.

Family.

She would have been filled with so much happiness except for one thought: River.

'Don't worry about me. We have to find River.' She tried to stand, but Adam held her tight.

'Adam. Let me go. I have to find River.'

'Jason's already taking care of it.' He indicated where Jason stood giving instructions to those who had already touched her with their love.

A moment later, the majority of the pack turned and surged off into the undergrowth in wolf and human form.

'Where's Cain?' She hoped they hadn't hurt or killed him.

'Don't worry,' Adam said, jerking his head to the left where a man was tied to a tree at the edge of the field. His arms were bound, his head hanging on his chest.

Sick dread filled her. Had she broken her promise to Eloise? 'What happened to him?'

'He's not dead, if that's what you're worried about. Jason managed to incapacitate him and we got him tied up to stop him from hurting any more of us. He got hit by your wave of Healer juice, or whatever it was, but it didn't seem to do anything for him.'

Bron tried to speak, coughed, tried again. 'He's full of dark magic. It's wrapped around his heart. But even so, what I just sent to all of you should have got through. He must be fighting it.'

'Yeah, well, he's got a death wish then because he's pretty seriously hurt.' He brushed her hair away from her damp forehead.

A well of sadness filled her chest at the thought of someone filled with that much hatred—that he'd rather die than accept a Healing from someone he considered an enemy.

She glanced at Eloise. Hope surged inside her. Maybe all wasn't lost.

Clouds moved in the dark night sky above their heads and a shaft of moonlight lit the scene. Bron suddenly became aware that Eloise was naked, her skin glistening and pale in the moonlight. As was Adam. 'You two need some clothes.'

Adam gestured and one of the pack, who hadn't changed, stepped forward and took off his jacket, placing it over the woman. Someone threw Adam a pair of tracksuit pants.

A howl sounded in the distance. 'What's that?'

'Jason sent the others to follow the cat's scent.'

She looked up at him, understanding dawning. 'They've found Morrigan's base.'

'Sounds like it.'

She turned from her worries over Eloise—the young Were was taking care of her. She would be safe for now. 'Take me there, Adam. I need to go to River now.' She took a step and almost crumpled to the ground as her knees gave way under her.

'Whoa. You're not going anywhere. Not until you've recovered.'

'I have to stop him from doing anything else he'll regret. I have to bring him back.' Bron met Adam's gaze, fear gripping her as she thought of River, how the Beast had taken him over.

'You're going to be no good to anyone like this. Wait until Jason and Skye bring back the chocolate and juice for you. That should pep you up. And hopefully the pack will have everything contained by then. Patrick is there. He'll bring River back.'

'River will kill him. The Beast has taken him over.'

'Patrick's tougher than he looks.'

'Fuck, Adam. You're not listening. The Beast. It's strong. Stronger than any one of you. And if he kills even one of you, we'll never get River back because he won't forgive himself. You have to let me get to him. I know I can help him now. I know what to do.'

'But you've exhausted yourself. How can you help?'

'I can't explain it. I just know there's more inside me. Please, Adam. Trust me.' Adam gritted his teeth. 'Adam. Please.'

He let out a tight breath. 'Fine.' He scooped her up in his arms. 'But if you get yourself hurt or killed, I'm not going to forgive you.'

Bron smiled, despite her tension. 'Noted.'

'I'll just let Jason know where we're going.' His eyes lost focus as he walked towards the fields where the pack had disappeared. After a moment, he winced.

'What is it?'

'He's not happy. Neither is Skye. They want me to stay until they get here, to talk you out of it until you've recovered.'

'There's no time, Adam.' He glanced down at her. 'I can feel it. There's something wrong. We can't wait here. We need to hurry.'

Adam grimaced, but nodded, despite the push and pull of opposing orders from his Alpha and Pack Healer.

'I'm sorry. I don't mean to cause you pain,' she said, touching his face.

He flinched. 'Don't waste your power on me. I'll get over it. So will Jason.' He pushed through brush and began to jog.

She clung to his broad shoulders, even though she knew he wouldn't drop her. It never ceased to surprise her how strong the Were were. It encompassed more than simple muscular strength. They were strong in mind, strong in body, and that strength was fuelled and sustained by their link to each other, ever growing. The strength of the Alpha resonated down through the pack: the stronger his bond, the stronger the pack.

The McVale Pack was fast becoming one of the strongest packs around. They were a force to be reckoned with. Pride resonated through her, as it did through the Packbond. A pride that would sustain her through whatever was to come that night.

Adam jogged through a dense stretch of bush, tangled bracken, ferns and gum trees, into a small field. Moonlight lit the space, turning the long grass silver. Cattle lowed on the other side of the field; a clump of them sleeping together, a few with their heads lowered to chomp lazily on the dewy grass.

It was so peaceful until a howl sounded in the distance, followed by another. The cows mooed, startled, and began to stampede across the field.

'He's that way,' Bron said as Adam began to run along the edge of the field away from the stampeding herd.

'But the rogue coven's base is that way.'

Bron shook her head. 'He's not there.'

'Have you got the link back?'

'No. Not like before. I can't explain it. But I know he's that way.'

Adam changed direction, leapt over a fence and plunged into another thicket of trees and ferns. Foliage broke, the snapping echoing through the still night alongside her tight breaths. The sense of foreboding was growing with every step. The howls in the distance, the knowledge that the pack was already at the hideout, didn't alleviate that feeling at all. It only grew. Her breath came in short, sharp gasps. Her heart pounded in her chest, the beat of it a painful throb in her throat, her head. The acidic copper taste was back in her throat as if she'd bitten her tongue and swallowed blood.

Her fingers were digging into Adam's shoulders. She couldn't seem to loosen their hold even though it might hurt him. 'Hurry, Adam. Something terrible is happening.'

He darted through more trees to come out on the edge of a clearing.

Long shadows stretched across the grass. The taste of blood in Bron's throat increased. She gagged.

Adam stopped, his head lifting as he took in a deep breath. 'Fuck.'

Her gaze followed his across the field, to the edge of the clearing where the shadows were thickest. At first she couldn't see anything and then ...

A glint of silvery white hide in the gloom. A cow. It was lying on its side, its head at an odd angle. A darker shadow hung over it.

There was a feral ripping and tearing sound.

The taste of blood rushed into her mouth, the warm salty tang quenching a thirst she didn't know she had.

'River.' He was here.

29

The shadow hanging over the dead cow moved, its head snapping up.

Ember red eyes pierced her through the gloom.

'Fuck,' Adam repeated as the Beast slowly straightened from its kill, his vicious snarl tearing across the clearing. Goosebumps prickled over her entire body.

Without taking his eyes off the Beast, Adam lowered Bron to her feet and pushed her behind him. 'Run.'

She shook her head. 'I can't leave him.'

Adam's teeth glinted white in the moonlight as he snarled, 'Bron. Do what I say.'

'No.'

'This isn't a—'

The Beast howled, then charged.

With a harsh, 'Bron, run,' Adam leapt forward to meet the Beast.

'Adam, no!'

In mid-leap, Adam changed, the glowing rainbow pulse lighting the surrounds in brilliant relief so that for a moment, Bron saw what the Beast had done. Blood and flesh and limbs littered the area around the cow. No, not just one cow. Many cows. Shredded into unrecognisable chunks of steaming flesh and snapped bone. Vomit rushed up her throat. Bron clapped her hand to her mouth, doubt swamping her.

River would never have killed like that.

She swallowed, the taste of blood thick in her mouth, overriding the bitter taste of bile. It made her gasp, reminded her of her certainty of before. If she could taste the blood the Beast had drunk, then River was still there. She dragged her eyes from the horror of slaughtered cattle to watch as Adam and the Beast met in the middle of the clearing.

The Beast howled, swiping a viciously clawed hand at Adam's wolf. Despite his size, Adam moved like water and slipped under the swipe, biting at the Beast's leg as he went past.

Bron bit down on a scream as a tearing pain slashed through her leg, her cry melding with the Beast's snarl as it spun and lashed out at the black wolf. Adam darted in again, scoring a bite, teeth tearing through flesh.

Bron couldn't hold in the scream this time as pain bloomed in her side, bright and horrible.

Adam turned at the scream. The Beast lunged, its jaws wide, ready to sink into the black wolf's neck.

'No!' she cried out, staggering forward. 'River, no!'

The Beast faltered mid-step and crashed into Adam. Adam howled as claws dug into his side, but then twisted and bit into the Beast's arm. Bron tried to muffle the scream at the echoed pain of Adam's teeth tearing through muscle and flesh. She clapped her hand over her arm, blood trickling through her fingers.

She wasn't simply feeling River's pain, she was experiencing the injuries. But why?

And then she knew—the mating bond. She'd accepted it and now it was fully formed. And even though most of it was blocked because the Beast had consumed River, it hadn't consumed all of him. The Beast and River didn't share much, but they both felt pain and because of her Healer empathy, she was feeling it with him a hundredfold because of the bond.

She suddenly didn't care about the pain. This was her way in.

The Beast swiped at Adam. The black wolf let go his grip on the Beast's arm and rolled away before the strike could connect. Beast and wolf spun to face each other, lips curled. Hatred and tension strung between them. Each of Adam's bites was designed to weaken the Beast so it could be captured, but he was still hurting the Beast, enraging it. It meant to kill.

Bron couldn't let either happen. She staggered forward just as Adam leapt at the Beast again.

'Adam, no!' Jason stepped into the moonlight on the far side of the clearing. Skye appeared just behind him.

Adam snarled but changed direction.

The Beast swiped at him as he went past. There was a loud thump and crunch of bone. But Adam didn't go down. He rolled and was on his feet an instant later on the opposite side of the clearing, his growl low and threatening as he faced the Beast again.

'You can't kill him,' Jason said.

Another snarl. Bron almost laughed at the sound, because she knew that Adam was berating Jason for telling him something he already knew, but the sound turned into a sob in her throat as the pain in her side sharpened.

The sound caught the Beast's attention. It straightened, head cocked as it sniffed the air. Then, without warning, it charged towards her.

'River, stop,' Jason shouted, moving to intercept as Adam sprang forward, trying to catch the Beast from behind.

The Beast didn't respond to the Alpha-command. It didn't so much as slow him down. His lips curled back in a snarl, his glowing eyes snapped hatred with every pounding step.

Her breath was a harsh catch in her throat, her wounds throbbed with every step the Beast took. Jason and Adam couldn't stop the Beast from reaching her, but with lightning certainty born from all she'd realised tonight, Bron knew what she had to do.

As the Beast charged at her, she said, 'River. I love you.' Then she dug her hand into the wound in her side.

The Beast howled and faltered, then, snarling, resumed his charge.

Bron dug her fingers in harder, the pain slicing into her chest, making her breath catch in her throat. Sweat prickled, nausea swirled. Her heart thumped painfully, but she didn't let go.

The Beast howled but didn't stop. It lifted a clawed hand. Blood, dark and thick and red, glistened on its nails in the moonlight. She curled her fingers into damaged flesh and then pulled. Prickling black swirled in her eyes.

The Beast made a noise like the screech of metal twisting and breaking.

She waited for the swipe that would tear her in half, would end her life, and muttered under her breath again, 'River, I love you.'

Nothing happened.

She opened her eyes. The Beast stood before her, nostrils dilated, blood-soaked breath panting over her. It was trembling, its mouth working, lips pulled back in a snarl. Its hand was still raised as if to swipe, but it didn't move.

She stared up into its eyes. They were gold-flecked hazel, not the glowing coal red of the Beast. 'River?'

'Bronwyn,' he groaned.

'Bron?'

The Beast trembled at the sound of the other Weres' voices, a snarl deep in its chest.

She held out her hand towards Adam and Jason. 'Don't come any closer. River is in control again, but the threat of you might tip him over the edge.' They stopped moving, but their tension was obvious and she knew they could spring forward at a moment's notice.

'Bron?'

Jason held his hand out as Skye called out from the other side of the clearing. 'Stay there, Skye.'

'But River—'

'I can't afford for you to get hurt,' Jason said. 'Please, Skye. I know it goes against the grain, but I need you to stay where you are.'

She stopped. 'What about Bron?'

He nodded. 'I know.' He turned back. 'Bron. Move away.'

She shook her head slowly.

'Listen to them, Bronwyn,' River rasped, his voice strange, the words distorted by the muzzle and long teeth. 'Run. For fuck's sake, run.'

'No.' She took a pained step closer so she could touch River's chest. Blood ran from a wound that mirrored hers. 'I'm here to heal you.'

'You can't heal me. The Darkness won't let you.' His face twisted. 'This is all my fault. I invited it in the night my parents were killed and now I'm lost.'

'No.' A tear tumbled down her cheek. 'You're not lost. I'm here. I will always be here.' She touched his chest over his heart. 'I will always find you.'

He trembled. 'I can't hold it back. It wants to kill you. Wants to kill all the pack, but especially you.'

'Why?'

'Because you are the only thing truly holding me here.'

'And that's why I will never leave.' Her lips widened in a smile as she stared up into eyes that belonged to the man she loved. 'Do you believe me?'

'I wish I didn't, but ... Yes.'

'Good. Now, let me do what I need to do to help you.'

'How are you going to do that when you haven't been able to before?'

'Because I am more than I was before. I know who I am now. And I know what I'm supposed to do.'

His lips pulled tight over his teeth; the fight inside him was causing him incredible pain—a pain reflected in her. But she was used to taking on the pain of others, and there was something far more important to concentrate on.

She could see what Morrigan had done to him now. The moondust glistening in his skin. She wasn't sure why the moon-dust had changed him into the Beast rather than his wolf, as it had done to the Were in her vision quest, but she knew the moondust had to be removed from him first; knew the words she had to speak.

Reaching one hand towards the sky and the other towards River, she cried out,

'To the Goddess of the Moon I speak,
Your help to release this Were I seek
Release him from your influence, I implore
Return to him the strength that is nature's law
Three times three times three times three,
As I will, so mote it be.'

The night held its breath. No movement. No sound.

Then slowly, so slowly, moondust rose from the Beast.

It tipped back its head and let out a mighty roar. Hatred flashed in its eyes as it fought what was happening: the loss of its power. Its features flashed from the Beast to River's and then back again. It trembled harder as more moondust lifted from its skin and rose, sparkling white and pure, into the night sky.

The battle inside it started shifting in River's favour.

'I love you,' Bron whispered. 'Come back to me.'

For an instant, the reflection of her love was mirrored in River's eyes, then just as quickly, an inky black shadow fell across his eyes and the hatred of the Beast was back.

Bron gasped. The Darkness!

The Beast's lips curled back on a silent, vicious snarl just before the last of the moondust lifted from it, its claw slashing towards her.

Behind her, Adam howled as Jason shouted a warning. Skye's power sizzled in the air. But they were all too late. With the last of his power, the Beast, energised by the Darkness, sought to take revenge against its greatest enemy—the male whose body he had taken over.

Bron threw her arm up to protect her face, her chest.

River's pained cry rang along her nerve-endings as the Beast's claws raked across her arm.

Pain bloomed, bright and hot, but nowhere near as bad as she'd thought it would be. There was an *oof* of noise in front of her, a thump as bodies hit the ground.

Clutching her arm to her chest, she stared at it. Blood beaded from four scratches. Just scratches. Her arm hadn't been shredded by claws.

River had pulled back.

A smile trembling on her lips, she spun to see what had happened.

Jason had dived at River and taken him on a rolling tumble across the field, grass and dirt spitting up in their wake.

The Alpha rolled to his feet, hands raised to defend, to attack.

But there was no need. River lay on the grass, blood dripping from the injuries on his chest, side and arms. The Beast was gone. His hazel eyes were no longer red-black and hate filled. Instead, they were wide with horror, his gaze pinned on her arm.

On the slashing cuts his claws had torn in her skin.

'I'm so sorry, Bronwyn. I'm so sorry. I couldn't stop.'

His pain and distress tore at her. She rushed over to him, stopped only by the body of the black wolf pushing between them. 'Adam, get out of the way.' He growled at her. 'I've not finished yet. The Darkness is still here. Cloying. Grasping. Can't you feel it?'

River held out his hand. 'And that's why you can't come near me. The Beast isn't fully gone. I can't guarantee I won't hurt you again.' Grief dulled his eyes as he gazed at her; but the longing was still there. A longing she felt in her core. Had always felt—she'd just been too stupid and stubborn to realise it until almost too late.

But it wasn't too late. She loved him and he loved her. It was enough.

Bron nodded. 'I know. I saw it. In a vision quest. It's ancient and evil and it's been inside you all along.'

'What are you talking about?' Skye said as she joined them.

Jason swore and moved so that he stood between her and River.

'Jason!'

'I asked you to stay away,' her growled at his mate.

Hands on hips, Skye stared him down. 'I had to make sure River and Bron were fine. Now let me through.'

He rolled his eyes but didn't move to stop her as she walked over to Bron, gaze focused on the Healer's injured arm. 'Your arm should be shredded.'

'I know. River pulled back.'

Skye's gaze darted between River and Bron. 'What did you mean when you said, "it explains so much"?'

'I didn't know what the dark smudge was that I could see in River's aura. I guessed it was the Darkness spoken about in the ancient diaries, but although I knew it was responsible for holding his wolf at bay and turning him into the Beast, I didn't know why or how it was doing it.'

'It could do it because there's something broken inside me,' River said, pushing slowly to his feet.

'No. You're wrong. That's what I wasn't seeing. The Darkness couldn't take full hold because there's nothing broken inside you. It's because of your strength, your purity, your love for your sister, your pack ... your love for me.' By the Goddess, she could see it now so clearly in his eyes. 'But not only that. It's the way you always see everything, including me, with such clarity. All of it allowed you to hold on.' She took a step closer to him. 'River, my love. You're not broken. You are more whole than anyone I've ever known.'

River stared at her, chest heaving. She could see in his eyes he wanted to believe her, but ...

'I feel it here,' he said, clenching his fist to his chest. 'Seething. Clawing at me to get out. It hurts and I don't think I can fight it anymore.'

'River,' Skye said, voice breaking. 'River, don't say that.'

'It's true. And I don't want to hurt any of you. That's why I have to go.'

'You can't go,' Jason said as Adam let out a pleading growl.

'I have to. I'm a danger to all of you.'

'But you can't go,' Skye said, reaching to touch her brother. River winced, jerking back. Skye's hands dropped to her sides, devastation clear on her face, but her voice remained resolute as she continued to speak. 'We have to look after you. You don't know how important you are. Not just to me. You know how important you are to me. And you're Bron's mate. But apart from that, Shelley discovered something in the diaries. Come back with us, River. Let us explain. You can't go.'

River stepped back, shaking his head. 'I know what you're talking about. Eloise overheard you.' He glanced at Bron. 'She's one of the rogue coven. She's a shapeshifter and she's been masquerading as your cat.'

'We know. She came to us. To lead us to you,' Bron said.

He nodded. 'She's a good person. She tried to help me. Tried to tell Morrigan what she'd heard.'

'Oh, no,' Skye said, her hand going to her mouth. 'She'll never leave you alone.'

River's lip twisted as if he were in pain. 'Eloise only told her I was related to her through Morghanna. She whispered to me later about what Shelley discovered, when she thought I was going to give up. She said I had to fight. And I will. I won't let it kill me. But if I stay here, I might hurt all of you.' His gaze flickered to Bron for a long, desire-filled moment. She tried to cling to that look, but his gaze moved to stare at the moon. 'I can't be here when the full moon comes. I have to be locked up. Far away.'

'No. That's where you're wrong. That's what I was trying to tell you before.' Bron stepped around Adam, but this time when he went to block her, Jason held his hand out.

'No, Adam. Let her.'

River edged away as she came close. 'Don't, Bronwyn. I don't want to hurt you.'

'And you won't. You haven't let the Beast hurt me yet, and you're not going to.' '

What do you call that?' he said, reaching out to touch her arm.

It was the softest, gentlest caress and it burned through her, made her want to curl up against him, secure in his strength. But she couldn't. Not until she'd freed him. 'I call it a scratch that could have been so much worse if you weren't so strong. If you weren't the male I love with all my heart, who loves me with all of yours, I'd probably be dead.'

'Bronwyn.'

Her name on his lips was a tortured sigh. She couldn't stand the sound of it. The Healer in her wouldn't allow it, let alone the woman who loved him. She reached out, laid her palm against his chest. He shuddered, seemed for a moment as if he would shift away as he'd so often done before. 'Do you trust me?'

'Yes. With my life. It's me I don't trust.'

'But you should. I do. With my life.'

'You shouldn't. I'm dangerous.'

'No. You're not. There's something inside you. You said it yourself. But you're wrong about how it got there. You didn't invite it in. Not really. It's drawn to anger and despair. It used the grief and pain of a little boy and pushed its way into you all those years ago.'

'How do you know?'

She shook her head. 'Partly the vision quest, partly instinct. Maybe some of what I'm getting through you from the mating bond. I didn't recognise it when I was trying to Heal you because its existence was hidden from everyone. But Bridgette Colliere knew of it. She banished it. She showed me in my vision quest. I didn't understand, but it just made the mistake of showing me what it was. I recognise it now. I might not be able to banish it like Bridgette Colliere did all those years ago, but I know what it hates. I know how to force it out of you.'

Without any warning, she slapped her other hand against his chest and pushed everything she was into him. The golden glow of a Healer's power fused her hands to his chest.

'Look at me, River. Look at me.'

His gaze snapped to hers and she held it, using the connection to enter his mind as her magic entered his body through her hands. She pushed her warmth, her empathy, her love, into him; filled her mind with how she saw him—his strength, his courage, the trust she had in him, their shared love, how that lifted her up beyond happiness and into bliss. She hooked into the mating bond—still so fragile but strengthening with every moment she believed in it.

She'd accepted it. Nothing on this earth could break it now that was done. Not even death.

The Darkness scrabbled against her efforts, fighting her. It had burrowed deep. She could burrow deeper, force it out. But only if River was ready to let go of the fear and anger that had called it in the first place. 'What happened was not your fault, River. You were a little boy torn from all he knew and loved. But that's not true anymore. You are safe. Your sister is safe. You are part of the pack again. And we have shared the gift of mating. You are mine and I am not going to let some evil Darkness take you from me. Now. Let. Me. In.'

She pressed her fingers into his skin, her gaze searing into his as she shoved more power into him.

He jolted, teeth snapping together with a grinding click as every muscle in his body tightened. The thing inside pushed back, try to take control again.

'Oh, no you don't.'

She had no idea where it came from, but she knew it. She knew it like the light knows the dark. Like goodness knows evil. Bridgette Colliere had seen and fought it all those years ago. It was the opposite of everything she stood for. It was envious of her power, her friendships, her love. But it also feared them.

And that was its weakness. That's why it had always given River pain whenever she'd tried to heal him directly. Why it had tried to kill her.

Her hope, her love, her goodness, was poison to it. Just like Bridgette's had been.

But it had learned from that time and it was stronger now. Wilier. And she had been weakened by the earlier Healing and the mirror injuries she'd sustained when River was hurt fighting Adam.

Her muscles trembled. Sweat prickled her brow and stung the wounds in her sides. She clenched her teeth, tasted blood. Blackness bloomed in the edges of her vision. Someone cried out her name. Blackness swirled in the growing void in her mind. Something was laughing at her, nasty and triumphant.

Then a warm, perfumed breeze fluttered past her, winding around her, tantalising her senses. It was filled with her favourite, energising scents: lemongrass, rosemary, frankincense and lavender with a hint of chilli chocolate like the little lilies River had planted in the garden he'd created for her.

'Don't give up on me, Bronwyn, my love.' River's voice sounded clear in her mind, echoing alongside another that said, *'Take what you need, my child. Take what is freely given.'*

Her eyes widened and she understood.

Searching out that connection she had to Skye and Shelley, she pulled on it. Pulled on all the bonds she'd pulled on before. She filled herself up with the strength of their connections, a strength freely given to her now and always. So much goodness and light and love. Not that there hadn't been hardships, old and new arguments, jealousy and dislike—they all lived alongside the good and the harmony in this astonishing ever-growing tree-like bond. But that disharmony didn't weaken the bond. It created nuances. Made it stronger because of the imperfections.

It filled her. It took her breath away with the glory of it. So much to discover. So much to understand. And it was all within her grasp if she could only do this one thing.

If she could only save this Were.

A Were who was not only essential to her, but who was essential to the pack in so many ways, not just for the reason Shelley had discovered. They loved him. They cared for him. He was family. He was pack.

Sliding her arms around him so she was chest to chest, heart to heart, her gaze on his, her lips a whisper from his, she said, 'I love you, River. They all love you. Feel that love.' And melding her lips to his, she pushed every bit of what she had just felt into him, through skin, through lips, through mind and bond.

He jerked as the thing inside him fought against what she was doing. She heard the scream of it in her mind, an agonising pierce that threatened to fracture her skull, but she didn't let go.

Hands pushed against her—on her shoulders, her back; Skye, Jason, Adam—as they supported her and fed her through touch. Shelley was also there, in her mind, and with her the ghosts of Adeline, Skye's grandpa, Harrison, and all the previous Pack Witches and Pack Warlocks with them. They were quickly followed by others; the pack opening themselves to her and giving up what she needed in her battle with this Darkness that wanted to take River.

She felt River in her mind, the pain in him, the love he had for her, the trust. He was fighting; for her, for himself, for Skye, for pack. 'That's right, River,' she whispered against his lips. 'Fight it. It's weakening. Can you feel it? Fight it, River. Fight.'

And he did. It was leaving him. The Darkness was being torn from between his auras, from around his heart, and pushed out. His arms tightened around her as he whispered words she'd longed to hear against her lips. 'I belong.'

She gloried in the sound of those words, the joy filling her, spilling out of her skin, her eyes, her hair, in her breath. It caressed her skin like a warm breeze, wrapping them both in a golden glow. She pulled back a little to stare up into his glorious eyes. 'Yes. You belong.'

He opened his mouth to say something else, but then he stiffened. He held still for a long moment, not breathing, not moving; she couldn't even hear his heartbeat.

'River?'

At the sound of his name, his body began to vibrate madly against hers. She held tighter, holding him up. The Darkness was fighting them. Oh Goddess. It was so strong. Stronger than she'd thought. But she was stronger than she'd thought too. And she was backed up by the strength of everyone who had ever cared for her. With the born strength she'd been given from the Goddess and never knew she had, she fought back. 'You're not going to take him from me. You're not.'

Froth bubbled on his lips, black and glistening. His skin was deathly pale, breathing jerky and shallow. She didn't stop, just pressed a kiss to his chin, his throat, his cheek, his chest, whispering with every caress, 'I love you. You're mine. You belong. We belong.'

His eyes turned pitch black and his head snapped back. Then he opened his mouth and roared.

She'd never heard anything like that sound and hoped to never hear anything like it again. It was agony incarnate; pain and hatred and fear and loneliness the like of which she had never imagined. The sound pierced her ears, her skin, chilling her so that, despite the warm summer air, she was colder than she'd ever been. She wanted to clap her hands to her ears, deny the sound, but she couldn't let go of River.

She wouldn't let go.

She held on tight, the touch of her friends and pack on her body, in her mind, never wavering. They wouldn't let go either. Pressing her cheek against River's cold chest, she kept up her words of love, her mantra, repeating them over and over, unable to hear them, but knowing they were there because of the warmth they left on her lips.

That warmth transferred to his skin, a small patch at first, but one that grew with every moment of belief. An ever-increasing circle, it turned his grey skin into the sun-kissed gold she loved so dearly.

He jerked and spasmed, so violently that if it hadn't been for the others holding her and him, she wouldn't have been able to ride such a storm. The ear-piercing sound increased until a final high-pitched scream tore through the night. River jerked up, as if something was being torn from him.

Then it was gone.

River sagged in her arms. She would have dropped him, except Jason and Adam were there.

Skye gasped. Bron looked up to see what her friend was staring at.

Above them something hovered, a dark sludge against the deep purple of the night's sky. It seethed, pulsing, looking like it was readying to attack.

'What the hell is that?' Adam muttered.

'That's what was inside River,' Skye said, her voice shaking with exhaustion and worry.

'It wants back in.'

'No. It wants us dead,' Jason said.

Bron shook her head as it quivered above them, gathering into a vicious, pulsing ball. 'No, it wants me dead.' Her words seemed to energise it. It whipped down, lashing towards her with a glistening dark tentacle.

In the circle of her arms, River straightened, lifted his head and roared at it, 'You will not touch her again!' He raised one arm, the rainbow glow of healthy Were change encasing his hand. It screeched, pulling back as the glow touched the edges of the ribbon of black.

Ash fell through the air from where the glow touched it.

It retreated, moving higher.

River tried to push Bron behind him. The Darkness shrieked again and swooped sideways, two tentacles shooting out from it, heading straight for Bron.

River spun out of her grasp, swiping at the tentacles. His nails, now elongated claws, glistened at the edges like they were filled with some gold-tipped poison. They slashed through the Darkness.

An ear-piercing shriek lit the night. The Darkness sucked up into itself. The air vibrated around it and then it was gone.

30

'What the hell just happened?'

Bron couldn't help but laugh as Adam's strident question broke the shocked silence. But as the laugh left her, so did all the strength she'd pulled on. Her knees turned into jelly and she began to tumble to the ground.

'No you don't,' a deep voice mumbled as strong arms wrapped around her, pulling her against a broadly muscled, sun-kissed chest.

Unlike when Adam had picked her up, she wasn't annoyed by it at all. River's arms were home. 'Oops,' she said, giggling a little, suddenly dizzy and carefree. 'I think I used up a little too much juice again.'

River smiled down at her, a warm, possessive smile. 'Then let me give you a little bit back.' He kissed her. But alongside the sexual buzz she had from being kissed by River, there was a familiar glow emanating from him and back into her.

She pulled away, shocked. 'How are you doing that?'

'The mating bond. What you give me, I can give back to you.'

'So I filled you with Healing light ...'

'And I'm giving a little of it back.'

She slapped her hand over his chest, holding him back. 'But you need it.' She touched his face where the scars he'd worn since he was ten still twisted, livid white tentacles across his cheek and into his hairline. 'It hasn't fully healed you yet.'

He turned his head, kissed her palm. 'That's because my scars aren't something I need healed. They're a part of me. I want them because they are a reminder.'

She swallowed hard. 'You want to be reminded of the Darkness?'

He nodded. 'Not just the Darkness. Someone far smarter than me said if we don't remember history we are certain to repeat it. I can't forget my history because it has led me to my future.' A bright smile flashed on his face, filled with wonder and his love for her. 'I never thought I'd get a future, and here I've been handed one better than any I could ever dream of.' He nuzzled his scarred cheek against her hand.

'So you won't let me heal your scars?'

'Do you mind them?'

She pulled his head down, kissed them. 'Only because I thought you did. I think they show your strength. They're one of the reasons I fell in love with you.'

'Then we're agreed, I get to keep my scars—for now.'

She nodded, understanding completely. He'd come so far tonight, but he had been locked in with the Darkness for so long, it had left deeper scars. Scars that would heal with love and time and belonging. And when he was ready, he would ask her to take away the last vestiges of that scarring and fully step into the skin of the Were he would have been if not for Morrigan and her machinations.

'So, about that power you need.' His lips curled into a wider smile as she opened her mouth to protest. 'Nobody needs as much as you just channelled into me. I don't think I'm going to ever be sick again.'

She chuckled, but his lips covered the sound and this time she gave herself up to it. 'Mm, that's good,' she murmured moments later as he pulled back a little. 'Better than chocolate for what ails you.'

His lips curved against hers.

There was a cough behind them. 'Sorry to interrupt this reunion moment,' Adam said. 'But is anyone going to answer my question?'

'I'm not sure myself,' Jason said. 'Bron?'

As River turned with her still in his arms so she could face those waiting patiently behind them, she laughed, bliss and wellbeing filling her. She could somehow feel through the pack that Iain and Gareth had been rescued. They were injured, but safe and being cared for until she had the strength to return and do a Healing on them. Part of her wanted to take care of them now, but the greater part wanted to stay right where she was, in River's arms, and that's where she would stay for tonight. Through the Packbond, there was a sensation of encouragement; for her to take her time and fulfil a much more important task.

The encouragement filled her with giddy bliss and she smiled at Adam, who was standing, peering around Jason, trying to hide his nudity. Not that she minded his nudity. But as a newly mated male, River would. 'We won,' she said in answer to his question.

'But against what?'

She shrugged and looked up at the sky where the Darkness had been only moments ago. 'The ancient witches called it the Darkness. What it is, other than evil, I don't know.'

'Did Morrigan send it?'

She sighed, her lips pressing together. 'No. At least, I don't think so.' She told them what she'd seen in her vision quest. 'It's far older than Morrigan. But it was most likely attracted by her need for revenge, as a small piece of it was attracted to River in a moment when he felt the same way—lost, frightened, alone and so grief-stricken he had no control over the rage that invited it in.'

'Will it be back?' River asked.

She cupped his face as she gazed up into his warm, hazel eyes. 'I don't think it's done with us yet, but if you're asking me if it will come back to claim you, no. I'm pretty sure that's impossible now. Not now you've fought it and won. And especially now you're filled with so much light and life.'

'And love.'

Her lips trembled. 'And love.'

'You saved me,' he whispered.

'You saved me first.' Her lips widened into a smile that mirrored his. 'We saved each other.'

'Yes, we did.'

'Always and forever.'

They were Were words of bonding, but said in front of others, they were words that sealed a mating in a pack. His eyes glowed as she said them, his arms trembled as they held her. 'You can't know how much I love to hear those words coming from you.' His lips pressed against hers in a soft, yielding kiss, offering, not taking. It was a giving, a promise.

She took up that promise and gave back one of her own.

After long moments, he leaned back, looked over Bron's shoulder. 'You will bear witness?'

Bron turned to see Jason, Skye at his side, eyes filled with tears of joy. Adam stood just behind them. The three of them nodded as one and intoned, 'We bear witness. With our hearts and souls and the love and bonds of pack, we bear witness.'

River gazed deeply into Bron's eyes. 'I love you, Bronwyn Kincaid. Always and forever will I be your mate.'

'I love you, River Collins. Always and forever will I be your mate.'

He bent his head as the words slipped from her mouth and sealed their bond with a kiss that stole her breath and her heart all over again.

JASON AND SKYE slipped from the clearing as Adam changed once again into his wolf and trotted off in the other direction. Skye risked a glance back to see her brother and her best friend entwined in each other, oblivious to everything else.

'Is it safe to leave them there?' She sniffed, wiping tears from her eyes.

'I have called to the lieutenants. A sentry has been set to make certain they won't be disturbed, just as we weren't disturbed when we mated.'

Skye blushed, knowing that Adam and Bron and Shelley had been witness to the start of that.

Jason pulled her to his side and pressed a kiss to her forehead. 'We could repeat it again tonight if you weren't so exhausted.'

Skye's lips bloomed into a smile, a seductive glint in her eyes. 'I'm never too exhausted for that.' He gave her a searing kiss of promise that made her sigh and tremble with longing. When he finally let her go, she whispered, 'No fair that you can do that to me.'

His brow shot up. 'You have no idea what you do to me.'

She slipped her hand down to cover the bulge in his jeans. 'I think I have a fair idea.'

'Witch,' he said, his grin a crooked slash on his face, lightning blue eyes glinting with the promise of so much more.

She laughed, the sound a crisp bell in the still night. A night filled with so much tension and grief and now filled with such happiness. She turned her attention to the moon and noticed that it held a gold tinge. 'Look at the moon. It's golden, not yellow, like Bron's Healer light.'

Jason's eyes glowed with wonder. 'Yes. There's no other colour quite like it. The Were call a moon such as that a Healer Moon. It's a good omen.' He looked down at her again. 'Let's go.' He headed them towards the cars they'd left behind.

'Shouldn't we go to the rogue coven's base? Help the others?'

'No. They have rounded up those who were left behind and Adam's gone to give final orders and make sure everyone gets home safe. My priority now is to look after you.'

He tugged her forward, but she didn't move. 'What do you mean, left behind?' He twisted his mouth and then firming it into a stubborn line, tried to pull her forward again. She dug her heels in. 'Jason. Tell me what happened.'

He let out a pent-up breath and then said, 'Morrigan wasn't there. It seemed she escaped again.'

Skye's gaze darted into the dark. 'She's out there?' He nodded. 'Will we ever be rid of her?'

He folded her into the safe strength of his arms before she had a chance to take a breath. 'I won't let her hurt you. I won't let her hurt River or Bron or anyone else in this pack ever again. Whatever she plans, we'll find her and we'll stop her.'

Skye cupped his face, staring into the eyes that had captured her soul and her heart from the first moment she'd looked into them. 'Yes, we will.' She pressed her lips against his, his love pouring through her as she poured her love through him; somehow brighter and more than it had ever been before.

After a long moment, passion-fuelled kiss, she pulled back a little to stare up at him. 'Tonight has changed us all.'

'Yes. It has. We are stronger.'

'Yes.' She frowned.

He reached out and touched her brow. 'What is it?'

'What about the Darkness? The thing that was inside River?'

He glanced back at the clearing where they'd left the newly mated pair. 'I think River and Bron are better suited to answer that question. But until we know more, let's just concentrate on what's before us.'

'Morrigan.'

'Yes. But I didn't mean that. If I've learned something from tonight, it's that love and friendship and the bonds that have held our pack together all these years are our greatest strengths. Let's build on that. If we do, Pack McVale will be formidable and nothing will be able to tear us apart.'

Skye smiled up at him. 'Nothing can tear us apart.'

He sealed her vow with a kiss.

———

RIVER LIFTED HIS HEAD. 'NOT HERE,' he whispered.

She nodded. As befitted a true mating, they would make love in the open, binding themselves to each other, but he couldn't allow that to happen in a place that still screamed of death, despite the Healing that had been done there tonight.

He carried her from the clearing where their battle was so

recently won, away from the cows the Beast had slaughtered. Thank the Moon he hadn't come across any more people or Were—the death of that rogue coven warlock at the hands of the Beast was enough to bear.

He pushed that thought away—the self-recrimination would keep for later. Now, he had Bronwyn in his arms and a mating to complete.

He entered a dell made up of ancient ash and elm trees. A stream trickled through a small, summer-scented clearing that was shielded from the outside world by a hedge of trees and brush that enclosed it on three sides. On the other side, the high grass of the nearby pasture created a fourth wall.

He didn't know how he knew, but somehow, he'd entered the McVale Packlands.

Packmates were nearby—close enough to come if danger threatened, but far enough away to give and ensure them complete privacy. But even so, he wanted Bronwyn to be safe in the knowledge they were shielded from the world as they gave themselves to each other.

He lay his beloved mate down on the soft, warm grass beside the stream, and after removing his shredded, blood-stained jeans, removed her clothes with a gentleness he had only ever given to his plants before her.

He had thought nothing could be more precious to him than his gardens—but Bronwyn was something far more special than he ever thought he deserved. She helped him to undress her, not seeming to mind his work-roughened hands as they brushed against the silk of her skin.

A tear of wonder welled in his eye.

She brushed it from his cheek and then touched her own cheek where a similar tear had left a track of pale silver in the moonlight. He kissed the tear from her skin, and then taking her clothes, made a pillow of them for her head.

She gazed up at him as if he were the centre of her universe. As she was the centre of his.

'Touch me,' she said. 'Love me.'

He moved his knuckles down her throat in a gentle caress, his fingers splaying wide over her breasts as he continued his wondering exploration. He stopped over her ribs where only the faintest hint of pink skin showed where the mirror injury to his had been. The injury she'd dug her fingers into, using her pain to reach him.

'It's healed,' he breathed, kissing her there, enjoying the sound of her moan and the way she arched up into his hand, into his lips.

'We're both healed.' She pulled him down to her and pressed her lips against his in a kiss that seared him from head to toes. His cock flexed against her. She laughed, the husky sound curling straight around his heart. 'Come inside me. Make us one.'

The scent of her warmth and her desire lifted to fill him with possessive heat. 'You are mine,' he said, slipping inside her with a long, steady glide.

'As you are mine,' she sighed, welcoming him home.

And as they joined together, light spilled out of them and over them, rivalling the glow of the golden Healer Moon.

In that moment, both of them were certain they could overcome anything, as long as they were One.

***

I HOPE you enjoyed Bron and River's story as much as I enjoyed writing it and can't wait to sink into the next instalment with Eloise and Iain's story in *Shifter Bound*. Read on for the first few chapters.

Before you do though, I just wanted to let you know that I also have a FREE ebook copy of **Witch Bound**, a novella set 40 years before the events in the current day *Pack Bound Series*, to give to you.

More on that after the first few chapters of *Shifter Bound* ...

SHIFTER BOUND

PACK BOUND SERIES BOOK 3

LEISL LEIGHTON

PROLOGUE

Northern Scotland, 1502

Weak, grieving, helpless, Bridgette watched as Morrigan rained fiery retribution down on the village. Like some Celtic Goddess, hair and gown blown back by a Fae wind, wrapped in Darkness, she poured her wrath down on the villagers responsible for the murder of her beloved sister.

Bridgette was the only one left who could stop Morrigan from falling into the abyss, and she'd tried, Goddess, she'd tried. But there was little she could do from the aether. It was like a wisp of fog standing in front of a ravaging storm. However, she had to try one last time. For the dead Morghanna, her newborn son, and all the generations of witch and Were who would follow—if she didn't succeed, all would suffer.

Fighting the exhaustion that made every movement through the aether torture, she cried out, 'Morrigan. Please. Do not do this. Morghanna would not wish it.' Morrigan didn't acknowledge she'd heard. But a tendril of the Darkness that surrounded Morrigan, coating her with its unreasoning hatred the way it had done the Were for centuries beyond remembering, broke free and rushed towards where Bridgette's astral self-floated. A whoosh, like the whisper of a thousand voices crying out in the void, followed in its wake.

She turned and fled, the electric cold of the Darkness nipping at her heels. She couldn't let it touch her. Not here. She tried to move faster, but she was too tired; the thread that connected her to her body stretched thin and weak, the aether now almost as thick as mud.

She wasn't going to make it.

An icy tendril caught her heel. Instant despair filled her, pushing aside her raging grief at Morghanna's loss. She almost stopped, almost gave in, but Malcolm's voice came to her out of the distance.

'*Mo ghrá*. Come back to me.'

'Malcolm!' She tore her foot from the tendril of Darkness and surged forward. It followed, sending a chill as cold as an ice shard through her nerves. 'Malcolm.'

'I am here. Follow my voice. I love ye. Come back to me.'

The Darkness behind her halted, quivered, then continued chasing her. Had it heard him? Goddess no! She couldn't let it get to Malcolm and Morghanna's baby son. There was only one choice to stop that from coming to pass.

Her heart lurched, sorrow almost swallowing her whole at the knowledge of what she must do.

They'd only had ten years—not enough. Not nearly enough—but to save them she'd give up every ounce of happiness she'd ever had. Touching her astral hand to the tether, she said, 'Forgive me, my love. Look after my children and Morghanna's son as if they were your own.' Then she wrapped her hand on the tether and pulled.

It was so thin, it gave with hardly any force. Pain shot through her, bright and sharp. Somehow—she knew not how, it should be impossible given what she'd just done—she could feel her body as if she was still attached to it.

Malcolm's arms were around her, her head pressed to his warm, strong chest. For a brief moment, she wanted to change what she'd done, return to her beloved, but the cold of the Darkness lingered too close.

She must protect the ones who meant the most to her. She would protect them forever.

The heart in her physical form shuddered. It tried to beat on, once, twice and then with a final throb it stopped.

Loss, grief—for Malcolm, for her children, for all she'd miss sharing with them, for the pain this would cause them—made her shriek into the aether as her astral self floated away.

Soon it would break apart, lost in the aether, lost to eternity.

She floated, aimless, sobbing, empty of everything except the pain of everything she'd lost, not even caring that the piece of Darkness that had chased her, was still in the aether with her.

Something touched her. She glanced up from her misery, not even caring if it was the Darkness come to claim her.

But it wasn't the Darkness. A lilac mist had appeared, surrounding her. Tendrils whispered out to her, inviting, caressing, coaxing.

All she was, all she wanted, all she had, was on the other side of that mist.

'For your sacrifice, I will reward you. You will not be lost here. Your essence will go on. Simply come to me. Embrace the possible future.'

The voice shivered through her, filling her with enough energy to dive towards it.

The Darkness screamed; a tearing sound that threatened to shred her mind of happiness and hope. But it was too late. It couldn't stop her from taking this one final leap of faith.

As she fell into the mist, Malcolm's voice rang through the aether. 'Come back to me, *mo ghrá*. Ye promised me forever.'

She hated the terrifying grief in the sound, hated that she'd made him cling to life to look after their family when she'd taken her own. But he would do it. For her. He'd understand how important his sacrifice—and hers—was.

He would live despite losing his mate.

And then after that ...

'Forever,' she whispered before her conscious thoughts broke apart in the embrace of the lilac mist.

1

'*Forever.*'

The word was a whispered breath of sound, so soft and low that Iain thought he'd misheard it. But then the little shifter's eyelids fluttered and her lips moved over the word again. He sat forward. 'Eloise?'

Her eyes snapped open—those beautiful golden-green peridot eyes—and she looked right at him. 'Mal? Where am I? What happened?'

'I'm not Mal. I'm Iain.'

'Iain?' She frowned.

'It's okay. You're safe.'

She smiled softly, lifted a hand as if to touch him. 'Of course I am safe. You are here.' Her eyes fluttered and then she was gone again.

'Damn it.' Iain thumped the arm of the chair.

'Did I miss something?' Bron asked, entering the room.

Iain gestured at the sleeping girl in the bed. 'She woke up again.'

'How long was she awake this time?' Bron bent over Eloise, putting one hand over her patient's forehead and the other over her chest.

'Not long.'

'Did she say anything?'

'She was whispering something about forever when she woke up, but not much else.' He sat forward, fingertips pressed to his lips. 'She looked right at me this time, and called me Mal.'

'Mal?'

'Must be someone in the rogue coven. I didn't get to ask because her eyes went foggy and she was gone again.'

Bron breathed in deeply and closed her eyes. Iain waited in silence, skin prickling at the use of her magic. Finally, she pulled her hands away from Eloise and straightened. 'She's asleep.' She smiled. 'Her body is healing itself in a natural way now. Finally.' She breathed out a sigh. 'She'll probably wake again soon and be awake longer next time.'

'That's good. You can start working with her then to control it.'

She looked thoughtful. 'Have there been any other episodes?'

He shook his head. 'Not like last time. Her heart's still thrumming like a hummingbird, though, especially when she's dreaming.'

'The dreaming isn't hurting her.'

'The flames don't seem to either.' Flames that resembled the flames of magic that surrounded Skye and Bron and Shelley when their power was building. Flames that usually were only found in witches with ties to the original lines. Flames that were indicators of significant power held within. 'Has Cordy figured out what they are yet?'

'No. She's as lost as we are. But she and Shelley are pouring through the diaries, trying to find out information.' She frowned. 'What they do agree on is that they are an expression of uncontrolled raw magical power, and that is never good.' She touched the leather cuff on Eloise's wrist. 'It seems this is working.'

'I thought Cordy said it was only a stopgap measure.'

'It is. She needs to wake up so we can truly help her.'

He took her hand in his as she stood. 'And we will.'

She touched his face, then brushed his hair off his brow. 'Yes, we will.'

His wolf hummed in pleasure at the caress, but it didn't make the urge inside him go away. He turned back to the bed and the woman in it.

Behind him, Bron sighed. 'If you want to take a break, I'll stay with her.'

'No. It's okay. I'll stay.' He avoided looking at her but could feel her gaze like a hand hovering just above his skin.

'She isn't your responsibility alone, Iain.'

'I know.'

'If I'd known you'd tie yourself to her when I asked you to stay, I wouldn't have asked.'

'I want to stay.'

'I don't want you damaging your wolf.'

'My wolf is fine.'

'I can feel your desire to roam. It's like an itch I can't quite reach.'

'It's my itch, though, and I'm fine with it.'

'Are you?' She touched Eloise's hand. 'And she has nothing to do with the dreams you've been having?'

His jaw twitched. He hated that she could see so much. 'Don't try to see more than is here, Bron. I'm simply here because it's the right thing to do.'

'There are many others who can protect the pack.'

He shrugged irritably. 'It's not just that. This little shifter helped save my life. I owe her. That's it.'

She watched him for a moment longer. He relaxed his shoulders, hoping she wouldn't question him further. He fought the desire to stretch his fingers, release the tension by cracking the knuckles. Bron knew him too well, knew his signs. He had to give nothing away. He didn't want to talk about why he was still here. He didn't fully understand it himself. He'd been so angry when Bron had kept him bedbound for longer than he thought was necessary. He hadn't wanted to wait until his wounds were fully healed. All he'd wanted was to run free. To forget that feeling of helplessness he'd been unable to shrug off since that night before Yule last year when Morrigan had taken him, River and Gareth prisoner and tortured them, almost killing him and Gareth.

He never wanted to feel like that again.

Then he'd found out Eloise was here, had seen her lying in this bed. Many of the pack had taken to referencing to her as 'the little shifter', mostly because of the size of the cat she'd turned into to spy on them, and not for the reasons he thought of her like that. Strangely she wasn't that little. In actual fact, she was on the taller side of average. Even so, she still managed to look small. No, not small. Fragile and delicate, like a little bird. Or like Sleeping Beauty. With her mane of tawny hair and the freckles splashed across her nose like little drops of brown sugar on cream, she did resemble the fairy-tale princess.

Except there was nothing restful about the expressions that crossed her face.

As the days passed, he'd spent more and more time at her side, watching, trying to figure her out, until it had got to the point where he'd been unable to make himself leave, even for more than the time it took to take a run.

It should have been torture to him, to his Lone Wolf soul, and yet his wolf didn't want to leave her either. It didn't make any sense.

His gaze slid back to her face as it so often did. He'd studied her for hours each day, and yet, every time he looked at her, he saw something new. Which was kind of surprising. There wasn't much to her. Fragile bones. Too-pale skin. Lips that held a stubborn pout even in sleep. She wasn't pretty—her eyes too big, mouth too wide, chin too pointed—and yet there was something about her that stayed in his mind even when he wasn't with her. Striking. That's what she was. Ethereal.

Purple smudges marked the skin under her eyes today. Every now and again she tossed her head, lips muttering words he couldn't catch. Her eyes moved constantly under almost translucent eyelids— eyes he'd been unable to forget since seeing them in Morrigan's cave that night. Eyes he'd seen so often in the cat that had watched him warily last year. She'd spied on them, giving Morrigan information that had almost allowed her to destroy them, but then she'd saved them all.

None of it made sense.

She didn't make sense.

He wanted her to wake up, to make her answer his questions, to help him put a stop to this endless fascination.

He realised he was leaning forward, fingers stroking the edges of her hair. Tawny like a lion's mane, it was thick and shiny and silken despite her having been in a coma for over two months.

A noise behind him made him realise the mistake he'd made. How had he forgotten she was there?

He made out like he was just re-settling Eloise's pillow—but when he glanced surreptitiously back at Bron, her raised brows told him she wasn't fooled. Damn.

Thankfully, she didn't say anything about that. 'Did she say anything to let you know who this Mal might have been to her?'

He shrugged. 'No. Although, possibly someone close. She seemed pleased to see me—him.'

'Curious. None of the ones we have are called Mal—although it could be one of the ones who got away with Morrigan.'

His gaze returned to Eloise. He wished he knew who Mal was and why that was the first name to her lips upon waking.

'How about you stop growling at me before River comes in here and shoves that growl down your throat,' Bron said.

He snapped off the growl. 'Sorry, I didn't realise.'

She stroked her hand over his hair. 'I know.'

He thought she was going to say something else, push him further about his need to be here with Eloise, but instead she bent and kissed his cheek. 'I'll bring you some lunch, but after you've eaten, I want you to go for a run. You've been in this room too long.' He opened his mouth to argue, but she held up a hand. 'River will sit with her.'

His mouth snapped closed. If anyone else had a right to look after Eloise, it was River.

'You're evil, you know that, don't you?'

She laughed. 'I try.' She pointed at him. 'Lunch, then run.'

'I promise.'

She flashed him a bright smile. 'Good.'

The door closed behind her. He returned to watching Eloise.

Bron brought him his lunch later and after eating it, he went for the promised run. He usually loved being out in the open spaces, the freedom of running under the clear blue sky, the brush of long grass against his legs, the briny scent of the ocean in his lungs. He could run forever, except ...

He didn't want to. There was a pull inside him, a pull to return to the Packhouse. To not go too far. But he didn't have to go far to let his wolf out to play.

He ran across Packland to the ocean, climbed down the cliff face. His feet pounded on the sand, the spray cold against the warmth of his skin as he ran. It was a private beach, accessible only from the McVale land, and there were sentries around to ensure it stayed that way. Knowing he would be left alone for as long as he wished, he shed his clothes and gave in to the press of his wolf under his skin. With a burst of rainbow glow, he transformed, black and silver fur shimmering in the breeze as he leapt down the beach, paws eating up the sand.

The joy as he ran was almost enough to rid him of the itchy need to return to his sentry duty. With a loud bark, he let his wolf completely off the leash, stretching out muscles that had only recently healed. He romped into the surf, snapped at the waves, chased seagulls off the sand and explored the rockpools at the far end of the bay. A crab snapped at his nose when he upset it sniffing at the seaweed it hid in. He jumped back with a yelp.

Chuckling, he pranced away to go and roll in the sand and enjoy the sun.

Too soon though, the drive to go back and check on Eloise became greater than the drive to keep running. He transformed back into his human skin, threw his clothes on and returned to the Packhouse.

He needed a shower but couldn't help going straight to Eloise's room. River—who was reading aloud to Eloise—looked up as he walked in. 'Hey man. You look better.'

Iain nodded, gaze sliding past the man who'd become his closest friend in the last six months, to the woman lying so quietly in the bed.

'She's fine. Has barely moved,' River said, fingers splayed out on his book. 'I'm happy to stay for longer if you want to take a shower. Or do something else.'

Iain shrugged. 'I might take a shower, but there's nothing else I need to do.'

'Not even making the bench and chair you promised me for the new garden?'

'What's the rush?'

River snapped his book shut and stood. 'No rush. It's just been a while since you did some serious sculpture or carpentry. I know if it was me, my fingers would be itching to get dirty after all this time.' He rubbed his hands on his jeans, as if he could feel the itch. 'Besides, those sketches you did for me were so intriguing, I'd love to see the reality. And there's all that wood Adam and Jason found on the beach just begging to be used. I saw how you were running your hand over the grain the other day. The way your eyes glazed over. I know that look.' His lips hitched into a lopsided smile. 'Have felt it on myself. I'm just a bit floored you can deny it, though.'

'I'm not denying it.' Iain shoved down the annoyance that flared at the other man's pushing. River meant well. And if anyone would understand, it would be River. But for some reason, he still couldn't tell the other Were what was stopping him from resuming his normal life. 'I just haven't felt the push, you know? Not like before. I was kind of waiting for it to come before I started. But you're right, that wood is prime now. I should use it.'

'Great. That's great.' River took a seat again and opened his book, *The Call of The Wild*—he insisted on reading it to Eloise; said it would speak to the animal nature that was at the heart of any shifter. 'I'll come get you if she stirs.'

River's eyes were on him, questions there as Iain hesitated. Seeing them, Iain shot one more look at Eloise and then forced himself to leave. He stood for a moment outside the door, fighting the urge to go back in.

No. He couldn't let the others know about the need, the pull to always seek out the shifter. Not until he understood it himself.

He forced himself to the side door then ran through the garden to his work shed.

The sketches he'd made were on his drafting table, the wood River mentioned piled in the corner. Running his hands over the smooth flotsam, he forced himself to see nothing but the grain, the knots and twists that could be used to form the rough structure of the bench he'd seen so clearly in his mind.

Actually, he'd seen the bench in his dreams. A dream his mind kept returning to, asleep and awake.

In the dream he'd come upon a glade in the middle of a wood. A woman sat there on a bench that looked as if it had grown from the twisted roots and branches of the trees around them. She'd been staring at the clear green pool of water at the centre of the glade, but turned as he entered, a blinding smile of happiness on her face as she'd seen him. That smile had filled him, made him whole in a way he'd never experienced before.

She'd held her hands out as if expecting him. He went to her, took her hand in his.

It felt like home.

A cracking sound snapped him from the dream memory. Blinking, he shook his head and looked down to see he'd gripped a piece of the wood so tightly it had crumbled in his hand. Cursing, he shoved the broken pieces aside. He really wasn't in the mood for this, but he couldn't return to the room. Not yet. Not with River there with that knowing look in his eyes.

How could he explain the inexplicable?

Lone Wolves did not get tied down. It was lore. And their lore had always held true. So, given that this pull he felt towards Eloise couldn't be the mating bond, what was it? And why was he having dreams that were so vivid, they felt real?

Smashing his fist against the bench, he gritted his teeth against the flare of pain and turned from the drawing. He couldn't start on that bench right now—emotion was a savaging rawness in his chest whenever he pictured it—but he could make something else.

A chair. Made out of this wood. He could do that.

Picking up his toolbelt, he strapped it around his waist, clamped a large piece of silky- soft wood onto the sawhorse and began to saw. He didn't need to draw the design out first because he could see it in his mind's eye. See exactly the dimensions it needed to be. Dimensions that would be perfect for a woman who was five foot ten and too thin. Yes, he could see it exactly.

The sun had begun its descent towards sunset and twilight when he finished and headed in to have a shower. He needed to thank River for making him use his hands. The tension locked inside him had been released for the time being. The runs hadn't been enough to smooth out the kinks in his temperament, but creating that chair had.

He couldn't wait to see it being used. He knew exactly where it should be placed. But that would have to wait until River finished what he was doing in that section of the garden—it should only be a few days.

'I know that look,' River said as Iain entered the room after his shower.

Iain laughed and clapped River on the shoulder. 'Thanks man.'

'My pleasure. Bronwyn kept me company for a few hours. She's just gone to check on our other guests but will be back later.'

'Tell her not to bother. I'll call if there's any need.' He took the chair as River stood, pulling it closer to the bed. 'You two deserve some alone-time.'

River halted at the door. 'You shouldn't stay here all night.'

'I'll be fine. I can sleep standing up if need be.'

River chuckled. 'Lone Wolf thing?'

He shared his friend's grin. 'Lone Wolf thing.' He nodded at the door. 'Go kiss your mate. I'll be fine.'

'I'm going to do more than kiss my mate,' River said, his mouth slanting, a glint in his eyes that was such a relief to see after the events of the year before.

But instead of making comments about it, Iain covered his ears. 'Lalalala. Too much information.'

River's laughter warmed him—it was a sound that had almost never come into being—and he waved the other man out the door then settled in for the night.

The room darkened soon after as the sun began to dip below the hills, the curtains a red flare for a brief few minutes. Iain closed his eyes against the glare, the red a blaze behind his eyes. Slumping in the chair, drowsiness took him over and before he could stop them, images—vicious, blood-tinged images—tore through his mind. Desperation clung to the images, the sound of a pleading voice sobbing nearby, the vibrant tang of copper in the air as warm liquid splashed over his face, down his side, thick and viscous. The sounds of wet tearing followed by an ear-piercing scream that brought bile to his throat, choking him.

He coughed, gagging, and sat bolt upright out of the nightmares that had plagued him since that night just before Yule. He shook, skin crawling, as he tried to shove down the terror that left a bitter tang in the back of his throat and constricted his chest. Helpless. He'd never felt so helpless.

A muffled moan caught his attention and he spun, eyes glowing in the dark, piercing the gloom. Eloise was twisting against the sheets, her hands held in front of her as if protecting herself from a blow, her mouth working to hold in a scream.

He was out of his chair in a moment, wanting desperately to touch her, but knowing somewhere deep inside that he shouldn't. Not now. Not yet. But he had to wake her up.

'Eloise.' She moaned again and thrashed against the sheets, hands raised in claws. He ducked, avoiding their swipe, and tried again. 'Eloise. Wake up. You're having a nightmare.' One to rival his nightmares by the look of it. 'Wake up.'

Her eyes fluttered and she stopped clawing at the air, her arms falling to her sides.

'That's it Eloise. You're safe. It's only a nightmare. Just wake up.'

Her eyes opened, focused on him, flared wide.

She screamed.

'She's awake.'

Jason looked up and smiled at Skye as she stood in the doorway. He lifted his arms and she walked to him, allowing him to gather her onto his lap. He didn't have to ask who was awake—there was only one 'her'. 'I'll call Marcus. He'll want to know.'

'Do you think he'll let Cordy come down and see her? She's going to need help. More help than Bron, Shelley and I can give her.' She smiled that little lopsided smile he so loved.

'We're still learning about our powers.'

He kissed her, loving the way she cupped his face when he did that. 'You're a fast learner, though.'

She smiled into his kiss. 'The best.'

A cough made Jason pull from the kiss. His brother stood in the doorway, a glint in his eye.

'Sorry for interrupting ...'

'No you're not,' Skye said, turning to face Adam.

Adam's smile widened. 'No. I'm not.' He sauntered into the room, leaned against the end of the couch. 'I hear our little prisoner is awake.'

'She's not our prisoner,' Skye said. 'She saved River's life. And Iain's and Gareth's for that matter.'

Jason smoothed his hand down her back. 'He knows that.'

Adam's eyebrow rose. 'Yes, she did, but we don't know why.'

'River says she was sorry for what she'd done. She was trying to do the right thing.'

'After spying on us and giving River up to Morrigan. What she did was almost destroy us.'

'You sound like Shelley,' Skye remarked.

Adam's brows rose. 'You mean Kitten actually agrees with me.' He snorted. 'That's one for the books.'

'If you stopped riding her like you do, she wouldn't be so keen to disagree with everything you say.'

'I enjoy "riding" her.'

Skye's growl was as menacing as a wolf's and Jason smiled. 'Now, now, you two. We're getting off topic.'

'Yes, we are.' Skye glared at Adam as she said to Jason, 'So, we need to go down there.'

'You're not going down there.' Adam snapped upright, his wolf so close to the surface his eyes glowed.

'Yes, I am,' Skye said. 'We've had this discussion before, Adam. I'm your Pack Witch and the leader of our new little coven. I have to do what I feel is best for the pack. And going down to see Eloise is what's best for the pack.'

'Jason?'

'Don't bring Jason into this. He's my mate, not my boss. Besides, I don't know what you're worried about. Eloise is hardly dangerous. Bron says she's frightened more than anything else.'

'But her powers—'

'Are contained for now. We have to go down to see her. And don't look at Jason that way. He agrees with me.'

'Well, that's just brilliant, isn't it?' Adam threw his hands up in the air. 'You're obviously pussy-whipped.' He jabbed his finger at Skye. 'And you're too stubborn to see sense. I'm going to talk to Shelley. I bet she can talk some sense into you.'

'Good luck with that,' Skye called out as he stalked from the room.

Jason chuckled. 'You enjoyed that, didn't you?'

She grinned. 'He's so happy-go-lucky most of the time. It's good for him to experience all of the emotions.'

'He's the pack's Trickster. From what I've been reading,' he tapped the old diary in his hand, 'he feels more than we can possibly understand.'

Her grin faded. 'I know. I don't want to lose him to that like others have been lost.'

'Neither do I.'

'Do you think he's right? That it's a mistake to go down to see Eloise?'

'No. We have to. But maybe we should give her some time to get acclimatised first.'

She nodded. 'Bron said she wanted to spend time bringing her up to date, let her get used to it all. It's going to be a shock for her to discover what happened and how much time has passed. Apparently when she finally woke up, it took Bron half an hour to stop her from screaming.'

Jason shook his head. He couldn't imagine what it must be like for the shifter to wake up and find her entire world had changed. 'Waiting is probably best.'

'Yes. Although Bron doesn't want us to wait too long. The bracelet has helped dampen the power fluctuations, but Bron's afraid it won't last for long now she's awake. She says she's going to need help to dampen the erratic powers while Eloise comes to terms with everything.'

'What about Iain?'

'Bron says he's determined to stay. And while she's worried, she also says that the power fluctuations aren't as bad when he's there. He seems to calm Eloise somehow.'

'Was he there when she woke?'

'Yes.'

'The screaming must have been pleasant for him.'

'Bron said he dealt with it really well. Which is kind of out of character, isn't it?'

Jason rubbed his nose against her neck, breathing in the scent that was nectar to him. 'Not really. He's a stubborn bastard when he gets his teeth into something, and for some reason, he's decided he wants to help Eloise.'

'I'm glad. She needs someone on her side. And he just needs someone.'

'He's a Lone Wolf, Skye.' He brushed his hand over her hair. 'It doesn't work like that for them.'

She smiled, a little secret smile. 'We'll see.'

He shook his head then kissed her neck. She shivered and made the little sound he loved. He smiled against her skin. 'So, when should we go down?'

'Bron says next week.' She sounded a little breathy.

He ran his lips up her neck to her ear. 'Next week it is.'

Skye shifted around to face him. 'Now, where were we before we were so rudely interrupted?'

Her smile warmed through him, the glint in her eye making him laugh out loud. He still couldn't believe this woman was his. 'I think we were here,' he said, as he cupped her face and brought her lips down to his.

I HOPE you enjoyed that sneak peek of *Shifter Bound*. If you want to read more, you can find buy-links with the QR code here:

If you don't want to miss out on news about books in this series or the new prequel **Dawn of the Curse Series**, set 500 years before the Pack Bound Series takes place, as well as special giveaways, sales, book signings and information on my other books, then sign up to my newsletter.

As an added bonus, when you join, you will get a FREE ebook copy of **Witch Bound**, a novella set 40 years before *Pack Bound*. Just turn the page to find out more:

LOVE A FREE BOOK?

YOUR FREE BOOK IS WAITING

One Fate, one mate, a bond too strong to deny ...

Paul Collins, duty-bound Pack Warlock and seer, must marry a strong witch for the good of Pack McVale. But his hidden feelings for his best-friend's sister, maternal wolf Ivy McVale, make this a more difficult pill to swallow every day. Especially when they begin to mate.

Then Paul has a vision: If they mate, Ivy will die. Desperate, Paul uses his powers to change destiny and make Ivy think she's always hated him. He can deal with any punishment the Fates make him pay for tampering with destiny, as long as Ivy lives.

After recovering from a bewildering month-long illness, Ivy notices her nemesis, Paul, is tormented by something. And strangely, she is the only one who can feel it. Unable to endure such unhappiness—even if he does call her Poison Ivy—she is determined to help him, no matter the cost. Because Pack McVale cannot survive without him, and curiously, neither can she …

Simply sign up to my newsletter and I will email your free copy of Witch Bound to you. You will also receive the latest on upcoming books, sales, giveaways and relevant bookish news.

Get My Free Copy of Witch Bound Here:

But wait! There's more …

If you're not into newsletters but think you might be into subscriptions that give you serialised content, exclusive chapters to new books, exclusive bonus content, signed print books and much more, then turn the page to find out about **Leisl's Legends** …

JOIN LEISL'S LEGENDS

Subscribe to (or follow) me (via the QR code) at my Leisl's Legends page on REAM—a new subscription app like Patreon except it's designed especially for readers and authors for an amazing reading experience—and you will get early access to *The Huntress and the Vampire King*, my hot enemies to lovers, witch-and-vampire-licious urban fantasy romance that readers over there are already in love with. It's the prequel novel to the first book in the Blood-Rites Series - *The Blood of the Seer*.

Be the first to find out where it all began with Anita and Hei's love story.
BECOME A LEGEND NOW!
https://reamstories.com/leislleightonauthor

You will also find serialised chapters of the next book in my popular **Gods Cursed Series** there and can comment on the story as I write it! Not to mention you will also get extra bonuses like exclusive NSFW Bonus Epilogues, Bonus Prologues and cut scenes and chapters from all of my books.

Be part of creating the stories you love AND get exclusive access to a whole range of goodies including other WIPs, bonus content, voting rights, signed books and more.

Read on to find out more about The Huntress and the Vampire King PLUS read the opening chapters ...

The Huntress and the Vampire King

She hates the vampire who saved her; he holds the key to her fate ...

Hunter-witch Anita Middleton wants revenge against the violent vampire cults that murdered her father and has worked hard to become one of the best vampire hunters there is. But on a difficult hunt she is caught in an ambush and is mortally wounded ... only to be saved by a mysterious warrior. A warrior with brilliant blue eyes and long silver-blonde hair who fights with a grace and violence like nothing she's seen. It is only after she wakes in the heart of his palazzo that she realises her saviour is a vampire - and according to her brother and mentor, this vampire king is their ally.

Lord Hei rules over an empire of witches, humans and vampires who have been trying to keep the vicious vampire cults, the Wild and Dark Brethren, at bay for centuries. Then he saves Anita and knows with one look she is the prophecied Huntress who could be his downfall or his salvation - and she is also his fated mate. But she struggles to trust him as her hatred of vampires is deep-seated. And she *needs* to trust him because only he can offer the specialised training a Huntress needs so her power won't overwhelm her.

But with the Dark Brethren mysteriously amassing, he has little time to win her over. And Anita must go on a crash course to learn how to control her Huntress magic ... or go slowly and violently insane.

The Huntress and the Vampire King is the exciting action-packed prequel novel to *The Blood of the Seer*.

If you love your vampires hot with a bit of The Witcher thrown in and your heroines as kick-arse as Buffy and even more tortured, if you love fated mates, enemies to lovers, chosen ones and epically hot romance mixed with action and mystery, then *The Huntress and the Vampire King* is what you've been waiting for.

Sign up to Leisl's Legends and start reading exclusive early release chapters of it now!

BECOME A LEGEND NOW!
https://reamstories.com/leislleightonauthor

ALSO BY LEISL LEIGHTON

PACK BOUND SERIES

Pack Bound

Moon Bound

Shifter Bound

Wolf Bound

Witch Bound

(A Pack Bound Series Prequel Novella -

FREE ebook copy to Newsletter Subscribers)

BOX SET

Pack Bound Series Collection Books 1-4

DAWN OF THE CURSE

A PACK BOUND PREQUEL SERIES

Soul Bound

Alpha Bound

Hunter Bound

Fae Bound

(Coming in 2027)

GODS CURSED SERIES

A Love Cursed Christmas Wish

Love Cursed

Soul Cursed

Blood Cursed

Hearts Cursed

Fates Cursed

Witch Cursed

Dragon Cursed

(Coming 2026)

Blood-Rites Series

The Blood of the Seer

The Blood of the Sire

The Blood of the Son

(Coming 2027)

Blood-Rites Prequel and Bonus Material

The Huntress and the Vampire King

The Middleton Manifesto

(Available now via Leisl's Legends subscription)

Anthologies

A Perfectly Paranormal Valentine

A Perfectly Paranormal Halloween

A Perfectly Paranormal Easter

A Perfectly Paranormal Christmas

A Perfectly Paranormal Prophecy

(Coming in 2027)

As well as writing sexy, epic and romantic paranormal novels, I write mysterious and emotional romantic suspense novels too. Check out the following titles for amazing, suspenseful reads:

STORM HAVEN SERIES

Need You Tonight

The Devil Inside

COALCLIFF STUD SERIES

Climbing Fear: Book 1

Blazing Fear: Book 2

ECHO SPRINGS SERIES

Dangerous Echoes: Book 1

Books 2-4 in this series, (written by Daniel deLorne, TJ Hamilton and Shannon Curtis) are also available now at all ebook retailers.

You can find all the buy links for Leisl's Books at her website:

ABOUT LEISL

Leisl Leighton is a tall red head with an overly large imagination. As a child, she identified strongly with Anne of Green Gables, and like Anne, is a voracious reader and born performer.

It came as no surprise when she went on to a career as a performer, script writer, script doctor, stage manager and musical director for cabaret and theatre restaurants.

After starting a family, Leisl stopped performing and began writing the stories plaguing her dreams. She now writes emotional stories mixed with mystery and a little bit of what goes bump in the night.

Her novels have won and placed in writing contests here and overseas. She is a passionate advocate for the romance genre, was President of Romance Writers of Australia from 2014-2017 and when she's not writing romantic stories of redemption, she is helping other authors reach their dreams with her Author Services. You can contact Leisl through her website via the QR Code above or here: https://www.leislleighton.com

And if you want to stay in touch and be the first to find out about new releases, appearances, special deals and exclusive content and give-

aways, sign up to her Newsletter and pick up your free copy of *Witch Bound* via the QR code.

Or sign up to *Leisl's Legends* via this QR code to get *Witch Cursed* plus serialised early access stories and bonus content including a bonus

NSFW ending for Love Cursed.

You can also follow her on social media:

f facebook.com/LeislLeightonAuthor

instagram.com/leislleightonauthor

BB bookbub.com/authors/leisl-leighton

a amazon.com/stores/Leisl-Leighton/author/BooDBYRGZY

ACKNOWLEDGMENTS

I couldn't have done this without my husband, Mark, who takes care of all things techie and listens to me ramble about characters and plot-lines that are as real to me as he is. Thankfully he loves me and knows I'm not insane.

Thanks to my two beautiful boys, Jacob and Nathaniel, for doing the same—it can be tough sometimes to have a mum who lives in another world!

Thanks to my family and close friends—especially my parents, Kerril and Jim—for their never-ending encouragement and support and helping me out with the kids when I have a deadline or just want to write a little bit more. Also thanks to my parents for letting me take over the study in your house as my new office—it has helped me be more productive and stop procrasto-cleaning/procrasto-cooking/pro-crasto-TV watching (it's just stopped procrastination!) plus it's just nice to have somewhere to work that's not my house.

Aside from great family and friends, a writer needs a Coven of writing peeps all their own. Thanks to my friends in my writing groups for encouraging me in this endeavour, through traditional publishing and into publishing my own stories my way—Marnie, Sam, Helen, Laura, Chris, Frana and Anita. I couldn't have gotten here without you.

Thanks especially to Marnie for all your editorial thoughts and advice. And to Sam for your brilliant covers. Love you both.

Thoughts and thanks also to my bestie, Helen, and to the first writing friend I ever had, Liz. You are both gone but never forgotten and a part of you will always live on in my stories. In fact, this series would never have been written without them (especially Liz who gave me endless encouragement and read many versions and gave me amazing feedback that helped get it to this published book right here.) I miss you both so much every day.

And a big shout out to all my friends in Romance Writers of Australia —you are inspiration and mentor rolled into a big ball of supportive writerly love. Thank you.

The final person I have to thank is my agent, Alex Adsett, for believing in me and my work and always backing every decision I make. Your confidence in me helps me believe I can actually do this writing thing. Eternal thanks.